Daffy Duck

YOU'RE DESPICABLE!

Written by:
Terry Collins
Michael Eury
Chuck Kim
Terry LaBan
Barry Liebmann
Bill Matheny
Jesse Leon McCann
Frank Strom
David Cody Weiss

Illustrated by:
David Alvarez
Jim Amash
Leo Batic
Mike DeCarlo
Horacio Saavedra
Javier Saavedra
Howard Simpson
Ruben Torreiro
Pablo Zamboni

Colored by:
Digital Chameleon
Bernie Mireault
Prismacolor
Dave Tanguay

Lettered by:
John Costanza
Daniel Griffo
Javier Saavedra

Dan DiDio
VP-Executive Editor

Joan Hilty
Dana Kurtin
Heidi MacDonald
Editors-original series

Chuck Kim
Harvey Richards
Assistant Editors-original series

Scott Nybakken
Editor-collected edition

Robbin Brosterman
Senior Art Director

Paul Levitz
President & Publisher

Georg Brewer
VP-Design & Retail Product
Development

Richard Bruning
Senior VP-Creative Director

Patrick Caldon
Senior VP-Finance & Operations

Chris Caramalis
VP-Finance

Terri Cunningham
VP-Managing Editor

Stephanie Fierman
Senior VP-Sales & Marketing

Alison Gill
VP-Manufacturing

Rich Johnson
VP-Book Trade Sales

Hank Kanalz
VP-General Manager, WildStorm

Lillian Laserson
Senior VP & General Counsel

Jim Lee
Editorial Director-WildStorm

Paula Lowitt
Senior VP-Business & Legal Affairs

David McKillips
VP-Advertising & Custom Publishing

John Nee
VP-Business Development

Gregory Noveck
Senior VP-Creative Affairs

Cheryl Rubin
Senior VP-Brand Management

Bob Wayne
VP-Sales

SEP 13 2005

3 9082 09930 2369

WB SHIELD ™ & © Warner Bros. Entertainment Inc.
(s05)

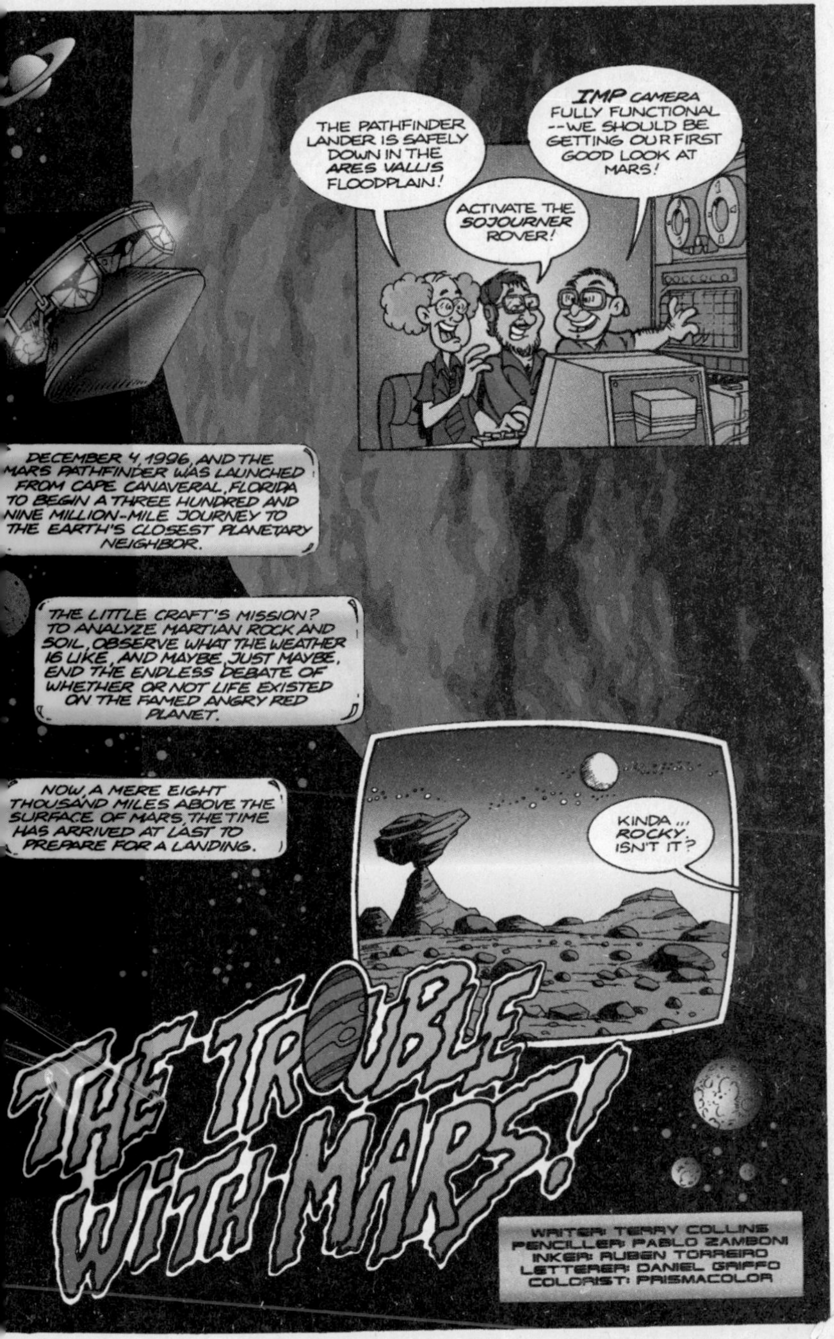
THE PATHFINDER LANDER IS SAFELY DOWN IN THE ARES VALLIS FLOODPLAIN!
ACTIVATE THE SOJOURNER ROVER!
IMP CAMERA FULLY FUNCTIONAL --WE SHOULD BE GETTING OUR FIRST GOOD LOOK AT MARS!
DECEMBER 4, 1996, AND THE MARS PATHFINDER WAS LAUNCHED FROM CAPE CANAVERAL, FLORIDA TO BEGIN A THREE HUNDRED AND NINE MILLION-MILE JOURNEY TO THE EARTH'S CLOSEST PLANETARY NEIGHBOR.
THE LITTLE CRAFT'S MISSION? TO ANALYZE MARTIAN ROCK AND SOIL, OBSERVE WHAT THE WEATHER IS LIKE, AND MAYBE, JUST MAYBE, END THE ENDLESS DEBATE OF WHETHER OR NOT LIFE EXISTED ON THE FAMED ANGRY RED PLANET.
NOW, A MERE EIGHT THOUSAND MILES ABOVE THE SURFACE OF MARS, THE TIME HAS ARRIVED AT LAST TO PREPARE FOR A LANDING.
KINDA... ROCKY. ISN'T IT?
THE TROUBLE WITH MARS!
WRITER: TERRY COLLINS
PENCILLER: PABLO ZAMBONI
INKER: RUBEN TORREIRO
LETTERER: DANIEL GRIFFO
COLORIST: PRISMACOLOR

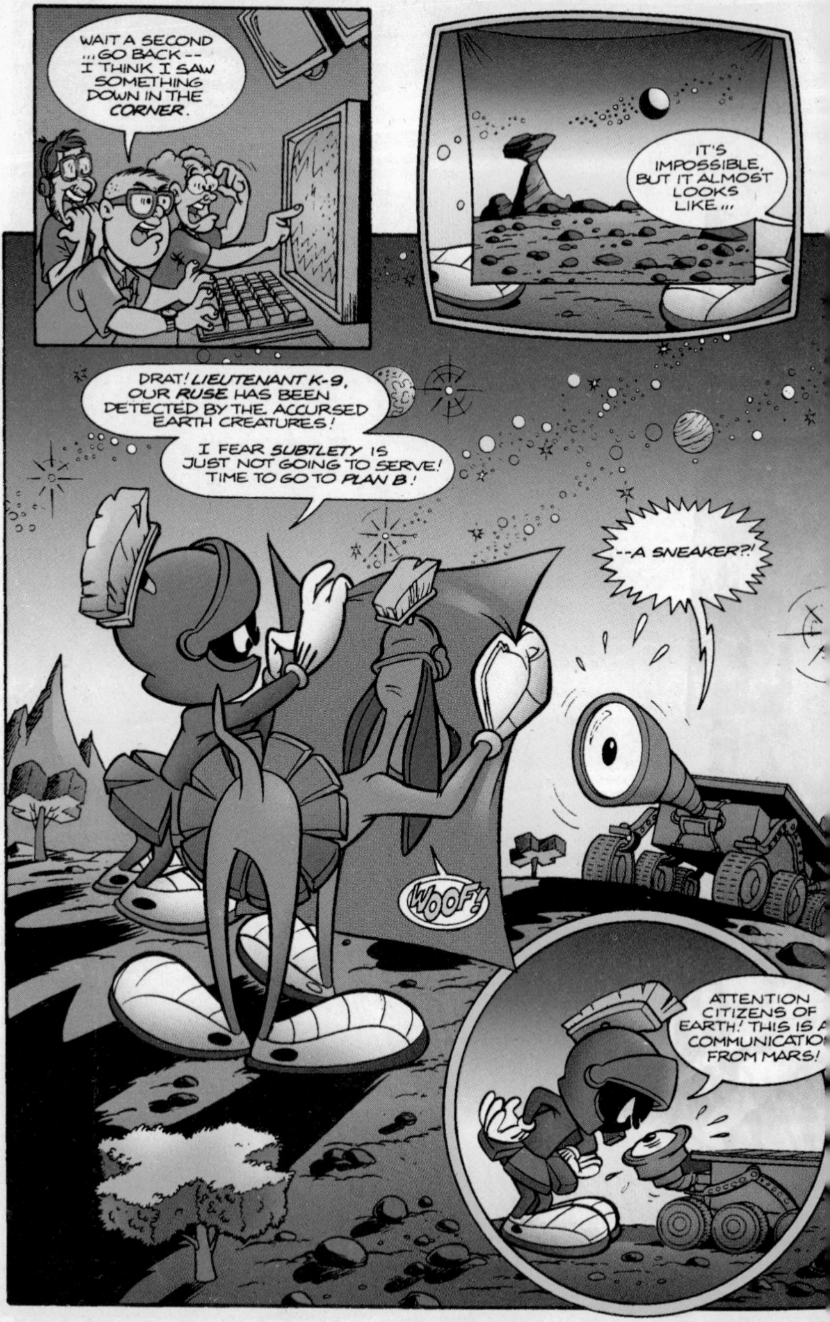
WAIT A SECOND ...GO BACK -- I THINK I SAW SOMETHING DOWN IN THE CORNER.
IT'S IMPOSSIBLE, BUT IT ALMOST LOOKS LIKE...
DRAT! LIEUTENANT K-9, OUR RUSE HAS BEEN DETECTED BY THE ACCURSED EARTH CREATURES!
I FEAR SUBTLETY IS JUST NOT GOING TO SERVE! TIME TO GO TO PLAN B!
--A SNEAKER?!
WOOF!
ATTENTION CITIZENS OF EARTH! THIS IS A COMMUNICATION FROM MARS!

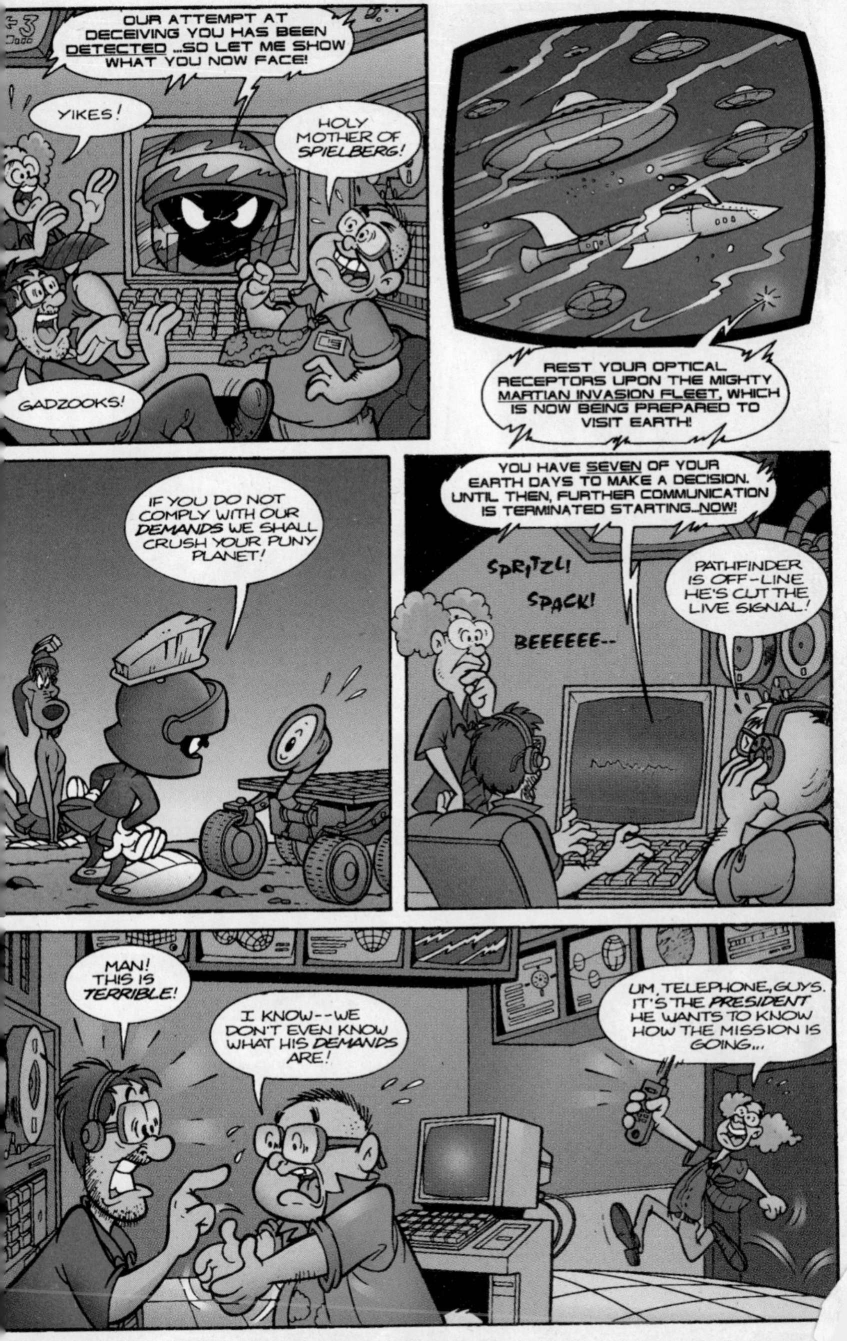
OUR ATTEMPT AT DECEIVING YOU HAS BEEN DETECTED ...SO LET ME SHOW WHAT YOU NOW FACE!
YIKES!
HOLY MOTHER OF SPIELBERG!
GADZOOKS!
REST YOUR OPTICAL RECEPTORS UPON THE MIGHTY MARTIAN INVASION FLEET, WHICH IS NOW BEING PREPARED TO VISIT EARTH!
IF YOU DO NOT COMPLY WITH OUR DEMANDS WE SHALL CRUSH YOUR PUNY PLANET!
YOU HAVE SEVEN OF YOUR EARTH DAYS TO MAKE A DECISION. UNTIL THEN, FURTHER COMMUNICATION IS TERMINATED STARTING...NOW!
SPRITZL!
SPACK!
BEEEEEE--
PATHFINDER IS OFF-LINE HE'S CUT THE LIVE SIGNAL!
MAN! THIS IS TERRIBLE!
I KNOW--WE DON'T EVEN KNOW WHAT HIS DEMANDS ARE!
UM, TELEPHONE, GUYS. IT'S THE PRESIDENT HE WANTS TO KNOW HOW THE MISSION IS GOING...

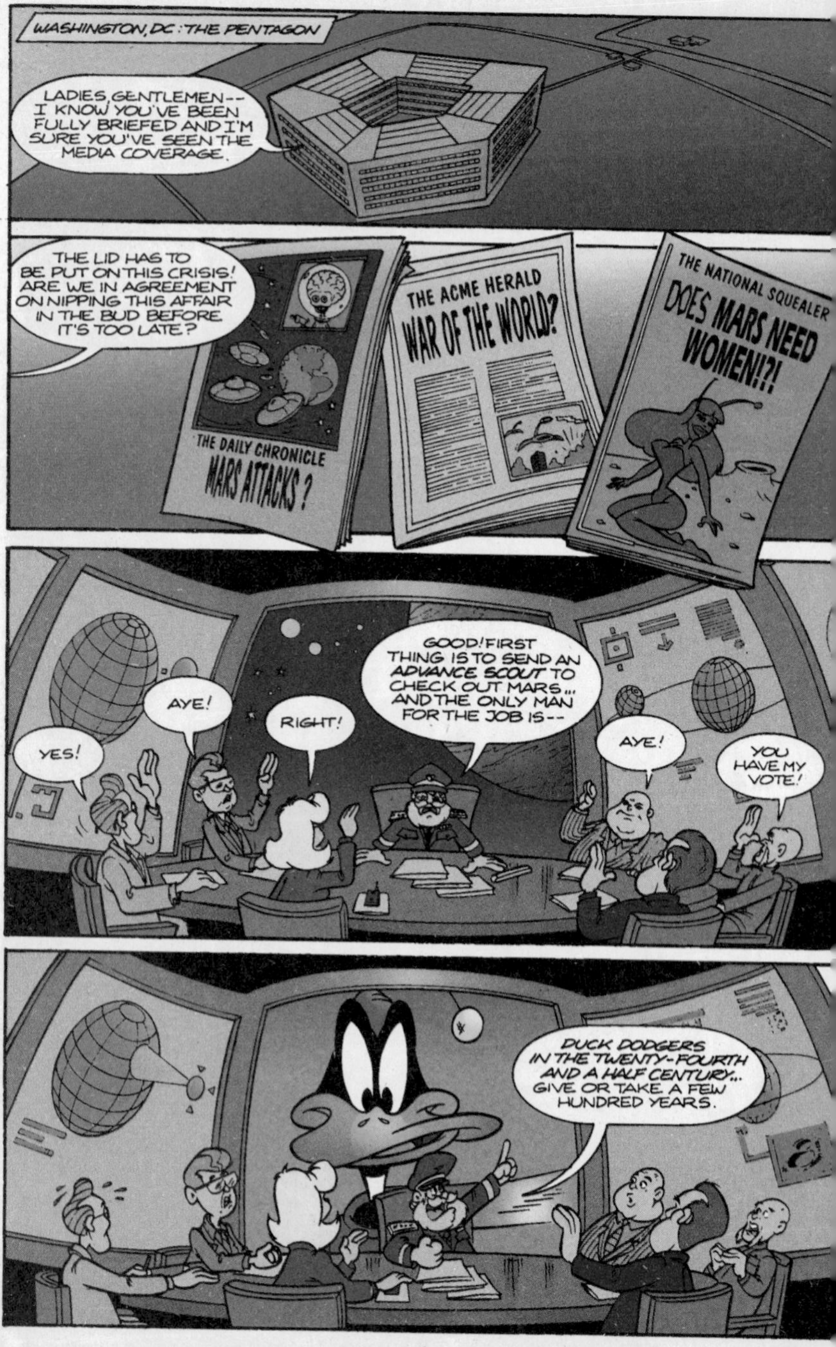
WASHINGTON, DC: THE PENTAGON
LADIES, GENTLEMEN-- I KNOW YOU'VE BEEN FULLY BRIEFED AND I'M SURE YOU'VE SEEN THE MEDIA COVERAGE.
THE LID HAS TO BE PUT ON THIS CRISIS! ARE WE IN AGREEMENT ON NIPPING THIS AFFAIR IN THE BUD BEFORE IT'S TOO LATE?
THE DAILY CHRONICLE
MARS ATTACKS?
THE ACME HERALD
WAR OF THE WORLD?
THE NATIONAL SQUEALER
DOES MARS NEED WOMEN!?!
YES!
AYE!
RIGHT!
GOOD! FIRST THING IS TO SEND AN ADVANCE SCOUT TO CHECK OUT MARS... AND THE ONLY MAN FOR THE JOB IS--
AYE!
YOU HAVE MY VOTE!
DUCK DODGERS IN THE TWENTY-FOURTH AND A HALF CENTURY... GIVE OR TAKE A FEW HUNDRED YEARS.

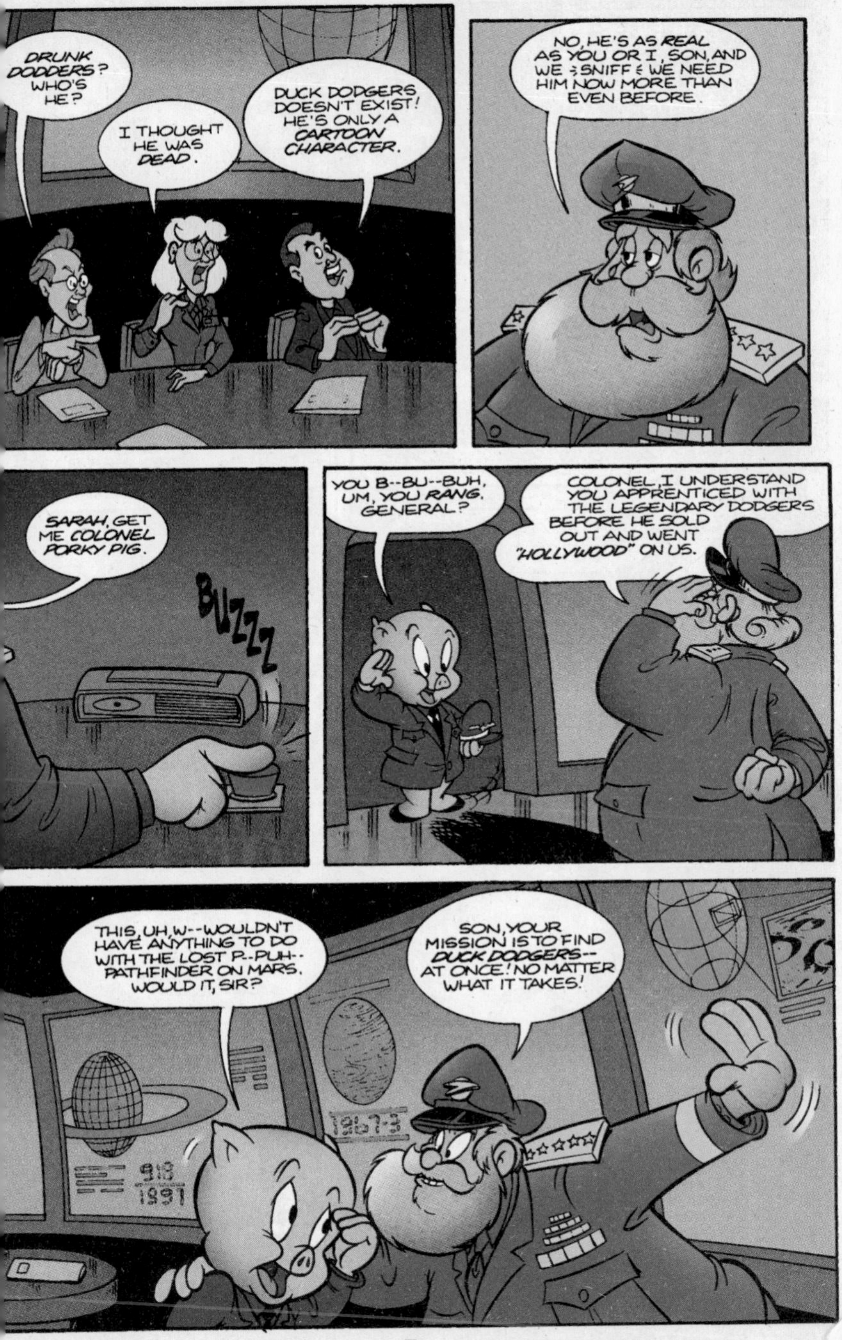

DRUNK DODDERS? WHO'S HE?
I THOUGHT HE WAS DEAD.
DUCK DODGERS DOESN'T EXIST! HE'S ONLY A CARTOON CHARACTER.
NO, HE'S AS REAL AS YOU OR I, SON, AND WE -SNIFF- WE NEED HIM NOW MORE THAN EVEN BEFORE.
SARAH, GET ME COLONEL PORKY PIG.
BUZZZZ
YOU B--BU--BUH, UM, YOU RANG, GENERAL?
COLONEL, I UNDERSTAND YOU APPRENTICED WITH THE LEGENDARY DODGERS BEFORE HE SOLD OUT AND WENT "HOLLYWOOD" ON US.
THIS, UH, W--WOULDN'T HAVE ANYTHING TO DO WITH THE LOST P--PUH--PATHFINDER ON MARS, WOULD IT, SIR?
SON, YOUR MISSION IS TO FIND DUCK DODGERS-- AT ONCE! NO MATTER WHAT IT TAKES!

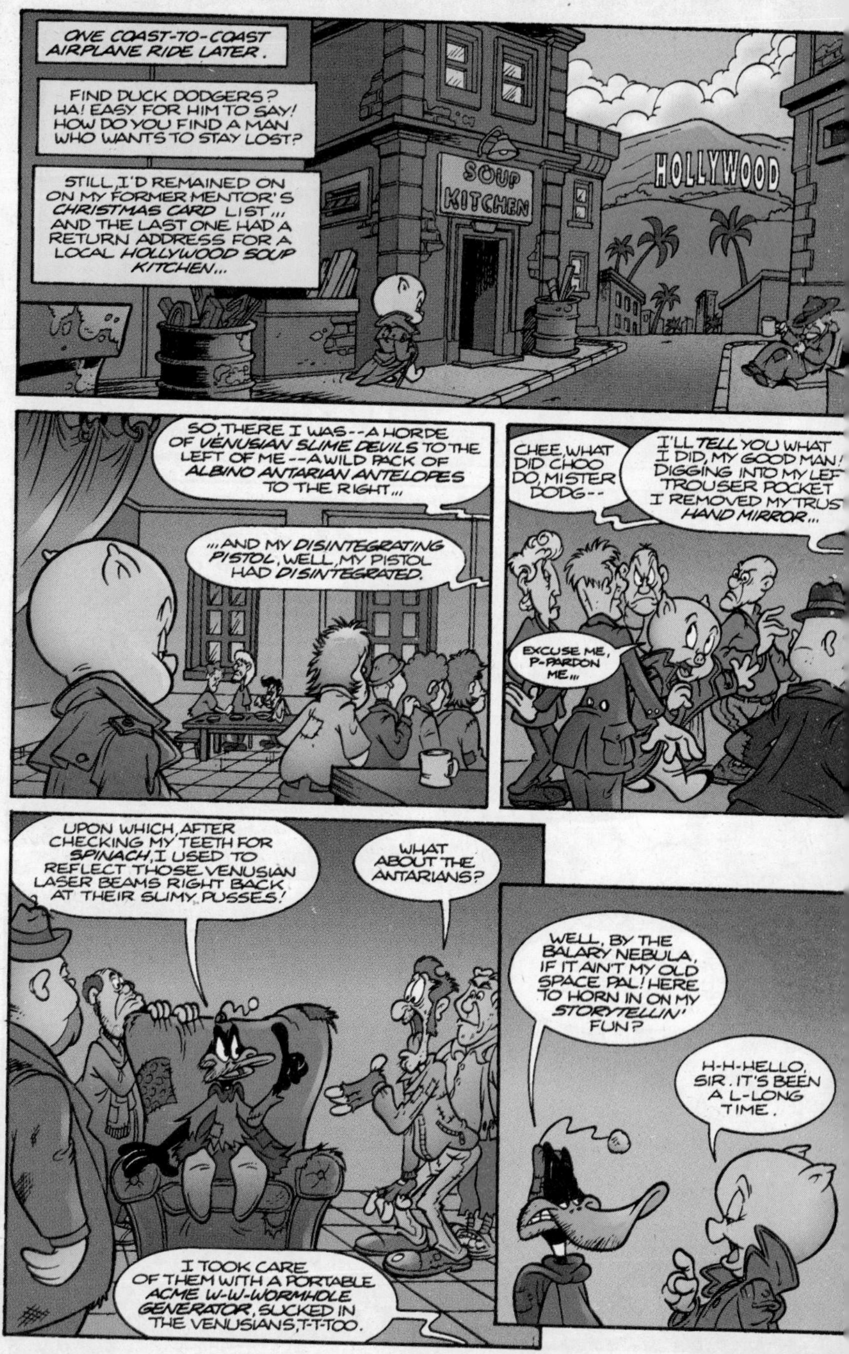
ONE COAST-TO-COAST AIRPLANE RIDE LATER.
FIND DUCK DODGERS? HA! EASY FOR HIM TO SAY! HOW DO YOU FIND A MAN WHO WANTS TO STAY LOST?
STILL, I'D REMAINED ON ON MY FORMER MENTOR'S CHRISTMAS CARD LIST... AND THE LAST ONE HAD A RETURN ADDRESS FOR A LOCAL HOLLYWOOD SOUP KITCHEN...
SOUP KITCHEN
HOLLYWOOD
SO, THERE I WAS--A HORDE OF VENUSIAN SLIME DEVILS TO THE LEFT OF ME--A WILD PACK OF ALBINO ANTARIAN ANTELOPES TO THE RIGHT...
...AND MY DISINTEGRATING PISTOL, WELL, MY PISTOL HAD DISINTEGRATED.
CHEE, WHAT DID CHOO DO, MISTER DODG--
I'LL TELL YOU WHAT I DID, MY GOOD MAN! DIGGING INTO MY LEF TROUSER POCKET I REMOVED MY TRUS HAND MIRROR...
EXCUSE ME, P-PARDON ME...
UPON WHICH, AFTER CHECKING MY TEETH FOR SPINACH, I USED TO REFLECT THOSE VENUSIAN LASER BEAMS RIGHT BACK AT THEIR SLIMY PUSSES!
WHAT ABOUT THE ANTARIANS?
I TOOK CARE OF THEM WITH A PORTABLE ACME W-W-WORMHOLE GENERATOR, SUCKED IN THE VENUSIANS, T-T-TOO.
WELL, BY THE BALARY NEBULA, IF IT AIN'T MY OLD SPACE PAL! HERE TO HORN IN ON MY STORYTELLIN' FUN?
H-H-HELLO, SIR. IT'S BEEN A L-LONG TIME.

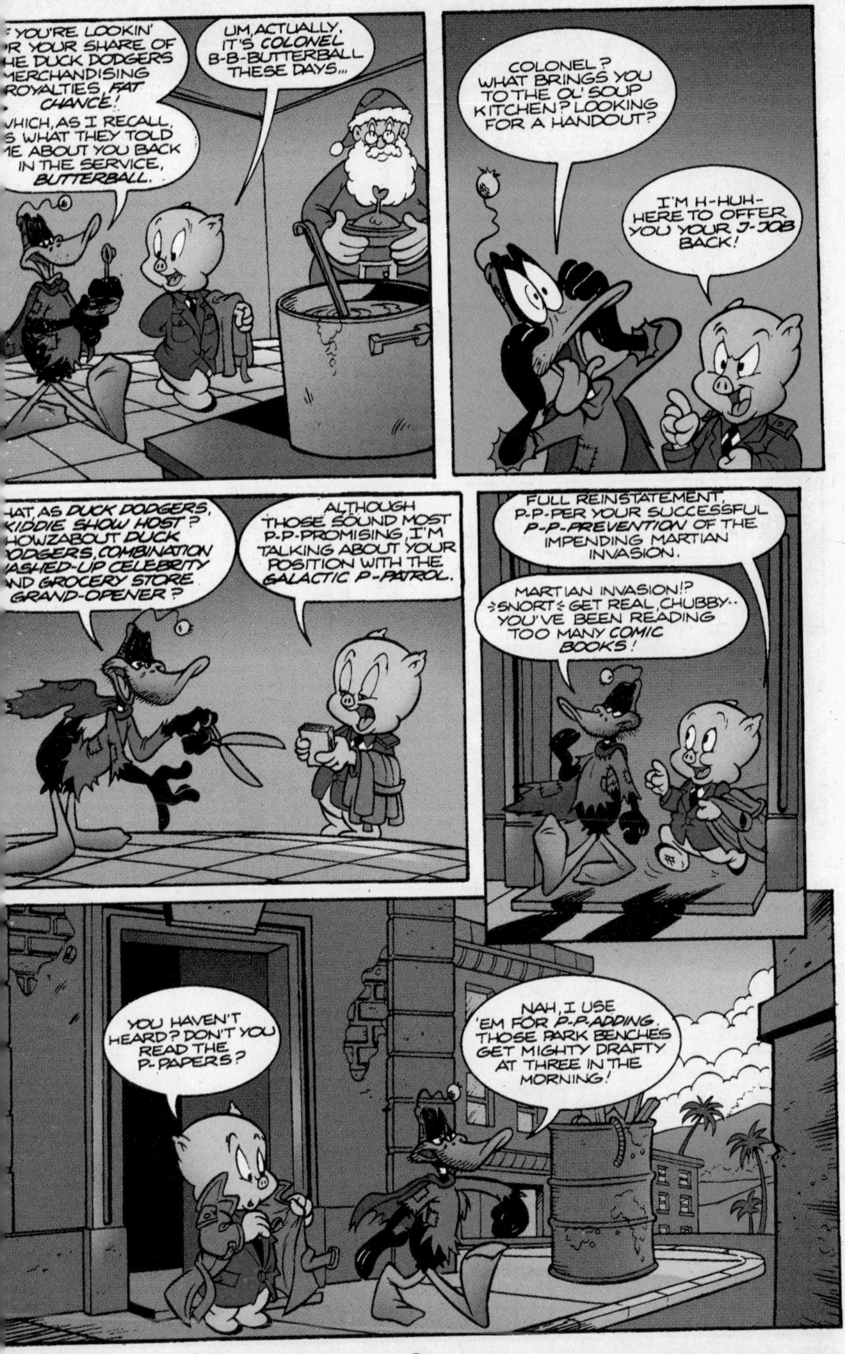
F YOU'RE LOOKIN' R YOUR SHARE OF HE DUCK DODGERS MERCHANDISING ROYALTIES, FAT CHANCE!
WHICH, AS I RECALL, S WHAT THEY TOLD ME ABOUT YOU BACK IN THE SERVICE, BUTTERBALL.
UM, ACTUALLY, IT'S COLONEL B-B-BUTTERBALL THESE DAYS...
COLONEL? WHAT BRINGS YOU TO THE OL' SOUP KITCHEN? LOOKING FOR A HANDOUT?
I'M H-HUH-HERE TO OFFER YOU YOUR J-JOB BACK!
HAT, AS DUCK DODGERS, KIDDIE SHOW HOST? HOWZABOUT DUCK DODGERS, COMBINATION WASHED-UP CELEBRITY ND GROCERY STORE GRAND-OPENER?
ALTHOUGH THOSE SOUND MOST P-P-PROMISING, I'M TALKING ABOUT YOUR POSITION WITH THE GALACTIC P-PATROL.
FULL REINSTATEMENT, P-P-PER YOUR SUCCESSFUL P-P-PREVENTION OF THE IMPENDING MARTIAN INVASION.
MARTIAN INVASION!? ≥SNORT≤ GET REAL, CHUBBY.. YOU'VE BEEN READING TOO MANY COMIC BOOKS!
YOU HAVEN'T HEARD? DON'T YOU READ THE P-PAPERS?
NAH, I USE 'EM FOR P-P-ADDING. THOSE PARK BENCHES GET MIGHTY DRAFTY AT THREE IN THE MORNING!

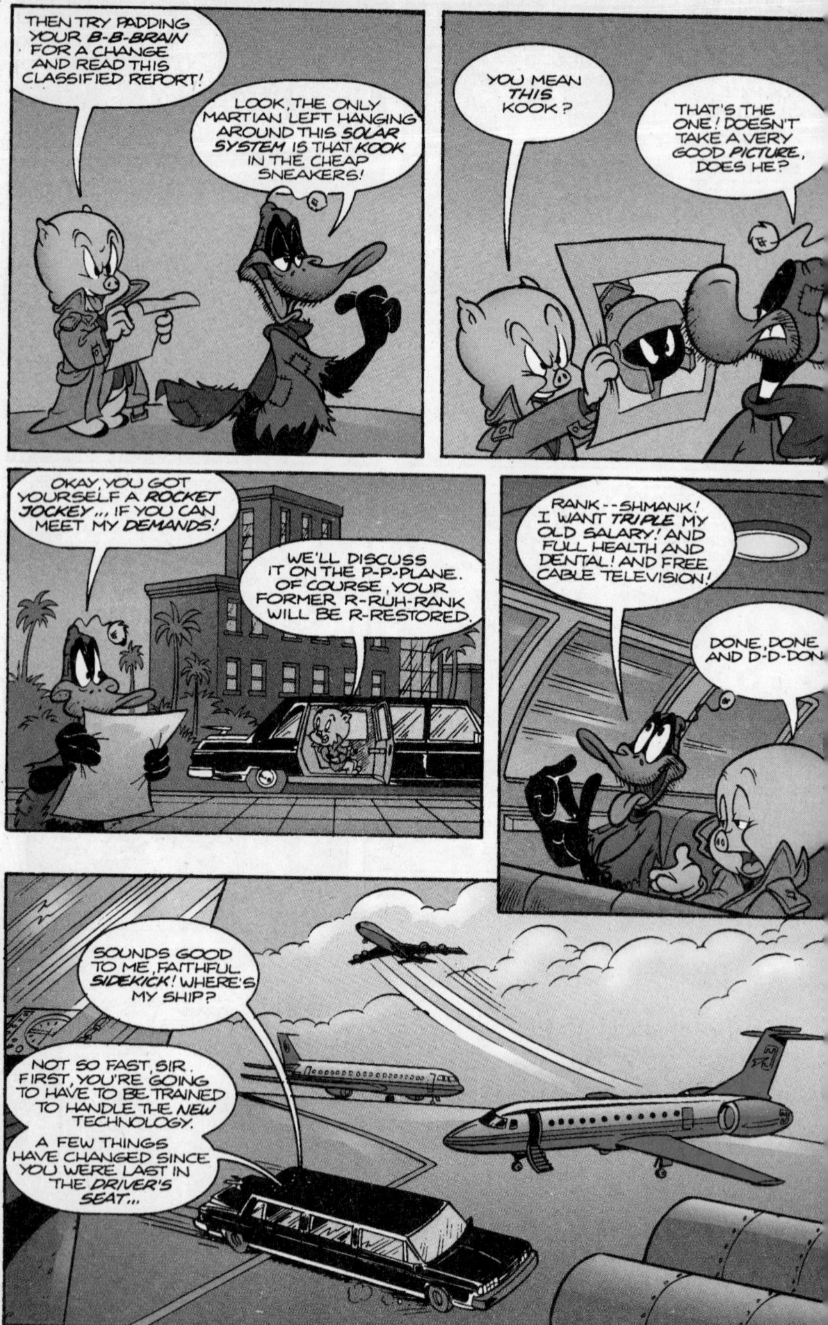
THEN TRY PADDING YOUR B-B-BRAIN FOR A CHANGE AND READ THIS CLASSIFIED REPORT!
LOOK, THE ONLY MARTIAN LEFT HANGING AROUND THIS SOLAR SYSTEM IS THAT KOOK IN THE CHEAP SNEAKERS!
YOU MEAN THIS KOOK?
THAT'S THE ONE! DOESN'T TAKE A VERY GOOD PICTURE, DOES HE?
OKAY, YOU GOT YOURSELF A ROCKET JOCKEY... IF YOU CAN MEET MY DEMANDS!
WE'LL DISCUSS IT ON THE P-P-PLANE. OF COURSE, YOUR FORMER R-RUH-RANK WILL BE R-RESTORED.
RANK--SHMANK! I WANT TRIPLE MY OLD SALARY! AND FULL HEALTH AND DENTAL! AND FREE CABLE TELEVISION!
DONE, DONE AND D-D-DON
SOUNDS GOOD TO ME, FAITHFUL SIDEKICK! WHERE'S MY SHIP?
NOT SO FAST, SIR. FIRST, YOU'RE GOING TO HAVE TO BE TRAINED TO HANDLE THE NEW TECHNOLOGY.
A FEW THINGS HAVE CHANGED SINCE YOU WERE LAST IN THE DRIVER'S SEAT...

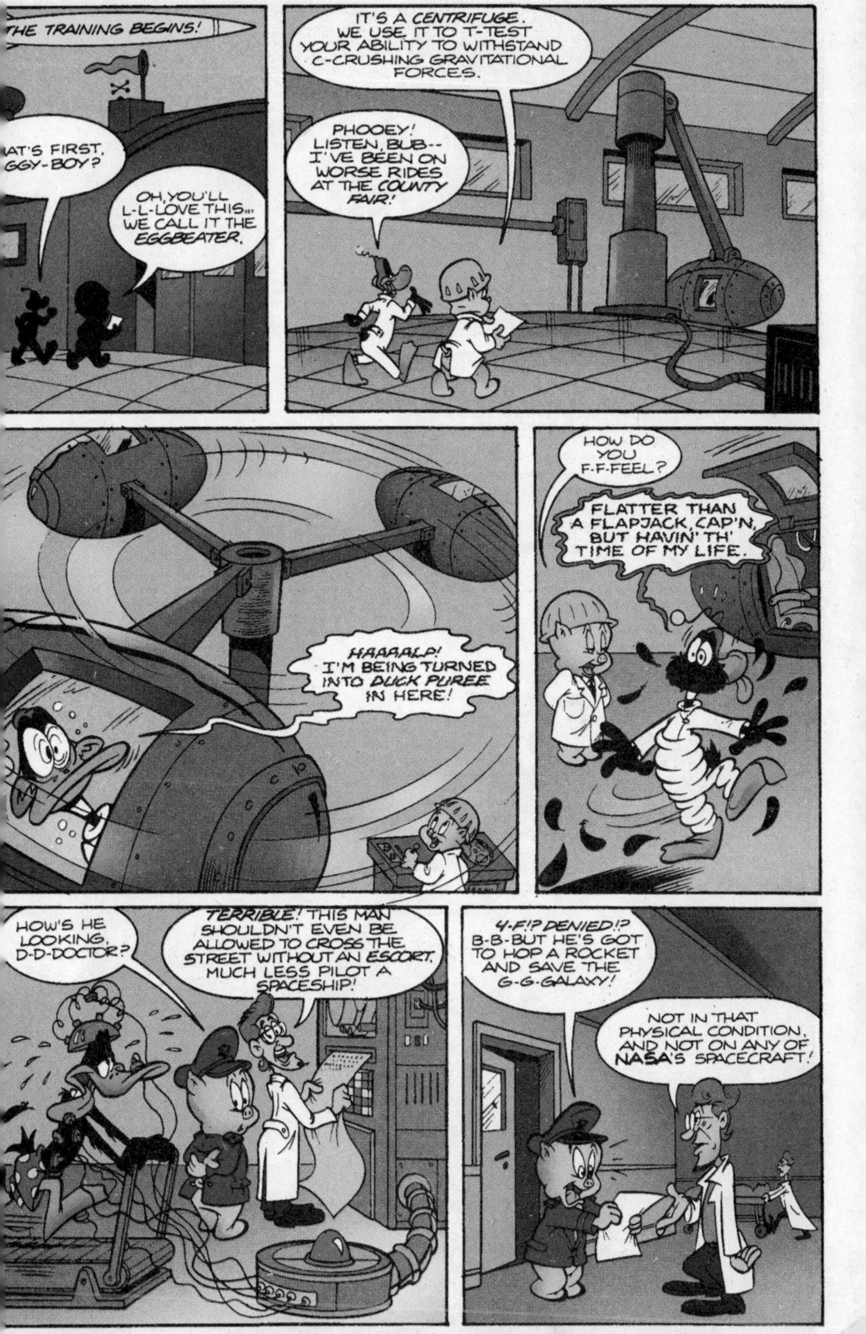
THE TRAINING BEGINS!
...AT'S FIRST, ...GGY-BOY?
OH, YOU'LL L-L-LOVE THIS... WE CALL IT THE EGGBEATER.
IT'S A CENTRIFUGE. WE USE IT TO T-TEST YOUR ABILITY TO WITHSTAND C-CRUSHING GRAVITATIONAL FORCES.
PHOOEY! LISTEN, BUB-- I'VE BEEN ON WORSE RIDES AT THE COUNTY FAIR!
HAAALP! I'M BEING TURNED INTO DUCK PUREE IN HERE!
HOW DO YOU F-F-FEEL?
FLATTER THAN A FLAPJACK, CAP'N, BUT HAVIN' TH' TIME OF MY LIFE.
HOW'S HE LOOKING, D-D-DOCTOR?
TERRIBLE! THIS MAN SHOULDN'T EVEN BE ALLOWED TO CROSS THE STREET WITHOUT AN ESCORT. MUCH LESS PILOT A SPACESHIP!
4-F!? DENIED!? B-B-BUT HE'S GOT TO HOP A ROCKET AND SAVE THE G-G-GALAXY!
NOT IN THAT PHYSICAL CONDITION, AND NOT ON ANY OF NASA'S SPACECRAFT!

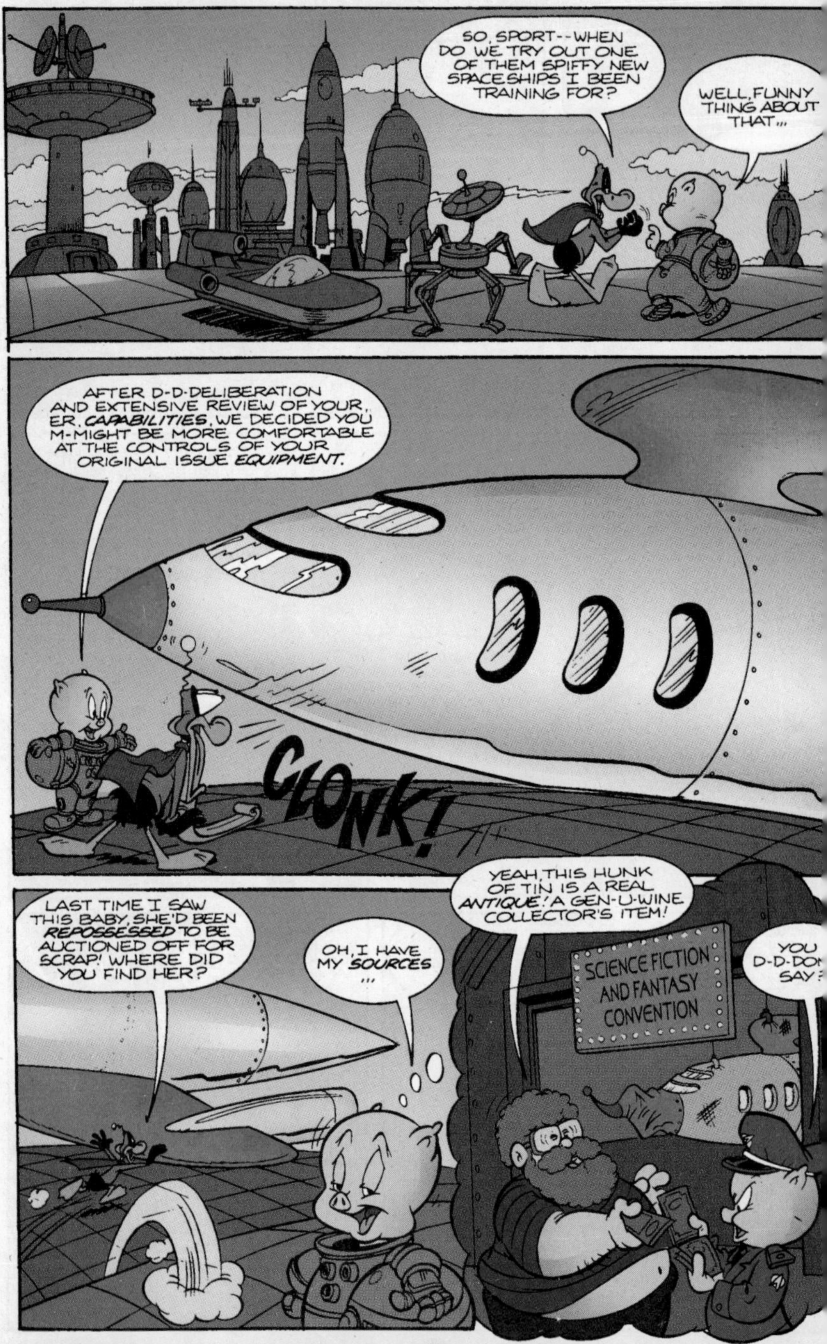

SO, SPORT--WHEN DO WE TRY OUT ONE OF THEM SPIFFY NEW SPACESHIPS I BEEN TRAINING FOR?
WELL, FUNNY THING ABOUT THAT...
AFTER D-D-DELIBERATION AND EXTENSIVE REVIEW OF YOUR, ER, CAPABILITIES, WE DECIDED YOU M-MIGHT BE MORE COMFORTABLE AT THE CONTROLS OF YOUR ORIGINAL ISSUE EQUIPMENT.
CLONK!
LAST TIME I SAW THIS BABY, SHE'D BEEN REPOSSESSED TO BE AUCTIONED OFF FOR SCRAP! WHERE DID YOU FIND HER?
OH, I HAVE MY SOURCES ...
YEAH, THIS HUNK OF TIN IS A REAL ANTIQUE! A GEN-U-WINE COLLECTOR'S ITEM!
SCIENCE FICTION AND FANTASY CONVENTION
YOU D-D-DON SAY?

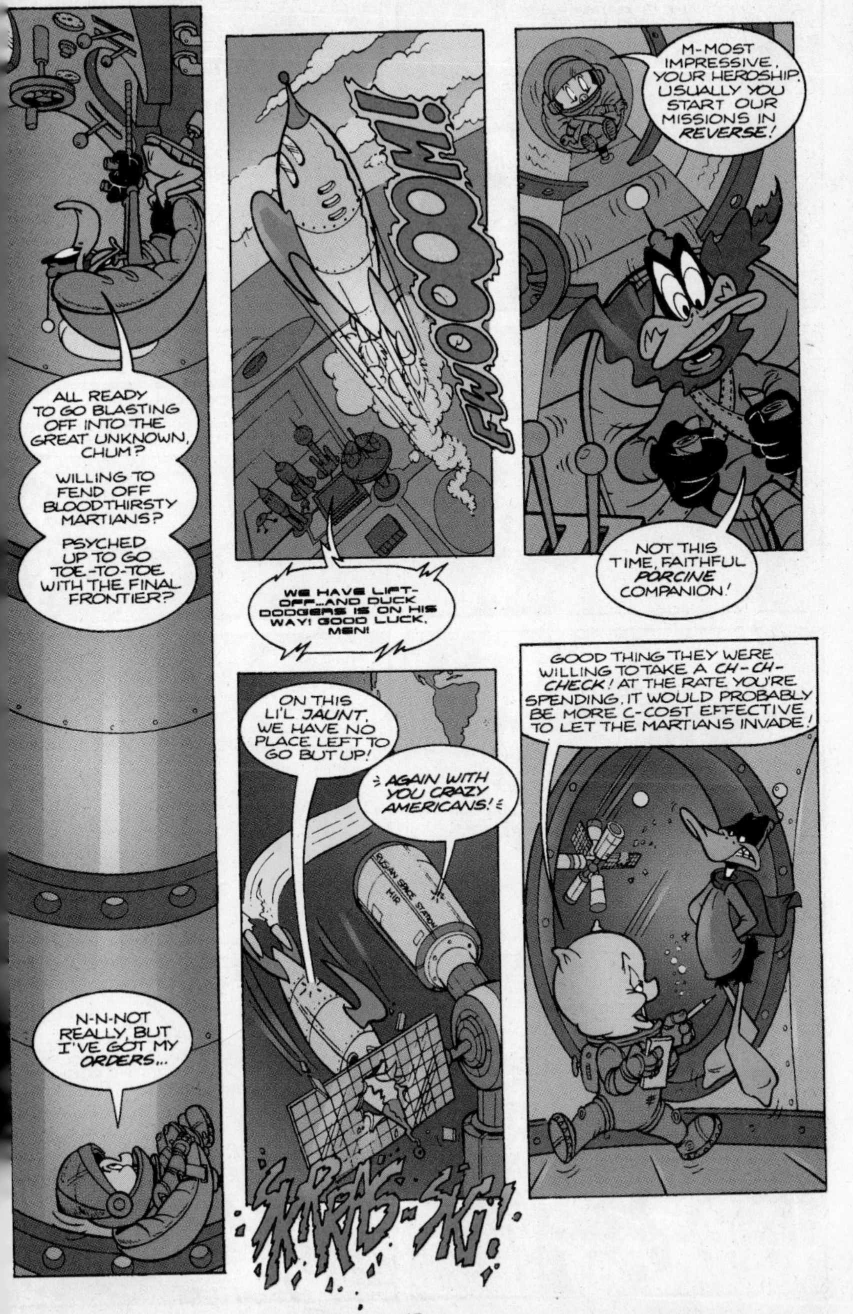
ALL READY TO GO BLASTING OFF INTO THE GREAT UNKNOWN, CHUM?
WILLING TO FEND OFF BLOODTHIRSTY MARTIANS?
PSYCHED UP TO GO TOE-TO-TOE WITH THE FINAL FRONTIER?
N-N-NOT REALLY, BUT I'VE GOT MY ORDERS...
FWOOOM!
WE HAVE LIFT-OFF...AND DUCK DODGERS IS ON HIS WAY! GOOD LUCK, MEN!
M-MOST IMPRESSIVE, YOUR HEROSHIP. USUALLY YOU START OUR MISSIONS IN REVERSE!
NOT THIS TIME, FAITHFUL PORCINE COMPANION!
ON THIS LI'L JAUNT, WE HAVE NO PLACE LEFT TO GO BUT UP!
AGAIN WITH YOU CRAZY AMERICANS!
MIR
SKRAS-SK!
GOOD THING THEY WERE WILLING TO TAKE A CH-CH-CHECK! AT THE RATE YOU'RE SPENDING, IT WOULD PROBABLY BE MORE C-COST EFFECTIVE TO LET THE MARTIANS INVADE!

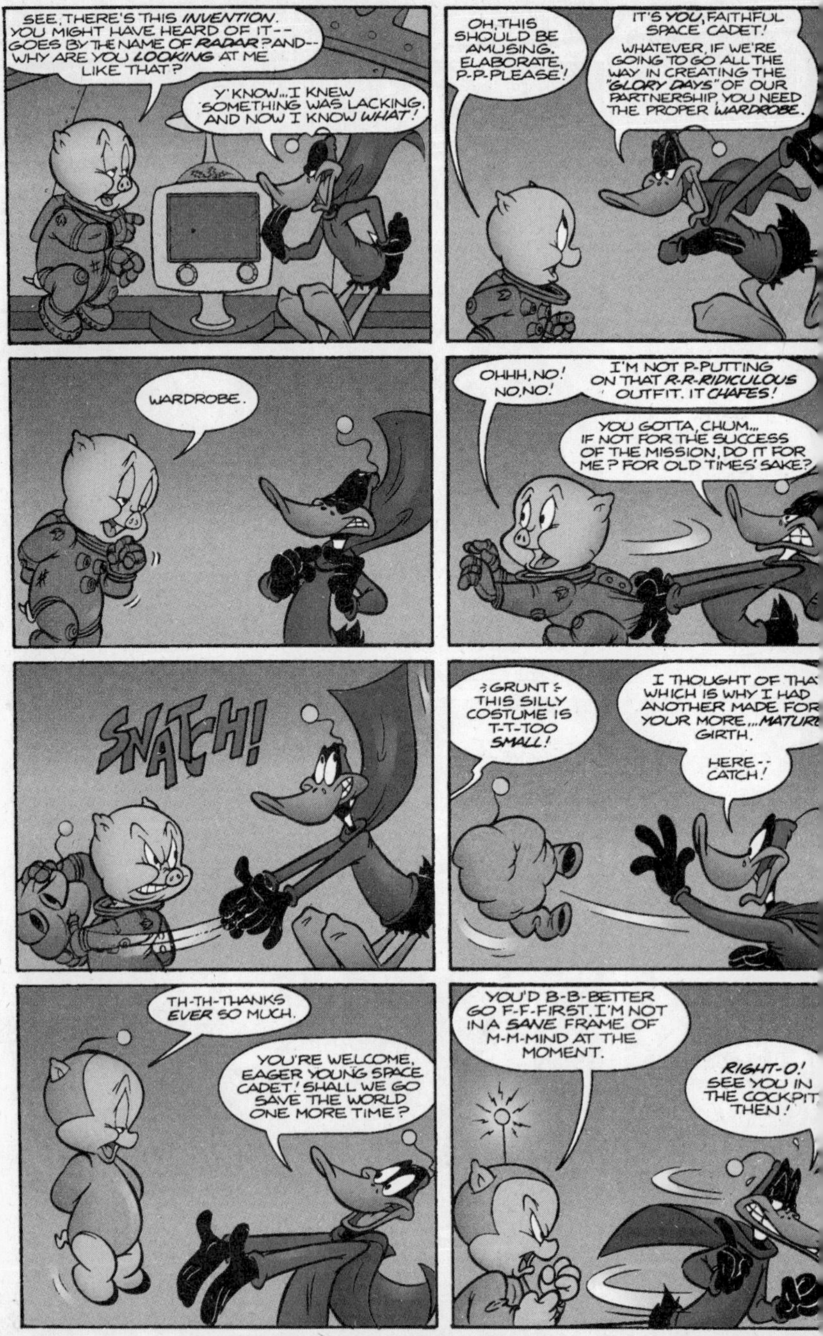
SEE, THERE'S THIS INVENTION. YOU MIGHT HAVE HEARD OF IT-- GOES BY THE NAME OF RADAR? AND-- WHY ARE YOU LOOKING AT ME LIKE THAT?
Y'KNOW...I KNEW SOMETHING WAS LACKING. AND NOW I KNOW WHAT!
OH, THIS SHOULD BE AMUSING. ELABORATE, P-P-PLEASE!
IT'S YOU, FAITHFUL SPACE CADET!
WHATEVER, IF WE'RE GOING TO GO ALL THE WAY IN CREATING THE "GLORY DAYS" OF OUR PARTNERSHIP, YOU NEED THE PROPER WARDROBE.
WARDROBE.
OHHH, NO! NO, NO!
I'M NOT P-PUTTING ON THAT R-R-RIDICULOUS OUTFIT. IT CHAFES!
YOU GOTTA, CHUM... IF NOT FOR THE SUCCESS OF THE MISSION, DO IT FOR ME? FOR OLD TIMES' SAKE?
SNATCH!
GRUNT THIS SILLY COSTUME IS T-T-TOO SMALL!
I THOUGHT OF THA WHICH IS WHY I HAD ANOTHER MADE FOR YOUR MORE... MATUR GIRTH.
HERE-- CATCH!
TH-TH-THANKS EVER SO MUCH.
YOU'RE WELCOME, EAGER YOUNG SPACE CADET! SHALL WE GO SAVE THE WORLD ONE MORE TIME?
YOU'D B-B-BETTER GO F-F-FIRST. I'M NOT IN A SANE FRAME OF M-M-MIND AT THE MOMENT.
RIGHT-O! SEE YOU IN THE COCKPIT THEN!

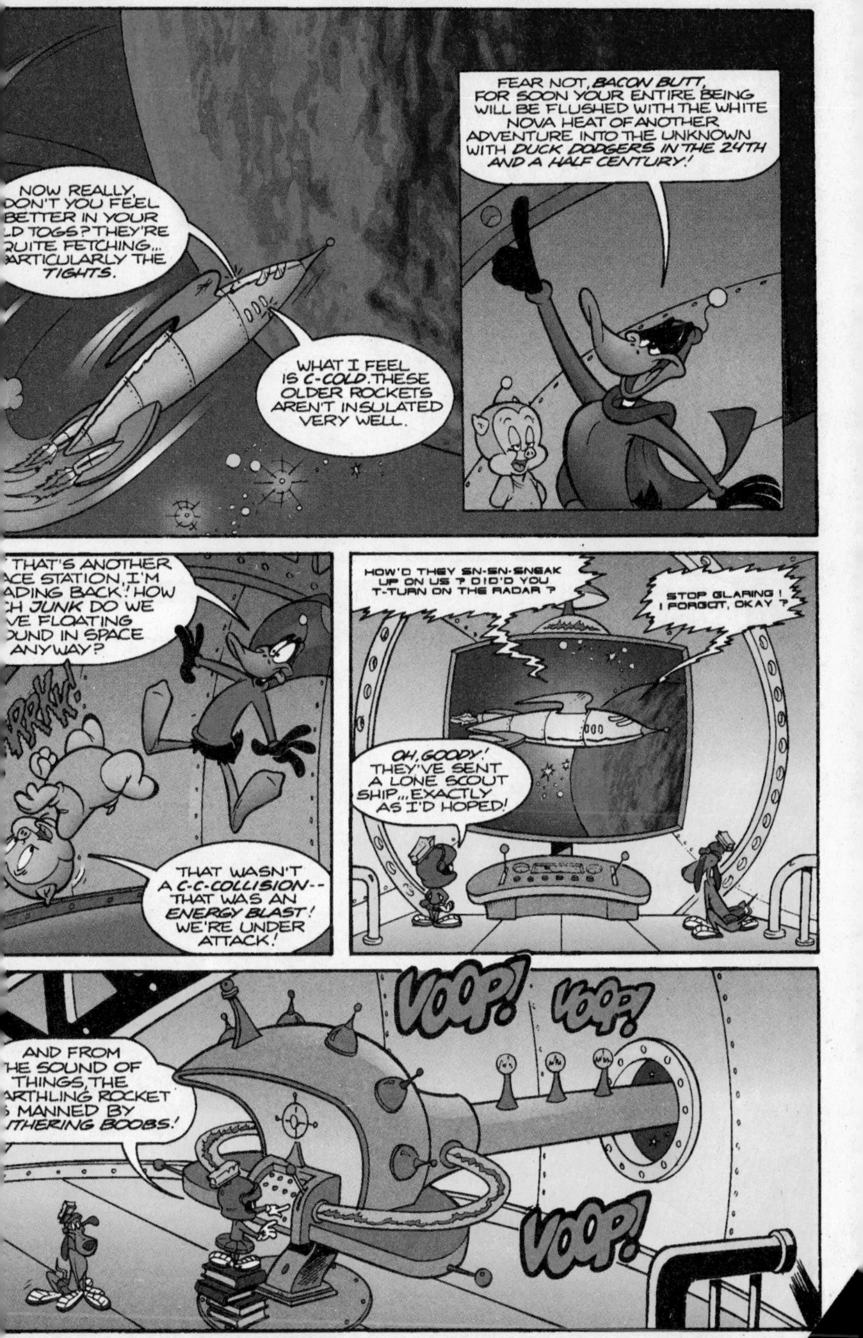
NOW REALLY, DON'T YOU FEEL BETTER IN YOUR LD TOGS? THEY'RE QUITE FETCHING... PARTICULARLY THE TIGHTS.
WHAT I FEEL IS C-COLD. THESE OLDER ROCKETS AREN'T INSULATED VERY WELL.
FEAR NOT, BACON BUTT, FOR SOON YOUR ENTIRE BEING WILL BE FLUSHED WITH THE WHITE NOVA HEAT OF ANOTHER ADVENTURE INTO THE UNKNOWN WITH DUCK DODGERS IN THE 24TH AND A HALF CENTURY!
THAT'S ANOTHER ACE STATION, I'M ADING BACK! HOW CH JUNK DO WE VE FLOATING OUND IN SPACE ANYWAY?
THAT WASN'T A C-C-COLLISION-- THAT WAS AN ENERGY BLAST! WE'RE UNDER ATTACK!
HOW'D THEY SN-SN-SNEAK UP ON US? DID'D YOU T-TURN ON THE RADAR?
STOP GLARING! I FORGOT, OKAY?
OH, GOODY! THEY'VE SENT A LONE SCOUT SHIP,,, EXACTLY AS I'D HOPED!
VOOP! VOOP!
AND FROM HE SOUND OF THINGS, THE ARTHLING ROCKET S MANNED BY THERING BOOBS!
VOOP!

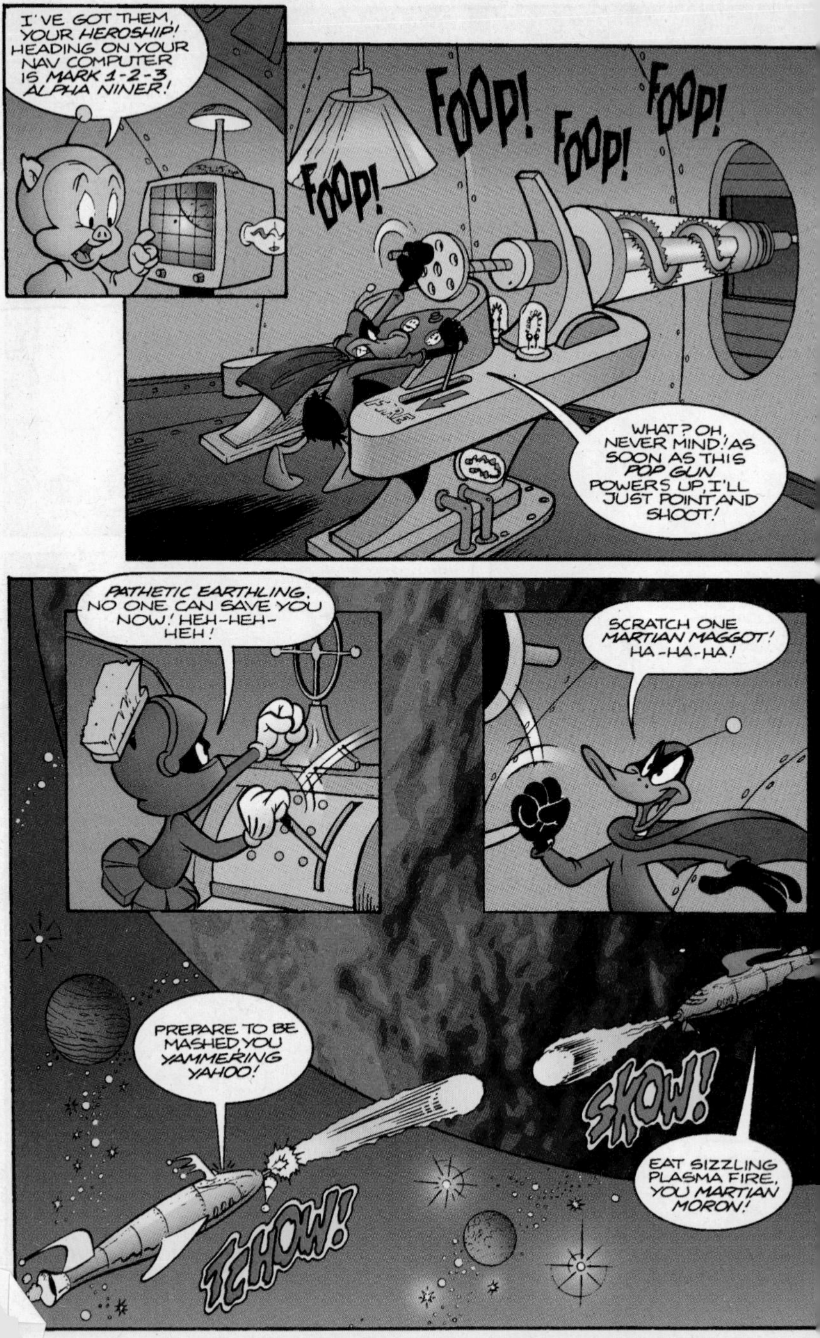

I'VE GOT THEM, YOUR HEROSHIP! HEADING ON YOUR NAV COMPUTER IS MARK 1-2-3 ALPHA NINER!
FOOP!
FOOP!
FOOP!
FOOP!
WHAT? OH, NEVER MIND! AS SOON AS THIS POP GUN POWERS UP, I'LL JUST POINT AND SHOOT!
PATHETIC EARTHLING. NO ONE CAN SAVE YOU NOW! HEH-HEH-HEH!
SCRATCH ONE MARTIAN MAGGOT! HA-HA-HA!
PREPARE TO BE MASHED YOU YAMMERING YAHOO!
TCHOW!
SKOW!
EAT SIZZLING PLASMA FIRE, YOU MARTIAN MORON!

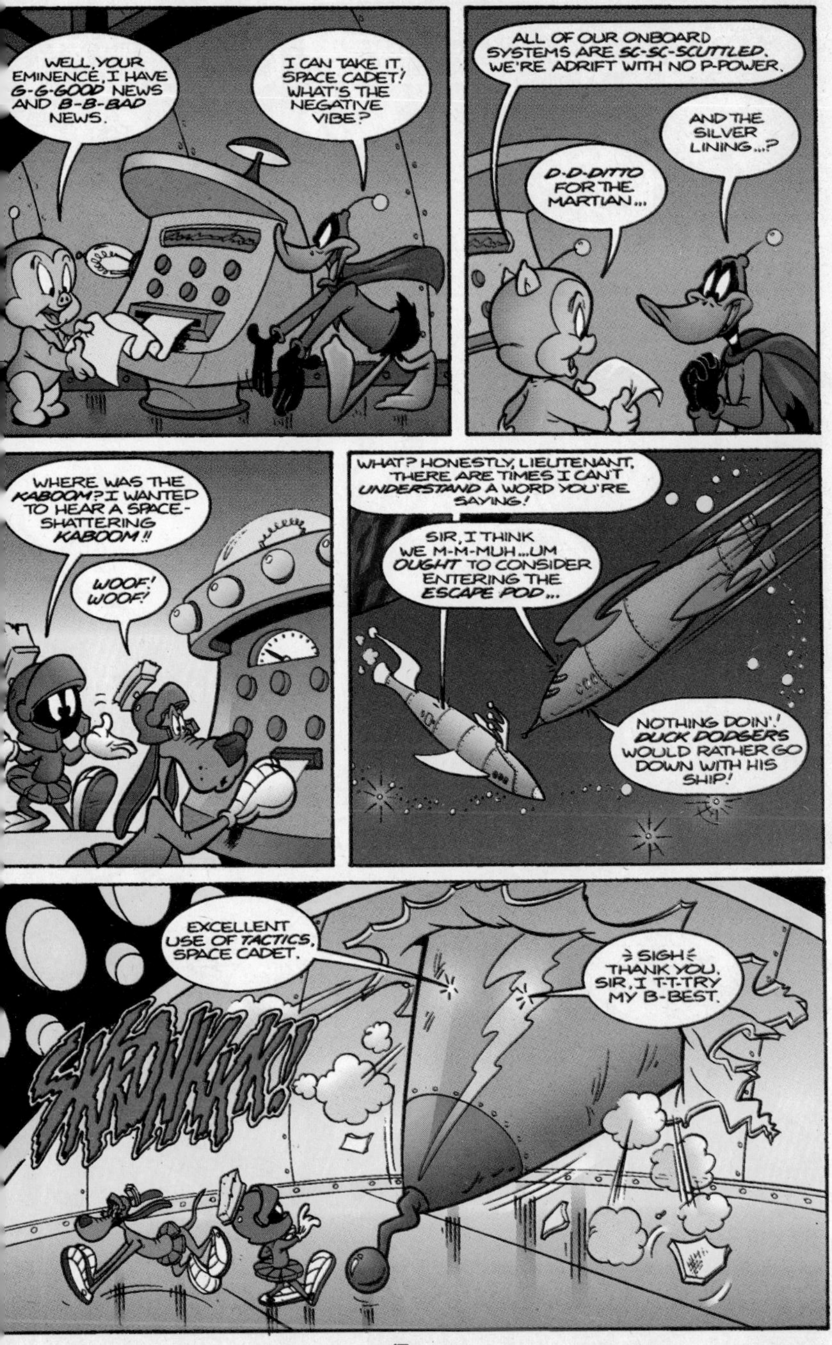
WELL, YOUR EMINENCE, I HAVE G-G-GOOD NEWS AND B-B-BAD NEWS.
I CAN TAKE IT, SPACE CADET! WHAT'S THE NEGATIVE VIBE?
ALL OF OUR ONBOARD SYSTEMS ARE SC-SC-SCUTTLED. WE'RE ADRIFT WITH NO P-POWER.
AND THE SILVER LINING...?
D-D-DITTO FOR THE MARTIAN...
WHERE WAS THE KABOOM? I WANTED TO HEAR A SPACE-SHATTERING KABOOM!!
WOOF! WOOF!
WHAT? HONESTLY, LIEUTENANT, THERE ARE TIMES I CAN'T UNDERSTAND A WORD YOU'RE SAYING!
SIR, I THINK WE M-M-MUH...UM OUGHT TO CONSIDER ENTERING THE ESCAPE POD...
NOTHING DOIN'! DUCK DODGERS WOULD RATHER GO DOWN WITH HIS SHIP!
EXCELLENT USE OF TACTICS, SPACE CADET.
SHOWWK!!
SIGH THANK YOU, SIR, I T-T-TRY MY B-BEST.

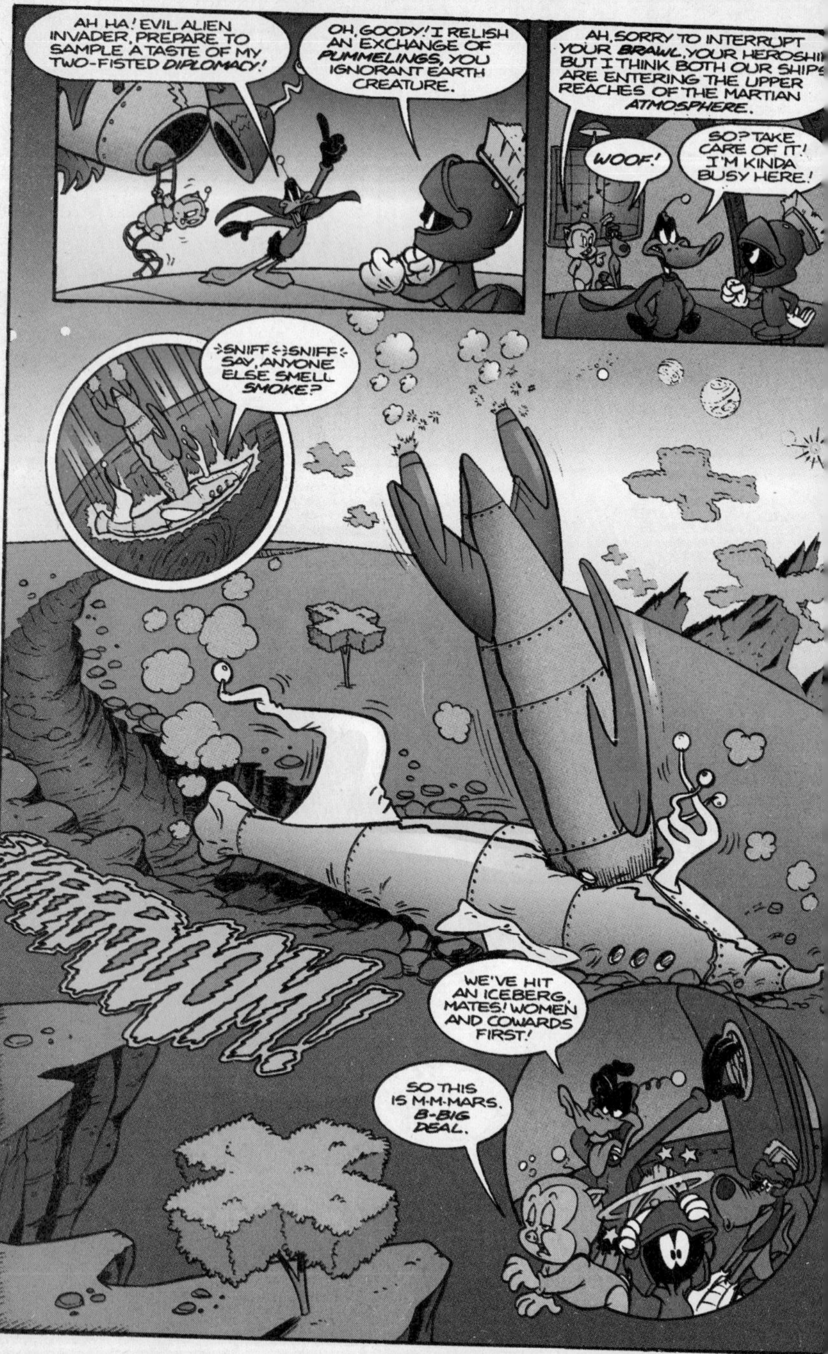
AH HA! EVIL ALIEN INVADER, PREPARE TO SAMPLE A TASTE OF MY TWO-FISTED *DIPLOMACY!*
OH, GOODY! I RELISH AN EXCHANGE OF *PUMMELINGS*, YOU IGNORANT EARTH CREATURE.
AH, SORRY TO INTERRUPT YOUR *BRAWL*, YOUR HEROSHI BUT I THINK BOTH OUR SHIP ARE ENTERING THE UPPER REACHES OF THE MARTIAN *ATMOSPHERE*.
WOOF!
SO? TAKE CARE OF IT! I'M KINDA BUSY HERE!
SNIFF SNIFF SAY, ANYONE ELSE SMELL *SMOKE?*
WE'VE HIT AN ICEBERG, MATES! WOMEN AND COWARDS FIRST!
SO THIS IS M-M-MARS. *B-BIG DEAL.*

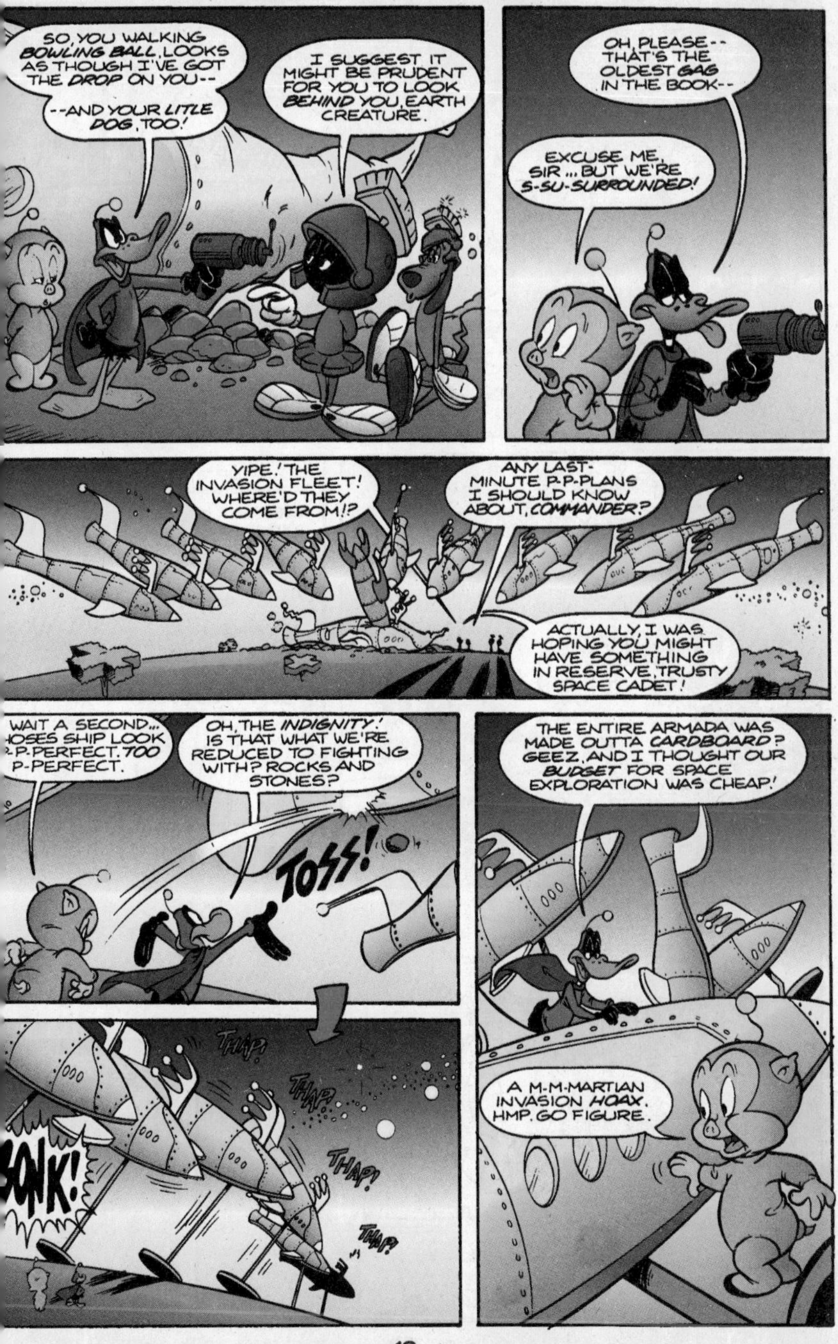
SO, YOU WALKING BOWLING BALL, LOOKS AS THOUGH I'VE GOT THE DROP ON YOU--
--AND YOUR LITLE DOG, TOO!
I SUGGEST IT MIGHT BE PRUDENT FOR YOU TO LOOK BEHIND YOU, EARTH CREATURE.
OH, PLEASE-- THAT'S THE OLDEST GAG IN THE BOOK--
EXCUSE ME, SIR ... BUT WE'RE S-SU-SURROUNDED!
YIPE! THE INVASION FLEET! WHERE'D THEY COME FROM!?
ANY LAST-MINUTE P-P-PLANS I SHOULD KNOW ABOUT, COMMANDER?
ACTUALLY, I WAS HOPING YOU MIGHT HAVE SOMETHING IN RESERVE, TRUSTY SPACE CADET!
WAIT A SECOND... HOSES SHIP LOOK P-P-PERFECT. TOO P-PERFECT.
OH, THE INDIGNITY! IS THAT WHAT WE'RE REDUCED TO FIGHTING WITH? ROCKS AND STONES?
TOSS!
THAP!
THAP!
THAP!
THAP!
SONK!
THE ENTIRE ARMADA WAS MADE OUTTA CARDBOARD? GEEZ, AND I THOUGHT OUR BUDGET FOR SPACE EXPLORATION WAS CHEAP!
A M-M-MARTIAN INVASION HOAX. HMP. GO FIGURE.

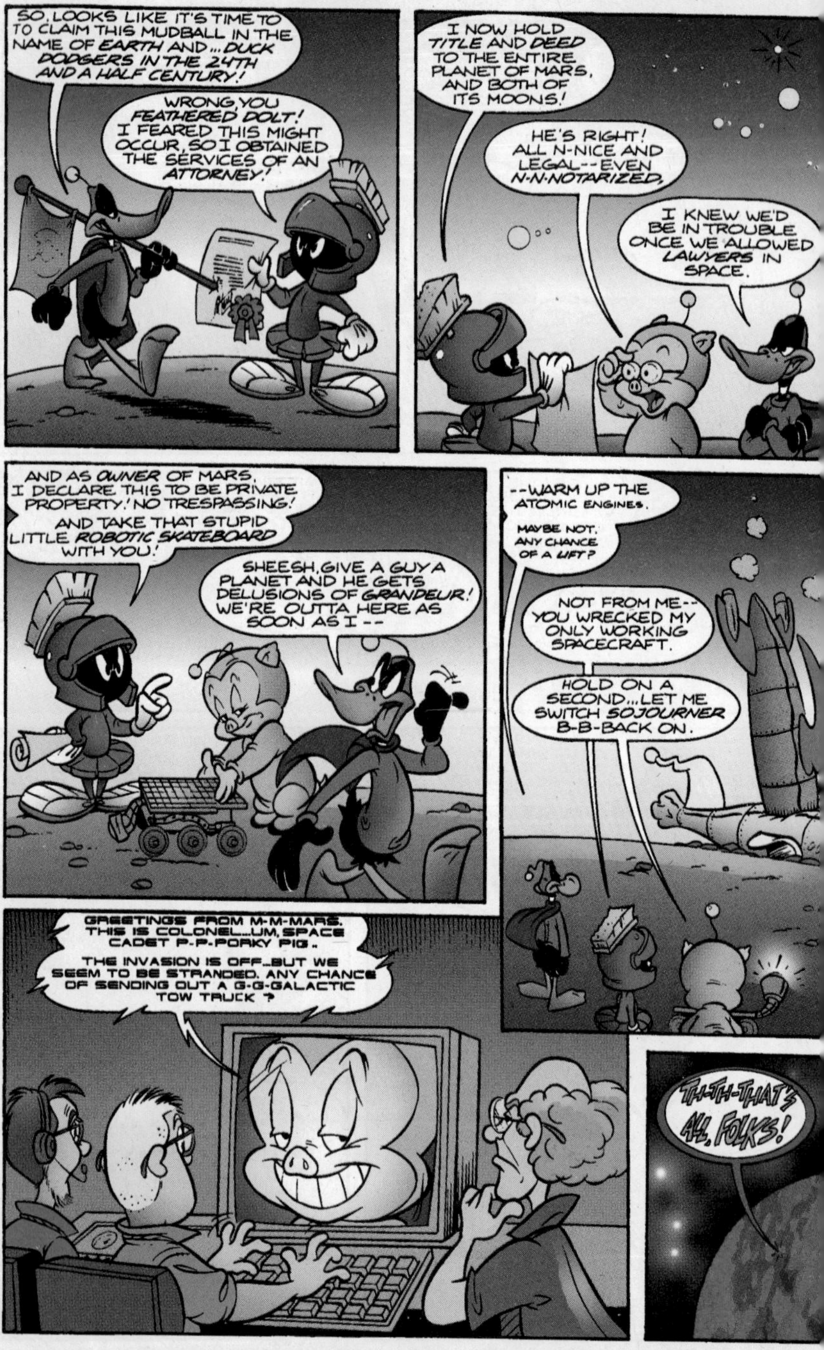
SO, LOOKS LIKE IT'S TIME TO TO CLAIM THIS MUDBALL IN THE NAME OF EARTH AND... DUCK DODGERS IN THE 24TH AND A HALF CENTURY!
WRONG, YOU FEATHERED DOLT! I FEARED THIS MIGHT OCCUR, SO I OBTAINED THE SERVICES OF AN ATTORNEY!
I NOW HOLD TITLE AND DEED TO THE ENTIRE PLANET OF MARS, AND BOTH OF ITS MOONS!
HE'S RIGHT! ALL N-NICE AND LEGAL--EVEN N-N-NOTARIZED.
I KNEW WE'D BE IN TROUBLE ONCE WE ALLOWED LAWYERS IN SPACE.
AND AS OWNER OF MARS, I DECLARE THIS TO BE PRIVATE PROPERTY! NO TRESPASSING!
AND TAKE THAT STUPID LITTLE ROBOTIC SKATEBOARD WITH YOU!
SHEESH, GIVE A GUY A PLANET AND HE GETS DELUSIONS OF GRANDEUR! WE'RE OUTTA HERE AS SOON AS I --
--WARM UP THE ATOMIC ENGINES.
MAYBE NOT. ANY CHANCE OF A LIFT?
NOT FROM ME--YOU WRECKED MY ONLY WORKING SPACECRAFT.
HOLD ON A SECOND...LET ME SWITCH SOJOURNER B-B-BACK ON.
GREETINGS FROM M-M-MARS. THIS IS COLONEL...UM, SPACE CADET P-P-PORKY PIG.
THE INVASION IS OFF...BUT WE SEEM TO BE STRANDED. ANY CHANCE OF SENDING OUT A G-G-GALACTIC TOW TRUCK?
TH-TH-THAT'S ALL, FOLKS!

A PIZZA MY MIND

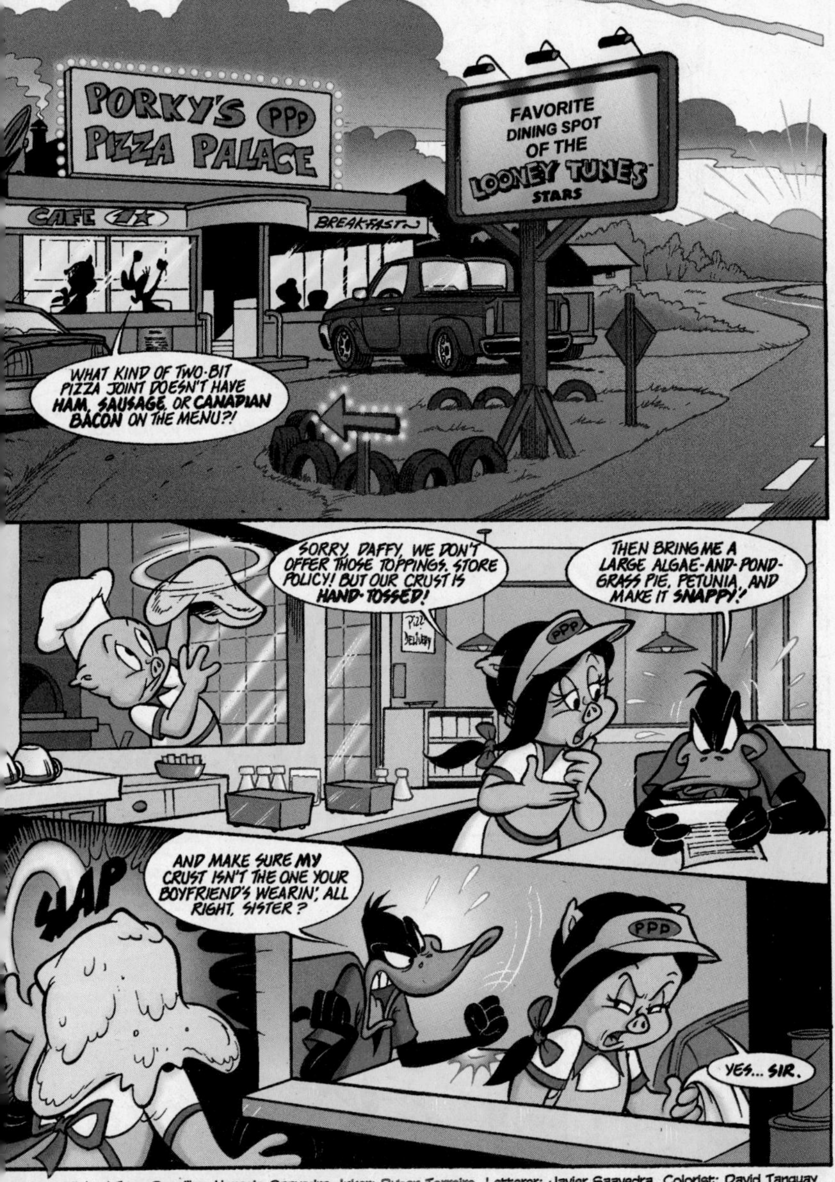
PORKY'S PPP PIZZA PALACE
CAFE
BREAKFAST
FAVORITE DINING SPOT OF THE LOONEY TUNES STARS
WHAT KIND OF TWO-BIT PIZZA JOINT DOESN'T HAVE HAM, SAUSAGE, OR CANADIAN BACON ON THE MENU?!
SORRY, DAFFY, WE DON'T OFFER THOSE TOPPINGS. STORE POLICY! BUT OUR CRUST IS HAND-TOSSED!
THEN BRING ME A LARGE ALGAE-AND-POND-GRASS PIE, PETUNIA, AND MAKE IT SNAPPY!
SLAP
AND MAKE SURE MY CRUST ISN'T THE ONE YOUR BOYFRIEND'S WEARIN', ALL RIGHT, SISTER?
YES... SIR.

Writer: Michael Eury Penciller: Horacio Saavedra Inker: Ruben Torreiro Letterer: Javier Saavedra Colorist: David Tanguay

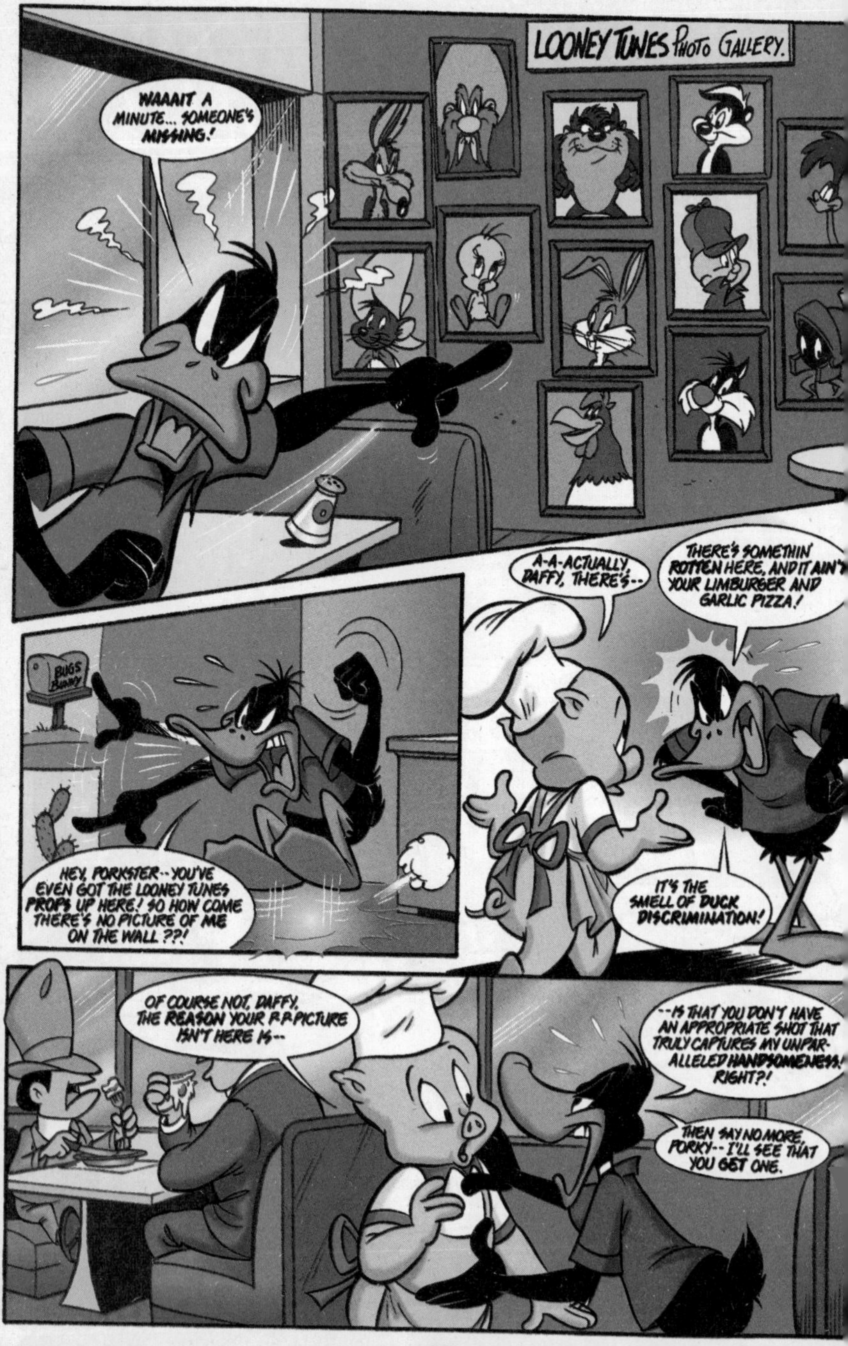
LOONEY TUNES PHOTO GALLERY.
WAAAIT A MINUTE... SOMEONE'S MISSING!
BUGS BUNNY
HEY, PORKSTER-- YOU'VE EVEN GOT THE LOONEY TUNES PROPS UP HERE! SO HOW COME THERE'S NO PICTURE OF ME ON THE WALL??!
A-A-ACTUALLY, DAFFY, THERE'S--
THERE'S SOMETHIN' ROTTEN HERE, AND IT AIN'T YOUR LIMBURGER AND GARLIC PIZZA!
IT'S THE SMELL OF DUCK DISCRIMINATION!
OF COURSE NOT, DAFFY. THE REASON YOUR P-P-PICTURE ISN'T HERE IS--
--IS THAT YOU DON'T HAVE AN APPROPRIATE SHOT THAT TRULY CAPTURES MY UNPARALLELED HANDSOMENESS! RIGHT?!
THEN SAY NO MORE, PORKY-- I'LL SEE THAT YOU GET ONE.

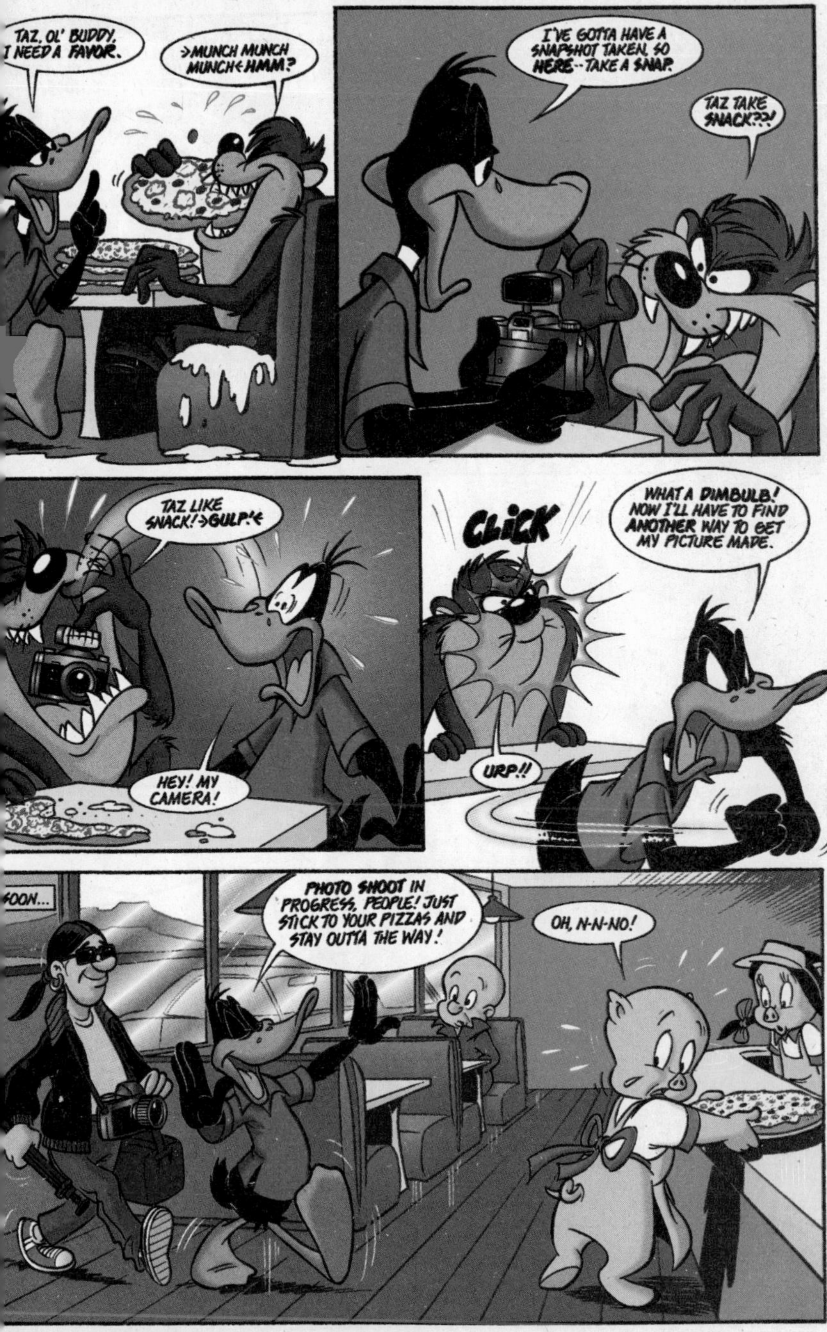
TAZ, OL' BUDDY, I NEED A FAVOR.
>MUNCH MUNCH MUNCH< HMM?
I'VE GOTTA HAVE A SNAPSHOT TAKEN, SO HERE--TAKE A SNAP.
TAZ TAKE SNACK??!
TAZ LIKE SNACK! >GULP!<
HEY! MY CAMERA!
CLICK
URP!!
WHAT A DIMBULB! NOW I'LL HAVE TO FIND ANOTHER WAY TO GET MY PICTURE MADE.
SOON...
PHOTO SHOOT IN PROGRESS, PEOPLE! JUST STICK TO YOUR PIZZAS AND STAY OUTTA THE WAY!
OH, N-N-NO!

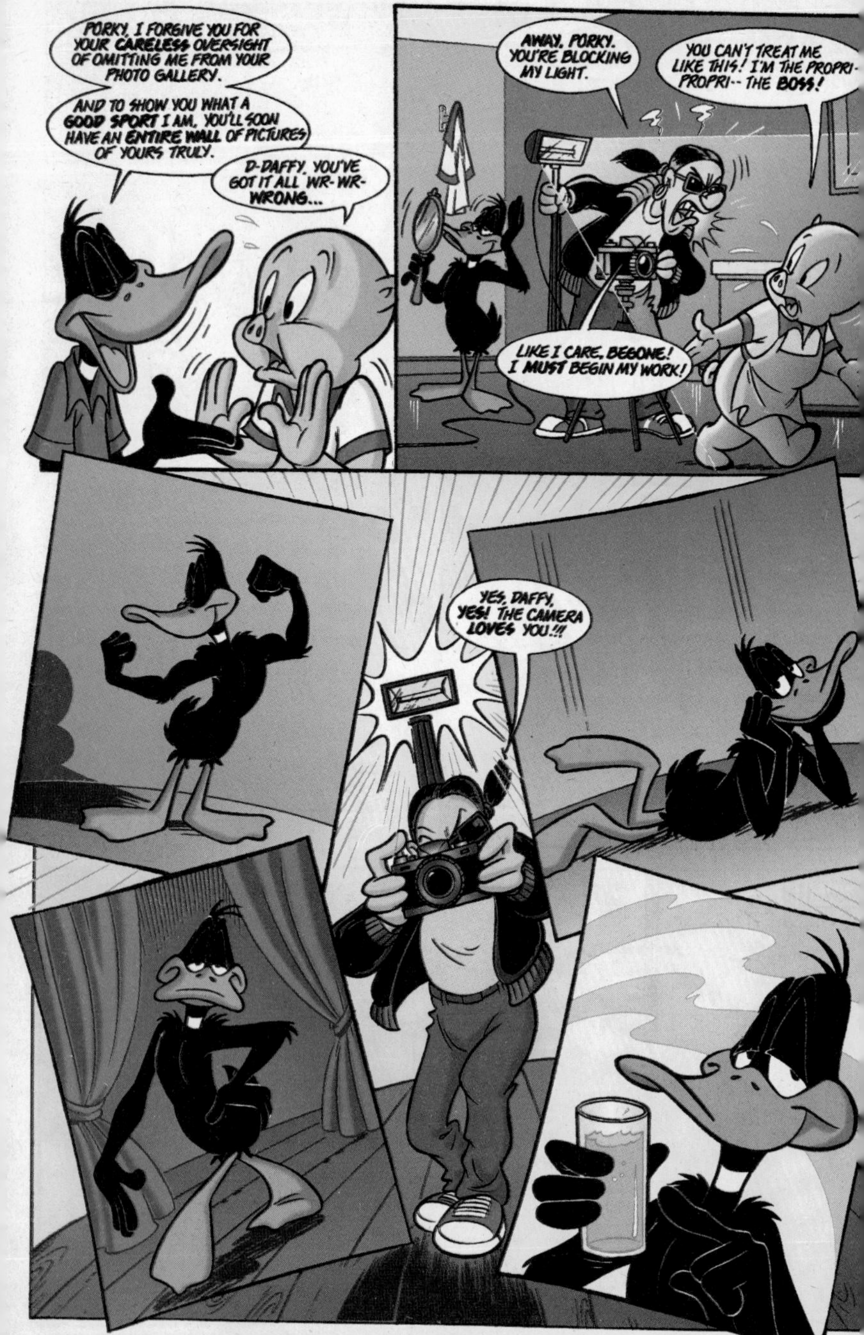
PORKY, I FORGIVE YOU FOR YOUR CARELESS OVERSIGHT OF OMITTING ME FROM YOUR PHOTO GALLERY.
AND TO SHOW YOU WHAT A GOOD SPORT I AM, YOU'LL SOON HAVE AN ENTIRE WALL OF PICTURES OF YOURS TRULY.
D-DAFFY, YOU'VE GOT IT ALL WR-WR-WRONG...
AWAY, PORKY. YOU'RE BLOCKING MY LIGHT.
YOU CAN'T TREAT ME LIKE THIS! I'M THE PROPRI-PROPRI-- THE BOSS!
LIKE I CARE. BEGONE! I MUST BEGIN MY WORK!
YES, DAFFY, YES! THE CAMERA LOVES YOU!!!

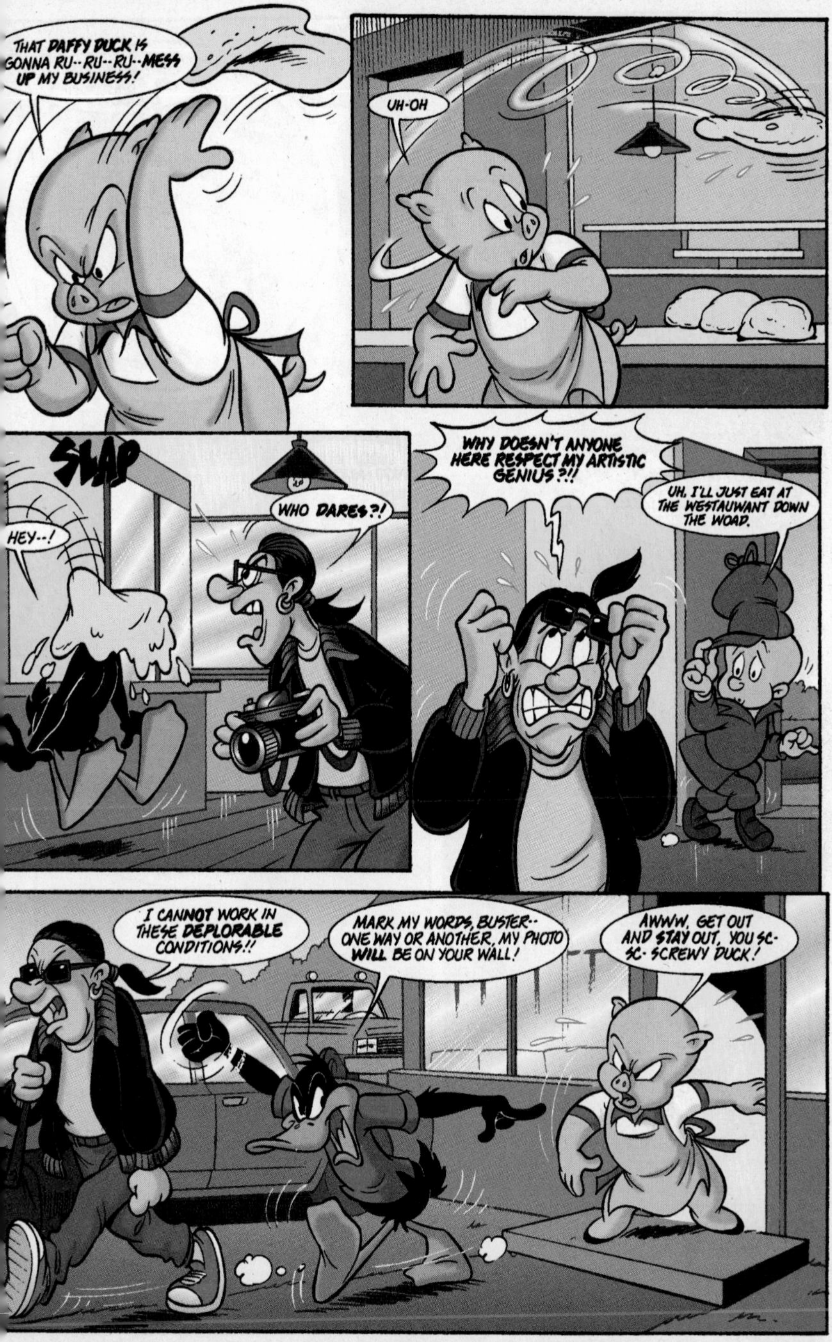
THAT DAFFY DUCK IS GONNA RU--RU--RU--MESS UP MY BUSINESS!
UH-OH
SLAP
HEY--!
WHO DARES?!
WHY DOESN'T ANYONE HERE RESPECT MY ARTISTIC GENIUS?!!
UH, I'LL JUST EAT AT THE WESTAUWANT DOWN THE WOAD.
I CANNOT WORK IN THESE DEPLORABLE CONDITIONS!!
MARK MY WORDS, BUSTER-- ONE WAY OR ANOTHER, MY PHOTO WILL BE ON YOUR WALL!
AWWW, GET OUT AND STAY OUT, YOU SC-SC- SCREWY DUCK!

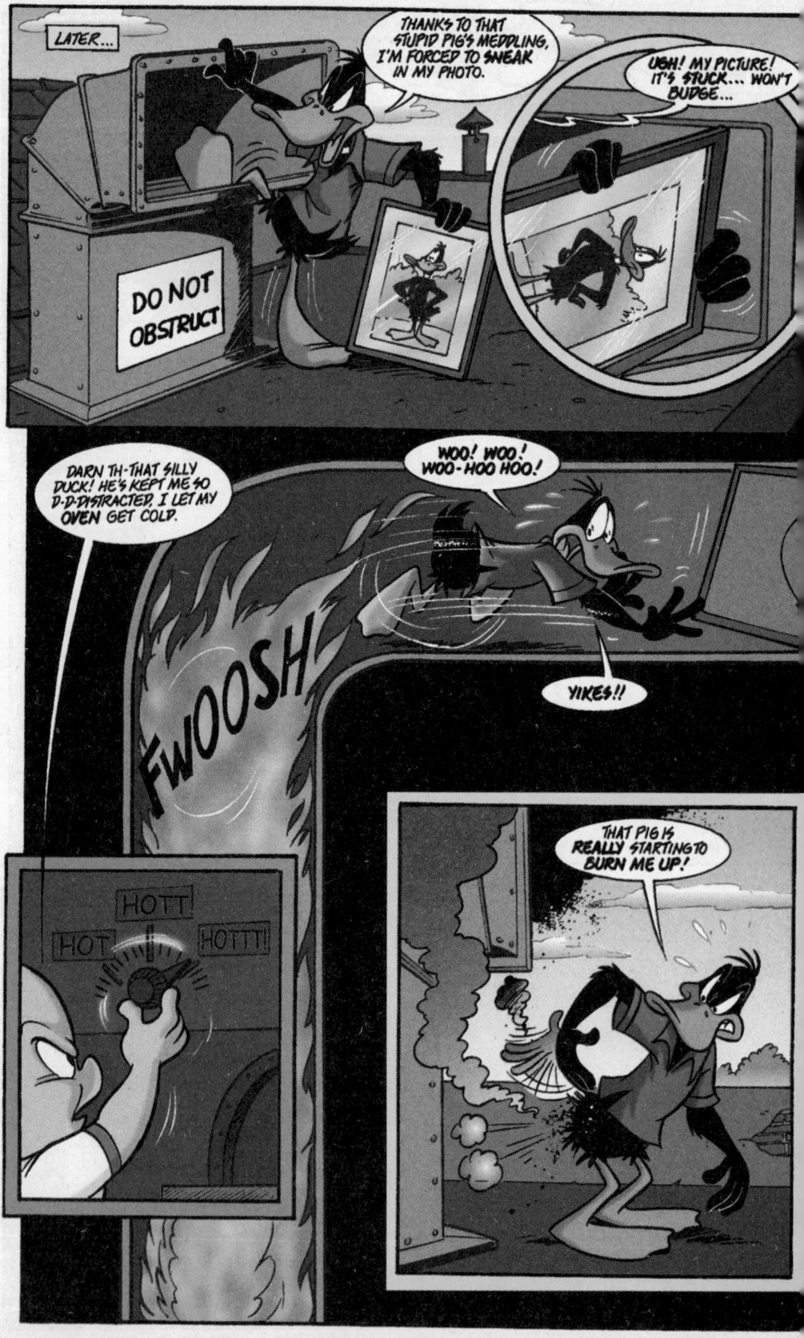
LATER...
THANKS TO THAT STUPID PIG'S MEDDLING, I'M FORCED TO SNEAK IN MY PHOTO.
UGH! MY PICTURE! IT'S STUCK... WON'T BUDGE...
DO NOT OBSTRUCT
DARN TH-THAT SILLY DUCK! HE'S KEPT ME SO D-D-DISTRACTED, I LET MY OVEN GET COLD.
WOO! WOO! WOO-HOO HOO!
YIKES!!
FWOOSH
HOT
HOTT
HOTTT!
THAT PIG IS REALLY STARTING TO BURN ME UP!

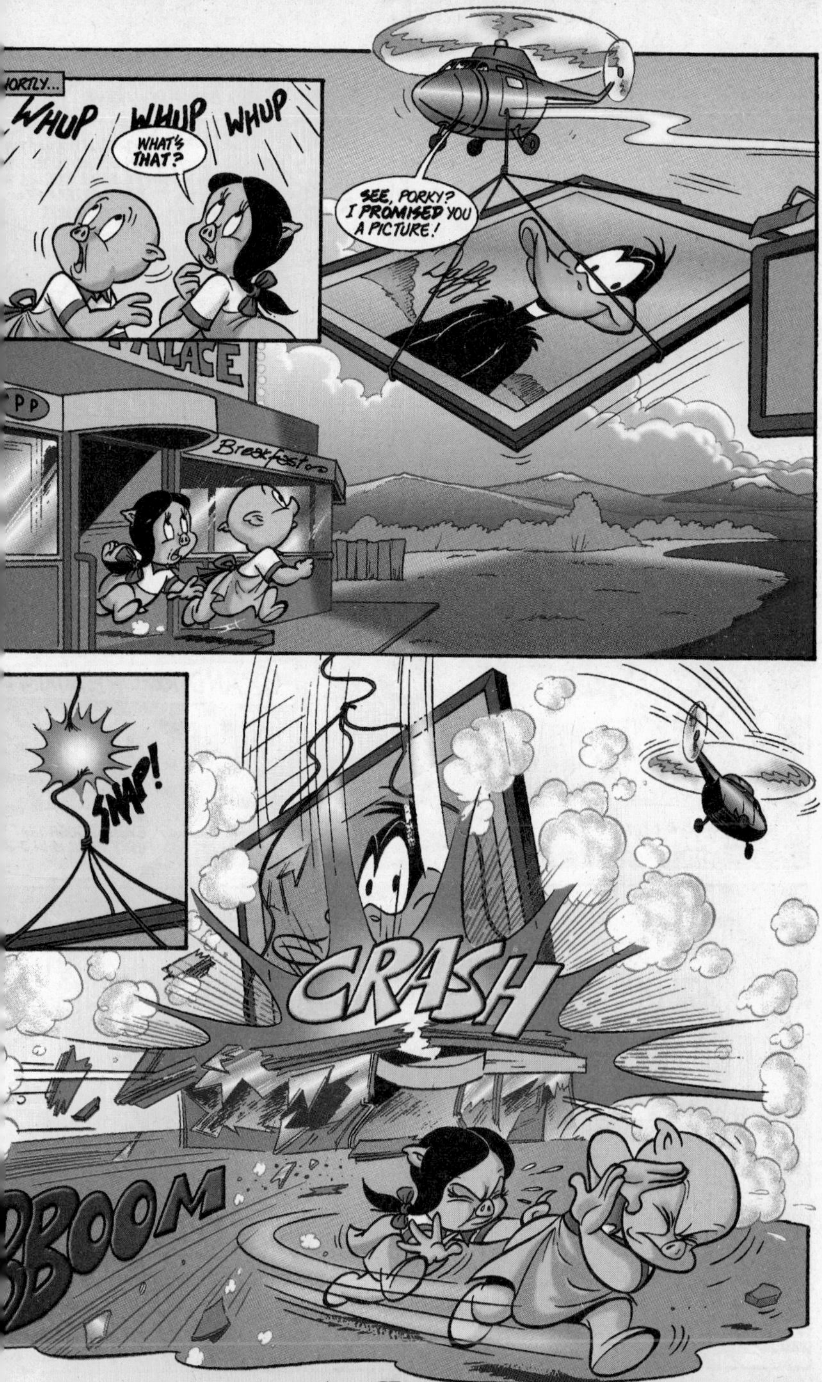

HORTLY...
WHUP WHUP WHUP
WHAT'S THAT?
SEE, PORKY? I PROMISED YOU A PICTURE!
PALACE
Breakfast
SNAP!
CRASH
BOOM

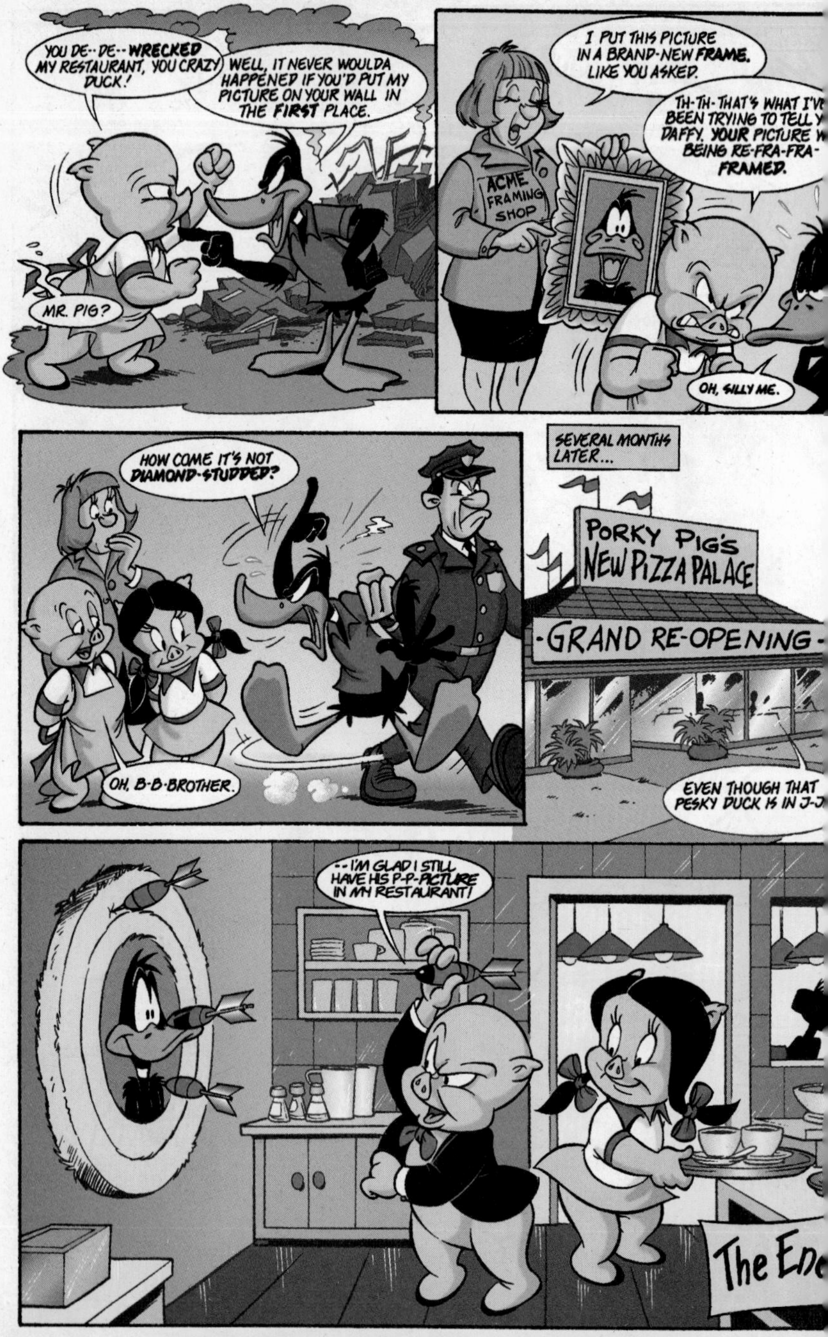
YOU DE--DE--WRECKED MY RESTAURANT, YOU CRAZY DUCK!
WELL, IT NEVER WOULDA HAPPENED IF YOU'D PUT MY PICTURE ON YOUR WALL IN THE FIRST PLACE.
MR. PIG?
I PUT THIS PICTURE IN A BRAND-NEW FRAME. LIKE YOU ASKED.
ACME FRAMING SHOP
TH-TH-THAT'S WHAT I'VE BEEN TRYING TO TELL Y DAFFY. YOUR PICTURE W BEING RE-FRA-FRA- FRAMED.
OH, SILLY ME.
HOW COME IT'S NOT DIAMOND-STUDDED?
OH, B-B-BROTHER.
SEVERAL MONTHS LATER...
PORKY PIG'S NEW PIZZA PALACE
-GRAND RE-OPENING-
EVEN THOUGH THAT PESKY DUCK IS IN J-J
--I'M GLAD I STILL HAVE HIS P-P-PICTURE IN MY RESTAURANT!
The End

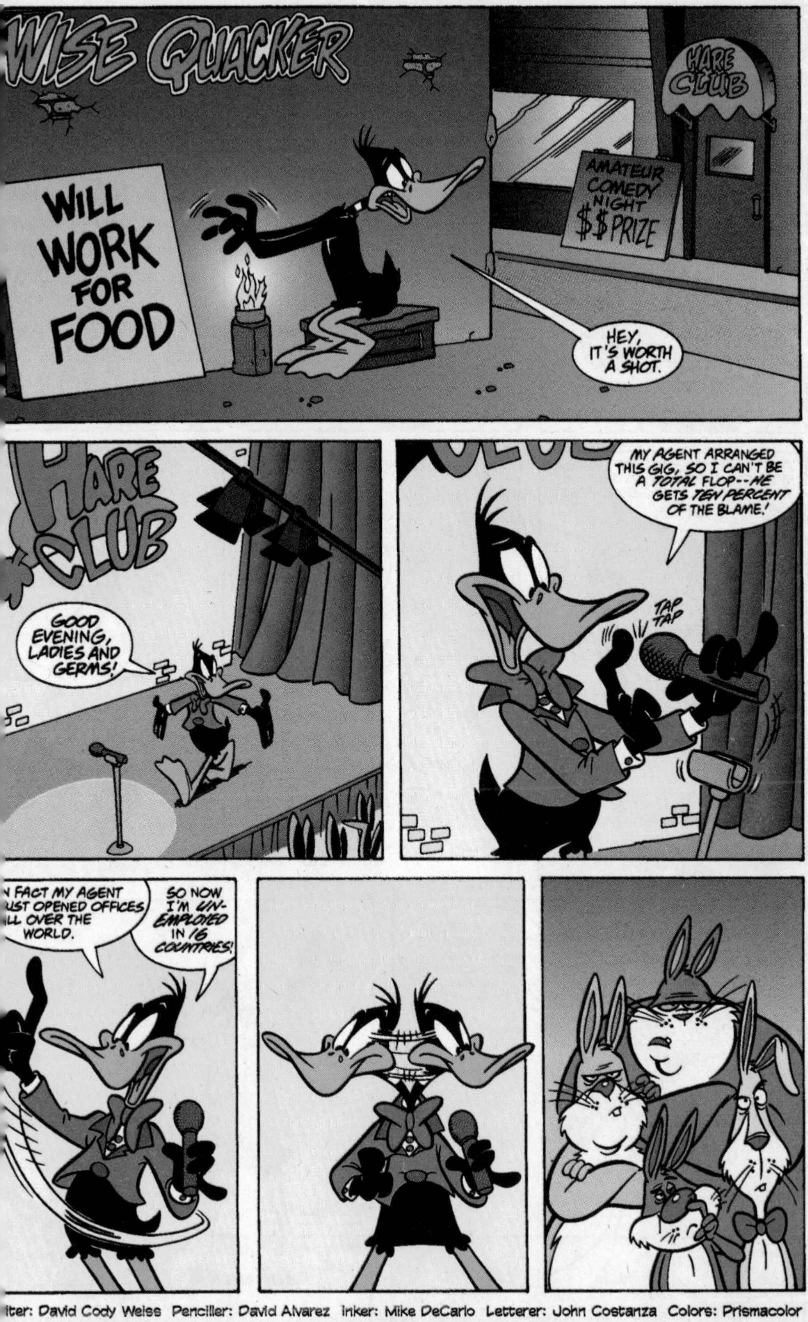
WISE QUACKER
WILL WORK FOR FOOD
HARE CLUB
AMATEUR COMEDY NIGHT $$ PRIZE
HEY, IT'S WORTH A SHOT.
HARE CLUB
GOOD EVENING, LADIES AND GERMS!
MY AGENT ARRANGED THIS GIG, SO I CAN'T BE A TOTAL FLOP--HE GETS TEN PERCENT OF THE BLAME!
TAP TAP
N FACT MY AGENT UST OPENED OFFICES LL OVER THE WORLD.
SO NOW I'M UN-EMPLOYED IN 16 COUNTRIES!

iter: David Cody Weiss Penciller: David Alvarez Inker: Mike DeCarlo Letterer: John Costanza Colors: Prismacolor

HMM, TOUGH CROWD. OKAY...

TWO *FLEAS* WANTED TO GO *TRAVELING*...

BUT THEY COULDN'T DECIDE WHETHER TO *WALK* OR TO CATCH A DOG!

SILKWORMS MAKE *THREAD*, *MOTHS* MAKE *HOLES*.

I CROSSED ONE WITH THE OTHER AND GOT A BUG THAT MAKES *LACE*.

THEN I CROSSED A *TERMITE* WITH A *PRAYING MANTIS*.

NOW I HAVE A BUG THAT SAYS *GRACE* BEFORE IT *EATS MY HOUSE!*

BZZZZZZZZZ

YAWN

ER... ACTUALLY, MY H IS IN SUCH BAD SHAPE THE *TERMITES* EA OUT.

IT'S A GREAT HOUSE, THOUGH--IT HAS HOT AND COLD RUNNING *MICE*.

Chirp... chirp... chirp...

30

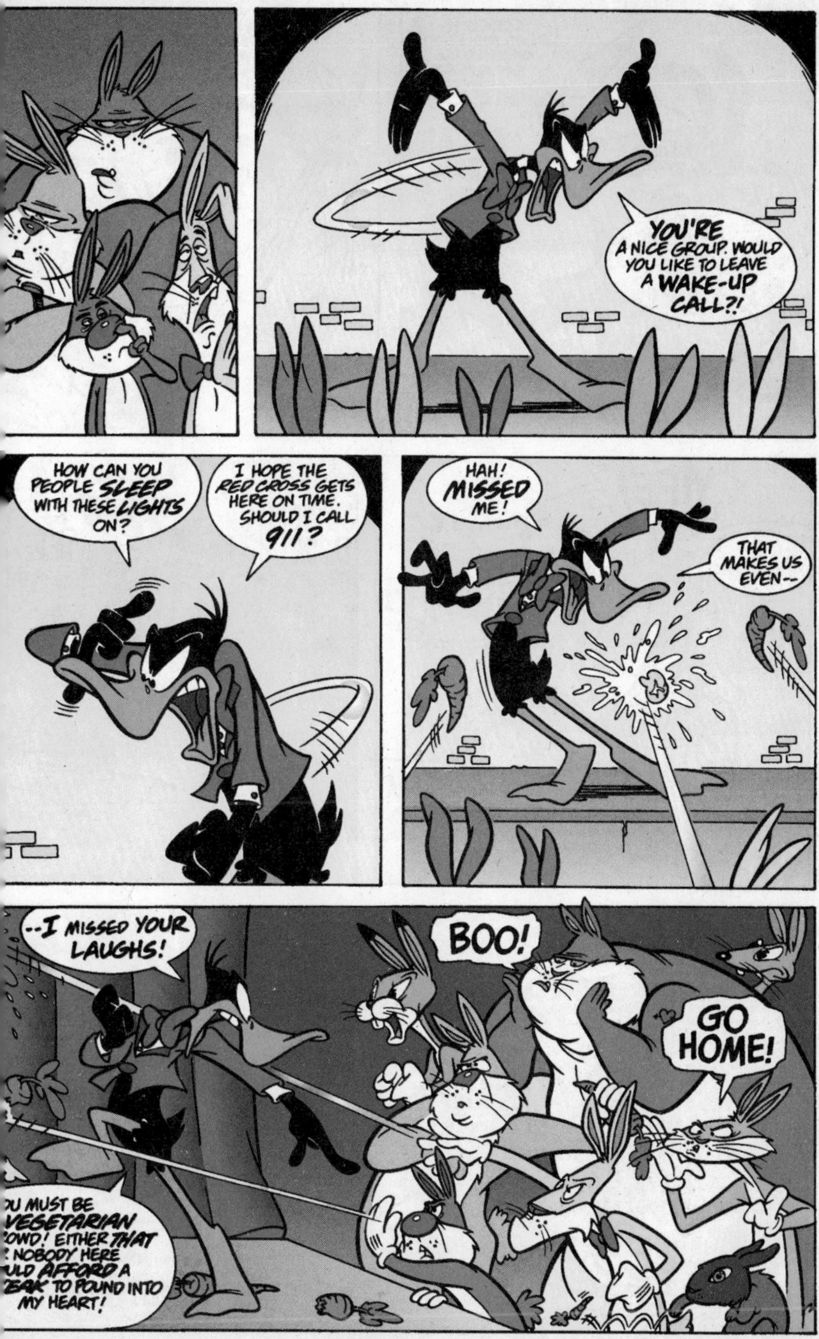
YOU'RE A NICE GROUP. WOULD YOU LIKE TO LEAVE A WAKE-UP CALL?!
HOW CAN YOU PEOPLE SLEEP WITH THESE LIGHTS ON?
I HOPE THE RED CROSS GETS HERE ON TIME. SHOULD I CALL 911?
HAH! MISSED ME!
THAT MAKES US EVEN--
--I MISSED YOUR LAUGHS!
BOO!
GO HOME!
OU MUST BE VEGETARIAN OWD! EITHER THAT NOBODY HERE ULD AFFORD A EAK TO POUND INTO MY HEART!

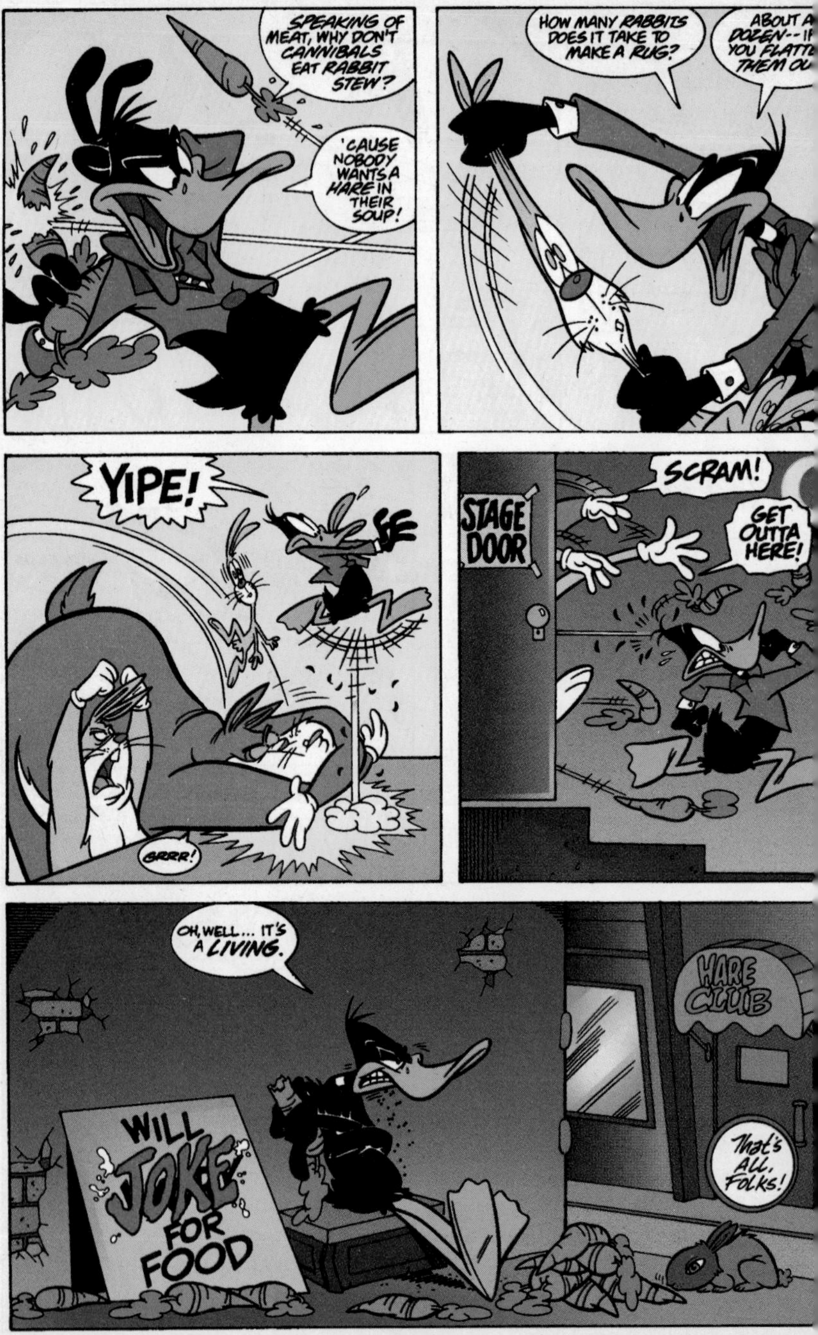
SPEAKING OF MEAT, WHY DON'T CANNIBALS EAT RABBIT STEW?
'CAUSE NOBODY WANTS A HARE IN THEIR SOUP!
HOW MANY RABBITS DOES IT TAKE TO MAKE A RUG?
YIPE!
GRRR!
STAGE DOOR
SCRAM!
GET OUTTA HERE!
OH, WELL... IT'S A LIVING.
HARE CLUB
WILL JOKE FOR FOOD
That's All, Folks!

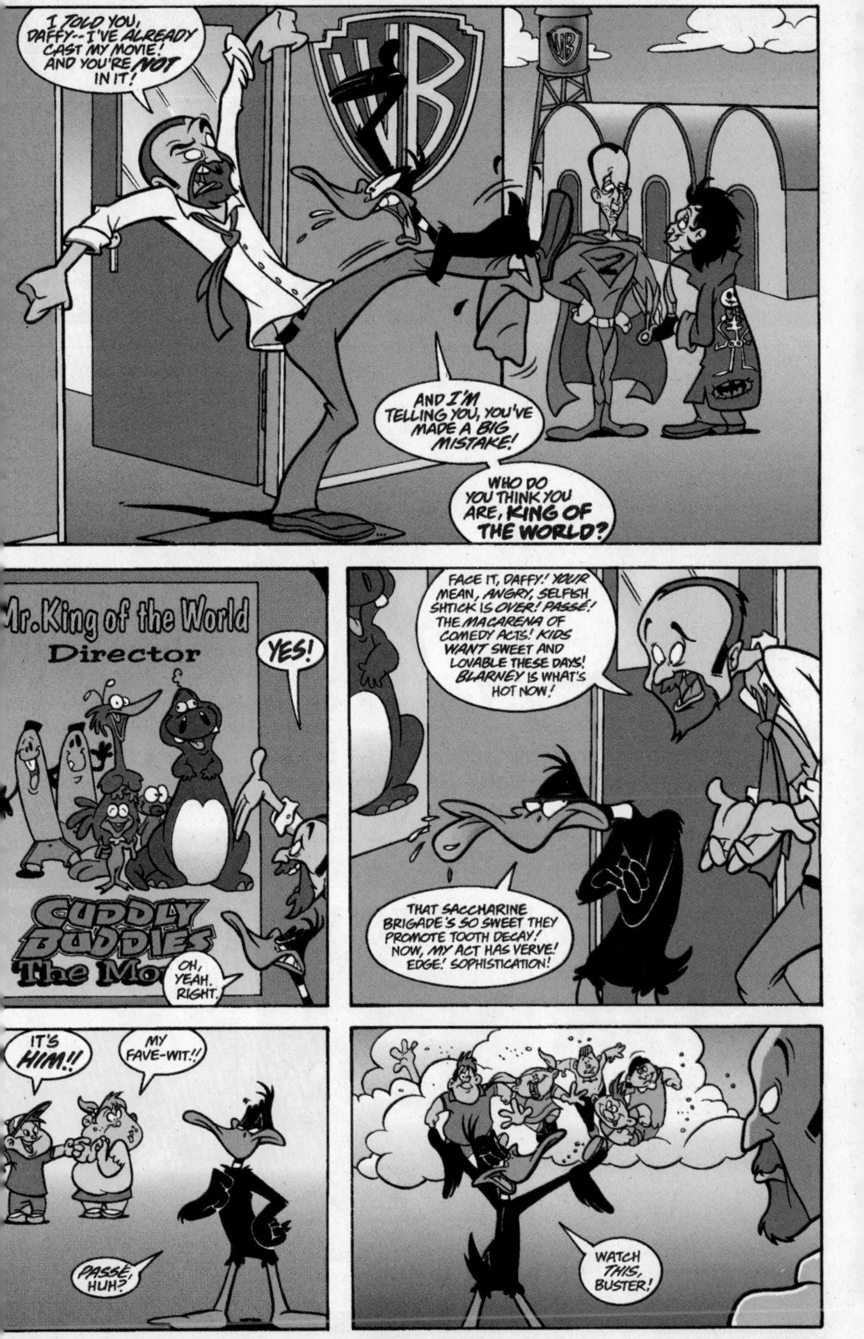
I TOLD YOU, DAFFY--I'VE ALREADY CAST MY MOVIE! AND YOU'RE NOT IN IT!
AND I'M TELLING YOU, YOU'VE MADE A BIG MISTAKE!
WHO DO YOU THINK YOU ARE, KING OF THE WORLD?
Mr. King of the World
Director
YES!
CUDDLY BUDDIES The Mo
OH, YEAH. RIGHT.
FACE IT, DAFFY! YOUR MEAN, ANGRY, SELFISH SHTICK IS OVER! PASSÉ! THE MACARENA OF COMEDY ACTS! KIDS WANT SWEET AND LOVABLE THESE DAYS! BLARNEY IS WHAT'S HOT NOW!
THAT SACCHARINE BRIGADE'S SO SWEET THEY PROMOTE TOOTH DECAY! NOW, MY ACT HAS VERVE! EDGE! SOPHISTICATION!
IT'S HIM!!
MY FAVE-WIT!!
PASSÉ, HUH?
WATCH THIS, BUSTER!

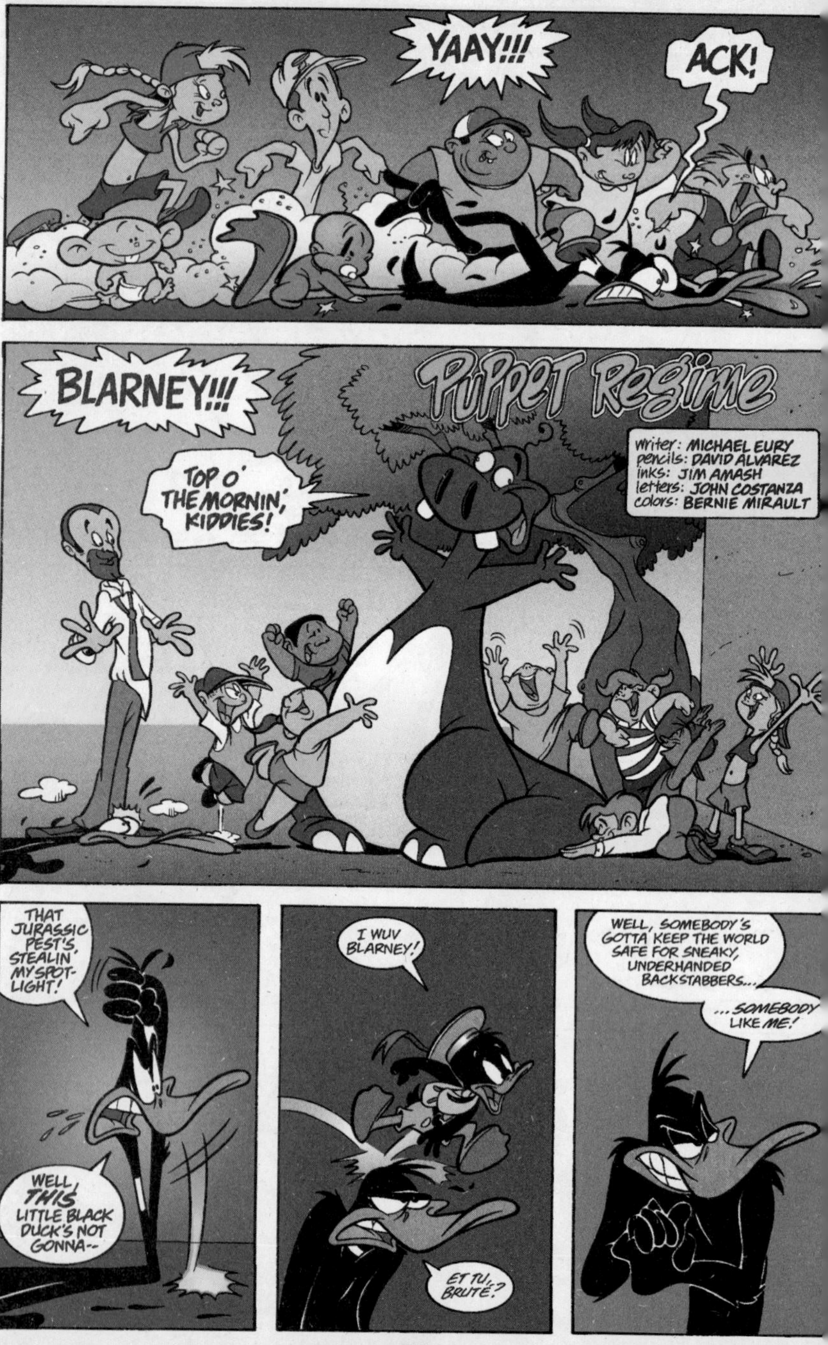
YAAY!!!
ACK!
BLARNEY!!!
Puppet Regime
writer: MICHAEL EURY
pencils: DAVID ALVAREZ
inks: JIM AMASH
letters: JOHN COSTANZA
colors: BERNIE MIRAULT
TOP O' THE MORNIN', KIDDIES!
THAT JURASSIC PEST'S, STEALIN' MY SPOT-LIGHT!
WELL, THIS LITTLE BLACK DUCK'S NOT GONNA--
I WUV BLARNEY!
ET TU, BRUTÉ?
WELL, SOMEBODY'S GOTTA KEEP THE WORLD SAFE FOR SNEAKY, UNDERHANDED BACKSTABBERS...
...SOMEBODY LIKE ME!

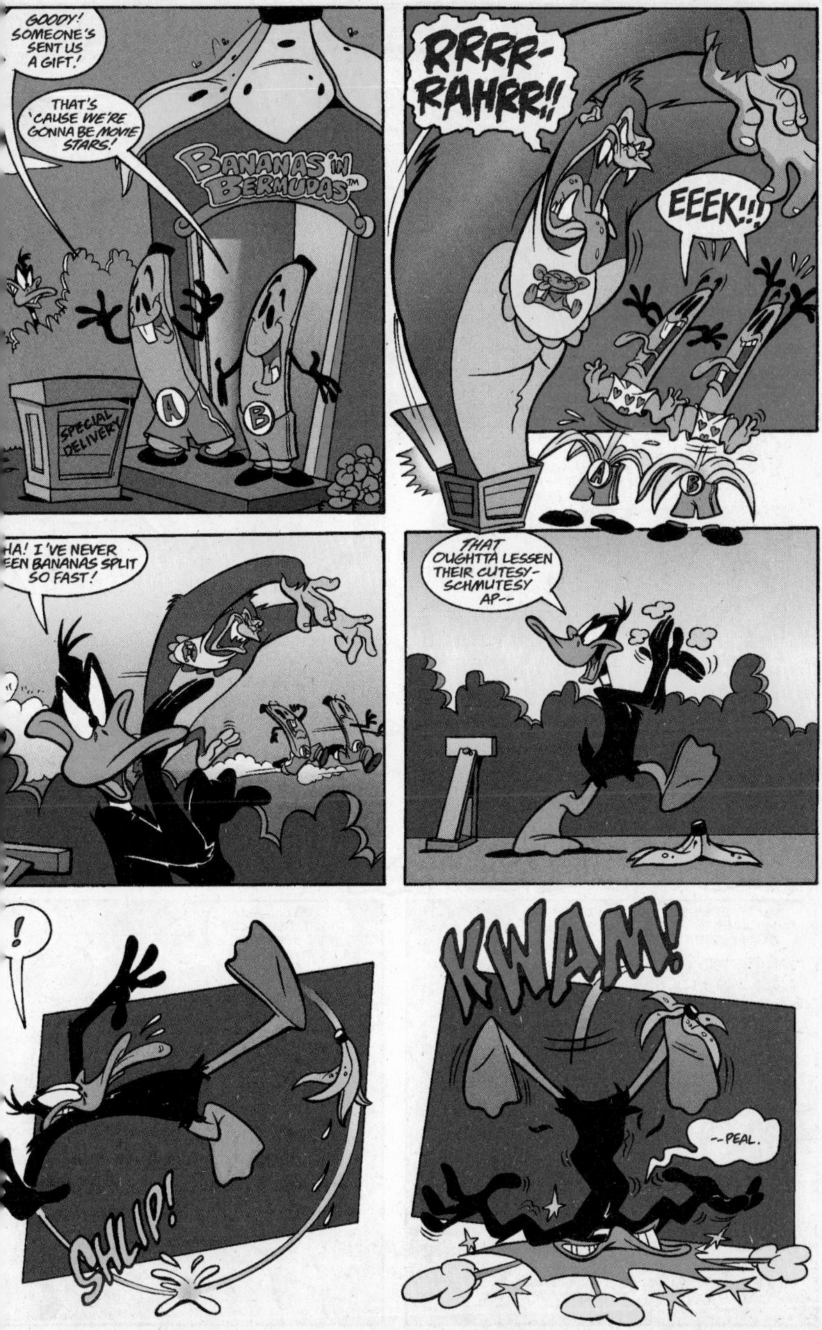
GOODY! SOMEONE'S SENT US A GIFT!
THAT'S 'CAUSE WE'RE GONNA BE MOVIE STARS!
BANANAS IN BERMUDAS™
SPECIAL DELIVERY
RRRR-RAHRR!!
EEEK!!!
HA! I'VE NEVER SEEN BANANAS SPLIT SO FAST!
THAT OUGHTTA LESSEN THEIR CUTESY-SCHMUTESY AP--
!
SHLIP!
KWAM!
--PEAL.

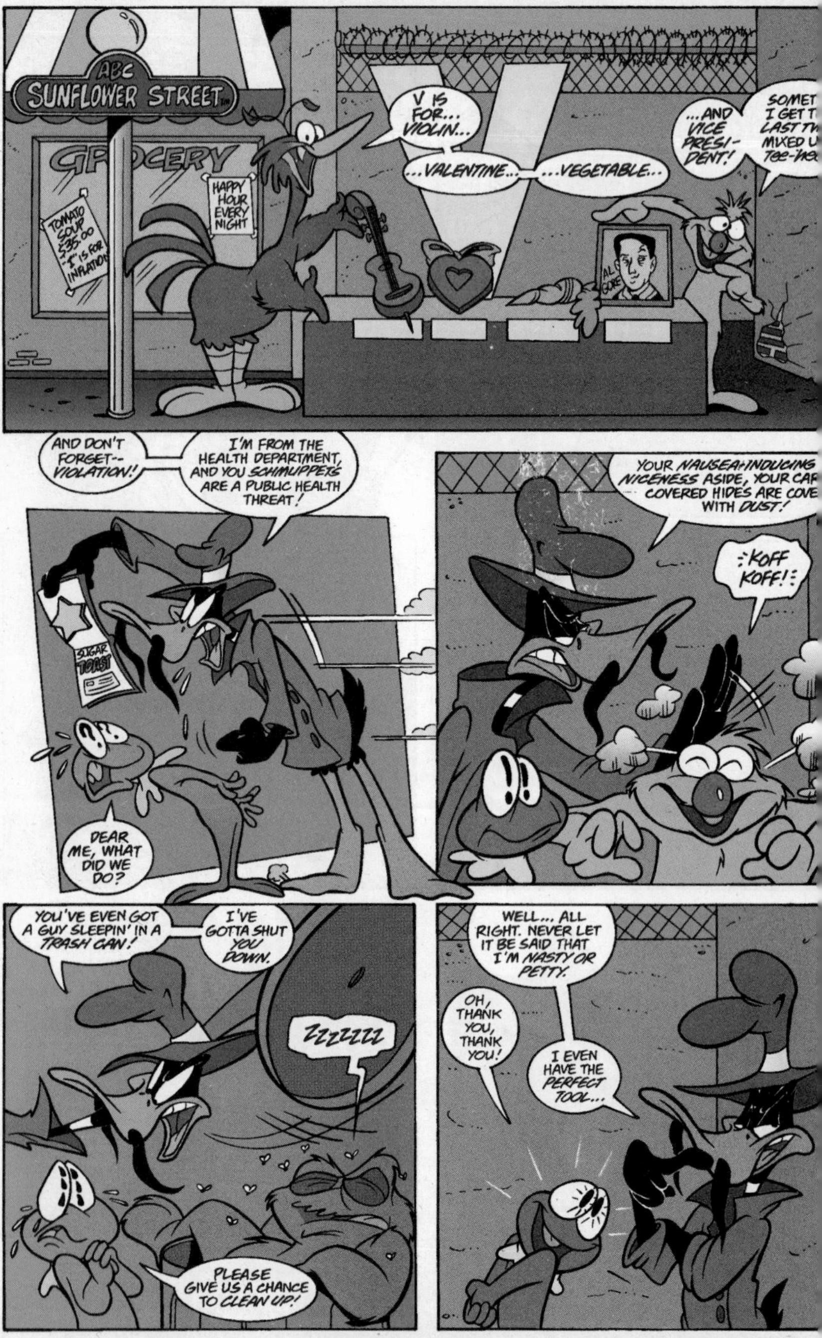
ABC
SUNFLOWER STREET
GROCERY
HAPPY HOUR EVERY NIGHT
TOMATO SOUP $35.00 "I" IS FOR INFLATION
V IS FOR... VIOLIN...
...VALENTINE...
...VEGETABLE...
...AND VICE PRESI-DENT!
AL GORE
AND DON'T FORGET-- VIOLATION!
I'M FROM THE HEALTH DEPARTMENT, AND YOU SCHMUPPETS ARE A PUBLIC HEALTH THREAT!
SUGAR TOAST
DEAR ME, WHAT DID WE DO?
YOUR NAUSEA-INDUCING NICENESS ASIDE, YOUR CAR COVERED HIDES ARE COVE WITH DUST!
KOFF KOFF!
YOU'VE EVEN GOT A GUY SLEEPIN' IN A TRASH CAN!
I'VE GOTTA SHUT YOU DOWN.
ZZZZZZZ
PLEASE GIVE US A CHANCE TO CLEAN UP!
WELL... ALL RIGHT. NEVER LET IT BE SAID THAT I'M NASTY OR PETTY.
OH, THANK YOU, THANK YOU!
I EVEN HAVE THE PERFECT TOOL...

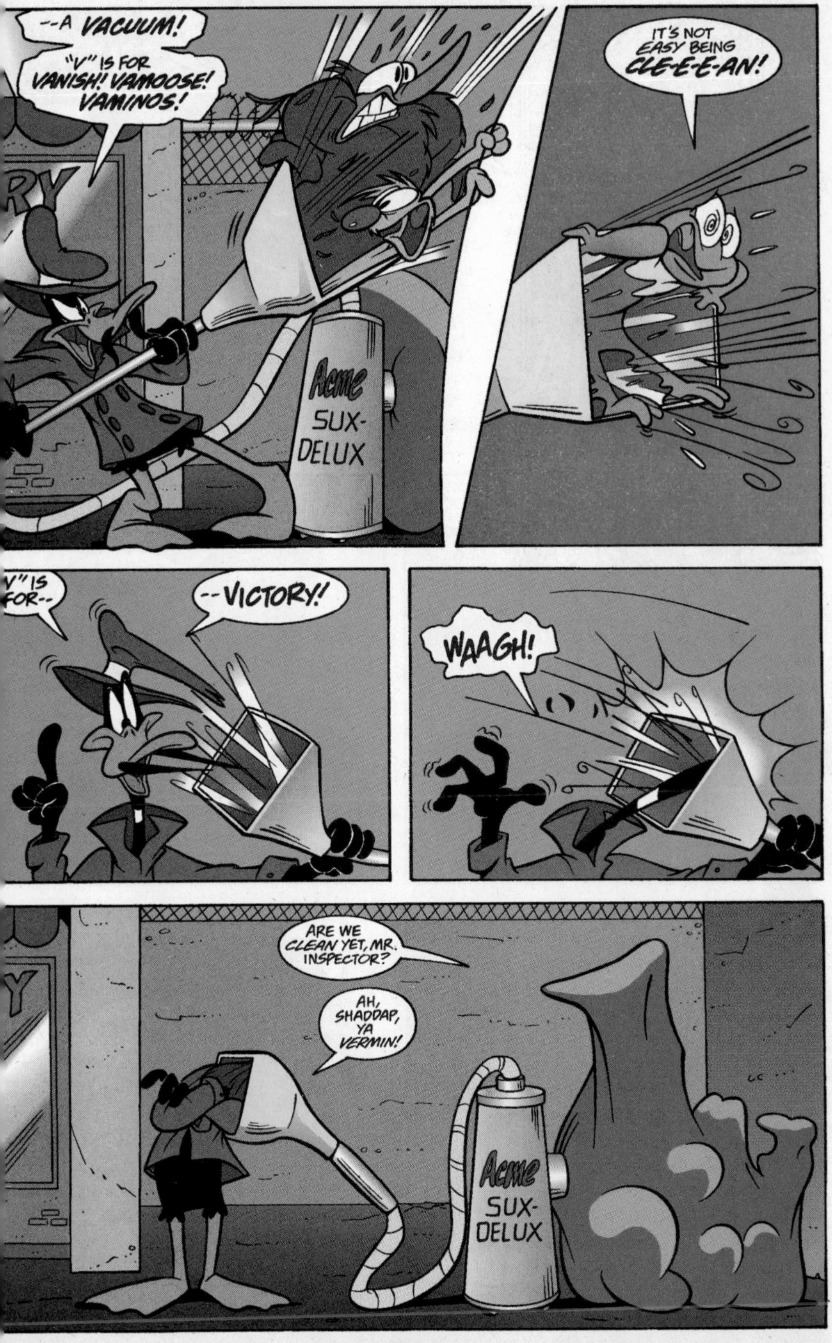
--A VACUUM!
"V" IS FOR VANISH! VAMOOSE! VAMINOS!
IT'S NOT EASY BEING CLE-E-E-AN!
SUX-DELUX
"V" IS FOR--
--VICTORY!
WAAGH!
ARE WE CLEAN YET, MR. INSPECTOR?
AH, SHADDAP, YA VERMIN!
SUX-DELUX

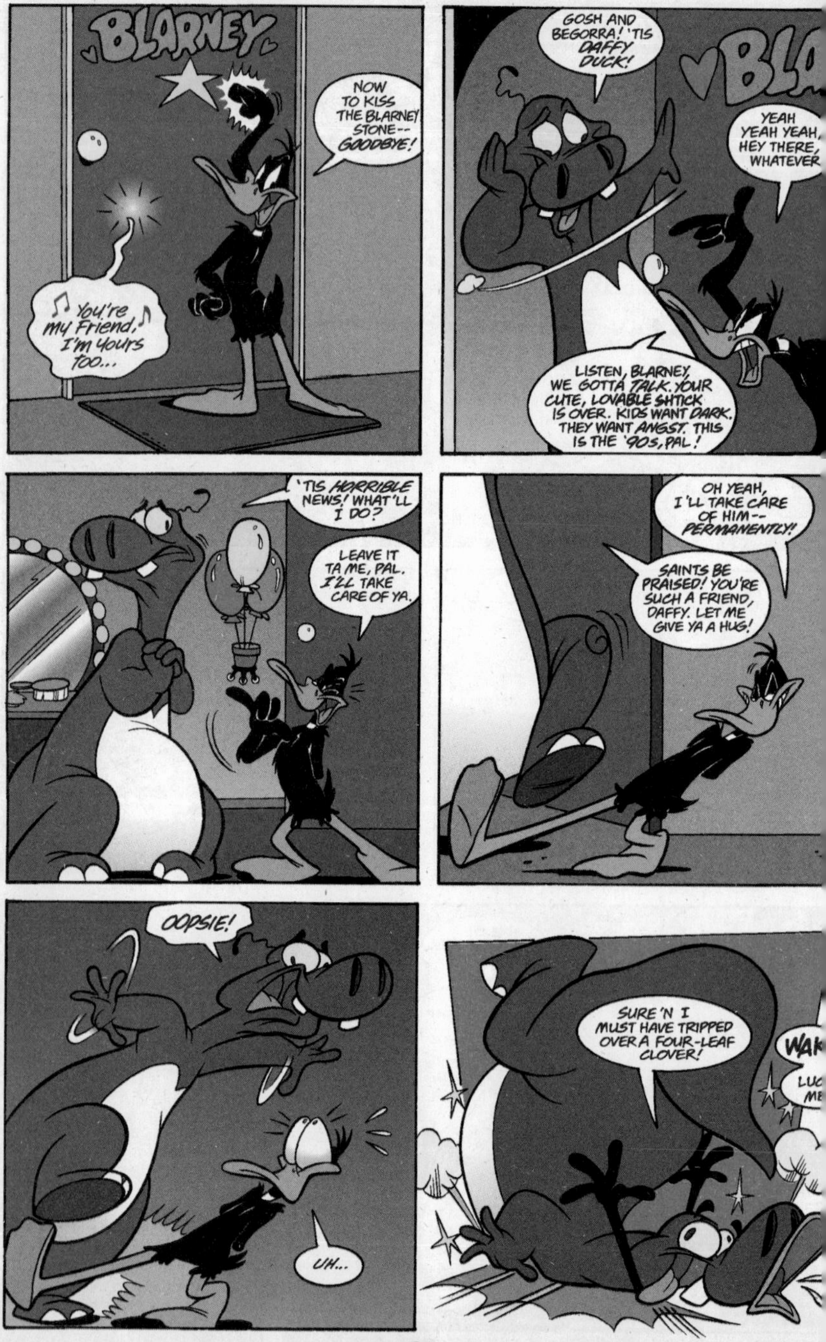
BLARNEY
NOW TO KISS THE BLARNEY STONE-- GOODBYE!
♫ You're my Friend, I'm Yours too... ♫
GOSH AND BEGORRA! 'TIS DAFFY DUCK!
YEAH YEAH YEAH, HEY THERE, WHATEVER
LISTEN, BLARNEY, WE GOTTA TALK. YOUR CUTE, LOVABLE SHTICK IS OVER. KIDS WANT DARK. THEY WANT ANGST. THIS IS THE '90S, PAL!
'TIS HORRIBLE NEWS! WHAT'LL I DO?
LEAVE IT TA ME, PAL. I'LL TAKE CARE OF YA.
OH YEAH, I'LL TAKE CARE OF HIM-- PERMANENTLY!
SAINTS BE PRAISED! YOU'RE SUCH A FRIEND, DAFFY. LET ME GIVE YA A HUG!
OOPSIE!
UH...
SURE 'N I MUST HAVE TRIPPED OVER A FOUR-LEAF CLOVER!

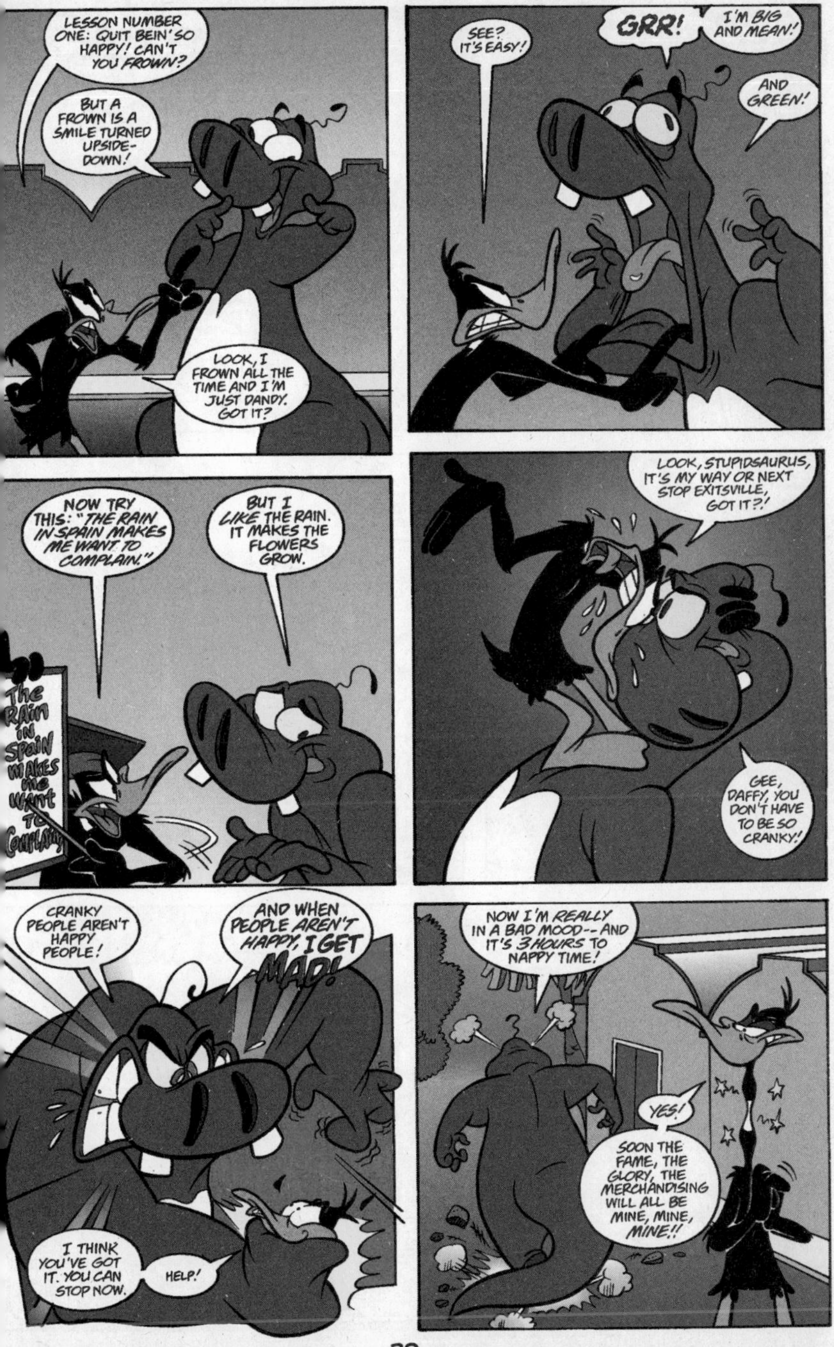
LESSON NUMBER ONE: QUIT BEIN' SO HAPPY! CAN'T YOU FROWN?
BUT A FROWN IS A SMILE TURNED UPSIDE-DOWN!
LOOK, I FROWN ALL THE TIME AND I'M JUST DANDY. GOT IT?
SEE? IT'S EASY!
GRR!
I'M BIG AND MEAN!
AND GREEN!
NOW TRY THIS: "THE RAIN IN SPAIN MAKES ME WANT TO COMPLAIN."
BUT I LIKE THE RAIN. IT MAKES THE FLOWERS GROW.
The RAIN IN SPAIN MAKES me WANT TO COMPLAIN
LOOK, STUPIDSAURUS, IT'S MY WAY OR NEXT STOP EXITSVILLE, GOT IT?!
GEE, DAFFY, YOU DON'T HAVE TO BE SO CRANKY!
CRANKY PEOPLE AREN'T HAPPY PEOPLE!
AND WHEN PEOPLE AREN'T HAPPY, I GET MAD!
I THINK YOU'VE GOT IT. YOU CAN STOP NOW.
HELP!
NOW I'M REALLY IN A BAD MOOD-- AND IT'S 3 HOURS TO NAPPY TIME!
YES!
SOON THE FAME, THE GLORY, THE MERCHANDISING WILL ALL BE MINE, MINE, MINE!!

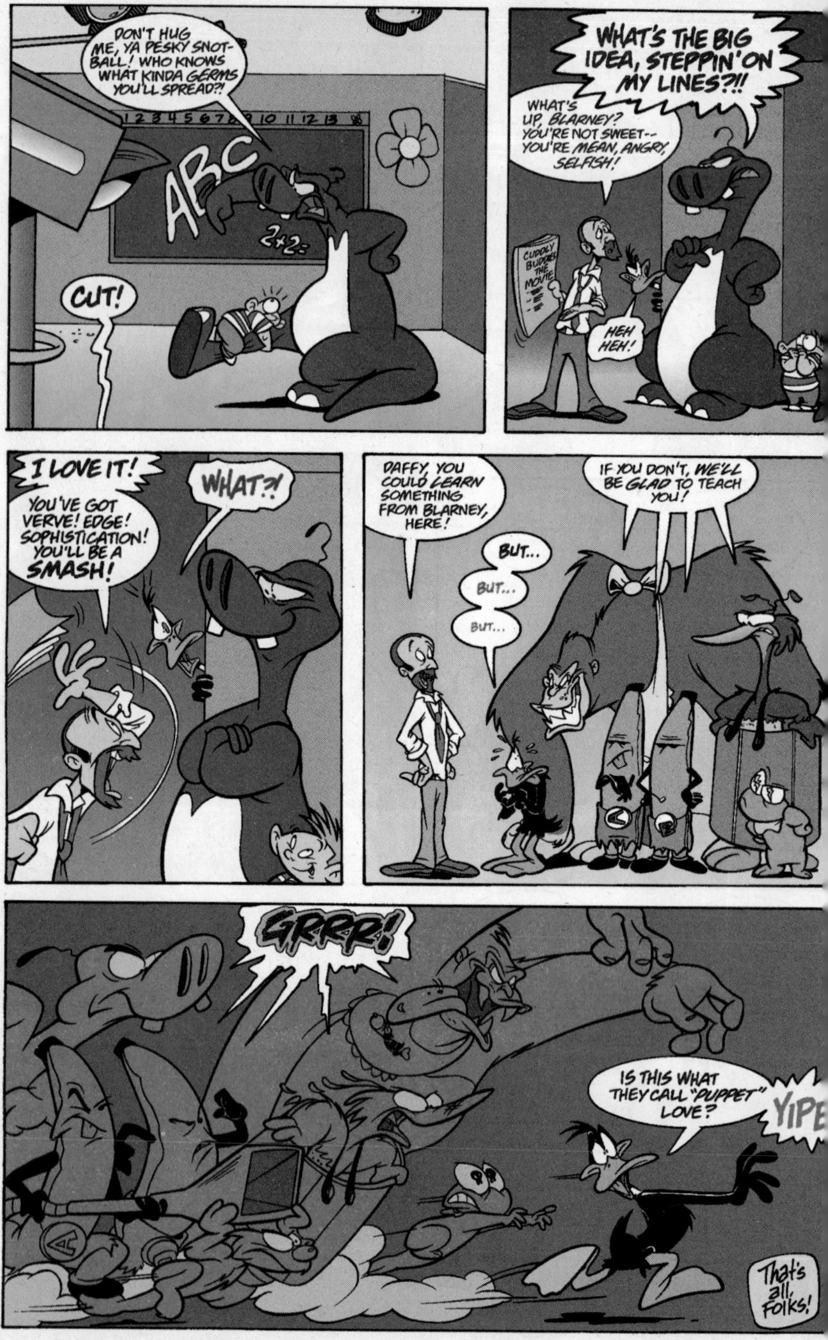

DON'T HUG ME, YA PESKY SNOT-BALL! WHO KNOWS WHAT KINDA GERMS YOU'LL SPREAD?!
1 2 3 4 5 6 7 8 9 10 11 12 13
ABC
2+2=
CUT!
WHAT'S THE BIG IDEA, STEPPIN' ON MY LINES?!!
WHAT'S UP, BLARNEY? YOU'RE NOT SWEET-- YOU'RE MEAN, ANGRY, SELFISH!
CUDDLY BUDDIES THE MOVIE
HEH HEH!
I LOVE IT!
YOU'VE GOT VERVE! EDGE! SOPHISTICATION! YOU'LL BE A SMASH!
WHAT?!
DAFFY, YOU COULD LEARN SOMETHING FROM BLARNEY, HERE!
IF YOU DON'T, WE'LL BE GLAD TO TEACH YOU!
BUT...
BUT...
BUT...
GRRR!
IS THIS WHAT THEY CALL "PUPPET" LOVE?
YIPE
That's all, Folks!

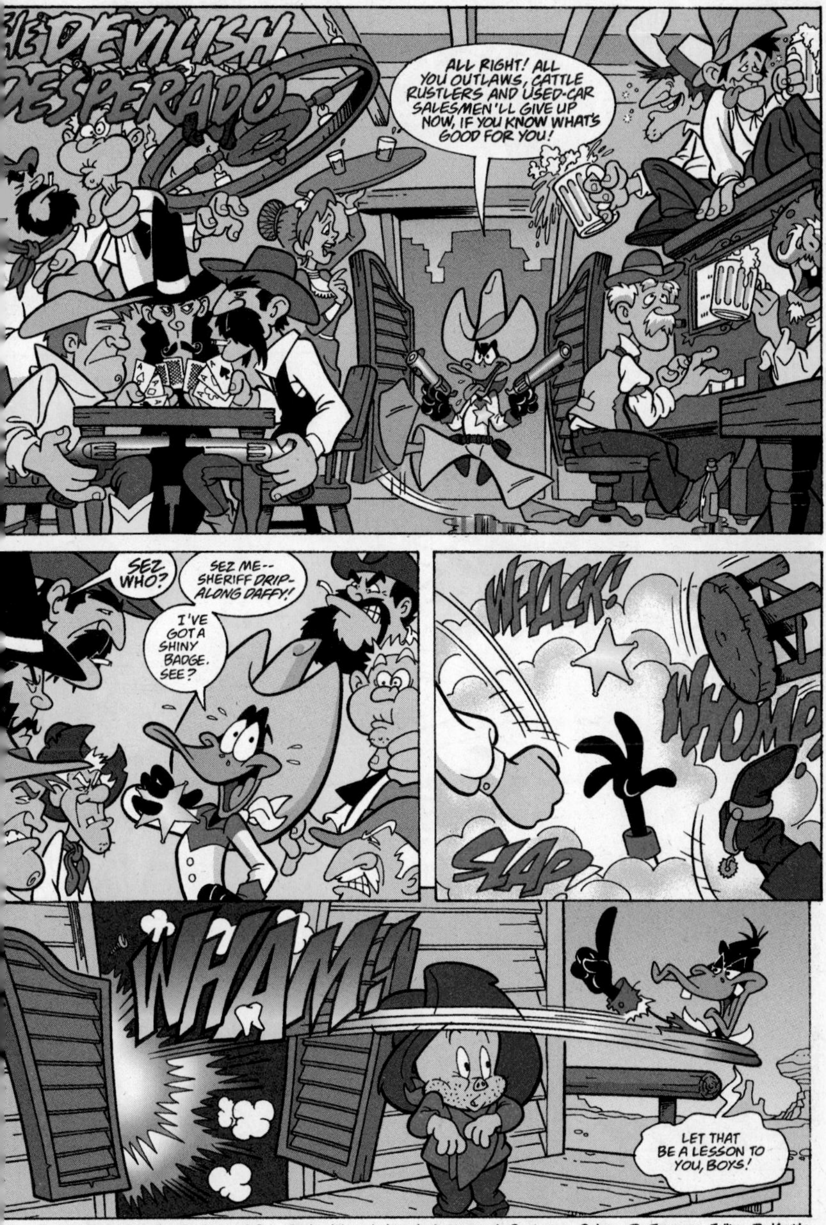
DEVILISH
DESPERADO
ALL RIGHT! ALL YOU OUTLAWS, CATTLE RUSTLERS AND USED-CAR SALESMEN'LL GIVE UP NOW, IF YOU KNOW WHAT'S GOOD FOR YOU!
SEZ WHO?
SEZ ME-- SHERIFF DRIP-ALONG DAFFY!
I'VE GOT A SHINY BADGE. SEE?
WHACK!
WHOMP!
SLAP
WHAM!!
LET THAT BE A LESSON TO YOU, BOYS!

riter: B. Mattheny Pencils: P. Zamboni & L. Batic Inks: J. Amash Letters: J. Costanza Colors: D. Tanguay Edits: D. Kurtin

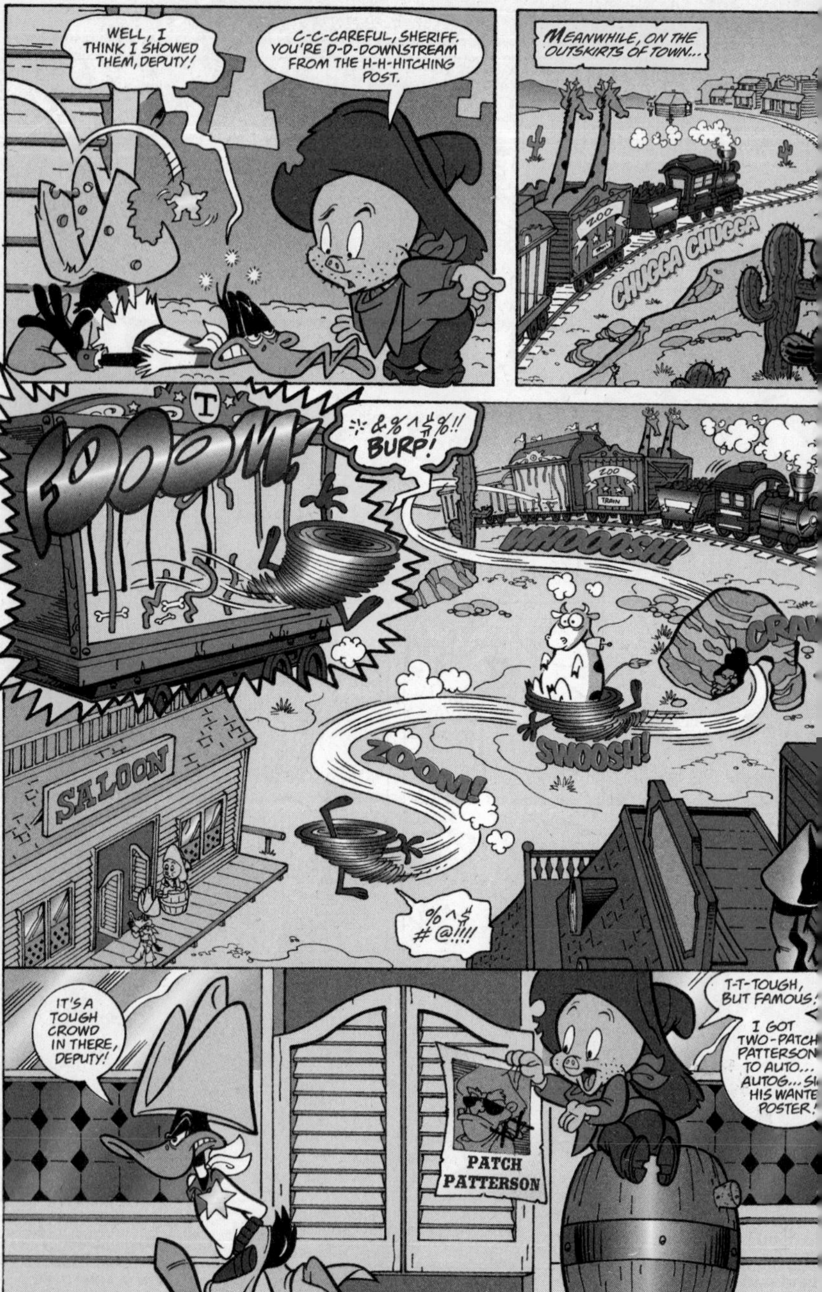
WELL, I THINK I SHOWED THEM, DEPUTY!
C-C-CAREFUL, SHERIFF. YOU'RE D-D-DOWNSTREAM FROM THE H-H-HITCHING POST.
MEANWHILE, ON THE OUTSKIRTS OF TOWN...
ZOO
CHUGGA CHUGGA
FOOOOM!
T
:*:&%^$%!! BURP!
ZOO
TRAIN
WHOOOOSH!
CRA
SWOOSH!
ZOOOM!
SALOON
%^$ #@!!!!
IT'S A TOUGH CROWD IN THERE, DEPUTY!
T-T-TOUGH, BUT FAMOUS!
I GOT TWO-PATCH PATTERSON TO AUTO... AUTOG... SI HIS WANTE POSTER!
PATCH PATTERSON

WOULD TAKE A
ENIUS TO STAND UP
THOSE HOODLUMS--
SPECIALLY THAT TWO-
ATCH PATTERSON!

W-W-WHAT THE--

ZZZZZZ

ZOUNDS! SOMEBODY'S TAKEN OUT TWO-PATCH PATTERSON!

CRASH THUD SMASH

GOOD THING I ALREADY GOT HIS AUTOG... AUTOG... SIGNATURE!

PATCH PATTERSON

ALL RIGHT, THAT'S ENOUGH, BUDDY!

IF THERE'S ANY RIFFRAFF TO BE ROUGHED UP, LET THE LAW HANDLE IT!

CRUNCH, CRUNCH! MMMM?

&%#@!!

HEY!

R-R-RIP!

WHAT'S THE BIG IDEA?

I HAD TO EAT 20 BOXES OF CEREAL TO WIN THAT BADGE!

GULP!

43

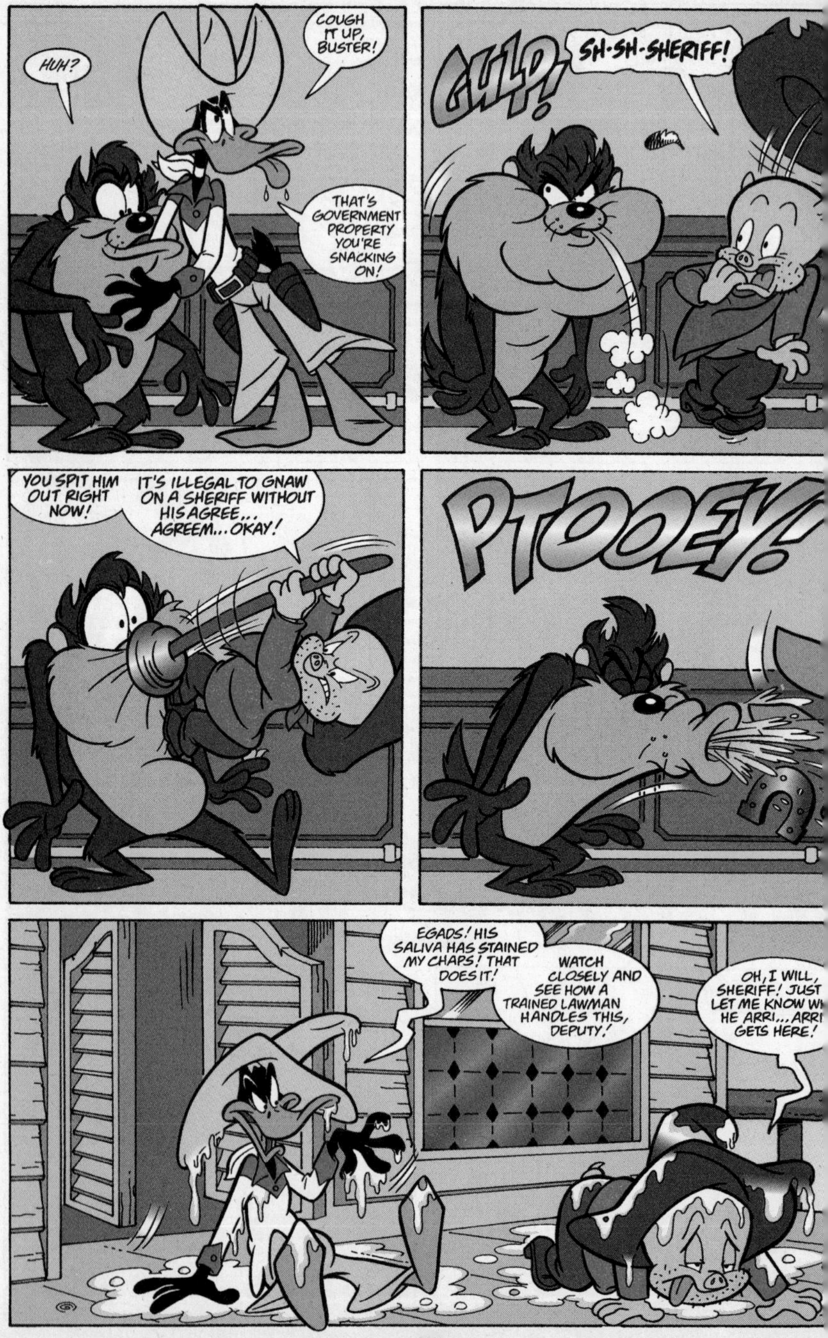
HUH?
COUGH IT UP, BUSTER!
THAT'S GOVERNMENT PROPERTY YOU'RE SNACKING ON!
GULP!
SH-SH-SHERIFF!
YOU SPIT HIM OUT RIGHT NOW!
IT'S ILLEGAL TO GNAW ON A SHERIFF WITHOUT HIS AGREE... AGREEM... OKAY!
PTOOEY!
EGADS! HIS SALIVA HAS STAINED MY CHAPS! THAT DOES IT!
WATCH CLOSELY AND SEE HOW A TRAINED LAWMAN HANDLES THIS, DEPUTY!
OH, I WILL, SHERIFF! JUST LET ME KNOW W HE ARRI... ARRI GETS HERE!

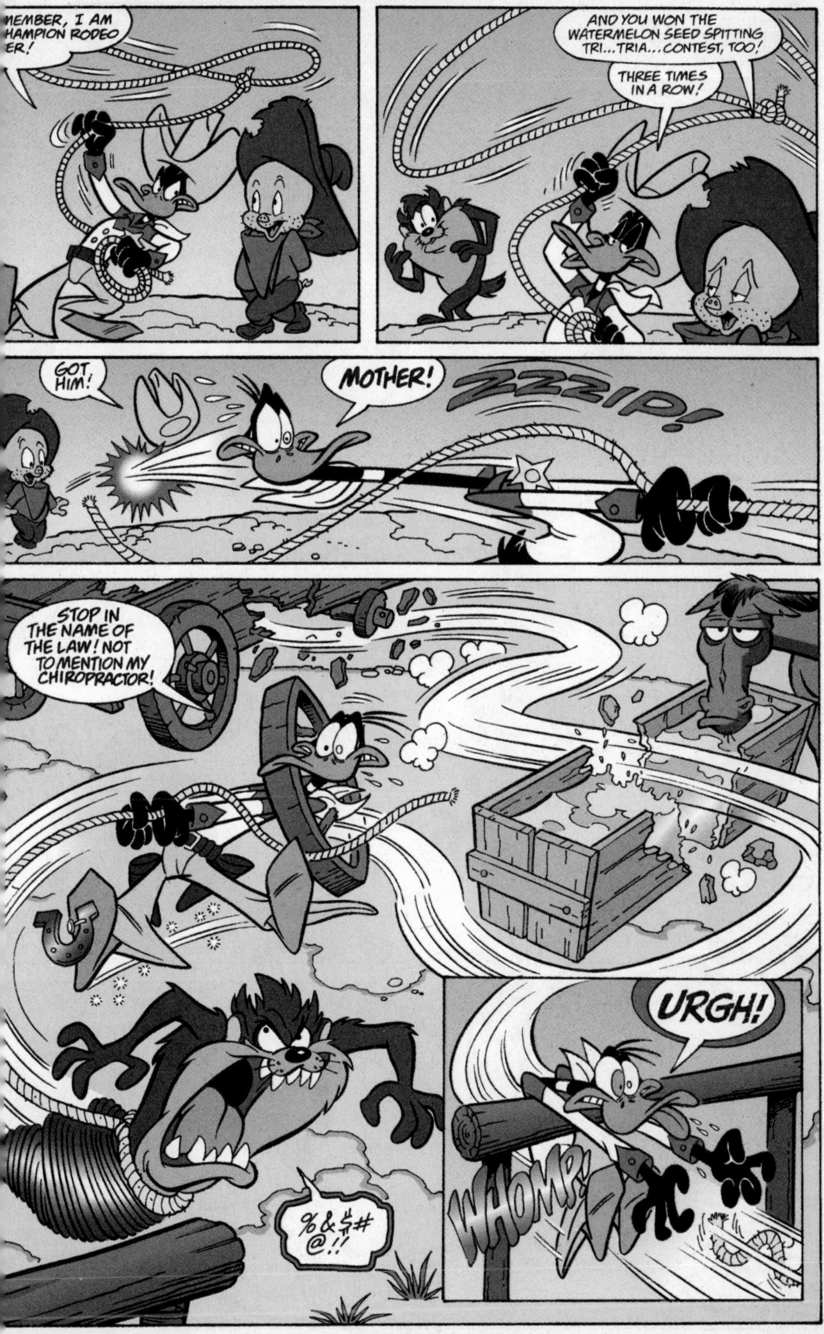
MEMBER, I AM
HAMPION RODEO
ER!
AND YOU WON THE WATERMELON SEED SPITTING TRI...TRIA...CONTEST, TOO!
THREE TIMES IN A ROW!
GOT HIM!
MOTHER!
ZZZIP!
STOP IN THE NAME OF THE LAW! NOT TO MENTION MY CHIROPRACTOR!
%&$#@!!
URGH!
WHOMP!

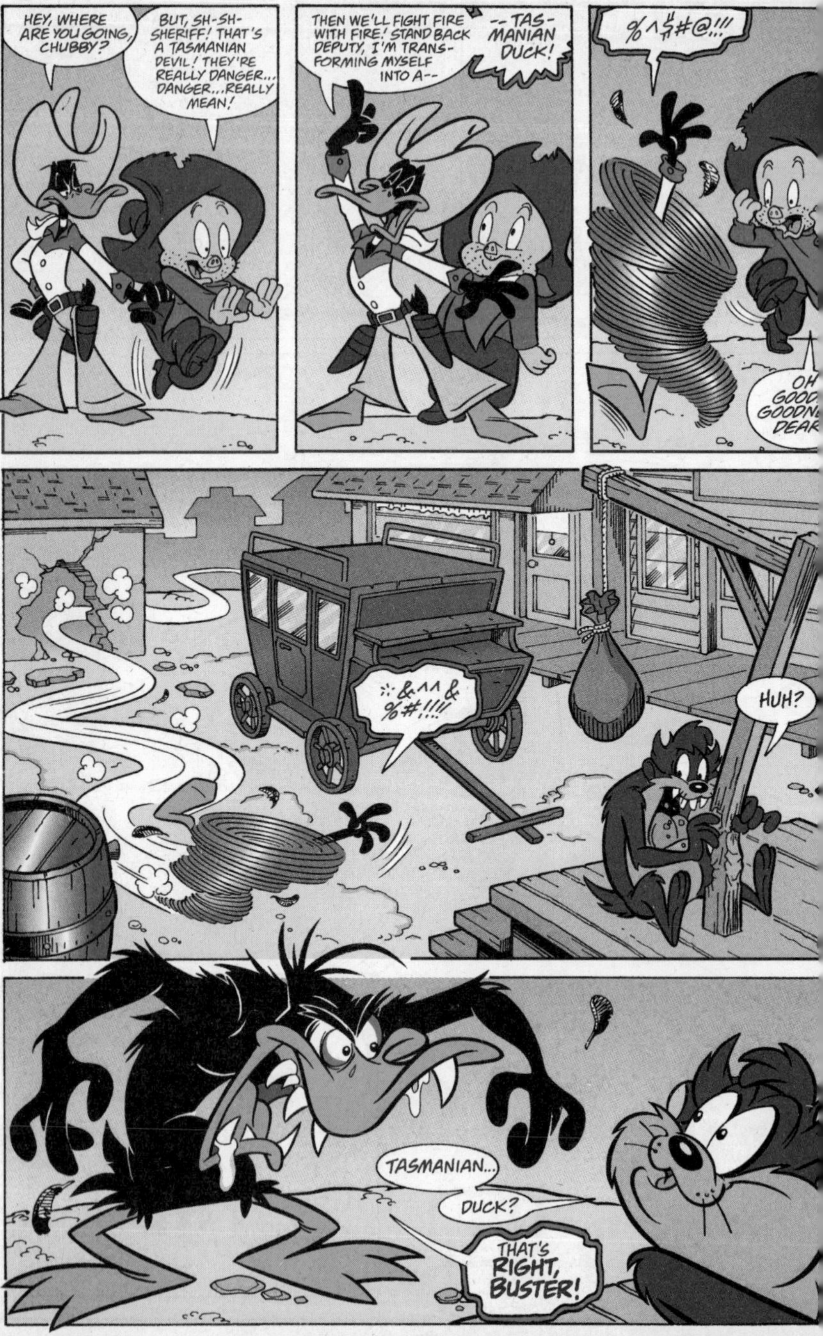
HEY, WHERE ARE YOU GOING, CHUBBY?
BUT, SH-SH-SHERIFF! THAT'S A TASMANIAN DEVIL! THEY'RE REALLY DANGER... DANGER... REALLY MEAN!
THEN WE'LL FIGHT FIRE WITH FIRE! STAND BACK DEPUTY, I'M TRANSFORMING MYSELF INTO A--
--TASMANIAN DUCK!
%^$#@!!!
OH GOOD GOODN DEAR
&^^& %#!!!!
HUH?
TASMANIAN...
DUCK?
THAT'S RIGHT, BUSTER!

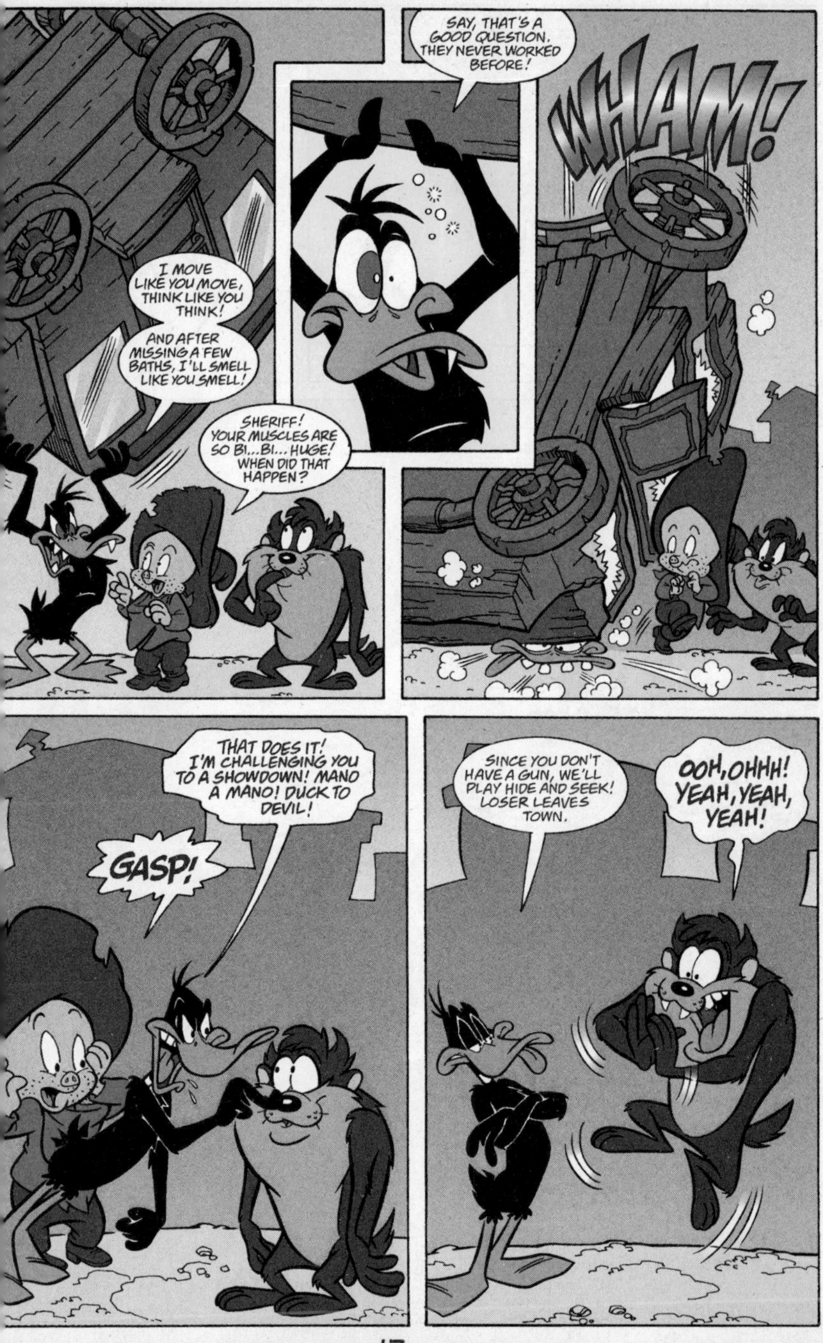
I MOVE LIKE YOU MOVE, THINK LIKE YOU THINK!
AND AFTER MISSING A FEW BATHS, I'LL SMELL LIKE YOU SMELL!
SHERIFF! YOUR MUSCLES ARE SO BI...BI... HUGE! WHEN DID THAT HAPPEN?
SAY, THAT'S A GOOD QUESTION. THEY NEVER WORKED BEFORE!
WHAM!
THAT DOES IT! I'M CHALLENGING YOU TO A SHOWDOWN! MANO A MANO! DUCK TO DEVIL!
GASP!
SINCE YOU DON'T HAVE A GUN, WE'LL PLAY HIDE AND SEEK! LOSER LEAVES TOWN.
OOH, OHHH! YEAH, YEAH, YEAH!

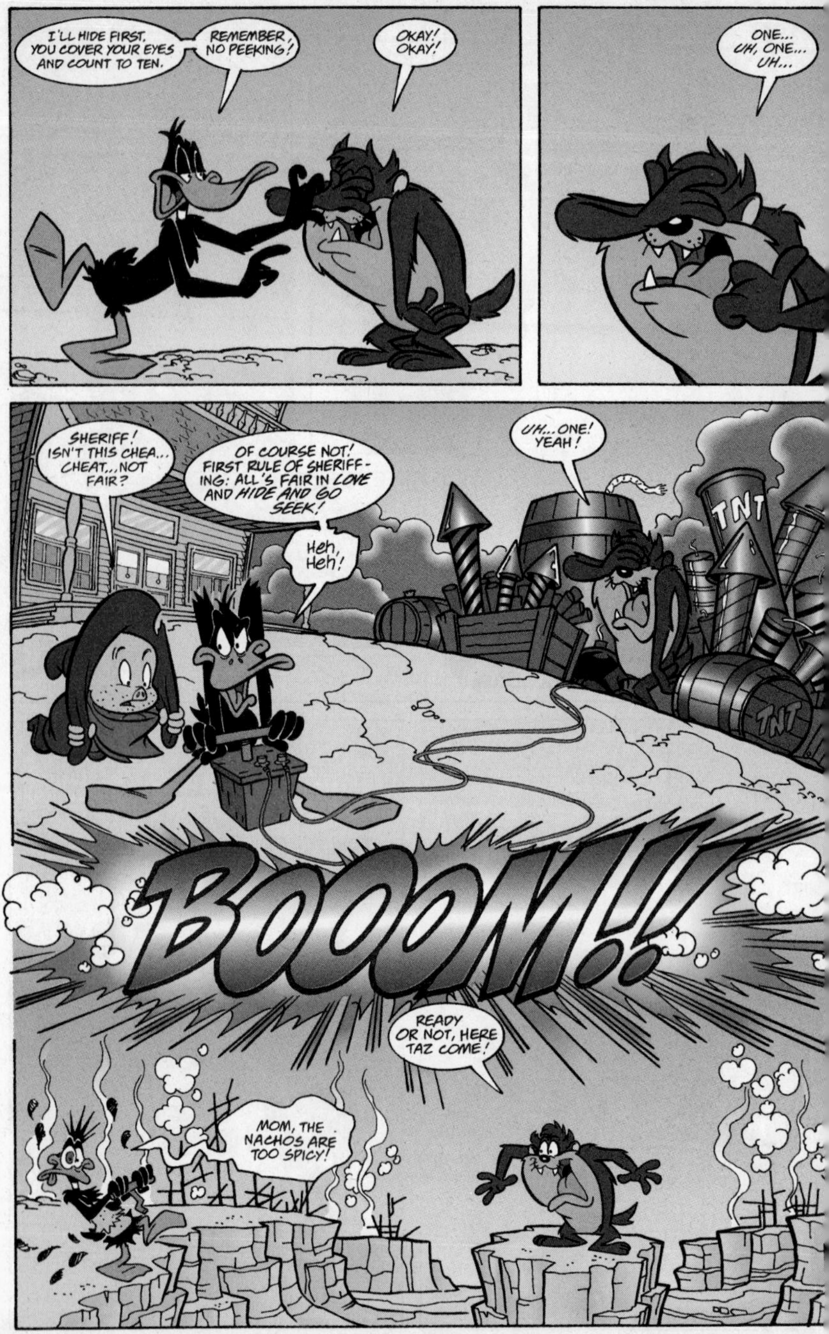
I'LL HIDE FIRST. YOU COVER YOUR EYES AND COUNT TO TEN.
REMEMBER, NO PEEKING!
OKAY! OKAY!
ONE... UH, ONE... UH...
SHERIFF! ISN'T THIS CHEA... CHEAT... NOT FAIR?
OF COURSE NOT! FIRST RULE OF SHERIFF-ING: ALL'S FAIR IN LOVE AND HIDE AND GO SEEK!
Heh, Heh!
UH... ONE! YEAH!
TNT
TNT
BOOOM!!
READY OR NOT, HERE TAZ COME!
MOM, THE NACHOS ARE TOO SPICY!

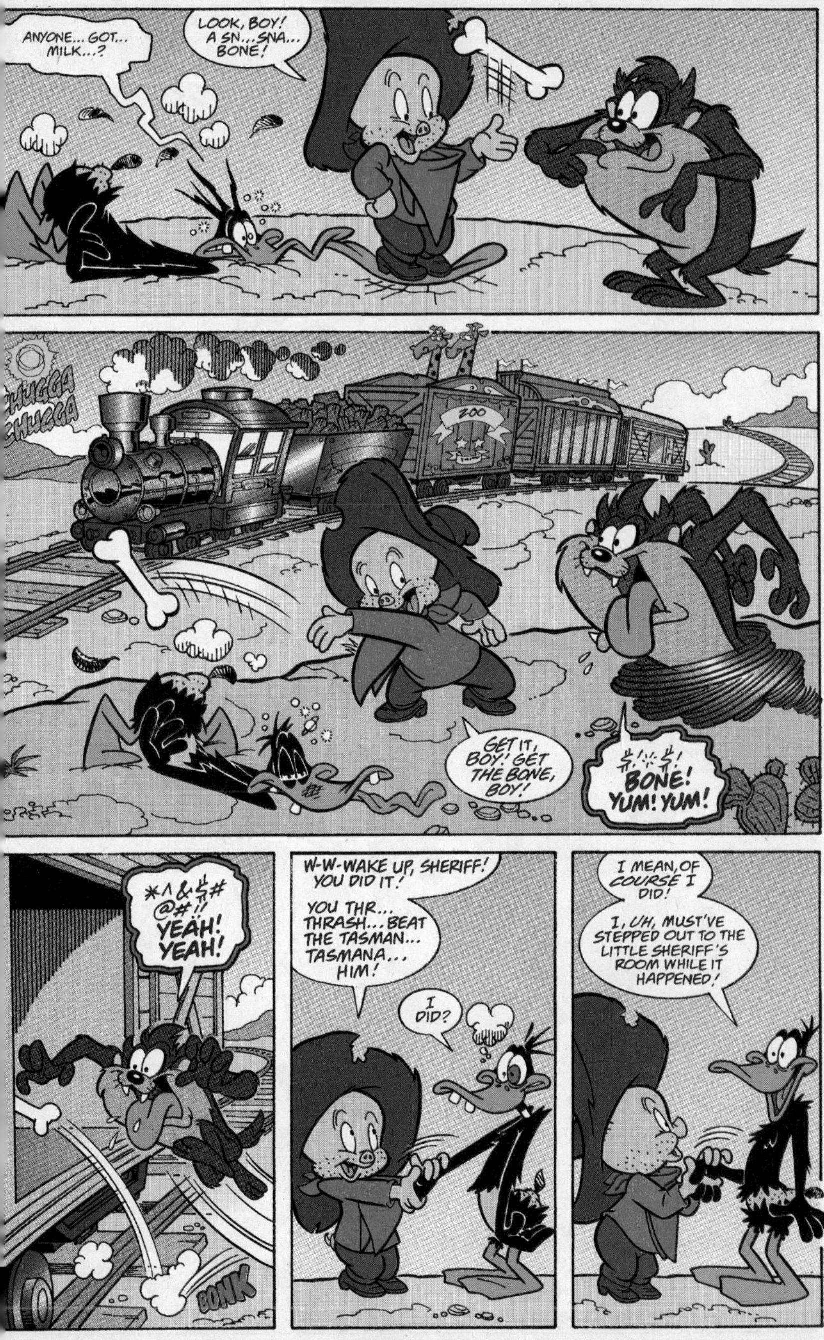
ANYONE... GOT... MILK...?
LOOK, BOY! A SN...SNA... BONE!
CHUGGA CHUGGA
ZOO
GET IT, BOY! GET THE BONE, BOY!
$!*$! BONE! YUM! YUM!
*^&$# @#!! YEAH! YEAH!
BONK
W-W-WAKE UP, SHERIFF! YOU DID IT!
YOU THR... THRASH... BEAT THE TASMAN... TASMANA... HIM!
I DID?
I MEAN, OF COURSE I DID!
I, UH, MUST'VE STEPPED OUT TO THE LITTLE SHERIFF'S ROOM WHILE IT HAPPENED!

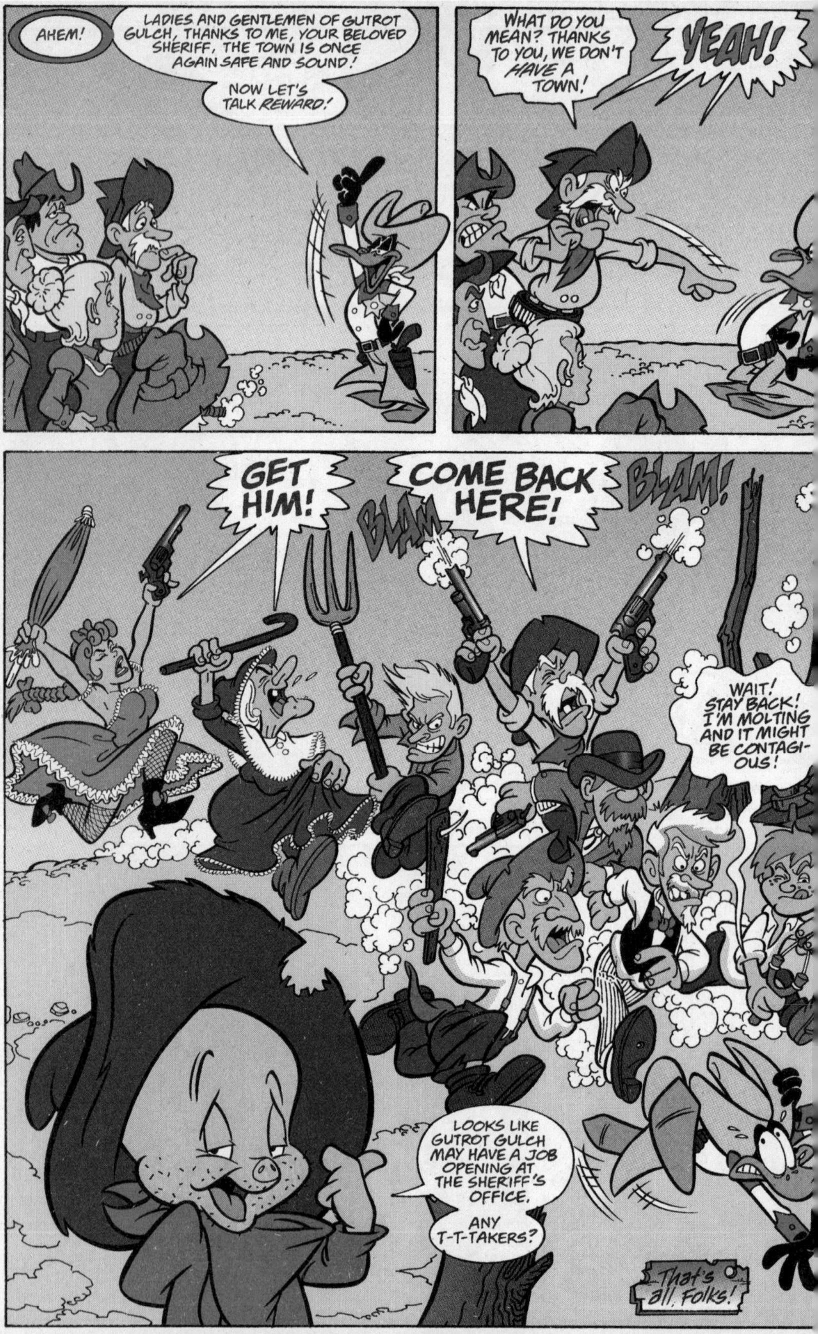
AHEM!
LADIES AND GENTLEMEN OF GUTROT GULCH, THANKS TO ME, YOUR BELOVED SHERIFF, THE TOWN IS ONCE AGAIN SAFE AND SOUND!
NOW LET'S TALK REWARD!
WHAT DO YOU MEAN? THANKS TO YOU, WE DON'T HAVE A TOWN!
YEAH!
GET HIM!
COME BACK HERE!
BLAM
BLAM!
WAIT! STAY BACK! I'M MOLTING AND IT MIGHT BE CONTAGIOUS!
LOOKS LIKE GUTROT GULCH MAY HAVE A JOB OPENING AT THE SHERIFF'S OFFICE.
ANY T-T-TAKERS?
That's all, Folks!

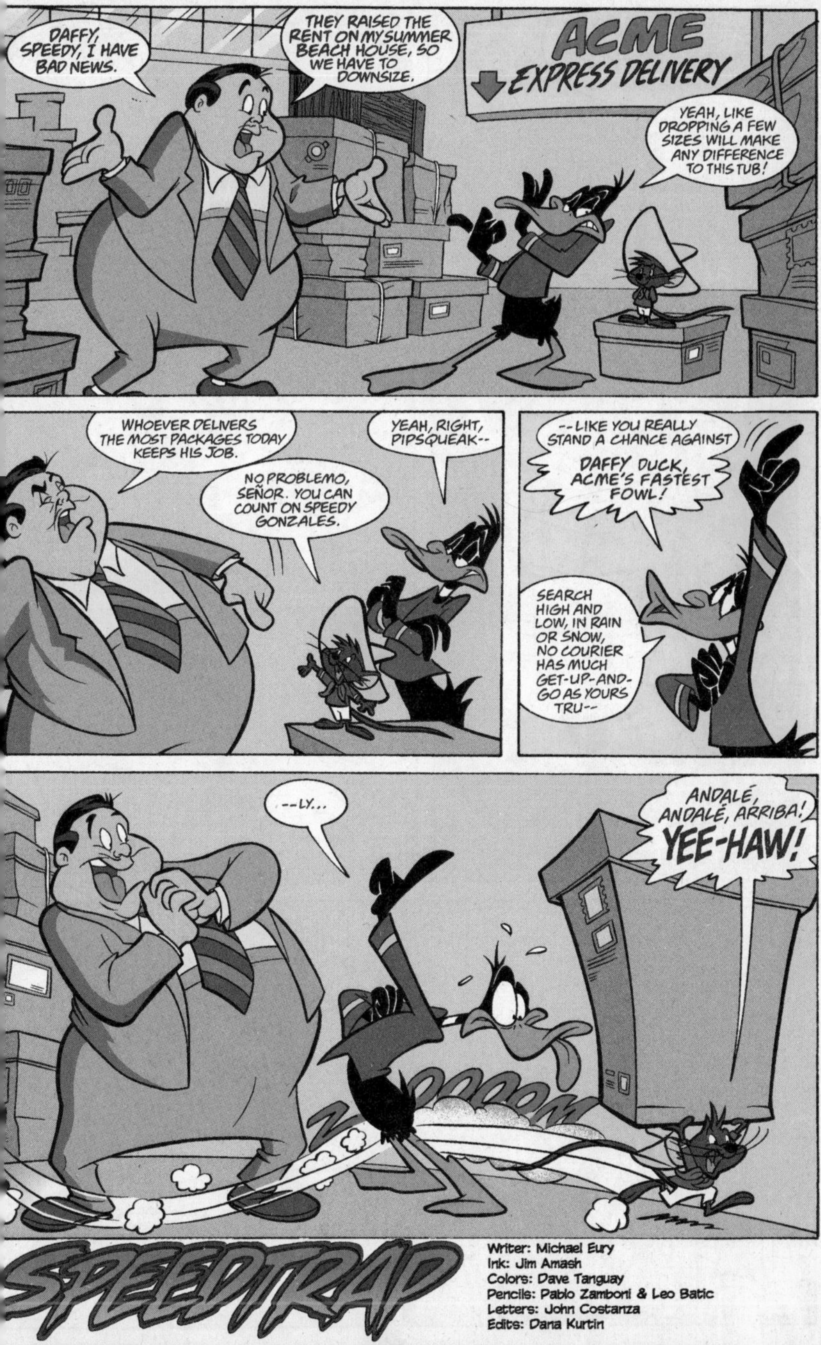
ACME
EXPRESS DELIVERY
DAFFY, SPEEDY, I HAVE BAD NEWS.
THEY RAISED THE RENT ON MY SUMMER BEACH HOUSE, SO WE HAVE TO DOWNSIZE.
YEAH, LIKE DROPPING A FEW SIZES WILL MAKE ANY DIFFERENCE TO THIS TUB!
WHOEVER DELIVERS THE MOST PACKAGES TODAY KEEPS HIS JOB.
NO PROBLEMO, SEÑOR. YOU CAN COUNT ON SPEEDY GONZALES.
YEAH, RIGHT, PIPSQUEAK--
--LIKE YOU REALLY STAND A CHANCE AGAINST
DAFFY DUCK, ACME'S FASTEST FOWL!
SEARCH HIGH AND LOW, IN RAIN OR SNOW, NO COURIER HAS MUCH GET-UP-AND-GO AS YOURS TRU--
--LY...
ANDALÉ, ANDALÉ, ARRIBA! YEE-HAW!
ZOOOOOOM

SPEEDTRAP

Writer: Michael Eury
Ink: Jim Amash
Colors: Dave Tanguay
Pencils: Pablo Zamboni & Leo Batic
Letters: John Costanza
Edits: Dana Kurtin

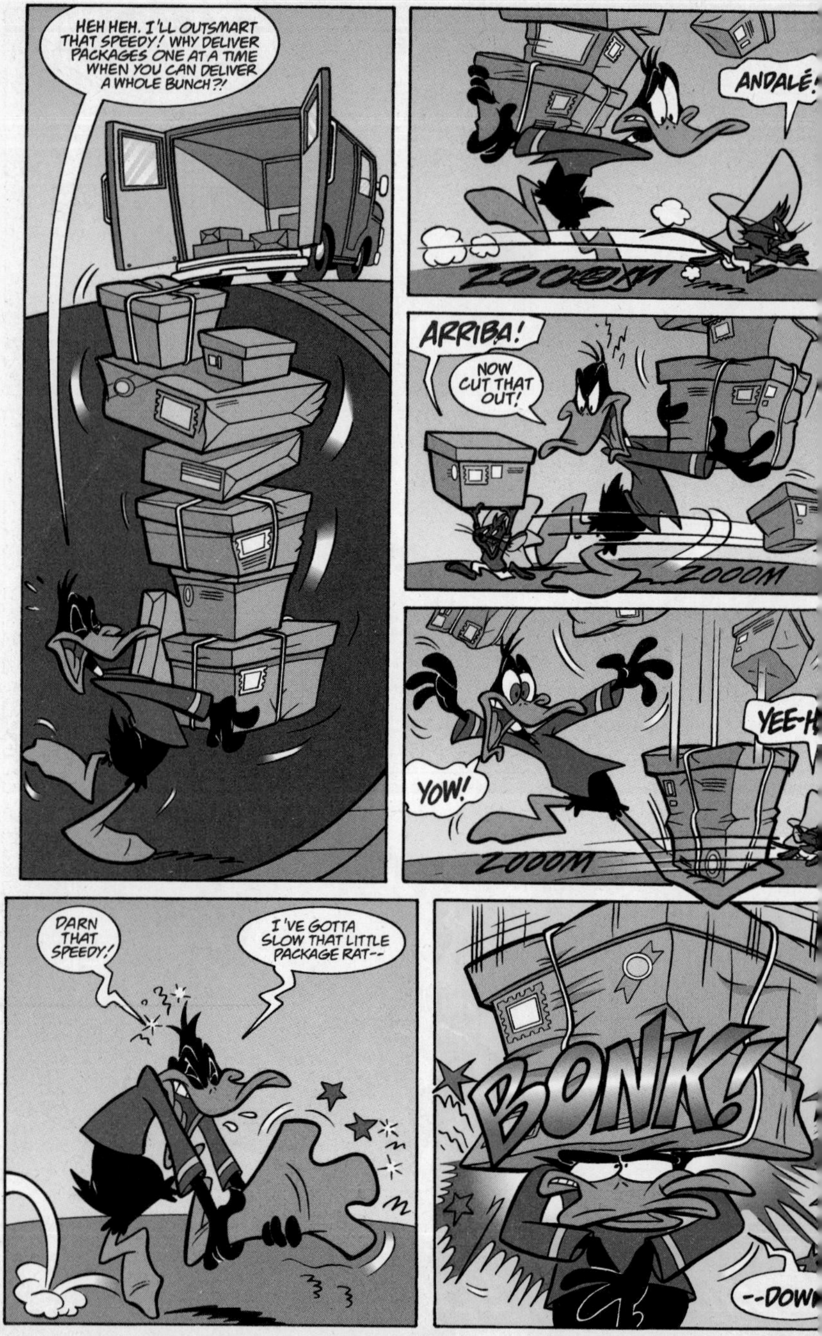
HEH HEH. I'LL OUTSMART THAT SPEEDY! WHY DELIVER PACKAGES ONE AT A TIME WHEN YOU CAN DELIVER A WHOLE BUNCH?!
ANDALÉ!
ZOOOOM
ARRIBA!
NOW CUT THAT OUT!
ZOOOM
YEE-H
YOW!
ZOOOM
DARN THAT SPEEDY!
I'VE GOTTA SLOW THAT LITTLE PACKAGE RAT--
BONK!
--DOW

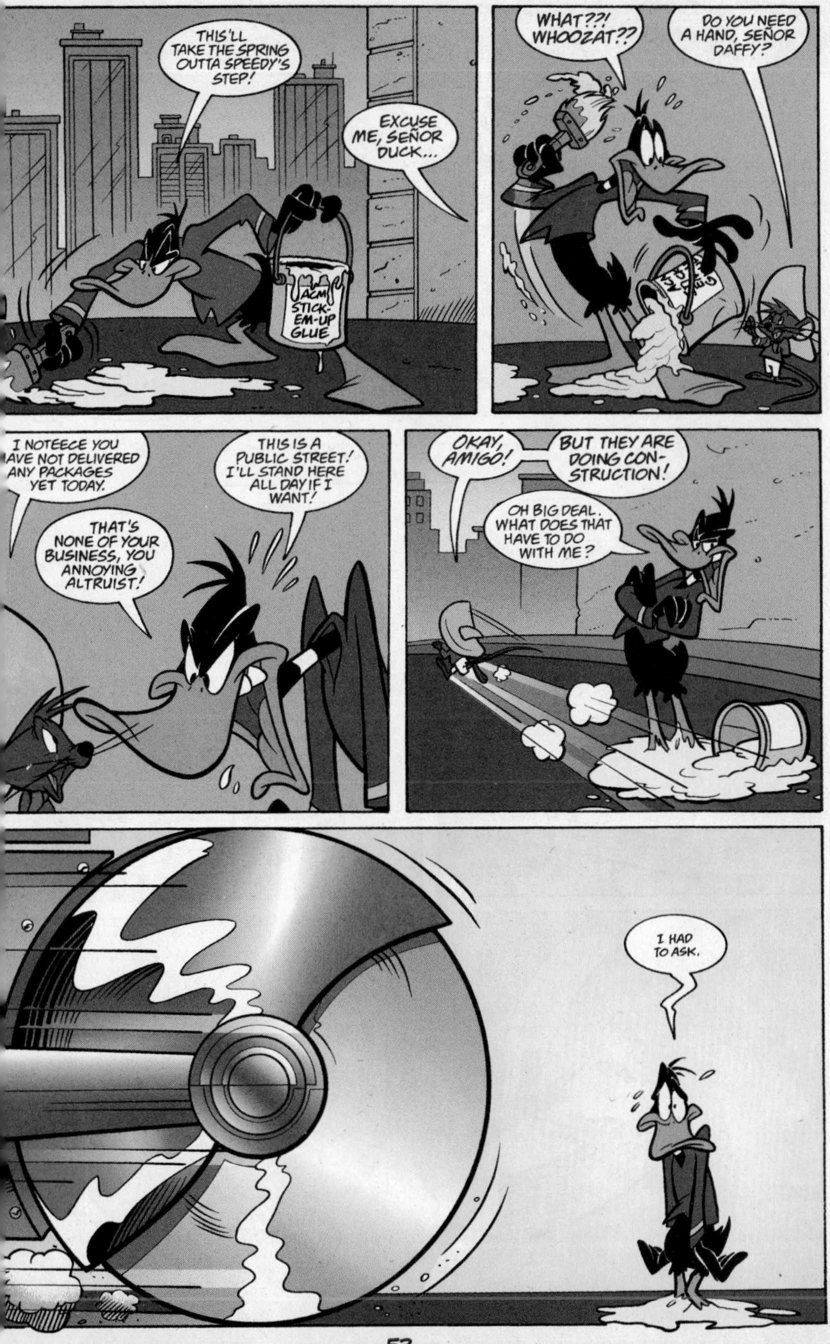
THIS'LL TAKE THE SPRING OUTTA SPEEDY'S STEP!
EXCUSE ME, SEÑOR DUCK...
ACM STICK-EM-UP GLUE
WHAT??! WHOOZAT??
DO YOU NEED A HAND, SEÑOR DAFFY?
I NOTEECE YOU AVE NOT DELIVERED ANY PACKAGES YET TODAY.
THAT'S NONE OF YOUR BUSINESS, YOU ANNOYING ALTRUIST!
THIS IS A PUBLIC STREET! I'LL STAND HERE ALL DAY IF I WANT!
OKAY, AMIGO!
BUT THEY ARE DOING CONSTRUCTION!
OH BIG DEAL. WHAT DOES THAT HAVE TO DO WITH ME?
I HAD TO ASK.

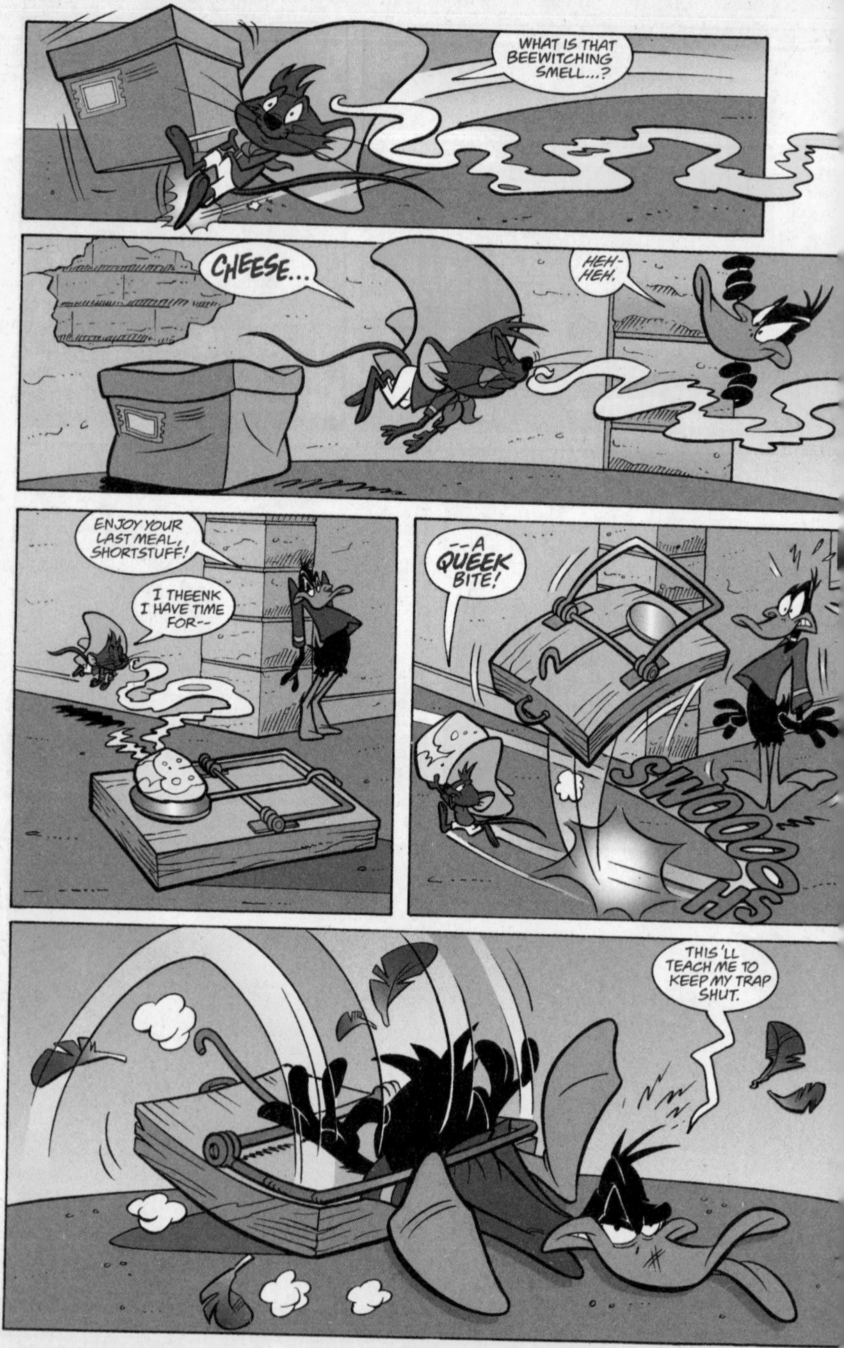

WHAT IS THAT BEEWITCHING SMELL...?
CHEESE...
HEH-HEH.
ENJOY YOUR LAST MEAL, SHORTSTUFF!
I THEENK I HAVE TIME FOR--
--A QUEEK BITE!
SHWOOOOOOSH
THIS'LL TEACH ME TO KEEP MY TRAP SHUT.

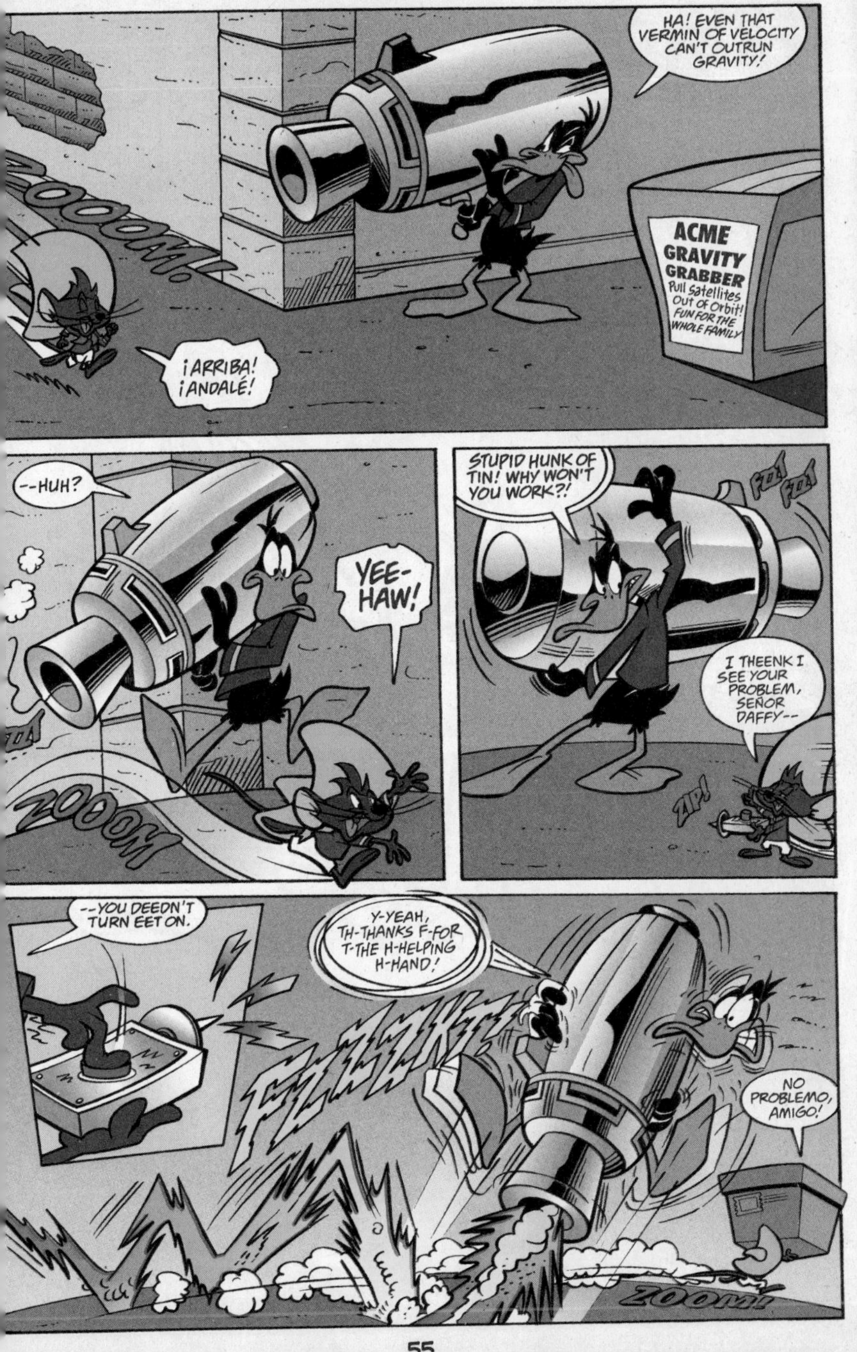
HA! EVEN THAT VERMIN OF VELOCITY CAN'T OUTRUN GRAVITY!
ACME GRAVITY GRABBER
Pull Satellites Out of Orbit!
FUN FOR THE WHOLE FAMILY
ZOOOOM!
¡ARRIBA! ¡ANDALÉ!
--HUH?
YEE-HAW!
ZOOOM
STUPID HUNK OF TIN! WHY WON'T YOU WORK?!
I THEENK I SEE YOUR PROBLEM, SEÑOR DAFFY--
ZIP!
--YOU DEEDN'T TURN EET ON.
Y-YEAH, TH-THANKS F-FOR T-THE H-HELPING H-HAND!
NO PROBLEMO, AMIGO!
ZOOM!

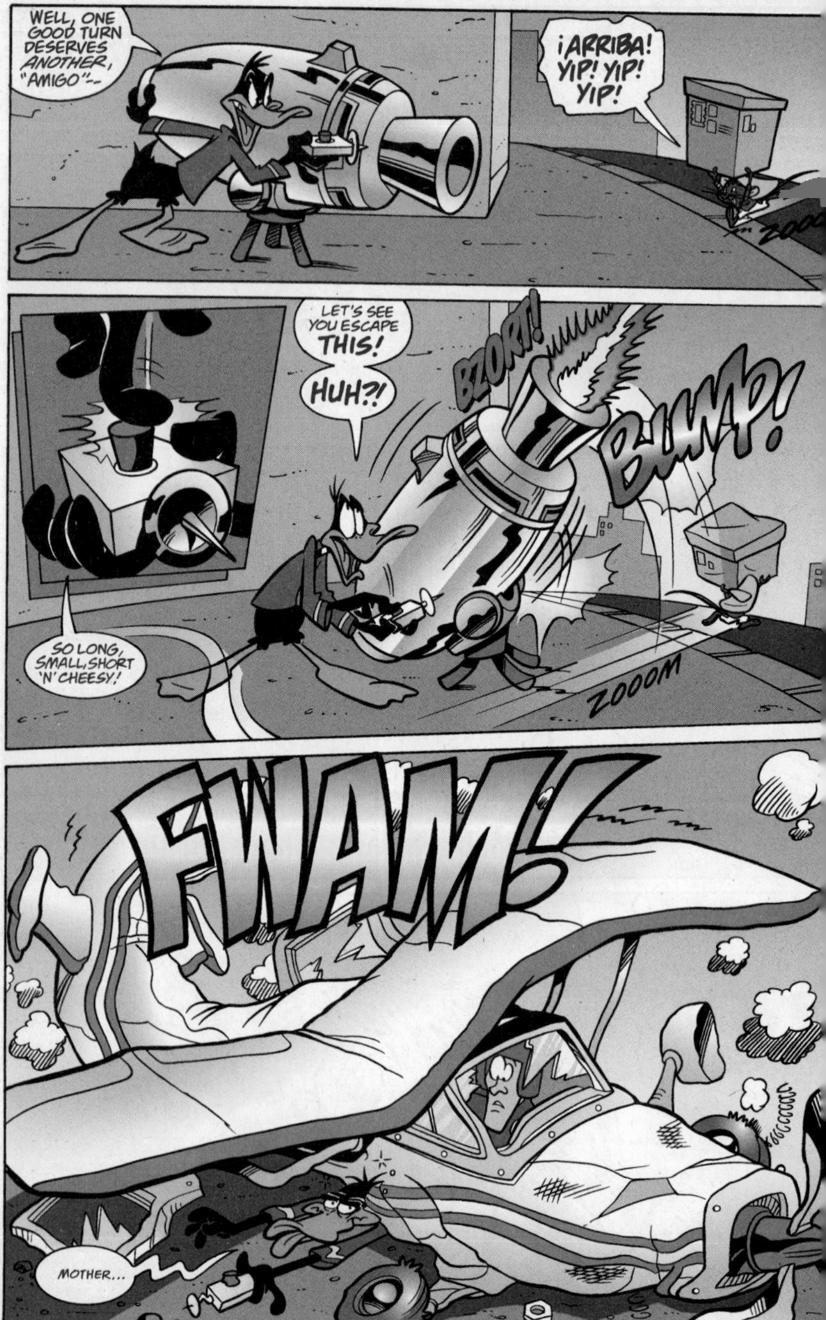
WELL, ONE GOOD TURN DESERVES ANOTHER, "AMIGO"--
¡ARRIBA! YIP! YIP! YIP!
ZOOO
LET'S SEE YOU ESCAPE THIS!
HUH?!
BZORT!
BUMP!
SO LONG, SMALL, SHORT 'N' CHEESY!
ZOOOM
FWAM!
MOTHER...

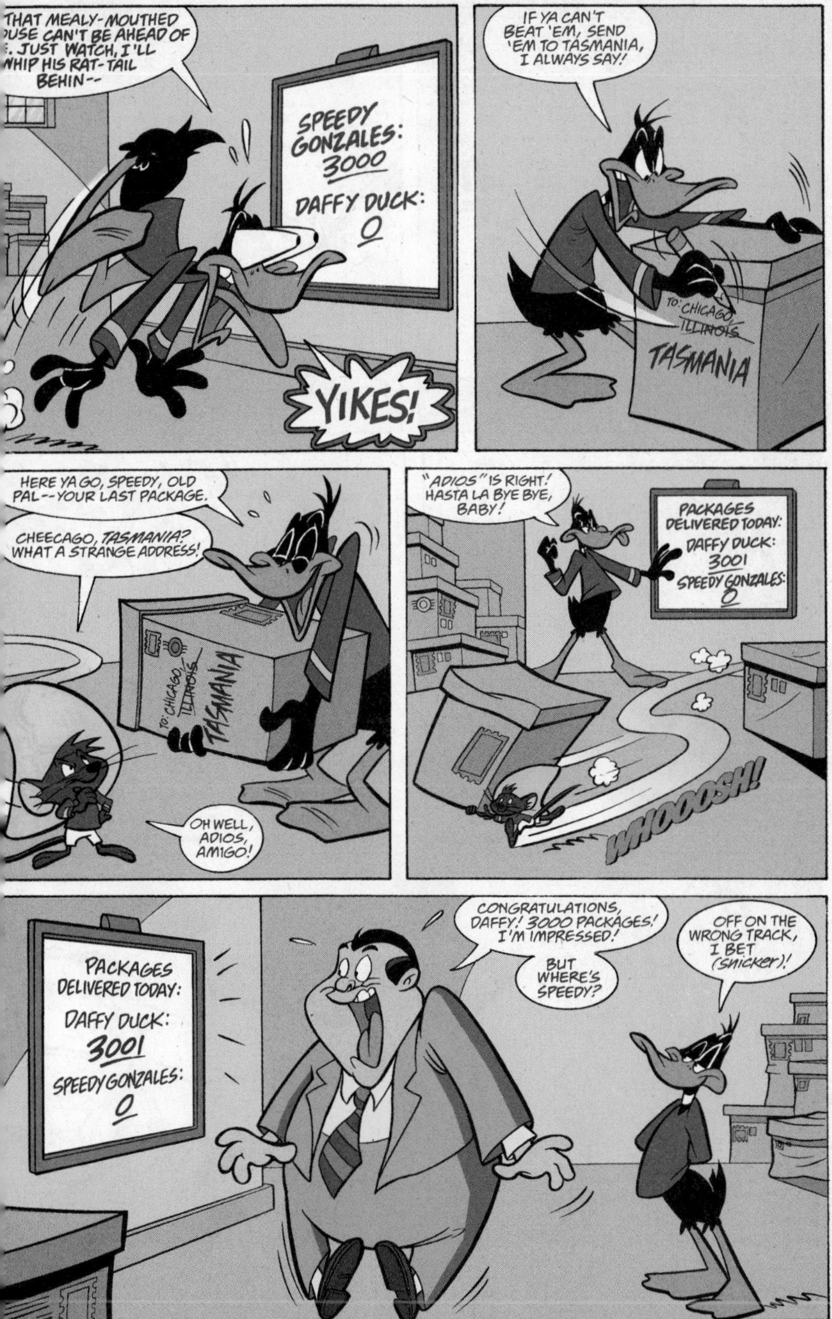
THAT MEALY-MOUTHED
OUSE CAN'T BE AHEAD OF
E. JUST WATCH, I'LL
WHIP HIS RAT-TAIL
BEHIN--
SPEEDY GONZALES: 3000
DAFFY DUCK: 0
YIKES!
IF YA CAN'T BEAT 'EM, SEND 'EM TO TASMANIA, I ALWAYS SAY!
TO: CHICAGO, ILLINOIS
TASMANIA
HERE YA GO, SPEEDY, OLD PAL--YOUR LAST PACKAGE.
CHEECAGO, TASMANIA? WHAT A STRANGE ADDRESS!
OH WELL, ADIOS, AMIGO!
"ADIOS" IS RIGHT! HASTA LA BYE BYE, BABY!
PACKAGES DELIVERED TODAY:
DAFFY DUCK: 3001
SPEEDY GONZALES: 0
WHOOOOSH!
CONGRATULATIONS, DAFFY! 3000 PACKAGES! I'M IMPRESSED!
BUT WHERE'S SPEEDY?
OFF ON THE WRONG TRACK, I BET (snicker)!
PACKAGES DELIVERED TODAY:
DAFFY DUCK: 3001
SPEEDY GONZALES: 0

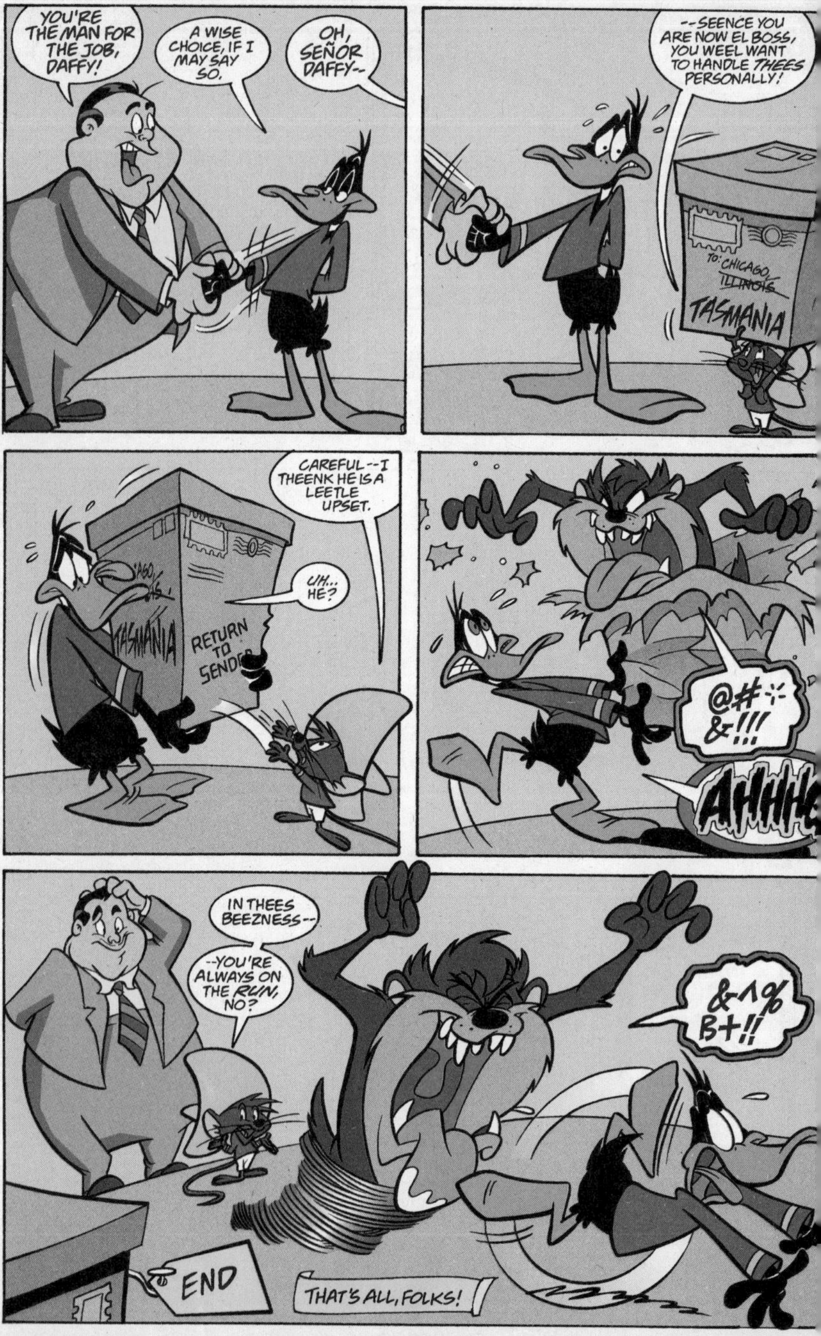

YOU'RE THE MAN FOR THE JOB, DAFFY!
A WISE CHOICE, IF I MAY SAY SO.
OH, SEÑOR DAFFY--
--SEENCE YOU ARE NOW EL BOSS, YOU WEEL WANT TO HANDLE THEES PERSONALLY!
TO: CHICAGO, ILLINOIS
TASMANIA
CAREFUL--I THEENK HE IS A LEETLE UPSET.
UH... HE?
TASMANIA
RETURN TO SENDER
@#*& !!!
AHHHH
IN THEES BEEZNESS--
--YOU'RE ALWAYS ON THE RUN, NO?
&^%B+!!
END
THAT'S ALL, FOLKS!

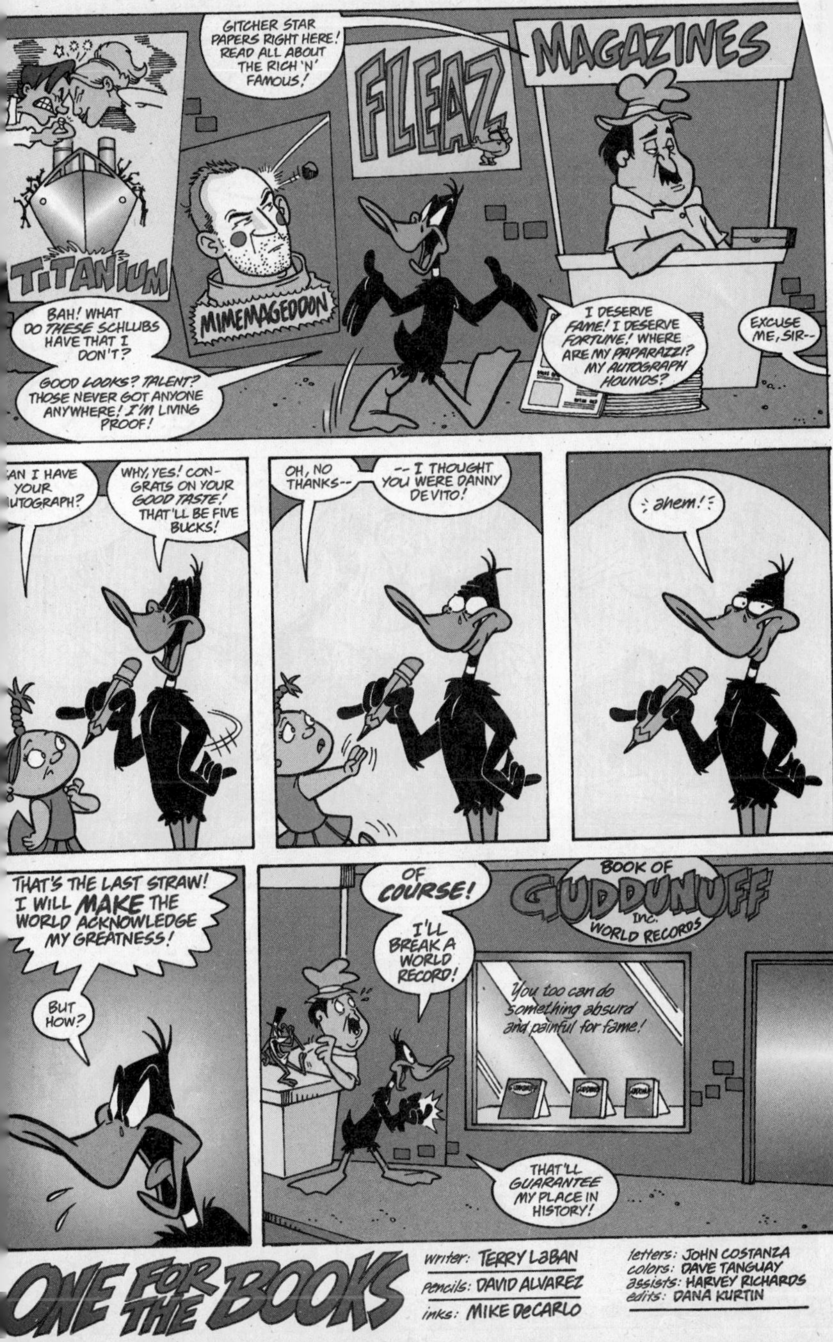
GITCHER STAR PAPERS RIGHT HERE! READ ALL ABOUT THE RICH 'N' FAMOUS!
MAGAZINES
FLEAZ
TITANIUM
MIMEMAGEDDON
BAH! WHAT DO THESE SCHLUBS HAVE THAT I DON'T?
GOOD LOOKS? TALENT? THOSE NEVER GOT ANYONE ANYWHERE! I'M LIVING PROOF!
I DESERVE FAME! I DESERVE FORTUNE! WHERE ARE MY PAPARAZZI? MY AUTOGRAPH HOUNDS?
EXCUSE ME, SIR--
AN I HAVE YOUR UTOGRAPH?
WHY, YES! CONGRATS ON YOUR GOOD TASTE! THAT'LL BE FIVE BUCKS!
OH, NO THANKS--
--I THOUGHT YOU WERE DANNY DEVITO!
ahem!
THAT'S THE LAST STRAW! I WILL MAKE THE WORLD ACKNOWLEDGE MY GREATNESS!
BUT HOW?
OF COURSE!
I'LL BREAK A WORLD RECORD!
BOOK OF GUDDUNUFF Inc. WORLD RECORDS
You too can do something absurd and painful for fame!
THAT'LL GUARANTEE MY PLACE IN HISTORY!

ONE FOR THE BOOKS

writer: TERRY LABAN
pencils: DAVID ALVAREZ
inks: MIKE DeCARLO
letters: JOHN COSTANZA
colors: DAVE TANGUAY
assists: HARVEY RICHARDS
edits: DANA KURTIN

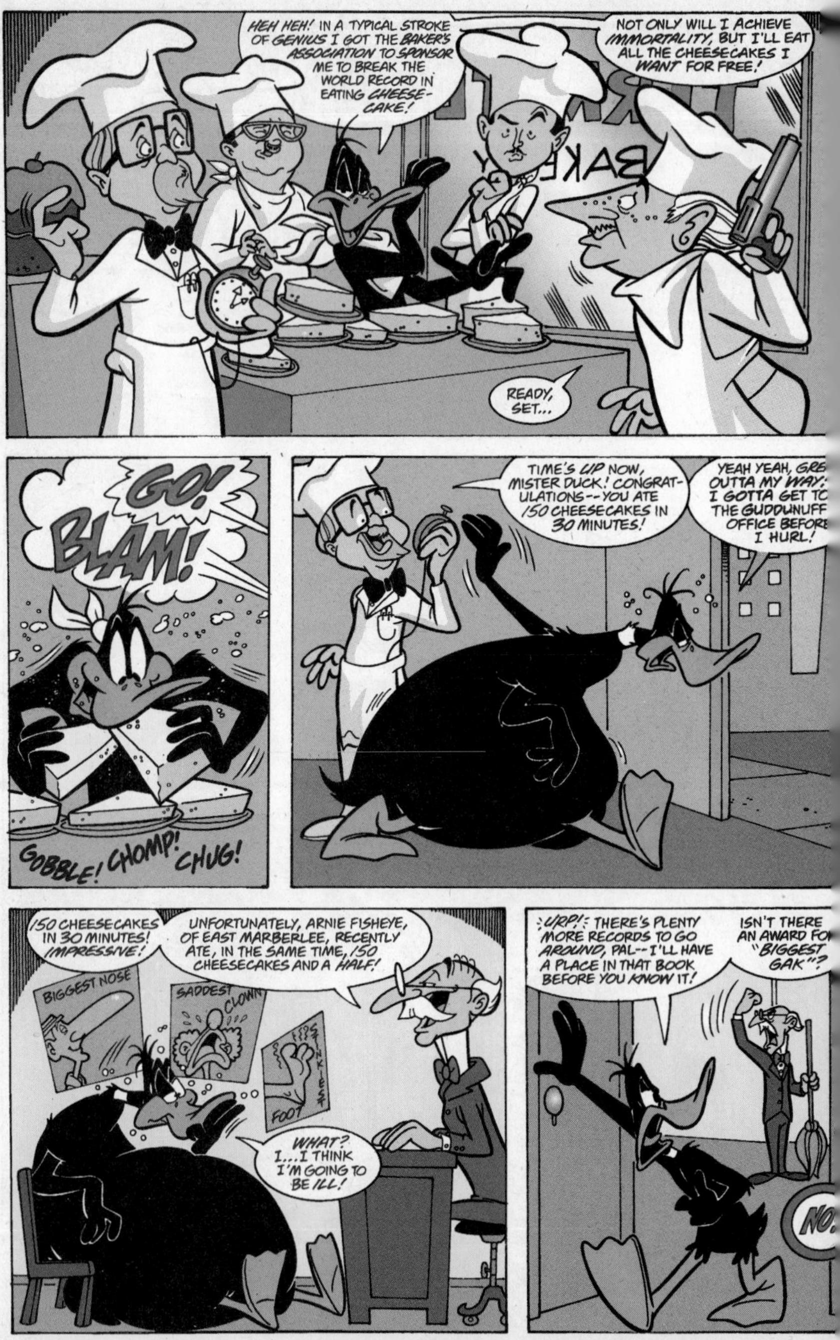

HEH HEH! IN A TYPICAL STROKE OF GENIUS I GOT THE BAKER'S ASSOCIATION TO SPONSOR ME TO BREAK THE WORLD RECORD IN EATING CHEESE-CAKE!
NOT ONLY WILL I ACHIEVE IMMORTALITY, BUT I'LL EAT ALL THE CHEESECAKES I WANT FOR FREE!
BAKE
READY, SET...
GO!
BLAM!
GOBBLE! CHOMP! CHUG!
TIME'S UP NOW, MISTER DUCK! CONGRAT-ULATIONS--YOU ATE 150 CHEESECAKES IN 30 MINUTES!
YEAH YEAH, GRE OUTTA MY WAY: I GOTTA GET TO THE GUDDUNUFF OFFICE BEFORE I HURL!
150 CHEESECAKES IN 30 MINUTES! IMPRESSIVE!
UNFORTUNATELY, ARNIE FISHEYE, OF EAST MARBERLEE, RECENTLY ATE, IN THE SAME TIME, 150 CHEESECAKES AND A HALF!
BIGGEST NOSE
SADDEST CLOWN
STINKIEST FOOT
WHAT? I...I THINK I'M GOING TO BE ILL!
URP! THERE'S PLENTY MORE RECORDS TO GO AROUND, PAL--I'LL HAVE A PLACE IN THAT BOOK BEFORE YOU KNOW IT!
ISN'T THERE AN AWARD FO "BIGGEST GAK"?
NO

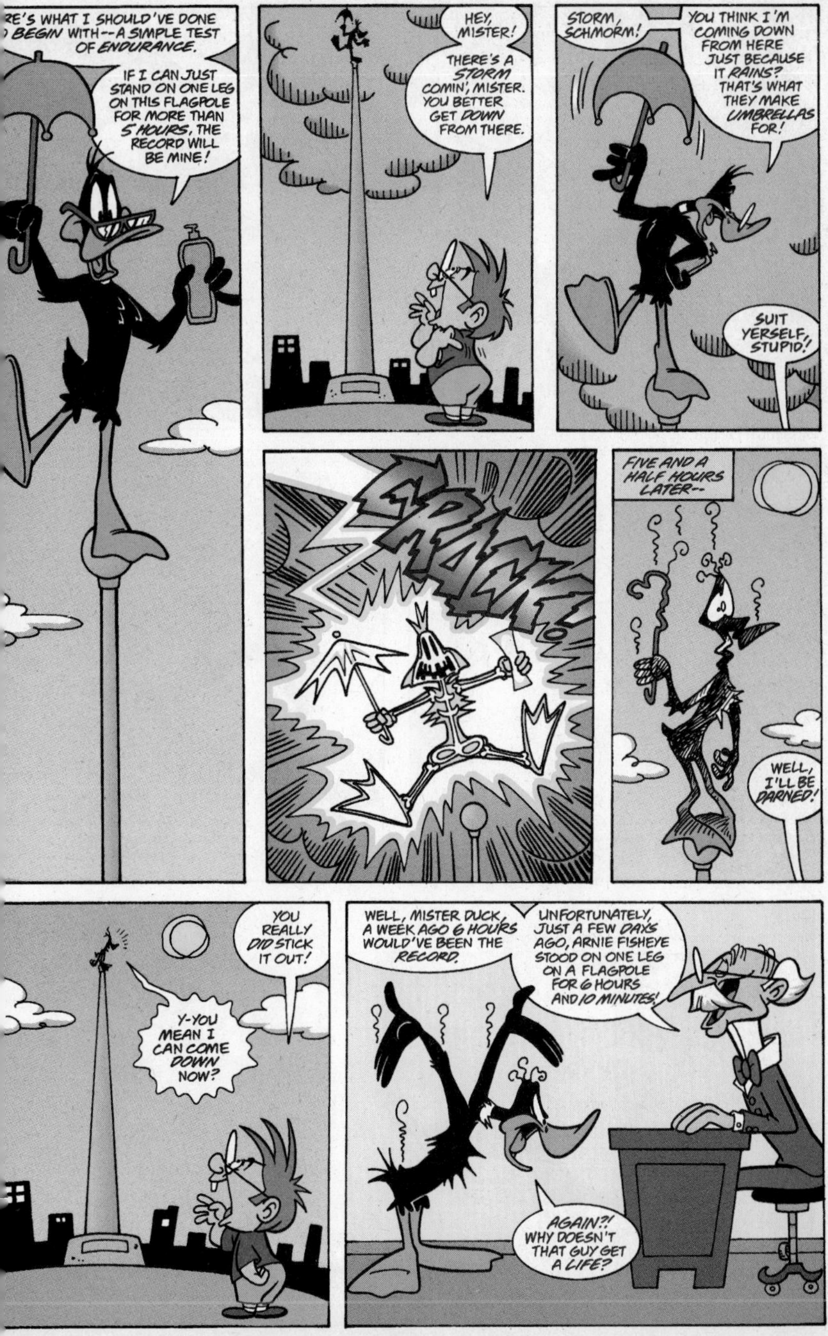

RE'S WHAT I SHOULD'VE DONE
BEGIN WITH--A SIMPLE TEST OF ENDURANCE.
IF I CAN JUST STAND ON ONE LEG ON THIS FLAGPOLE FOR MORE THAN 5 HOURS, THE RECORD WILL BE MINE!
HEY, MISTER!
THERE'S A STORM COMIN', MISTER. YOU BETTER GET DOWN FROM THERE.
STORM, SCHMORM!
YOU THINK I'M COMING DOWN FROM HERE JUST BECAUSE IT RAINS? THAT'S WHAT THEY MAKE UMBRELLAS FOR!
SUIT YERSELF, STUPID!
KRACK!
FIVE AND A HALF HOURS LATER--
WELL, I'LL BE DARNED!
YOU REALLY DID STICK IT OUT!
Y-YOU MEAN I CAN COME DOWN NOW?
WELL, MISTER DUCK, A WEEK AGO 6 HOURS WOULD'VE BEEN THE RECORD.
UNFORTUNATELY, JUST A FEW DAYS AGO, ARNIE FISHEYE STOOD ON ONE LEG ON A FLAGPOLE FOR 6 HOURS AND 10 MINUTES!
AGAIN?! WHY DOESN'T THAT GUY GET A LIFE?

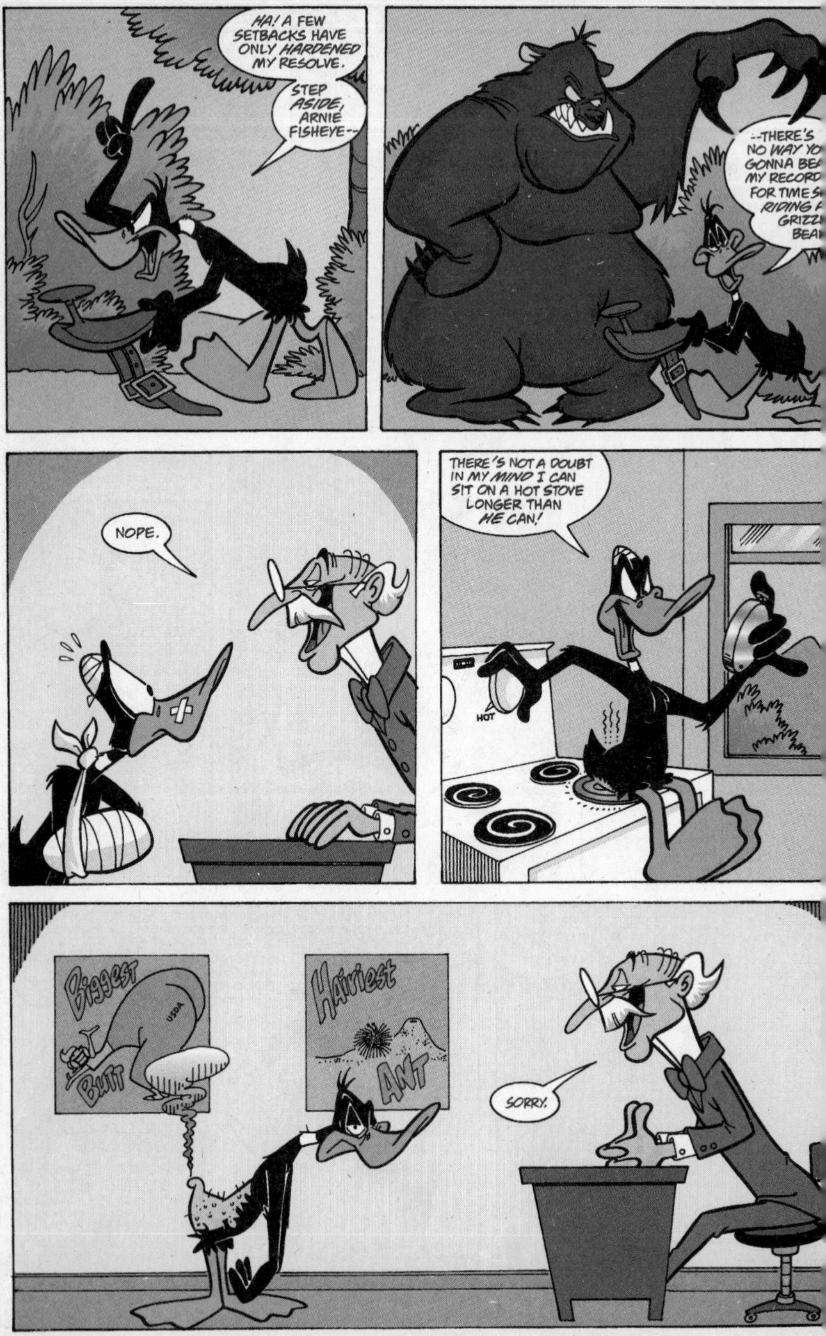
HA! A FEW SETBACKS HAVE ONLY HARDENED MY RESOLVE.
STEP ASIDE, ARNIE FISHEYE--
--THERE'S NO WAY YO GONNA BEA MY RECORD FOR TIME S RIDING A GRIZZ BEA
NOPE.
THERE'S NOT A DOUBT IN MY MIND I CAN SIT ON A HOT STOVE LONGER THAN HE CAN!
HOT
Biggest BUTT
USDA
Hairiest ANT
SORRY.

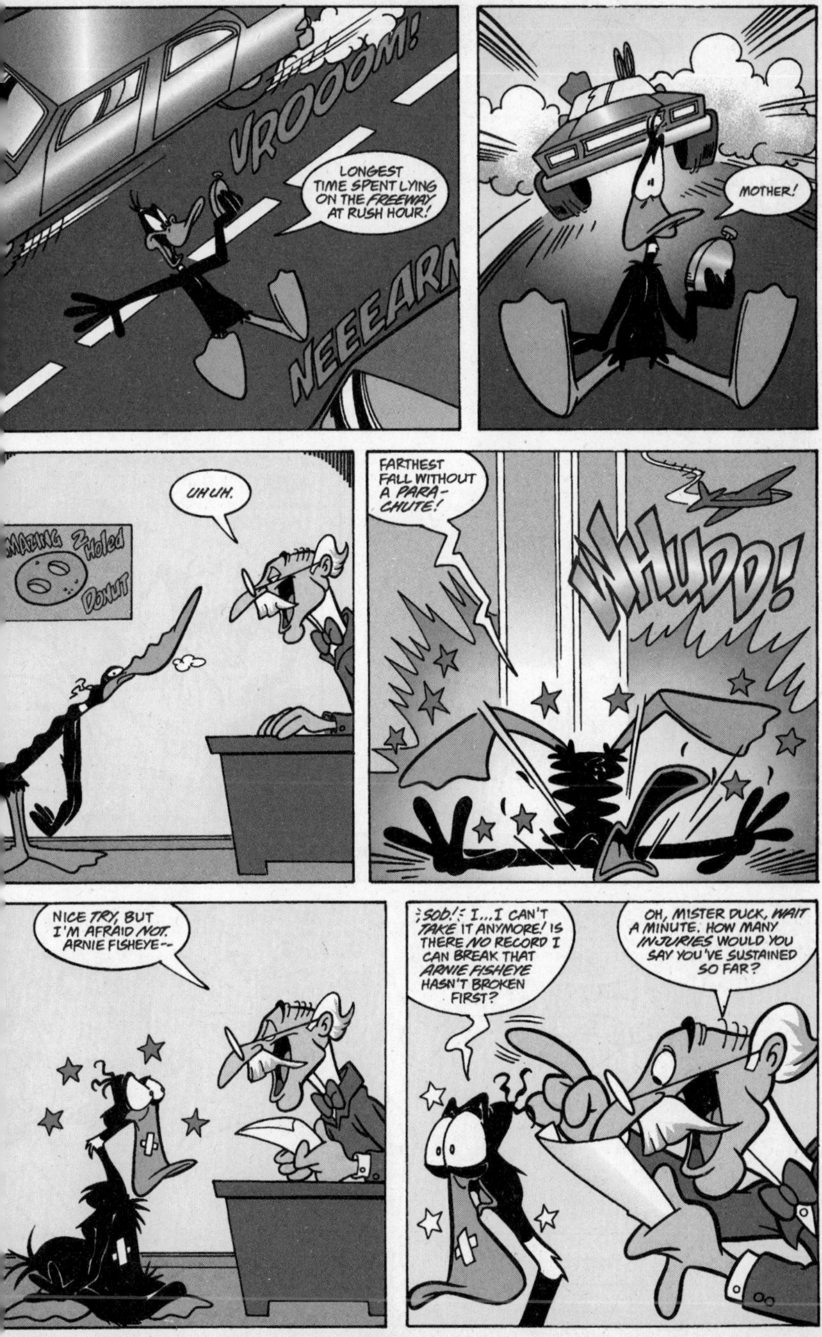

VROOOM!
LONGEST TIME SPENT LYING ON THE FREEWAY AT RUSH HOUR!
NEEEARN
MOTHER!
UH UH.
AMAZING 2 Holed DONUT
FARTHEST FALL WITHOUT A PARA-CHUTE!
WHUDD!
NICE TRY, BUT I'M AFRAID NOT. ARNIE FISHEYE--
SOB! I...I CAN'T TAKE IT ANYMORE! IS THERE NO RECORD I CAN BREAK THAT ARNIE FISHEYE HASN'T BROKEN FIRST?
OH, MISTER DUCK, WAIT A MINUTE. HOW MANY INJURIES WOULD YOU SAY YOU'VE SUSTAINED SO FAR?

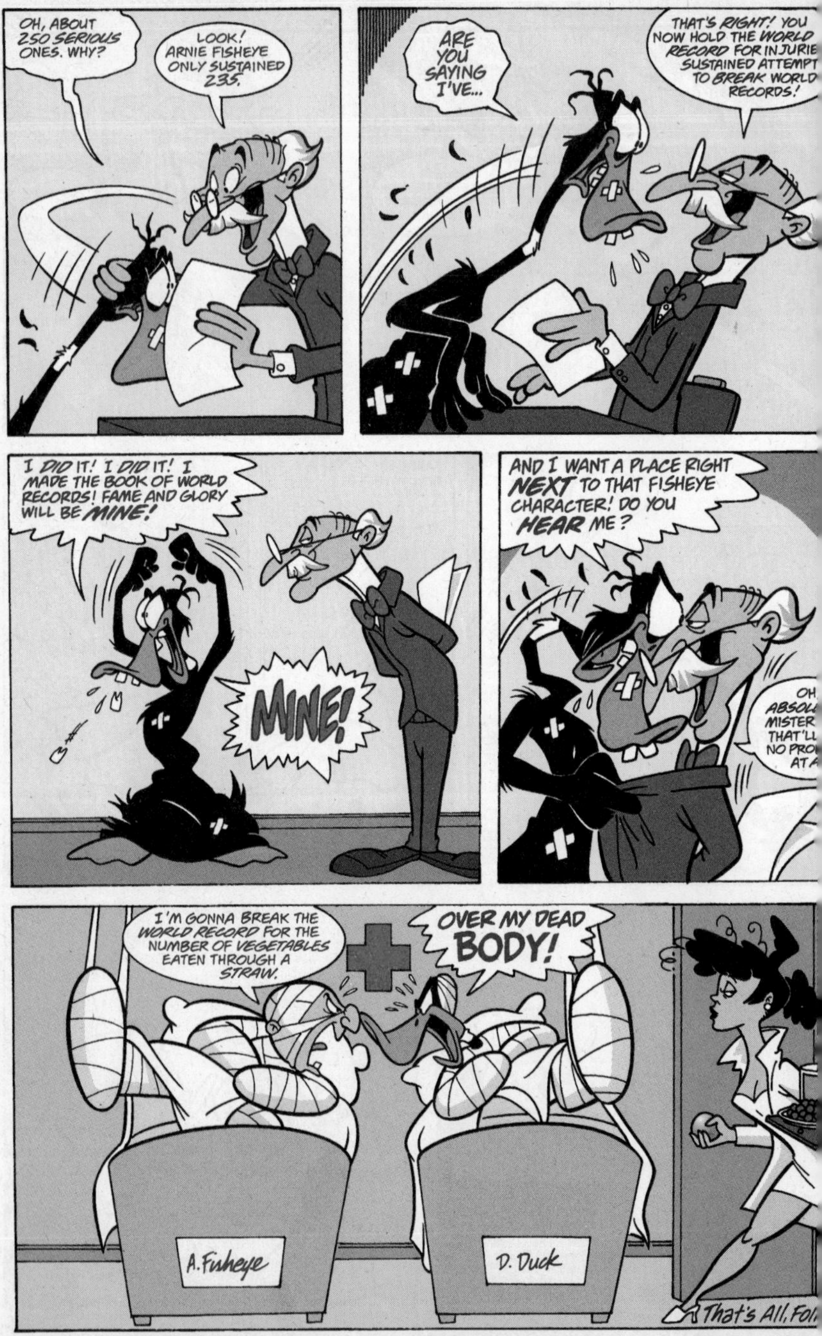
OH, ABOUT 250 SERIOUS ONES. WHY?
LOOK! ARNIE FISHEYE ONLY SUSTAINED 235.
ARE YOU SAYING I'VE...
THAT'S RIGHT! YOU NOW HOLD THE WORLD RECORD FOR INJURIE SUSTAINED ATTEMPT TO BREAK WORLD RECORDS!
I DID IT! I DID IT! I MADE THE BOOK OF WORLD RECORDS! FAME AND GLORY WILL BE MINE!
MINE!
AND I WANT A PLACE RIGHT NEXT TO THAT FISHEYE CHARACTER! DO YOU HEAR ME?
OH ABSOL MISTER THAT'L NO PRO AT A
I'M GONNA BREAK THE WORLD RECORD FOR THE NUMBER OF VEGETABLES EATEN THROUGH A STRAW.
OVER MY DEAD BODY!
A. Fisheye
D. Duck
That's All, Fol

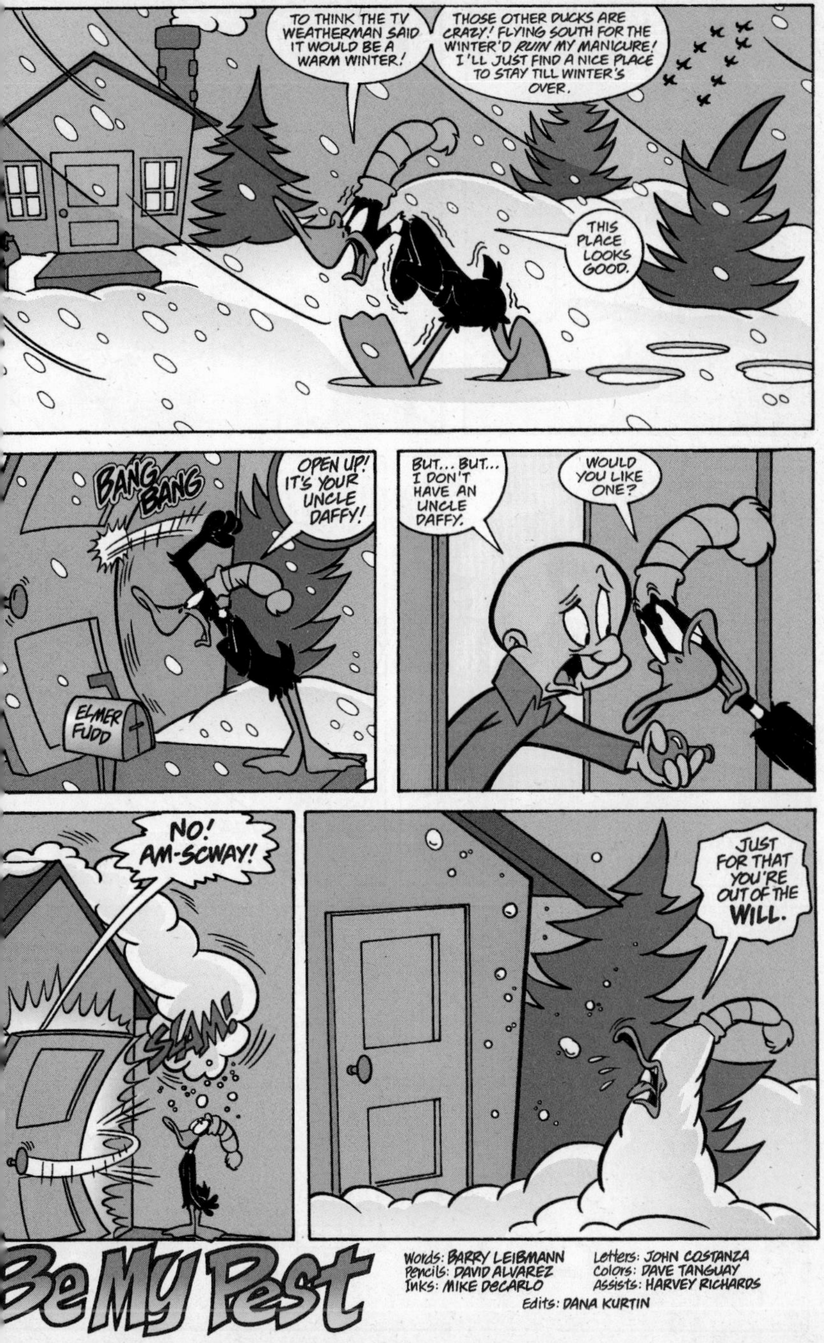
TO THINK THE TV WEATHERMAN SAID IT WOULD BE A WARM WINTER!
THOSE OTHER DUCKS ARE CRAZY! FLYING SOUTH FOR THE WINTER'D RUIN MY MANICURE! I'LL JUST FIND A NICE PLACE TO STAY TILL WINTER'S OVER.
THIS PLACE LOOKS GOOD.
BANG BANG
OPEN UP! IT'S YOUR UNCLE DAFFY!
ELMER FUDD
BUT... BUT... I DON'T HAVE AN UNCLE DAFFY.
WOULD YOU LIKE ONE?
NO! AM-SCWAY!
SLAM!
JUST FOR THAT YOU'RE OUT OF THE WILL.

Be My Pest

Words: BARRY LEIBMANN
Pencils: DAVID ALVAREZ
Inks: MIKE DeCARLO
Letters: JOHN COSTANZA
Colors: DAVE TANGUAY
Assists: HARVEY RICHARDS
Edits: DANA KURTIN

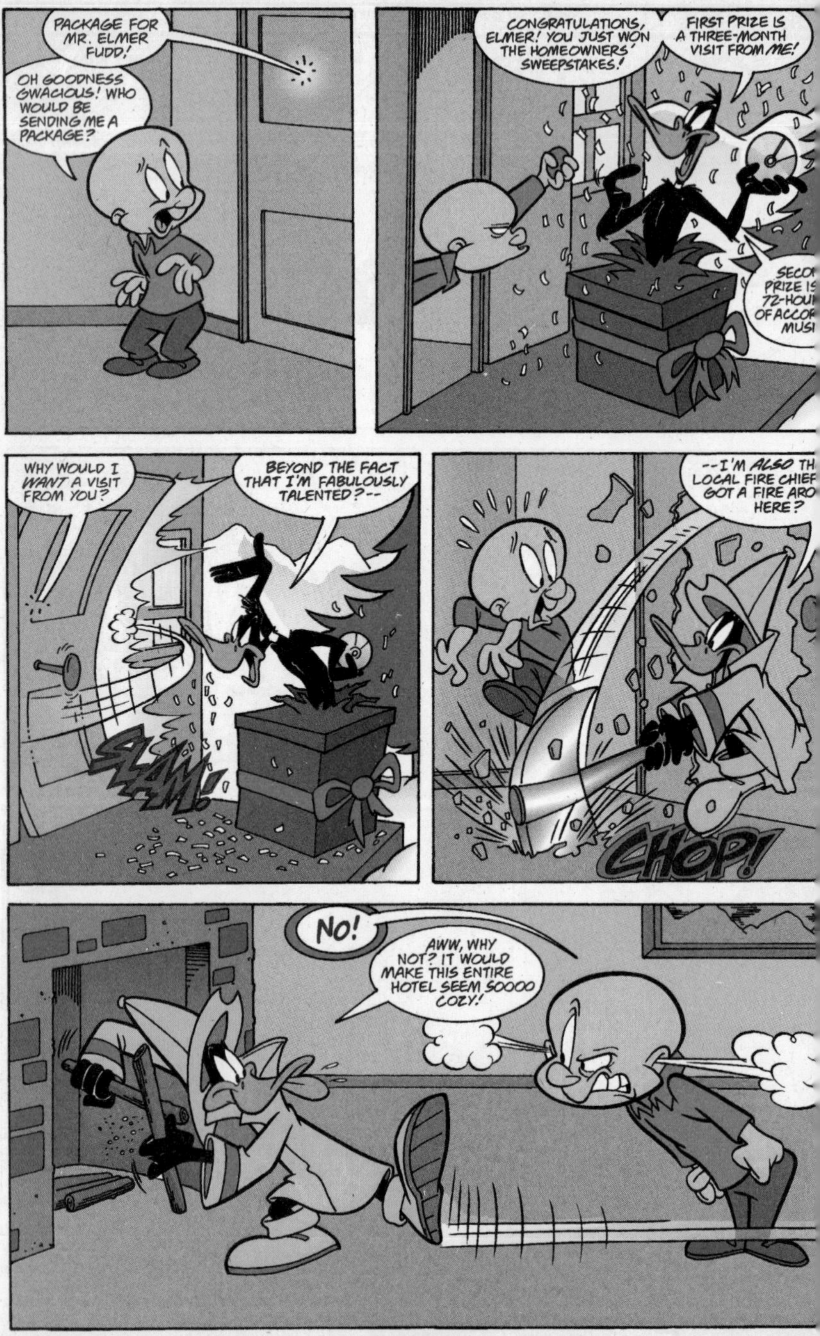

PACKAGE FOR MR. ELMER FUDD!
OH GOODNESS GWACIOUS! WHO WOULD BE SENDING ME A PACKAGE?
CONGRATULATIONS, ELMER! YOU JUST WON THE HOMEOWNERS' SWEEPSTAKES!
FIRST PRIZE IS A THREE-MONTH VISIT FROM ME!
SECON PRIZE IS 72-HOU OF ACCOR MUSI
WHY WOULD I WANT A VISIT FROM YOU?
BEYOND THE FACT THAT I'M FABULOUSLY TALENTED?--
SLAM!
--I'M ALSO TH LOCAL FIRE CHIEF GOT A FIRE ARO HERE?
CHOP!
NO!
AWW, WHY NOT? IT WOULD MAKE THIS ENTIRE HOTEL SEEM SOOOO COZY!

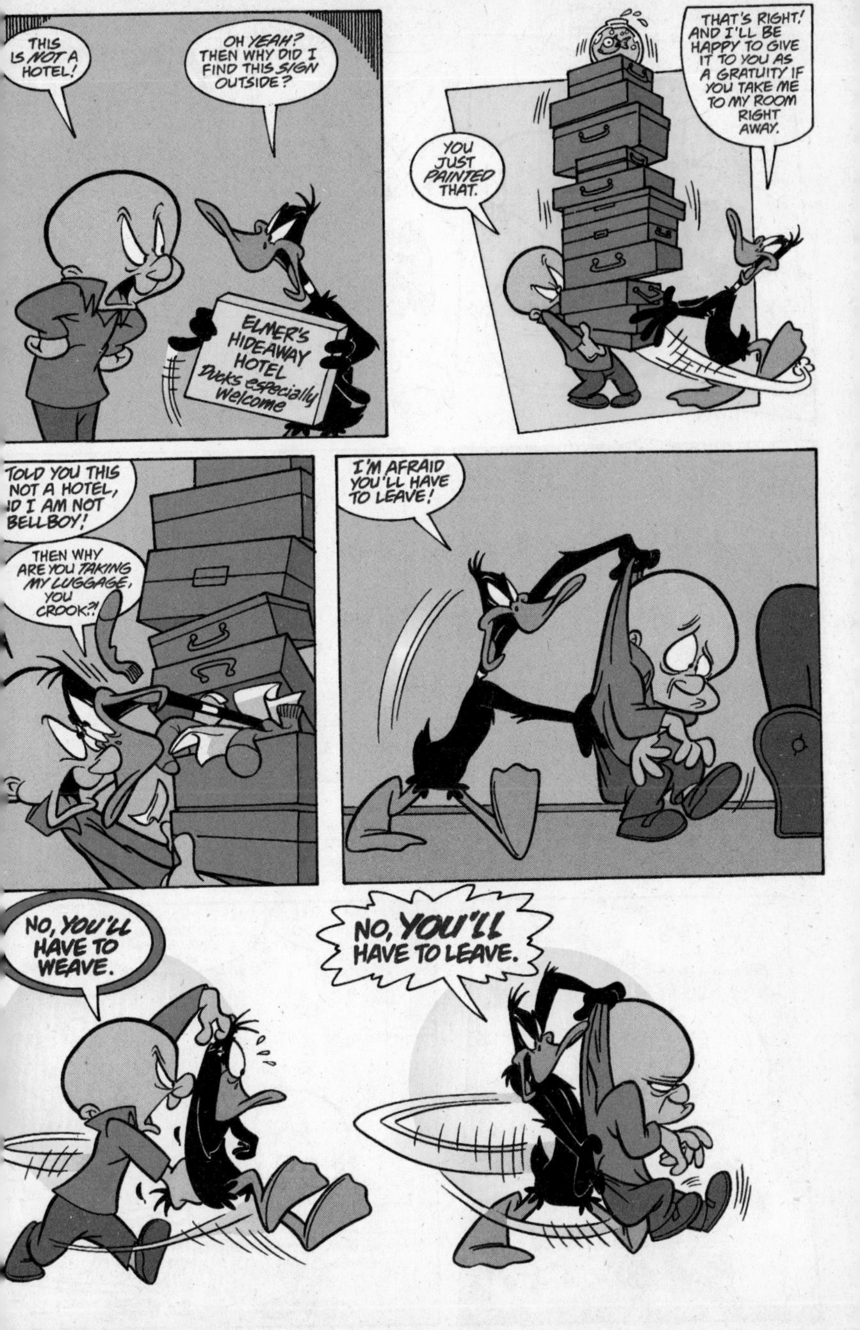
THIS IS NOT A HOTEL!
OH YEAH? THEN WHY DID I FIND THIS SIGN OUTSIDE?
ELMER'S HIDEAWAY HOTEL Ducks especially Welcome
YOU JUST PAINTED THAT.
THAT'S RIGHT! AND I'LL BE HAPPY TO GIVE IT TO YOU AS A GRATUITY IF YOU TAKE ME TO MY ROOM RIGHT AWAY.
TOLD YOU THIS NOT A HOTEL, ID I AM NOT BELLBOY!
THEN WHY ARE YOU TAKING MY LUGGAGE, YOU CROOK?!
I'M AFRAID YOU'LL HAVE TO LEAVE!
NO, YOU'LL HAVE TO WEAVE.
NO, YOU'LL HAVE TO LEAVE.

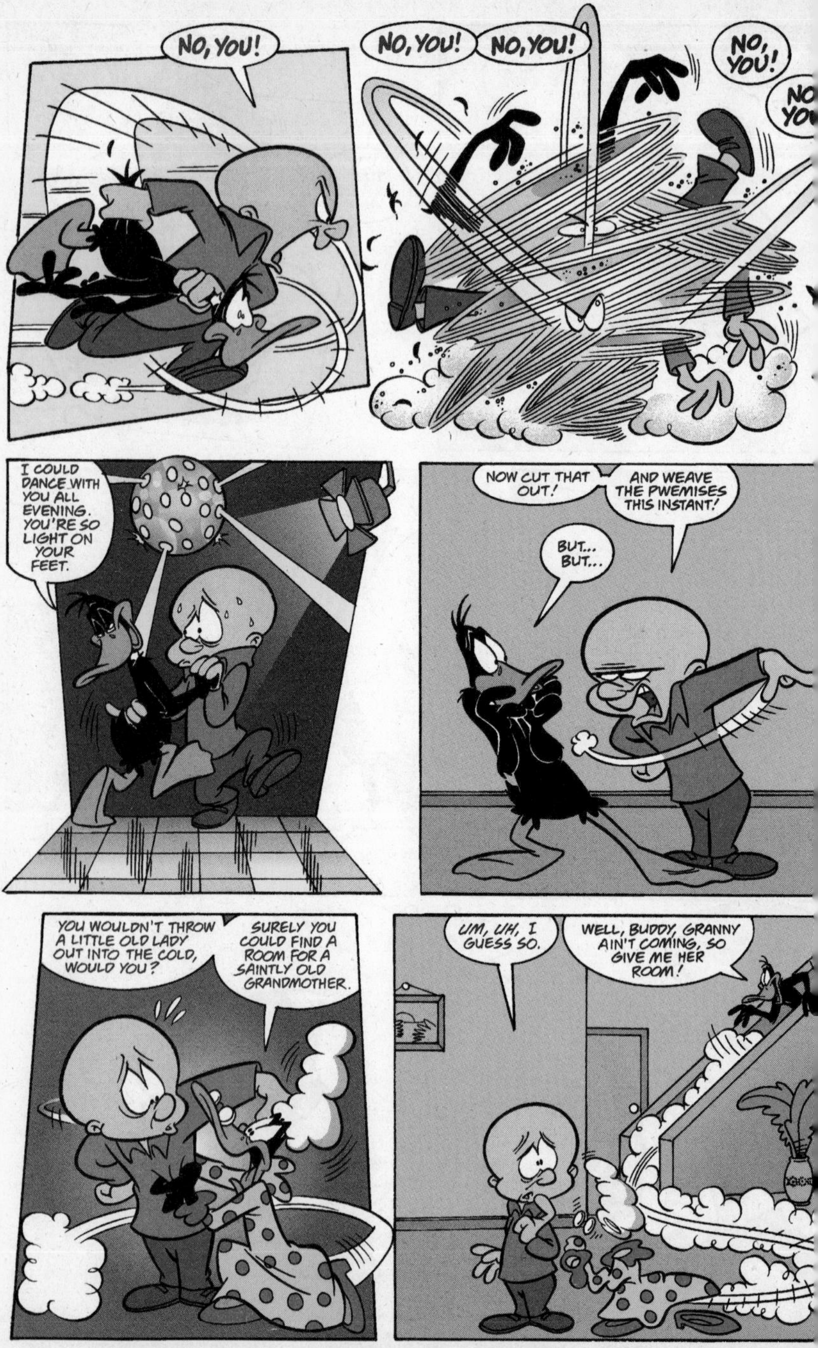
NO, YOU!
NO, YOU!
NO, YOU!
NO, YOU!
I COULD DANCE WITH YOU ALL EVENING. YOU'RE SO LIGHT ON YOUR FEET.
NOW CUT THAT OUT!
AND WEAVE THE PWEMISES THIS INSTANT!
BUT... BUT...
YOU WOULDN'T THROW A LITTLE OLD LADY OUT INTO THE COLD, WOULD YOU?
SURELY YOU COULD FIND A ROOM FOR A SAINTLY OLD GRANDMOTHER.
UM, UH, I GUESS SO.
WELL, BUDDY, GRANNY AIN'T COMING, SO GIVE ME HER ROOM!

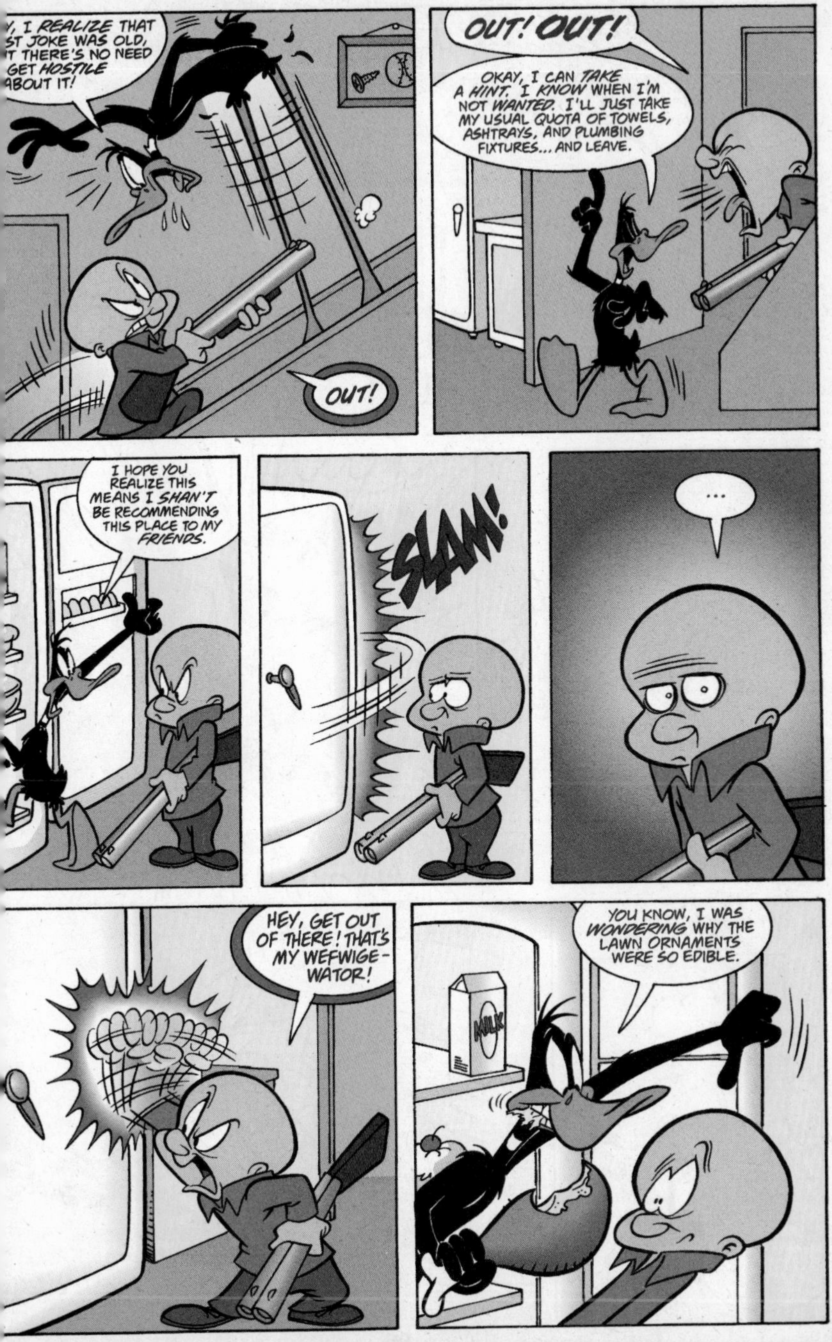
Y, I REALIZE THAT
ST JOKE WAS OLD,
T THERE'S NO NEED
GET HOSTILE
ABOUT IT!
OUT!
OUT! OUT!
OKAY, I CAN TAKE A HINT. I KNOW WHEN I'M NOT WANTED. I'LL JUST TAKE MY USUAL QUOTA OF TOWELS, ASHTRAYS, AND PLUMBING FIXTURES... AND LEAVE.
I HOPE YOU REALIZE THIS MEANS I SHAN'T BE RECOMMENDING THIS PLACE TO MY FRIENDS.
SLAM!
...
HEY, GET OUT OF THERE! THAT'S MY WEFWIGE-WATOR!
YOU KNOW, I WAS WONDERING WHY THE LAWN ORNAMENTS WERE SO EDIBLE.
MILK

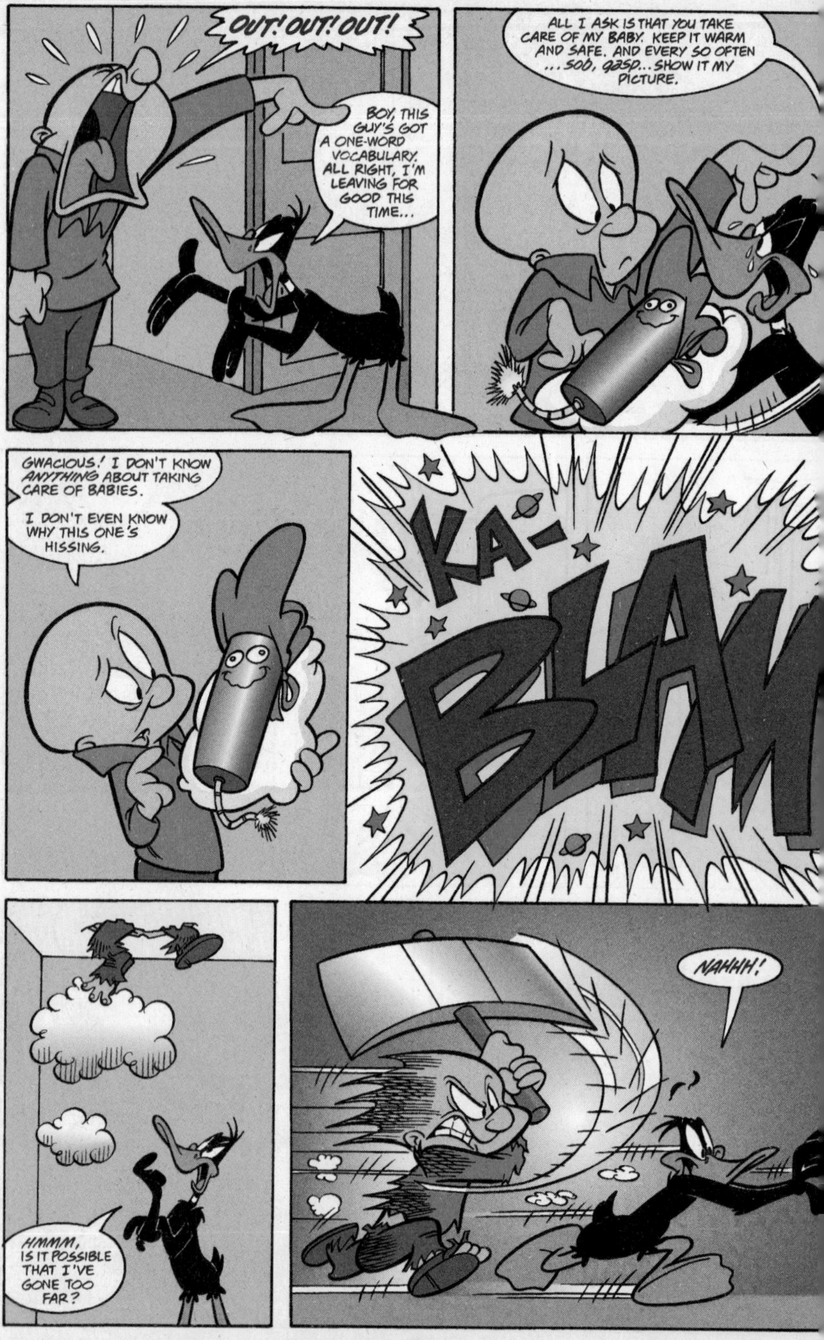
OUT! OUT! OUT!
BOY, THIS GUY'S GOT A ONE-WORD VOCABULARY. ALL RIGHT, I'M LEAVING FOR GOOD THIS TIME...
ALL I ASK IS THAT YOU TAKE CARE OF MY BABY. KEEP IT WARM AND SAFE. AND EVERY SO OFTEN ...sob, gasp... SHOW IT MY PICTURE.
GWACIOUS! I DON'T KNOW ANYTHING ABOUT TAKING CARE OF BABIES.
I DON'T EVEN KNOW WHY THIS ONE'S HISSING.
KA-
HMMM, IS IT POSSIBLE THAT I'VE GONE TOO FAR?
NAHHH!

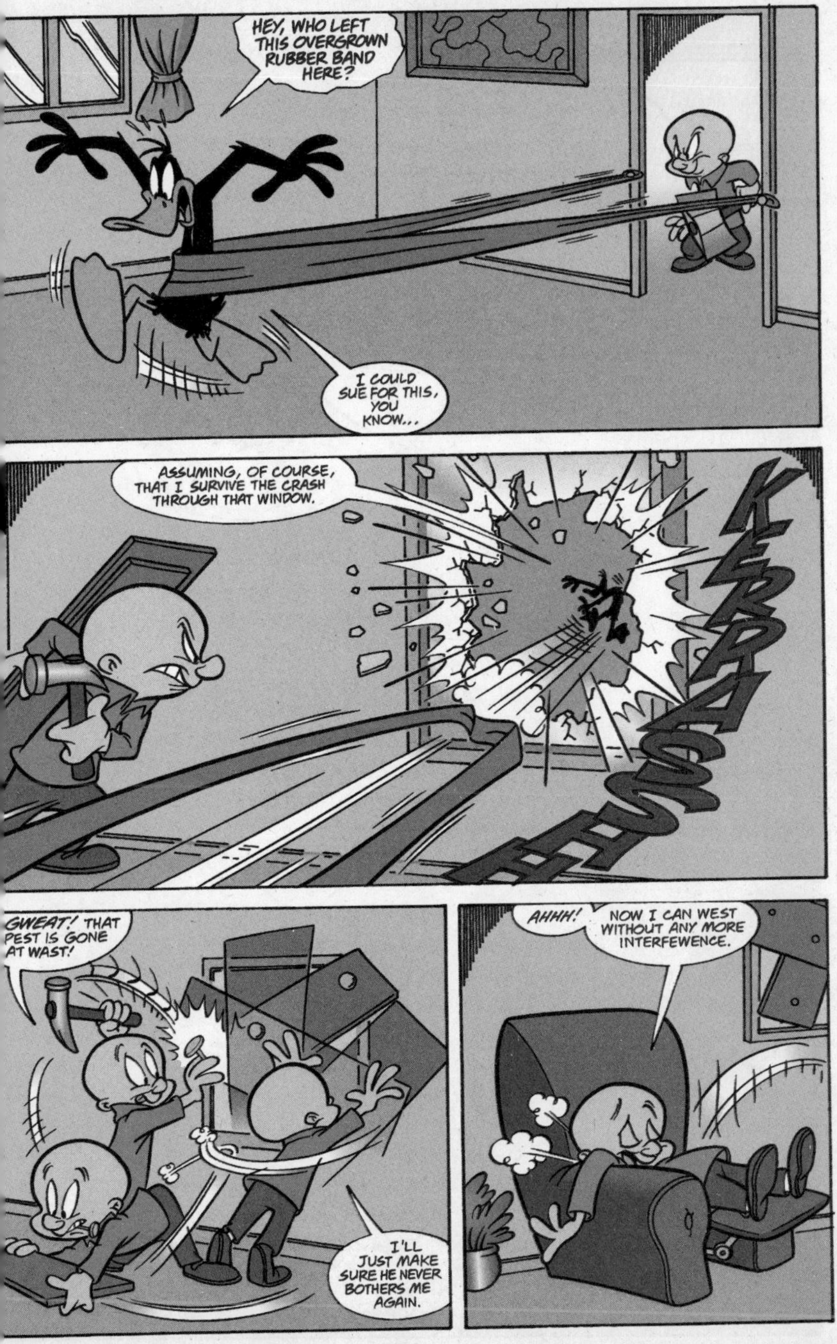
HEY, WHO LEFT THIS OVERGROWN RUBBER BAND HERE?
I COULD SUE FOR THIS, YOU KNOW...
ASSUMING, OF COURSE, THAT I SURVIVE THE CRASH THROUGH THAT WINDOW.
KERRASSHH
GWEAT! THAT PEST IS GONE AT WAST!
I'LL JUST MAKE SURE HE NEVER BOTHERS ME AGAIN.
AHHH!
NOW I CAN WEST WITHOUT ANY MORE INTERFEWENCE.

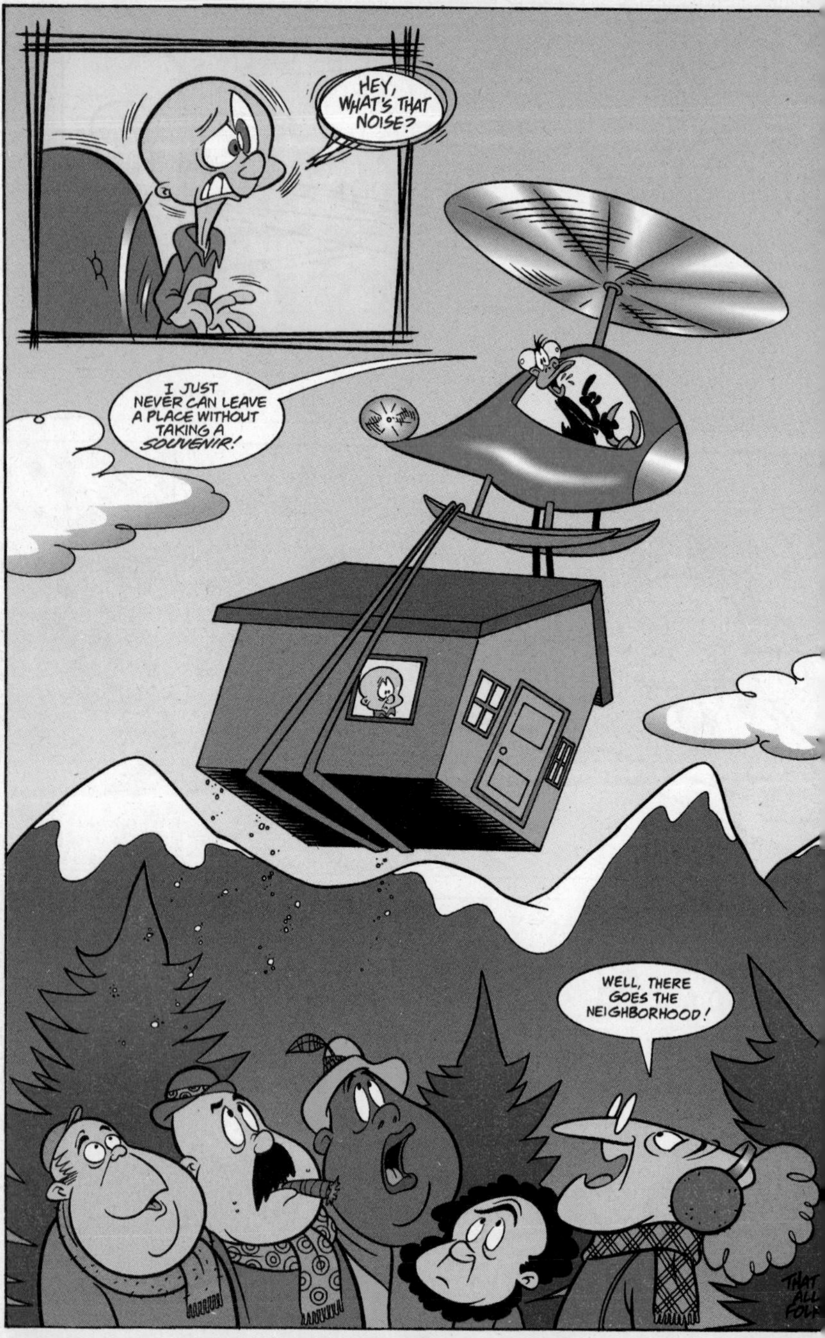
HEY, WHAT'S THAT NOISE?
I JUST NEVER CAN LEAVE A PLACE WITHOUT TAKING A SOUVENIR!
WELL, THERE GOES THE NEIGHBORHOOD!

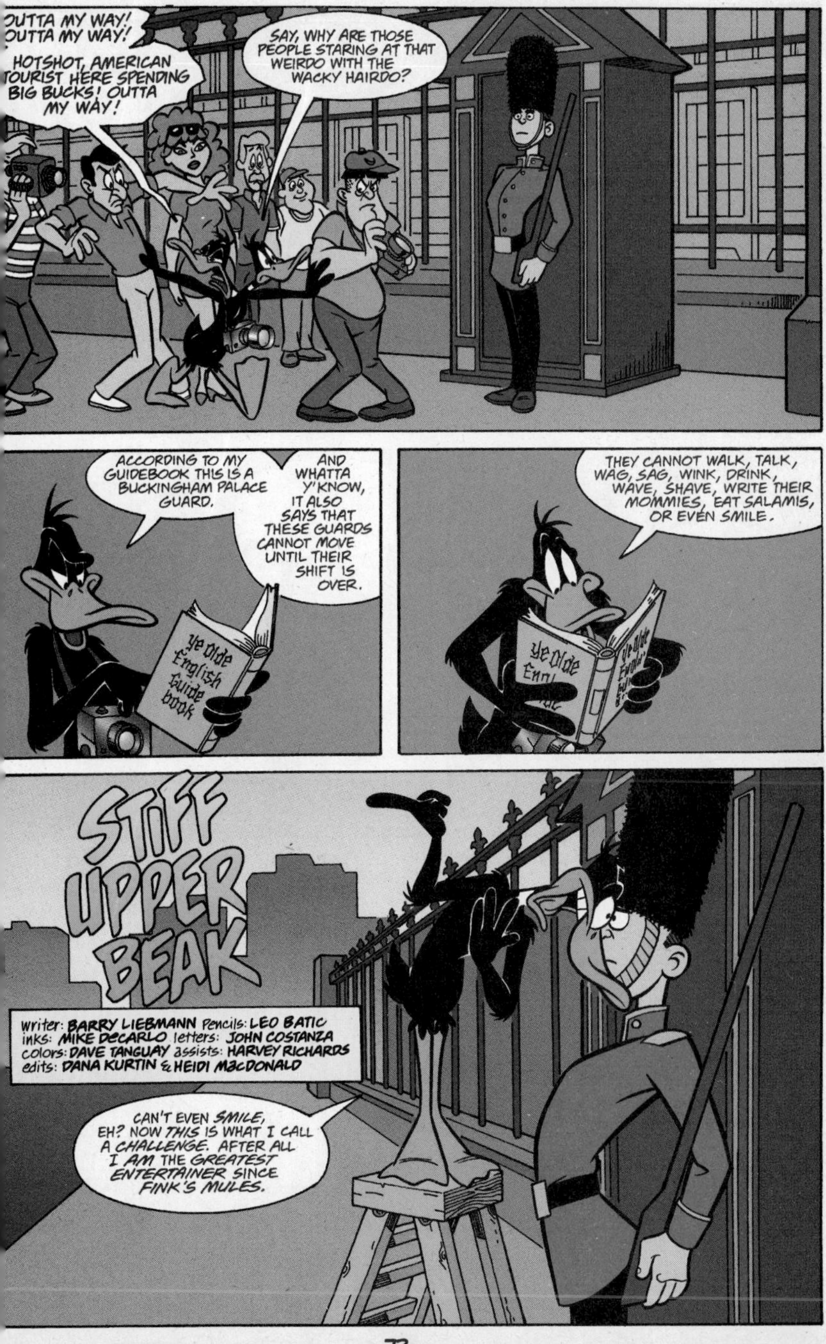
OUTTA MY WAY! OUTTA MY WAY!
HOTSHOT, AMERICAN TOURIST HERE SPENDING BIG BUCKS! OUTTA MY WAY!
SAY, WHY ARE THOSE PEOPLE STARING AT THAT WEIRDO WITH THE WACKY HAIRDO?
ACCORDING TO MY GUIDEBOOK THIS IS A BUCKINGHAM PALACE GUARD.
AND WHATTA Y'KNOW, IT ALSO SAYS THAT THESE GUARDS CANNOT MOVE UNTIL THEIR SHIFT IS OVER.
Ye Olde English Guide book
THEY CANNOT WALK, TALK, WAG, SAG, WINK, DRINK, WAVE, SHAVE, WRITE THEIR MOMMIES, EAT SALAMIS, OR EVEN SMILE.
STIFF UPPER BEAK
writer: BARRY LIEBMANN Pencils: LEO BATIC
inks: MIKE DECARLO letters: JOHN COSTANZA
colors: DAVE TANGUAY assists: HARVEY RICHARDS
edits: DANA KURTIN & HEIDI MACDONALD
CAN'T EVEN SMILE, EH? NOW THIS IS WHAT I CALL A CHALLENGE. AFTER ALL I AM THE GREATEST ENTERTAINER SINCE FINK'S MULES.

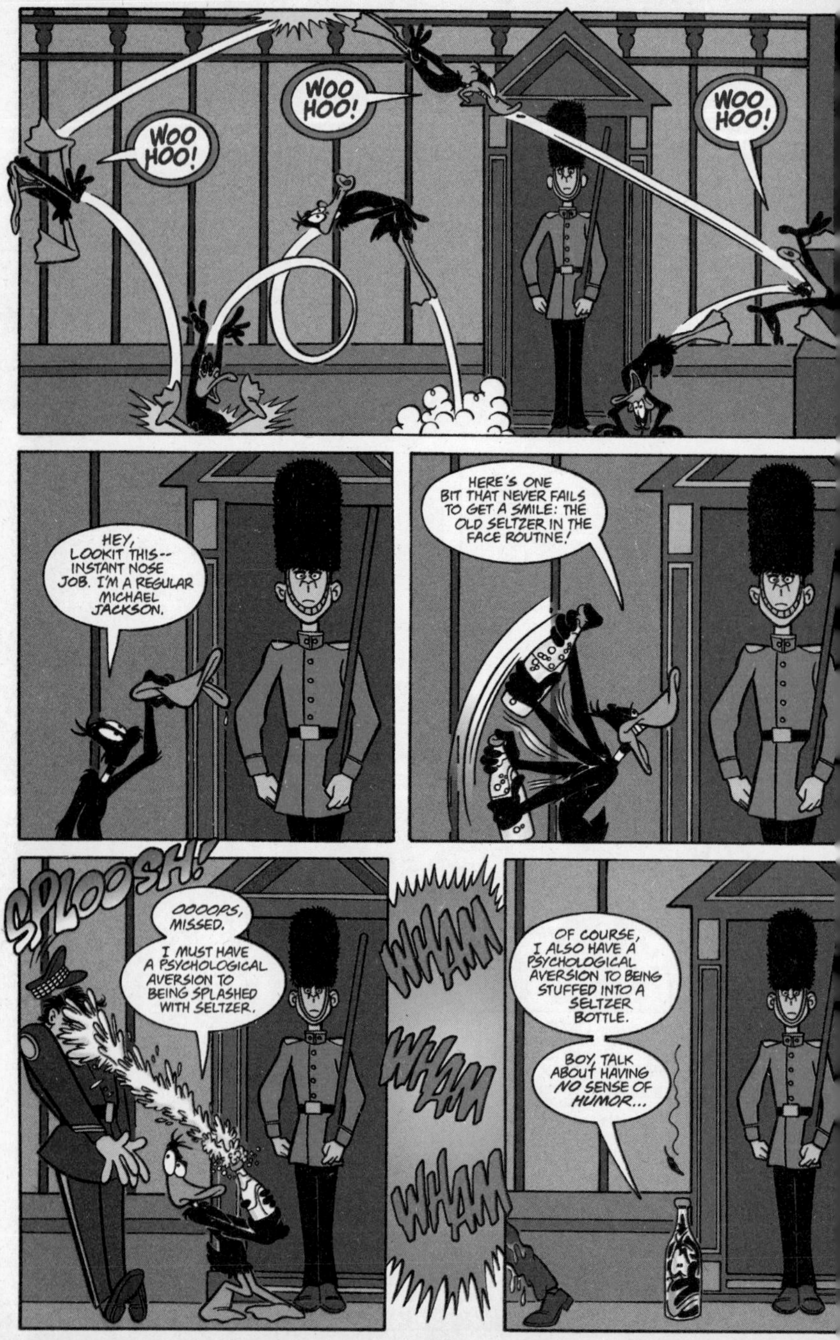
WOO HOO!
WOO HOO!
WOO HOO!
HEY, LOOKIT THIS-- INSTANT NOSE JOB. I'M A REGULAR MICHAEL JACKSON.
HERE'S ONE BIT THAT NEVER FAILS TO GET A SMILE: THE OLD SELTZER IN THE FACE ROUTINE!
SPLOOSH!
OOOOPS, MISSED.
I MUST HAVE A PSYCHOLOGICAL AVERSION TO BEING SPLASHED WITH SELTZER.
WHAM
WHAM
WHAM
OF COURSE, I ALSO HAVE A PSYCHOLOGICAL AVERSION TO BEING STUFFED INTO A SELTZER BOTTLE.
BOY, TALK ABOUT HAVING NO SENSE OF HUMOR...

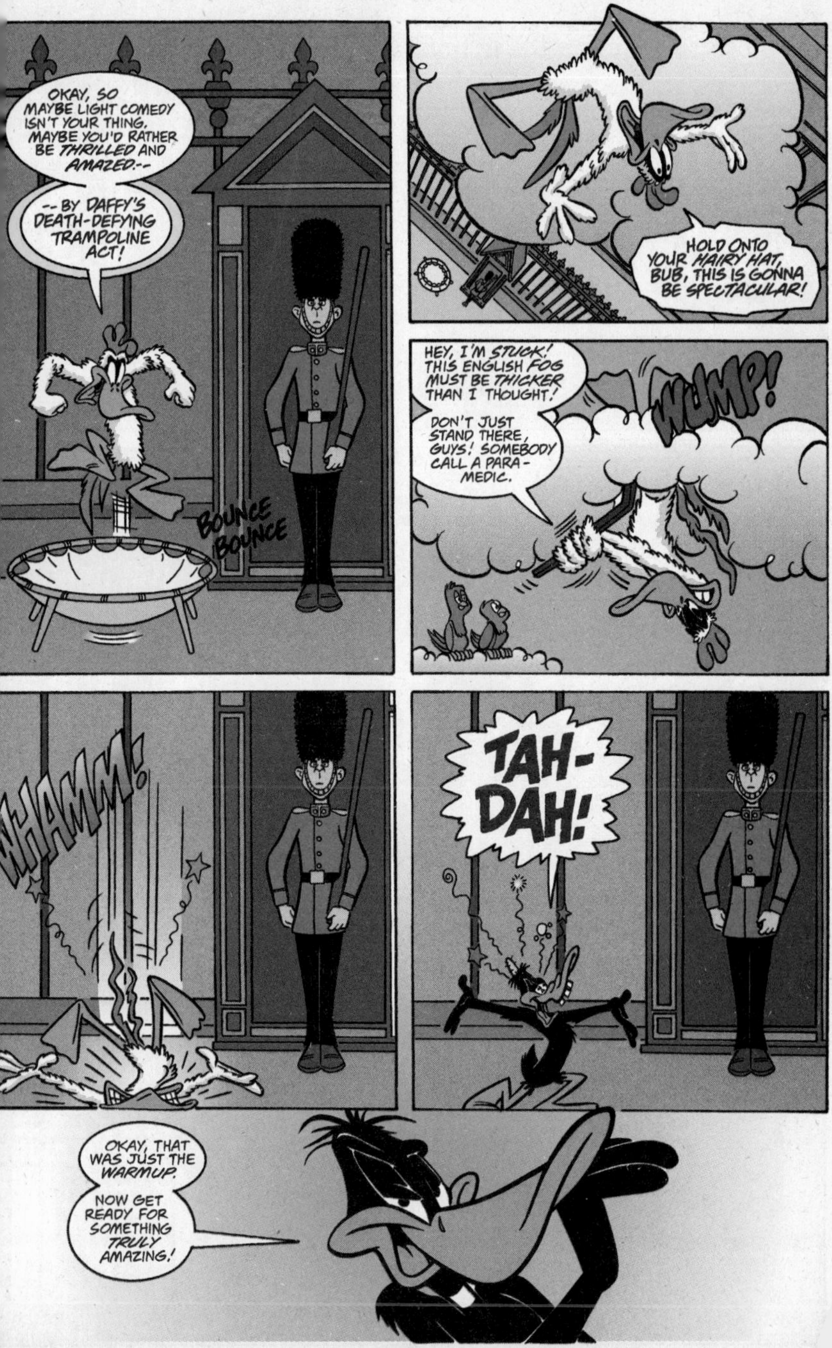
OKAY, SO MAYBE LIGHT COMEDY ISN'T YOUR THING, MAYBE YOU'D RATHER BE THRILLED AND AMAZED.--
-- BY DAFFY'S DEATH-DEFYING TRAMPOLINE ACT!
BOUNCE BOUNCE
HOLD ONTO YOUR HAIRY HAT, BUB, THIS IS GONNA BE SPECTACULAR!
HEY, I'M STUCK! THIS ENGLISH FOG MUST BE THICKER THAN I THOUGHT!
DON'T JUST STAND THERE, GUYS! SOMEBODY CALL A PARA-MEDIC.
WUMP!
WHAMM!
TAH-DAH!
OKAY, THAT WAS JUST THE WARMUP.
NOW GET READY FOR SOMETHING TRULY AMAZING!

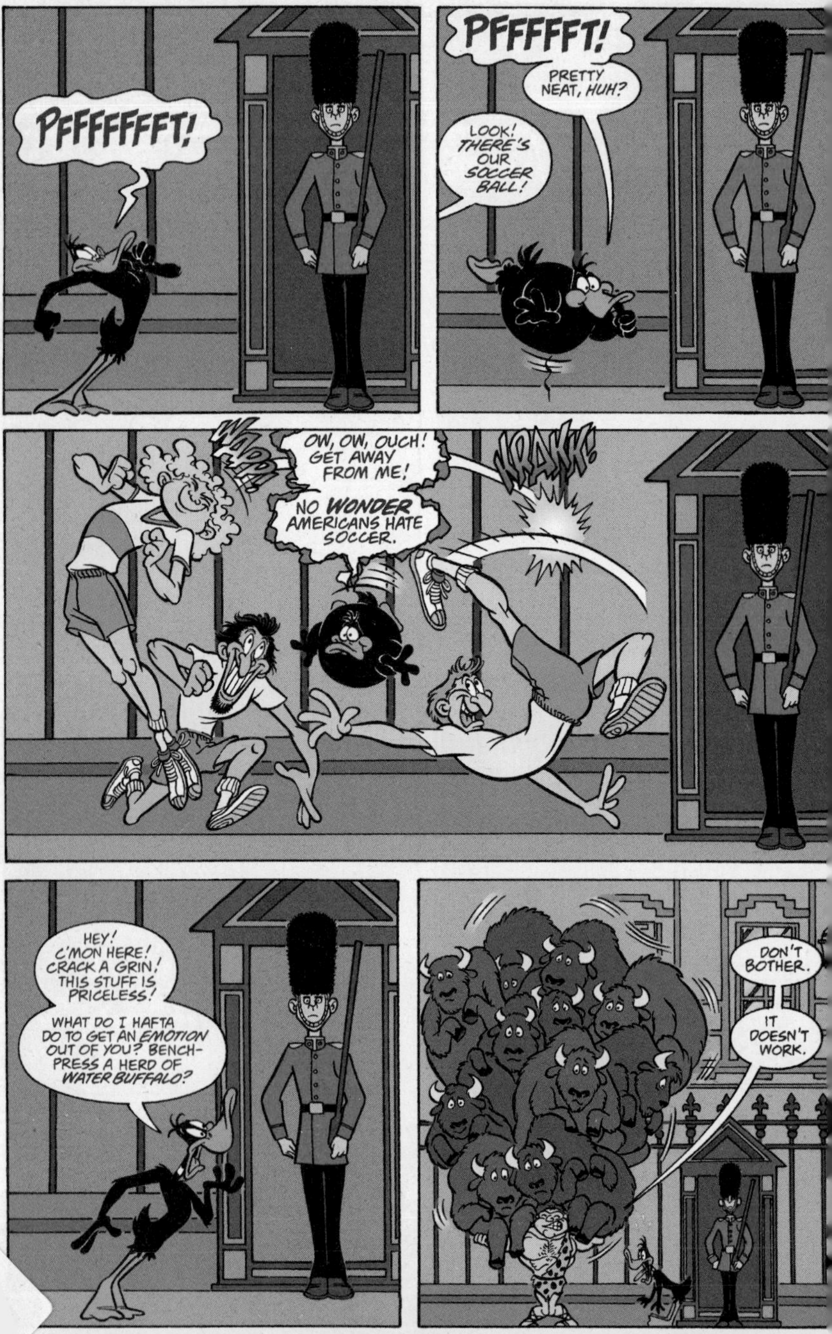
PFFFFFFFT!
PFFFFFT!
PRETTY NEAT, HUH?
LOOK! THERE'S OUR SOCCER BALL!
OW, OW, OUCH! GET AWAY FROM ME!
KRAKK!
NO WONDER AMERICANS HATE SOCCER.
HEY! C'MON HERE! CRACK A GRIN! THIS STUFF IS PRICELESS!
WHAT DO I HAFTA DO TO GET AN EMOTION OUT OF YOU? BENCH-PRESS A HERD OF WATER BUFFALO?
DON'T BOTHER.
IT DOESN'T WORK.

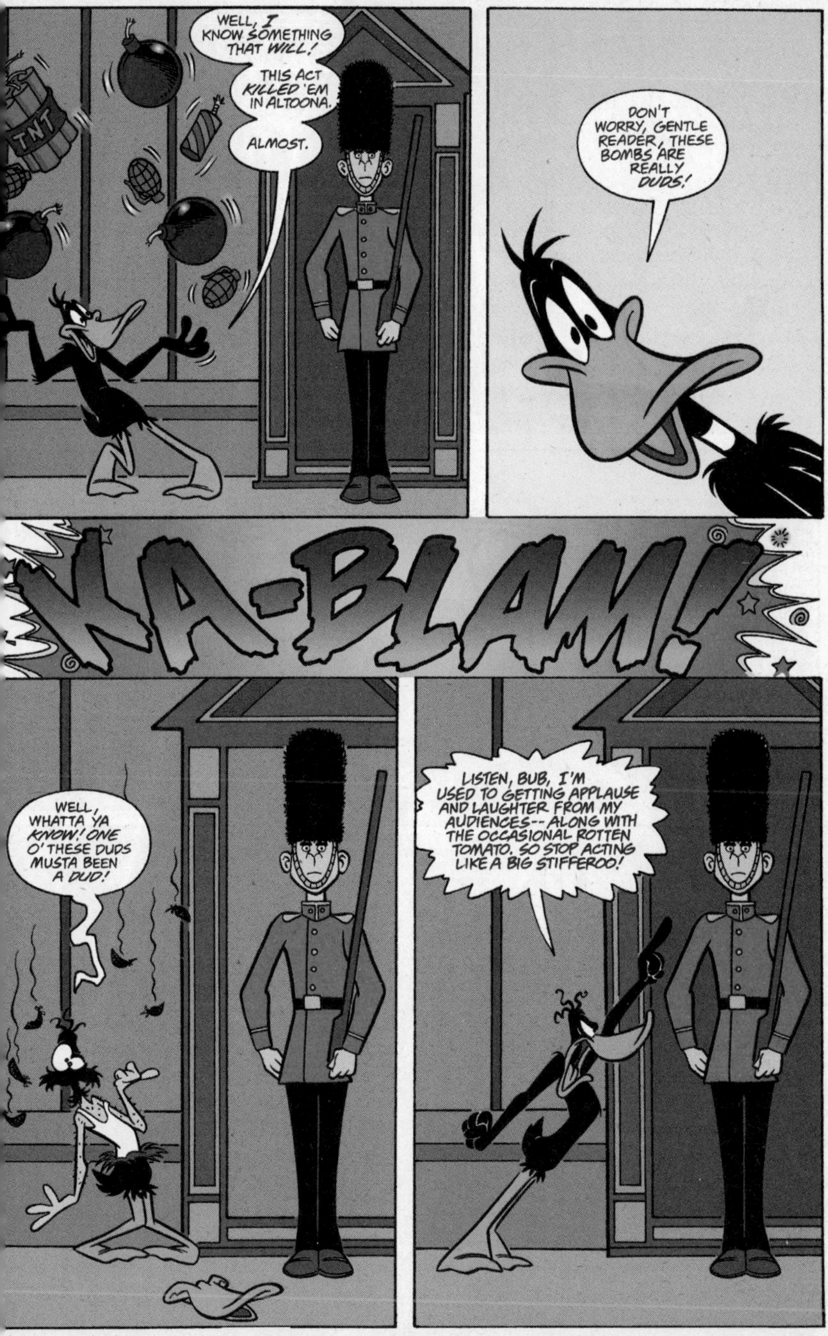
WELL, I KNOW SOMETHING THAT WILL!
THIS ACT KILLED 'EM IN ALTOONA.
ALMOST.
TNT
DON'T WORRY, GENTLE READER, THESE BOMBS ARE REALLY DUDS!
KA-BLAM!
WELL, WHATTA YA KNOW! ONE O' THESE DUDS MUSTA BEEN A DUD!
LISTEN, BUB, I'M USED TO GETTING APPLAUSE AND LAUGHTER FROM MY AUDIENCES-- ALONG WITH THE OCCASIONAL ROTTEN TOMATO. SO STOP ACTING LIKE A BIG STIFFEROO!

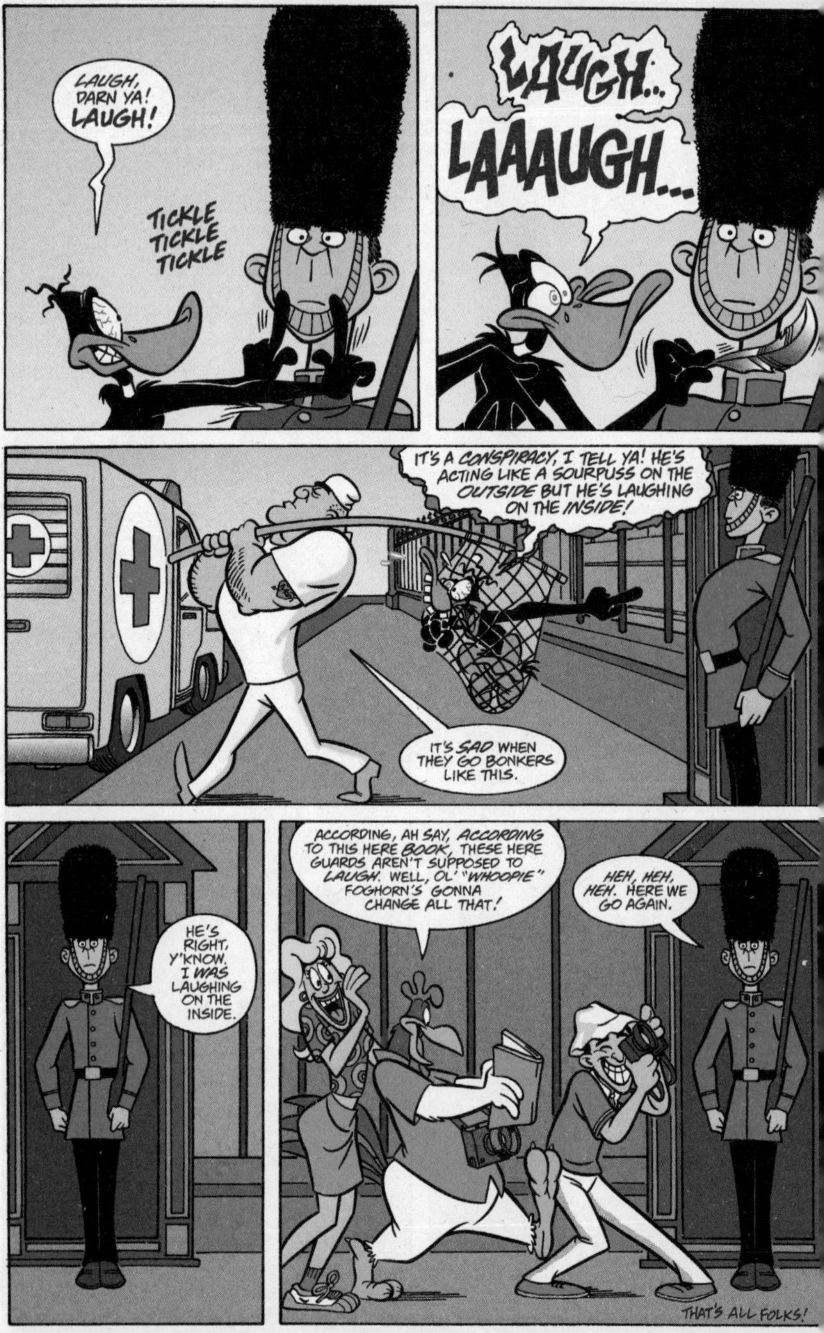
LAUGH, DARN YA! LAUGH!
TICKLE TICKLE TICKLE
LAUGH... LAAAUGH...
IT'S A CONSPIRACY, I TELL YA! HE'S ACTING LIKE A SOURPUSS ON THE OUTSIDE BUT HE'S LAUGHING ON THE INSIDE!
IT'S SAD WHEN THEY GO BONKERS LIKE THIS.
HE'S RIGHT, Y'KNOW. I WAS LAUGHING ON THE INSIDE.
ACCORDING, AH SAY, ACCORDING TO THIS HERE BOOK, THESE HERE GUARDS AREN'T SUPPOSED TO LAUGH. WELL, OL' "WHOOPIE" FOGHORN'S GONNA CHANGE ALL THAT!
HEH, HEH, HEH. HERE WE GO AGAIN.
THAT'S ALL FOLKS!

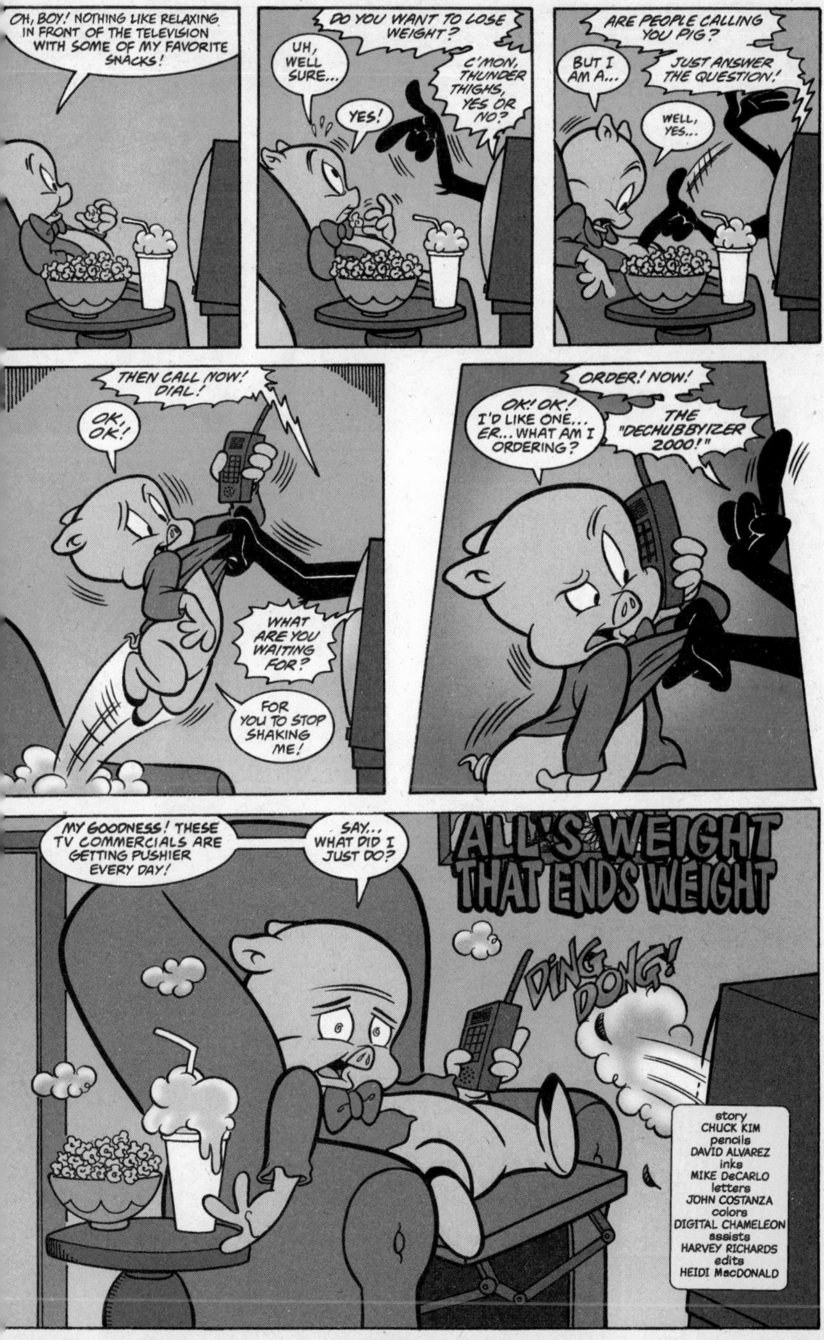
OH, BOY! NOTHING LIKE RELAXING IN FRONT OF THE TELEVISION WITH SOME OF MY FAVORITE SNACKS!
DO YOU WANT TO LOSE WEIGHT?
UH, WELL SURE...
C'MON, THUNDER THIGHS, YES OR NO?
YES!
ARE PEOPLE CALLING YOU PIG?
BUT I AM A...
JUST ANSWER THE QUESTION!
WELL, YES...
THEN CALL NOW! DIAL!
OK, OK!
WHAT ARE YOU WAITING FOR?
FOR YOU TO STOP SHAKING ME!
ORDER! NOW!
OK! OK! I'D LIKE ONE... ER... WHAT AM I ORDERING?
THE "DECHUBBYIZER 2000!"
MY GOODNESS! THESE TV COMMERCIALS ARE GETTING PUSHIER EVERY DAY!
SAY... WHAT DID I JUST DO?
ALL'S WEIGHT THAT ENDS WEIGHT
DING DONG!
story CHUCK KIM
pencils DAVID ALVAREZ
inks MIKE DeCARLO
letters JOHN COSTANZA
colors DIGITAL CHAMELEON
assists HARVEY RICHARDS
edits HEIDI MacDONALD

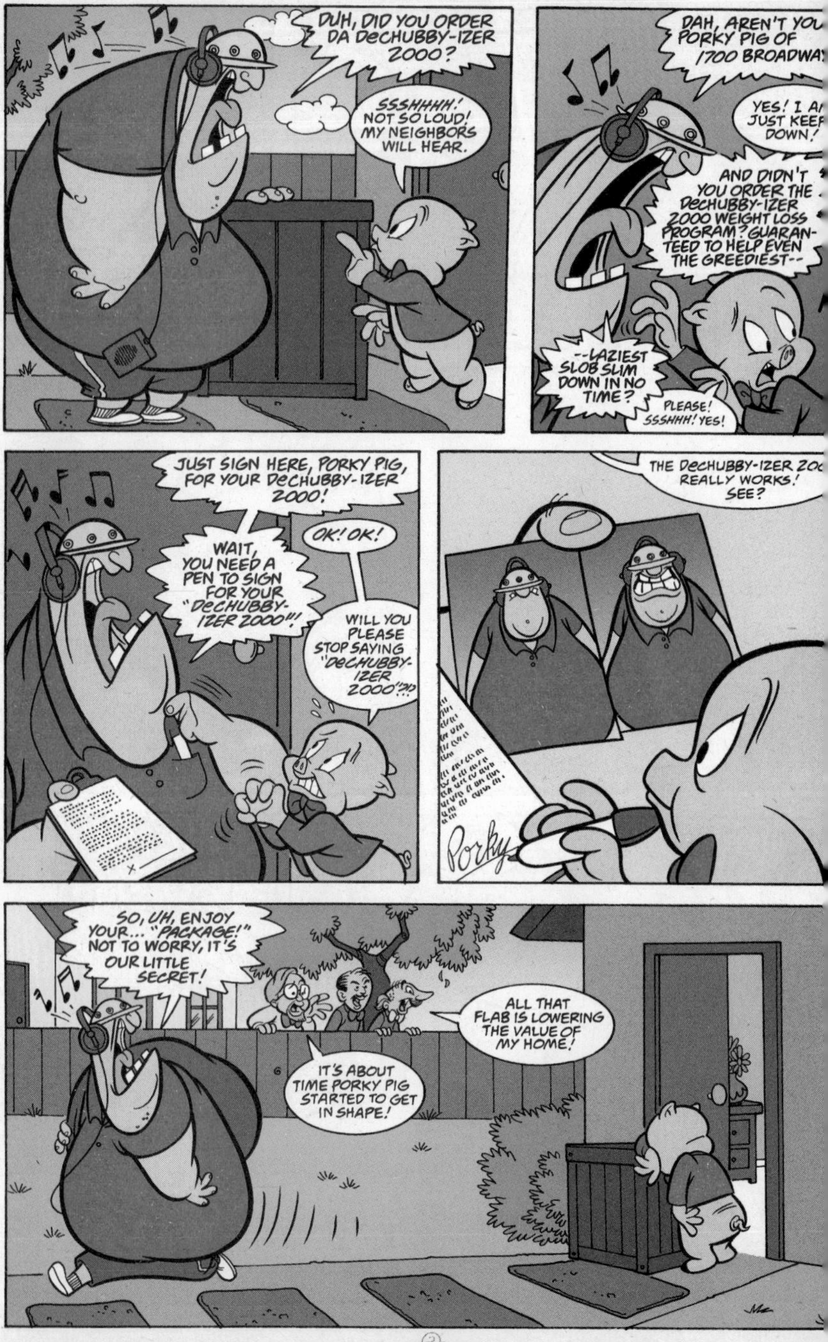
DUH, DID YOU ORDER DA DeCHUBBY-IZER 2000?
SSSHHHH! NOT SO LOUD! MY NEIGHBORS WILL HEAR.
DAH, AREN'T YOU PORKY PIG OF 1700 BROADWAY
YES! I AM JUST KEEP DOWN!
AND DIDN'T YOU ORDER THE DeCHUBBY-IZER 2000 WEIGHT LOSS PROGRAM? GUARANTEED TO HELP EVEN THE GREEDIEST--
--LAZIEST SLOB SLIM DOWN IN NO TIME?
PLEASE! SSSHHH! YES!
JUST SIGN HERE, PORKY PIG, FOR YOUR DeCHUBBY-IZER 2000!
OK! OK!
WAIT, YOU NEED A PEN TO SIGN FOR YOUR "DeCHUBBY-IZER 2000"!
WILL YOU PLEASE STOP SAYING "DeCHUBBY-IZER 2000"?!?
THE DeCHUBBY-IZER 2000 REALLY WORKS! SEE?
Porky
SO, UH, ENJOY YOUR... "PACKAGE!" NOT TO WORRY, IT'S OUR LITTLE SECRET!
ALL THAT FLAB IS LOWERING THE VALUE OF MY HOME!
IT'S ABOUT TIME PORKY PIG STARTED TO GET IN SHAPE!

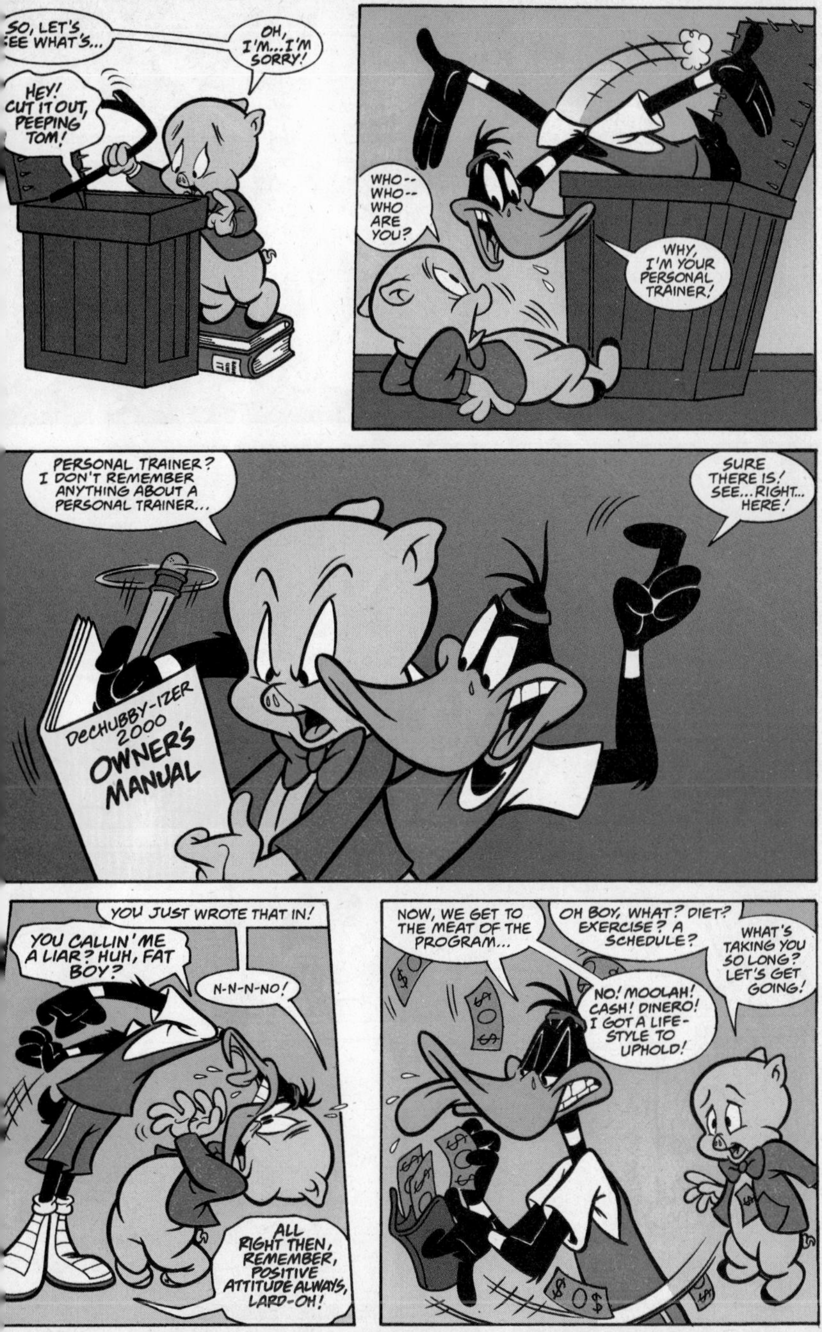
SO, LET'S SEE WHAT'S...
OH, I'M...I'M SORRY!
HEY! CUT IT OUT, PEEPING TOM!
WHO--WHO--WHO ARE YOU?
WHY, I'M YOUR PERSONAL TRAINER!
PERSONAL TRAINER? I DON'T REMEMBER ANYTHING ABOUT A PERSONAL TRAINER...
SURE THERE IS! SEE...RIGHT... HERE!
DeCHUBBY-IZER 2000 OWNER'S MANUAL
YOU JUST WROTE THAT IN!
YOU CALLIN' ME A LIAR? HUH, FAT BOY?
N-N-N-NO!
ALL RIGHT THEN, REMEMBER, POSITIVE ATTITUDE ALWAYS, LARD-OH!
NOW, WE GET TO THE MEAT OF THE PROGRAM...
OH BOY, WHAT? DIET? EXERCISE? A SCHEDULE?
NO! MOOLAH! CASH! DINERO! I GOT A LIFE-STYLE TO UPHOLD!
WHAT'S TAKING YOU SO LONG? LET'S GET GOING!

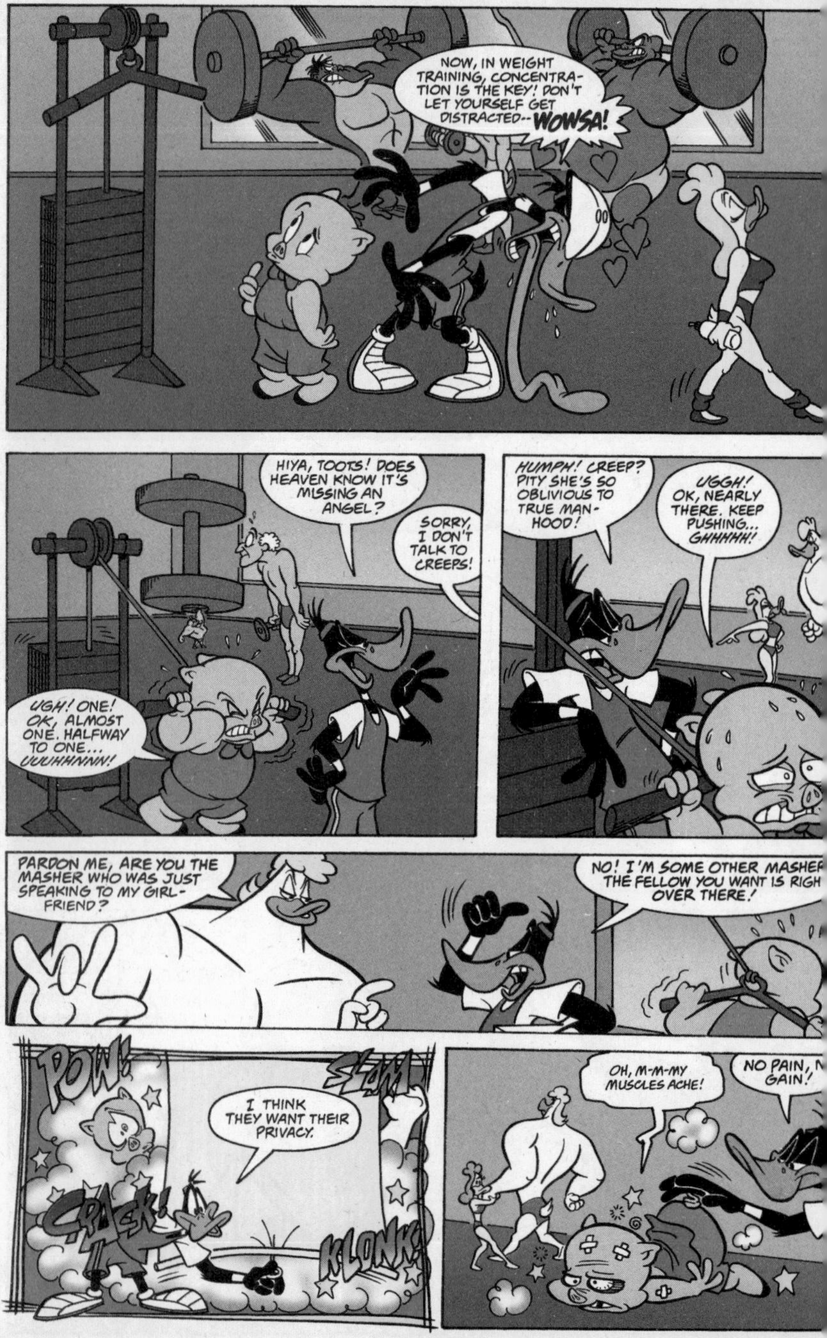
NOW, IN WEIGHT TRAINING, CONCENTRATION IS THE KEY! DON'T LET YOURSELF GET DISTRACTED-- WOWSA!
HIYA, TOOTS! DOES HEAVEN KNOW IT'S MISSING AN ANGEL?
SORRY, I DON'T TALK TO CREEPS!
UGH! ONE! OK, ALMOST ONE. HALFWAY TO ONE... UUUHHNNN!
HUMPH! CREEP? PITY SHE'S SO OBLIVIOUS TO TRUE MAN-HOOD!
UGGH! OK, NEARLY THERE. KEEP PUSHING... GHHHHH!
PARDON ME, ARE YOU THE MASHER WHO WAS JUST SPEAKING TO MY GIRL-FRIEND?
NO! I'M SOME OTHER MASHER THE FELLOW YOU WANT IS RIGH OVER THERE!
POW!
SLAM
I THINK THEY WANT THEIR PRIVACY.
CRACK!
KLONK!
OH, M-M-MY MUSCLES ACHE!
NO PAIN, GAIN!

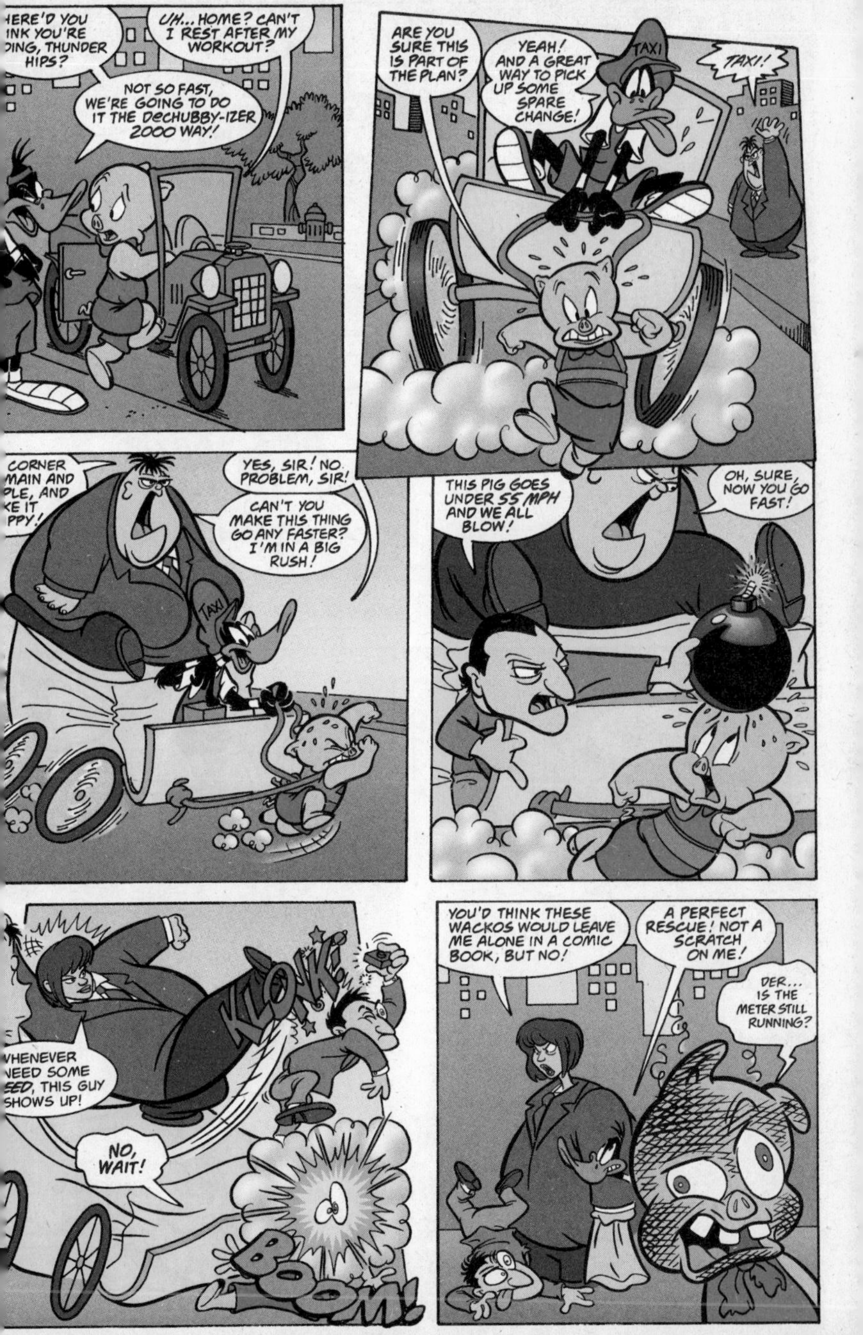
HERE'D YOU
INK YOU'RE
OING, THUNDER
HIPS?
UH... HOME? CAN'T I REST AFTER MY WORKOUT?
NOT SO FAST, WE'RE GOING TO DO IT THE DECHUBBY-IZER 2000 WAY!
ARE YOU SURE THIS IS PART OF THE PLAN?
YEAH! AND A GREAT WAY TO PICK UP SOME SPARE CHANGE!
TAXI!
CORNER
MAIN AND
PLE, AND
KE IT
PPY!
YES, SIR! NO PROBLEM, SIR!
CAN'T YOU MAKE THIS THING GO ANY FASTER? I'M IN A BIG RUSH!
THIS PIG GOES UNDER 55 MPH AND WE ALL BLOW!
OH, SURE, NOW YOU GO FAST!
KLONK!
WHENEVER
NEED SOME
EED, THIS GUY
SHOWS UP!
NO, WAIT!
BOOM!
YOU'D THINK THESE WACKOS WOULD LEAVE ME ALONE IN A COMIC BOOK, BUT NO!
A PERFECT RESCUE! NOT A SCRATCH ON ME!
DER... IS THE METER STILL RUNNING?

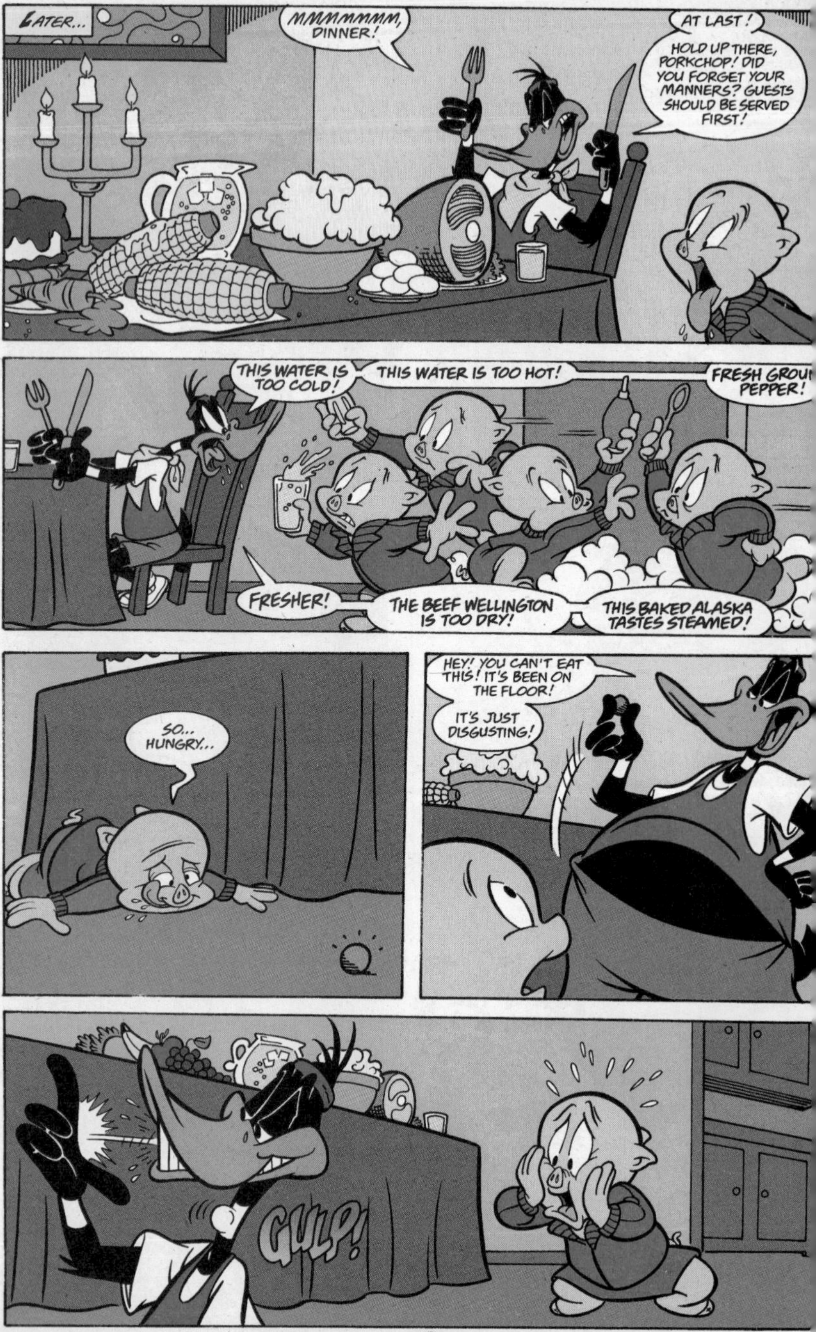
LATER...
MMMMMMM, DINNER!
AT LAST!
HOLD UP THERE, PORKCHOP! DID YOU FORGET YOUR MANNERS? GUESTS SHOULD BE SERVED FIRST!
THIS WATER IS TOO COLD!
THIS WATER IS TOO HOT!
FRESH GROU PEPPER!
FRESHER!
THE BEEF WELLINGTON IS TOO DRY!
THIS BAKED ALASKA TASTES STEAMED!
SO... HUNGRY...
HEY! YOU CAN'T EAT THIS! IT'S BEEN ON THE FLOOR!
IT'S JUST DISGUSTING!
GULP!

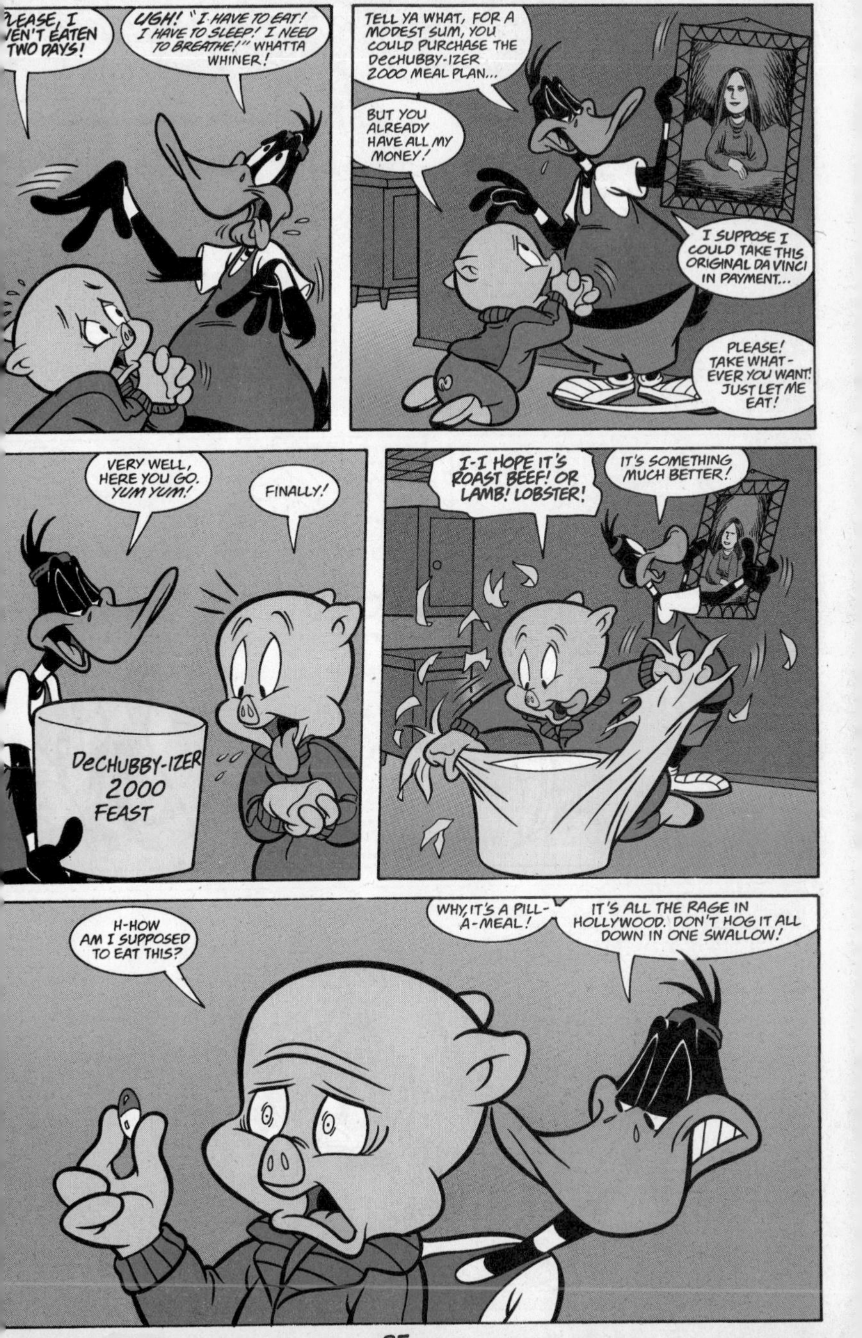

LEASE, I VEN'T EATEN TWO DAYS!
UGH! "I-HAVE TO EAT! I HAVE TO SLEEP! I NEED TO BREATHE!" WHATTA WHINER!
TELL YA WHAT, FOR A MODEST SUM, YOU COULD PURCHASE THE DeCHUBBY-IZER 2000 MEAL PLAN...
BUT YOU ALREADY HAVE ALL MY MONEY!
I SUPPOSE I COULD TAKE THIS ORIGINAL DA VINCI IN PAYMENT...
PLEASE! TAKE WHAT-EVER YOU WANT! JUST LET ME EAT!
VERY WELL, HERE YOU GO. YUM YUM!
FINALLY!
DeCHUBBY-IZER 2000 FEAST
I-I HOPE IT'S ROAST BEEF! OR LAMB! LOBSTER!
IT'S SOMETHING MUCH BETTER!
H-HOW AM I SUPPOSED TO EAT THIS?
WHY, IT'S A PILL-A-MEAL!
IT'S ALL THE RAGE IN HOLLYWOOD. DON'T HOG IT ALL DOWN IN ONE SWALLOW!

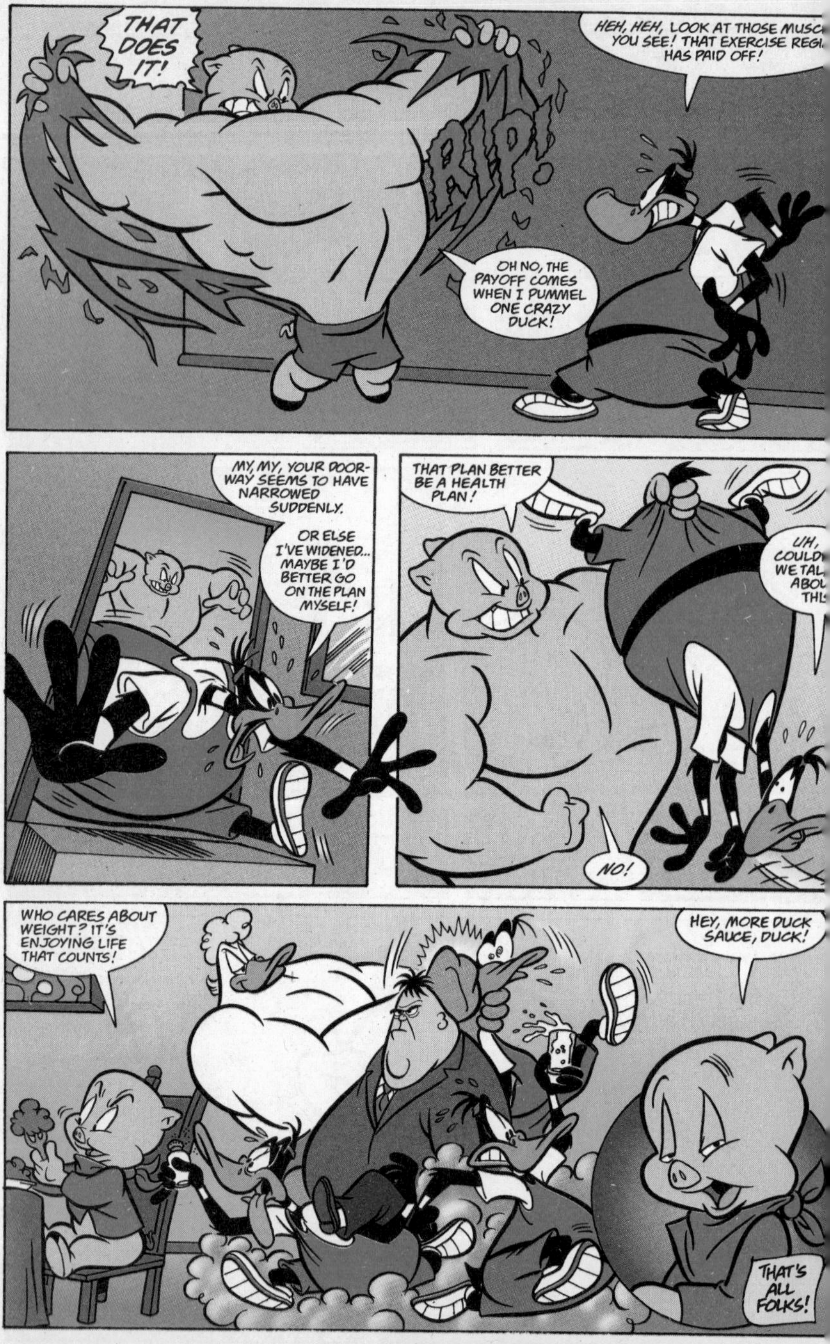
THAT DOES IT!
RIP!
HEH, HEH, LOOK AT THOSE MUSC
YOU SEE! THAT EXERCISE REGI
HAS PAID OFF!
OH NO, THE PAYOFF COMES WHEN I PUMMEL ONE CRAZY DUCK!
MY, MY, YOUR DOORWAY SEEMS TO HAVE NARROWED SUDDENLY.
OR ELSE I'VE WIDENED... MAYBE I'D BETTER GO ON THE PLAN MYSELF!
THAT PLAN BETTER BE A HEALTH PLAN!
NO!
WHO CARES ABOUT WEIGHT? IT'S ENJOYING LIFE THAT COUNTS!
HEY, MORE DUCK SAUCE, DUCK!
THAT'S ALL FOLKS!

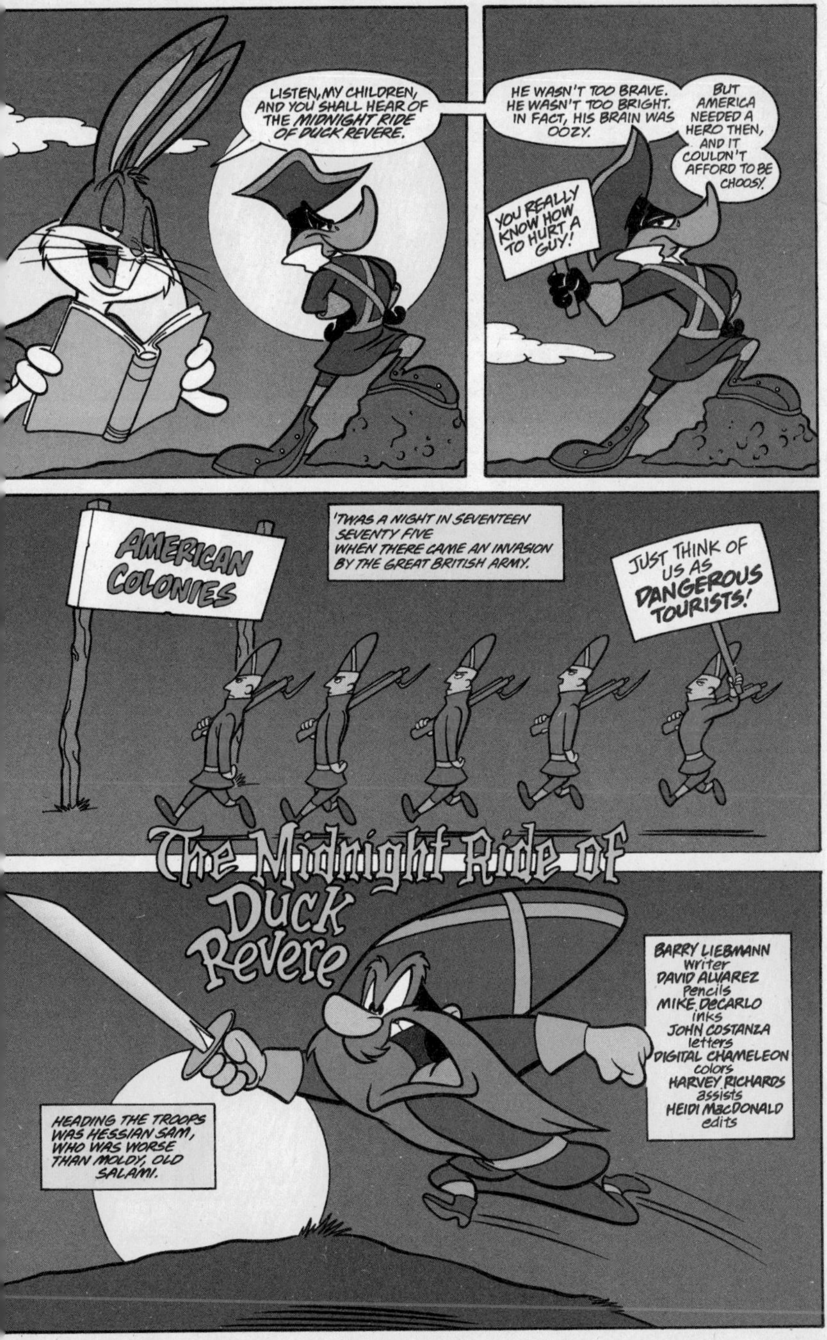
LISTEN, MY CHILDREN, AND YOU SHALL HEAR OF THE MIDNIGHT RIDE OF DUCK REVERE.
HE WASN'T TOO BRAVE. HE WASN'T TOO BRIGHT. IN FACT, HIS BRAIN WAS OOZY.
BUT AMERICA NEEDED A HERO THEN, AND IT COULDN'T AFFORD TO BE CHOOSY.
YOU REALLY KNOW HOW TO HURT A GUY!
AMERICAN COLONIES
'TWAS A NIGHT IN SEVENTEEN SEVENTY FIVE WHEN THERE CAME AN INVASION BY THE GREAT BRITISH ARMY.
JUST THINK OF US AS DANGEROUS TOURISTS!
The Midnight Ride of Duck Revere
BARRY LIEBMANN writer
DAVID ALVAREZ pencils
MIKE DeCARLO inks
JOHN COSTANZA letters
DIGITAL CHAMELEON colors
HARVEY RICHARDS assists
HEIDI MacDONALD edits
HEADING THE TROOPS WAS HESSIAN SAM, WHO WAS WORSE THAN MOLDY, OLD SALAMI.

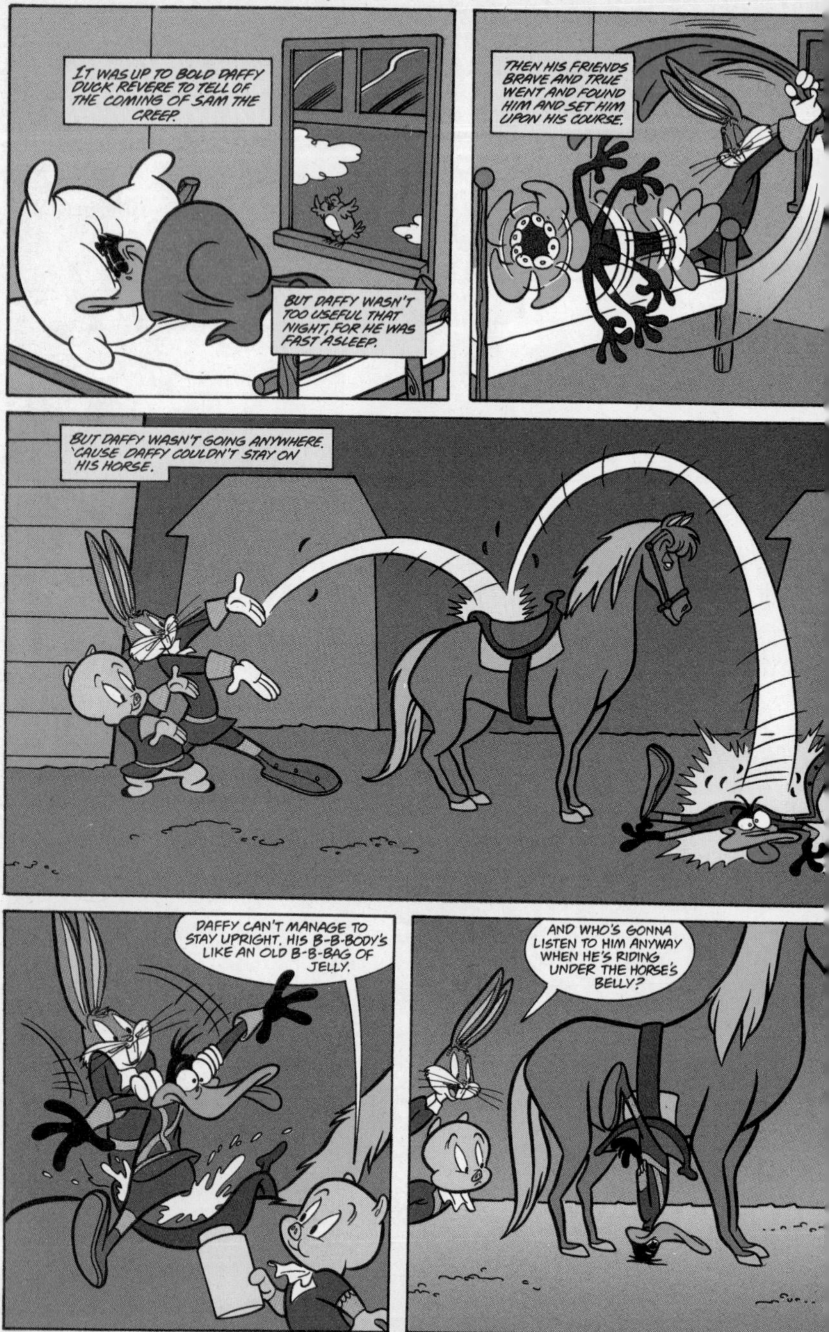
IT WAS UP TO BOLD DAFFY DUCK REVERE TO TELL OF THE COMING OF SAM THE CREEP.
BUT DAFFY WASN'T TOO USEFUL THAT NIGHT, FOR HE WAS FAST ASLEEP.
THEN HIS FRIENDS BRAVE AND TRUE WENT AND FOUND HIM AND SET HIM UPON HIS COURSE.
BUT DAFFY WASN'T GOING ANYWHERE. 'CAUSE DAFFY COULDN'T STAY ON HIS HORSE.
DAFFY CAN'T MANAGE TO STAY UPRIGHT. HIS B-B-BODY'S LIKE AN OLD B-B-BAG OF JELLY.
AND WHO'S GONNA LISTEN TO HIM ANYWAY WHEN HE'S RIDING UNDER THE HORSE'S BELLY?

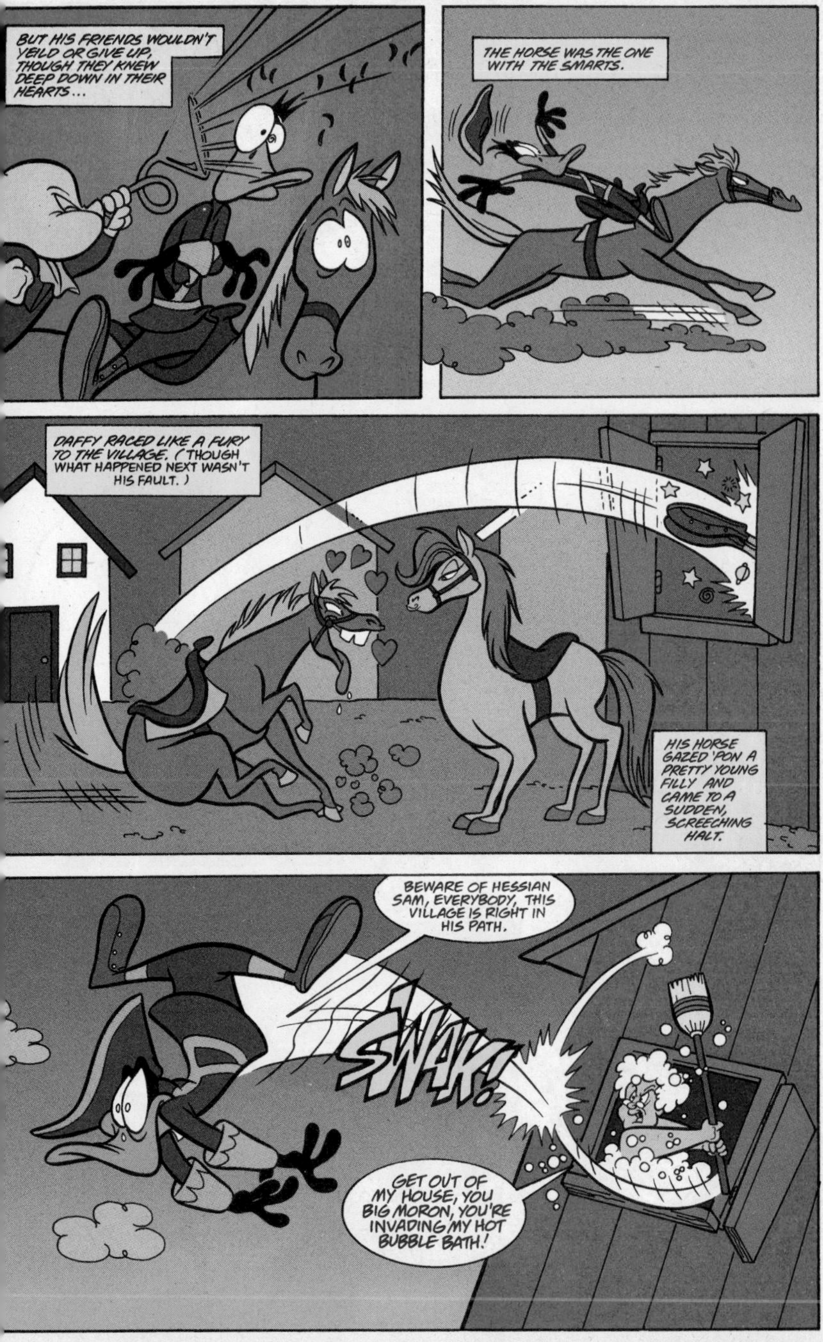

BUT HIS FRIENDS WOULDN'T YEILD OR GIVE UP, THOUGH THEY KNEW DEEP DOWN IN THEIR HEARTS...
THE HORSE WAS THE ONE WITH THE SMARTS.
DAFFY RACED LIKE A FURY TO THE VILLAGE. (THOUGH WHAT HAPPENED NEXT WASN'T HIS FAULT.)
HIS HORSE GAZED 'PON A PRETTY YOUNG FILLY AND CAME TO A SUDDEN, SCREECHING HALT.
BEWARE OF HESSIAN SAM, EVERYBODY, THIS VILLAGE IS RIGHT IN HIS PATH.
SWAK!
GET OUT OF MY HOUSE, YOU BIG MORON, YOU'RE INVADING MY HOT BUBBLE BATH!

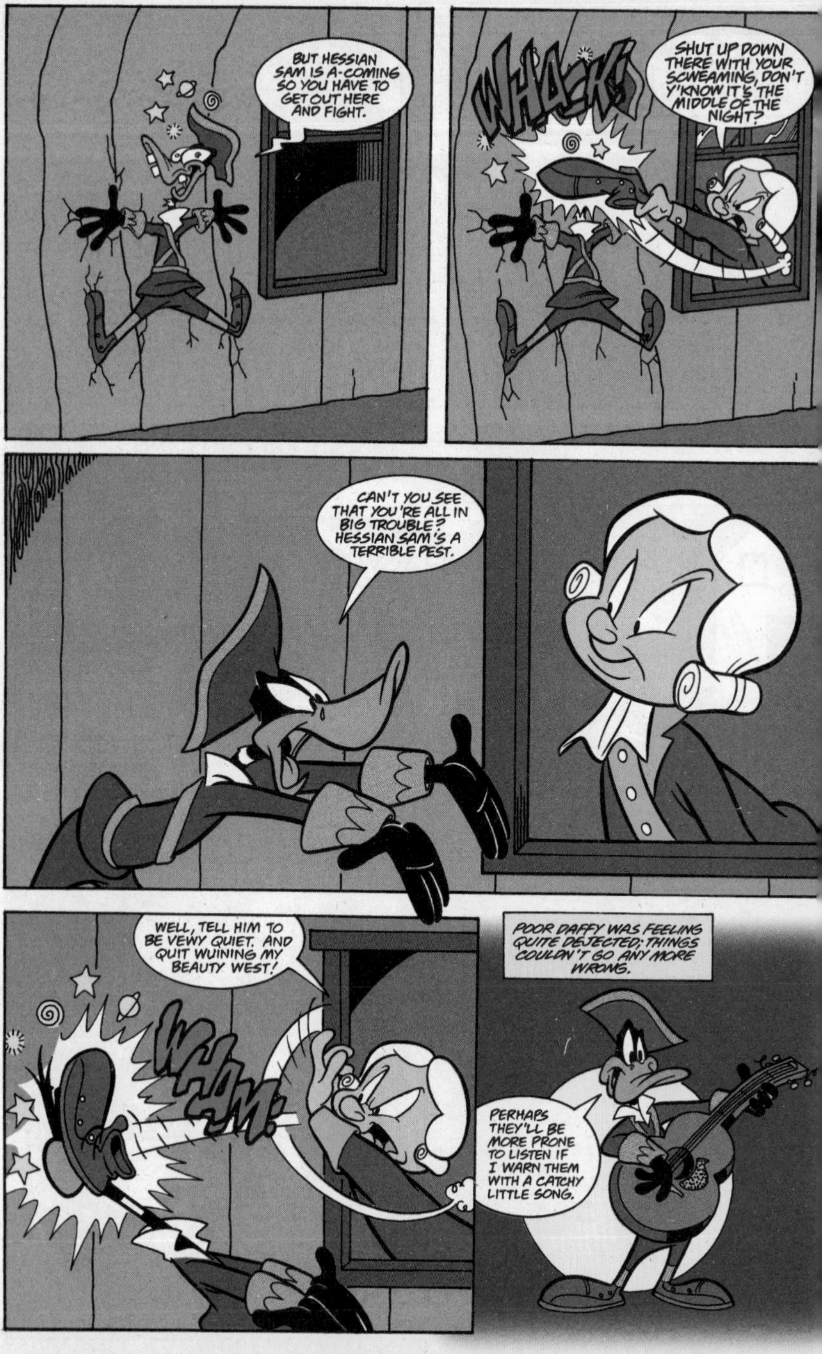
BUT HESSIAN SAM IS A-COMING SO YOU HAVE TO GET OUT HERE AND FIGHT.
WHACK!
SHUT UP DOWN THERE WITH YOUR SCWEAMING, DON'T Y'KNOW IT'S THE MIDDLE OF THE NIGHT?
CAN'T YOU SEE THAT YOU'RE ALL IN BIG TROUBLE? HESSIAN SAM'S A TERRIBLE PEST.
WELL, TELL HIM TO BE VEWY QUIET. AND QUIT WUINING MY BEAUTY WEST!
WHAM!
POOR DAFFY WAS FEELING QUITE DEJECTED; THINGS COULDN'T GO ANY MORE WRONG.
PERHAPS THEY'LL BE MORE PRONE TO LISTEN IF I WARN THEM WITH A CATCHY LITTLE SONG.

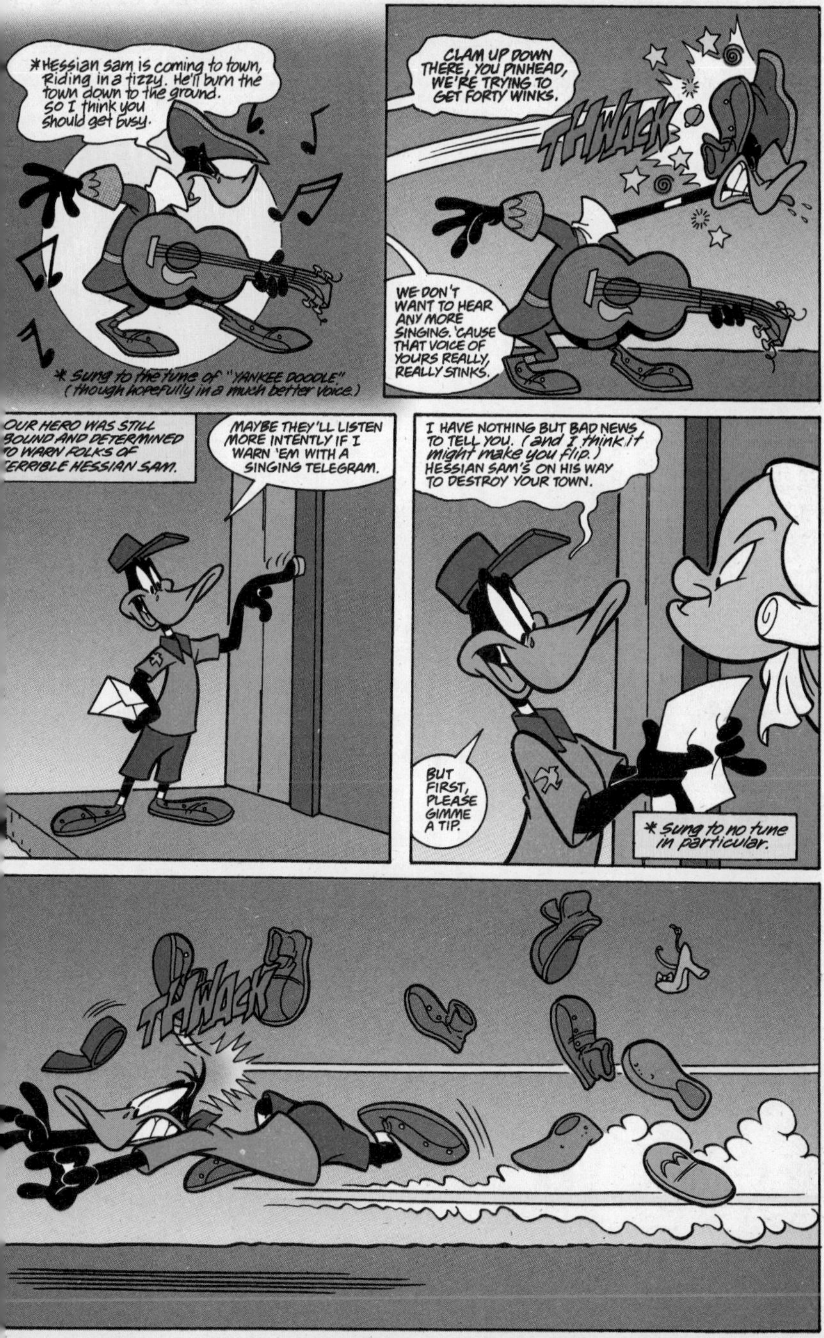

*Hessian sam is coming to town, Riding in a tizzy. He'll burn the town down to the ground. So I think you should get busy.
* Sung to the tune of "YANKEE DOODLE" (though hopefully in a much better voice.)
CLAM UP DOWN THERE, YOU PINHEAD, WE'RE TRYING TO GET FORTY WINKS.
THWACK
WE DON'T WANT TO HEAR ANY MORE SINGING. 'CAUSE THAT VOICE OF YOURS REALLY, REALLY STINKS.
OUR HERO WAS STILL BOUND AND DETERMINED TO WARN FOLKS OF TERRIBLE HESSIAN SAM.
MAYBE THEY'LL LISTEN MORE INTENTLY IF I WARN 'EM WITH A SINGING TELEGRAM.
I HAVE NOTHING BUT BAD NEWS TO TELL YOU. (and I think it might make you flip.) HESSIAN SAM'S ON HIS WAY TO DESTROY YOUR TOWN.
BUT FIRST, PLEASE GIMME A TIP.
* Sung to no tune in particular.
THWACK

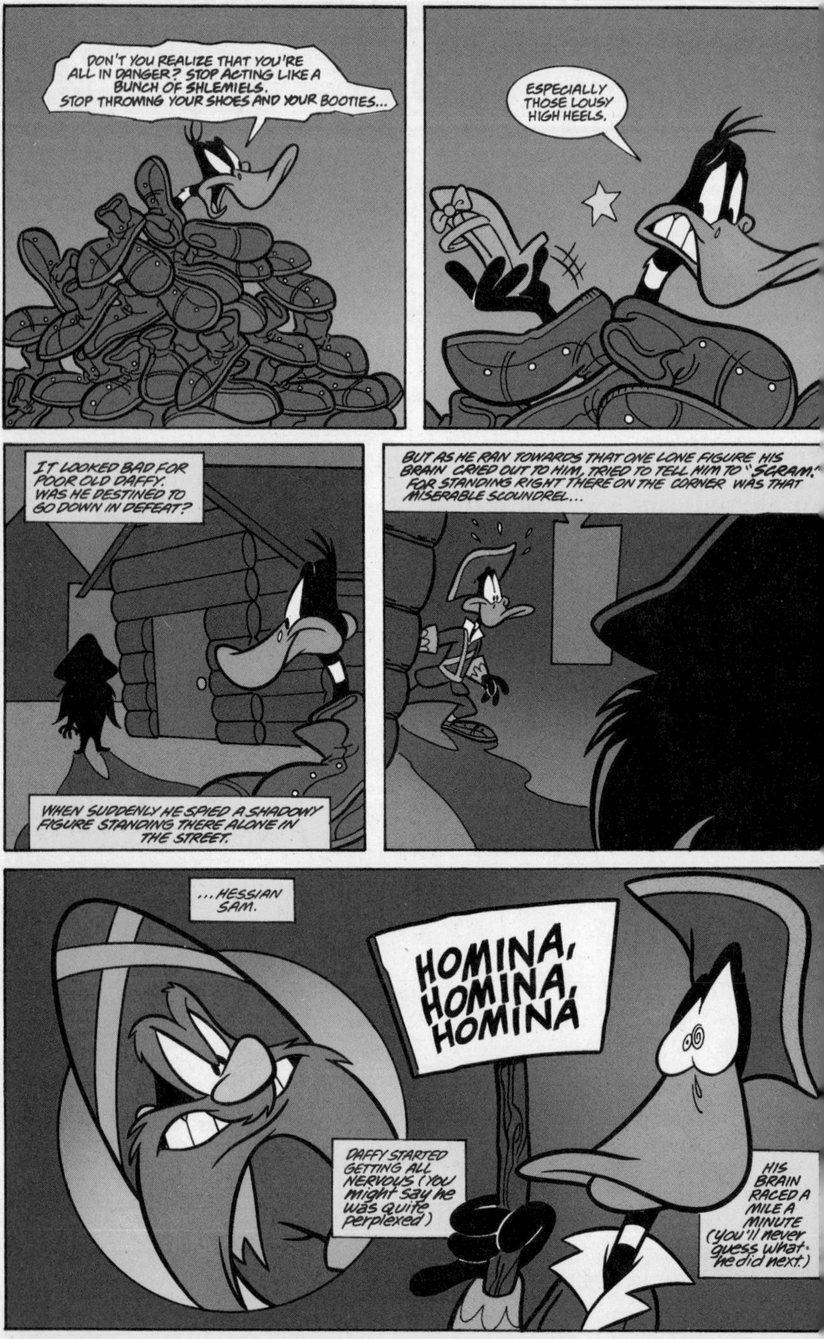

DON'T YOU REALIZE THAT YOU'RE ALL IN DANGER? STOP ACTING LIKE A BUNCH OF SHLEMIELS. STOP THROWING YOUR SHOES AND YOUR BOOTIES...
ESPECIALLY THOSE LOUSY HIGH HEELS.
IT LOOKED BAD FOR POOR OLD DAFFY. WAS HE DESTINED TO GO DOWN IN DEFEAT?
WHEN SUDDENLY HE SPIED A SHADOWY FIGURE STANDING THERE ALONE IN THE STREET.
BUT AS HE RAN TOWARDS THAT ONE LONE FIGURE HIS BRAIN CRIED OUT TO HIM, TRIED TO TELL HIM TO "SCRAM." FOR STANDING RIGHT THERE ON THE CORNER WAS THAT MISERABLE SCOUNDREL...
...HESSIAN SAM.
HOMINA, HOMINA, HOMINA
DAFFY STARTED GETTING ALL NERVOUS (YOU might say he was quite perplexed)
HIS BRAIN RACED A MILE A MINUTE (you'll never guess what he did next.)

OUR HERO TOOK OUT A BIG DRUM MADE OF STEEL AND THEN PROCEEDED TO SMACK IT, TILL EVERYONE IN THE HOOD CRIED OUT...

HEY, WHO THE HECK'S MAKIN' ALL THAT RACKET?

JUST LIKE OL' GEORGE WASHINGTON I CANNOT TELL A FIB.

IT WAS THE JERK RIGHT NEXT TO ME, THE ONE WITH THE HAIRY BIB.

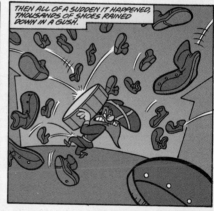

THEN ALL OF A SUDDEN IT HAPPENED, THOUSANDS OF SHOES RAINED DOWN IN A GUSH.

HESSIAN SAM WAS FORCED TO SURRENDER BEFORE HE WAS POUNDED TO MUSH.

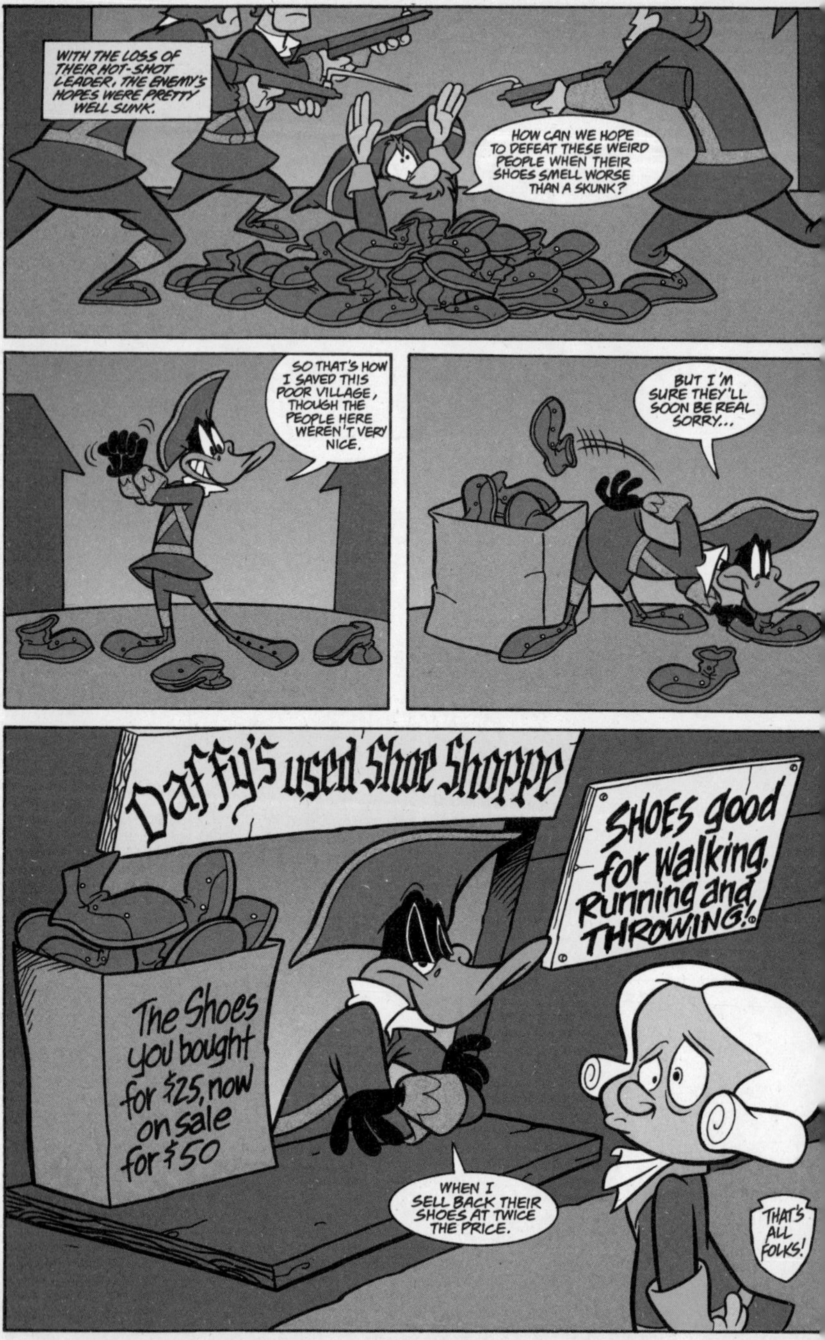
WITH THE LOSS OF THEIR HOT-SHOT LEADER, THE ENEMY'S HOPES WERE PRETTY WELL SUNK.
HOW CAN WE HOPE TO DEFEAT THESE WEIRD PEOPLE WHEN THEIR SHOES SMELL WORSE THAN A SKUNK?
SO THAT'S HOW I SAVED THIS POOR VILLAGE, THOUGH THE PEOPLE HERE WEREN'T VERY NICE.
BUT I'M SURE THEY'LL SOON BE REAL SORRY...
Daffy's used Shoe Shoppe
SHOES good for Walking, Running and THROWING!
The Shoes you bought for $25, now on sale for $50
WHEN I SELL BACK THEIR SHOES AT TWICE THE PRICE.
THAT'S ALL FOLKS!

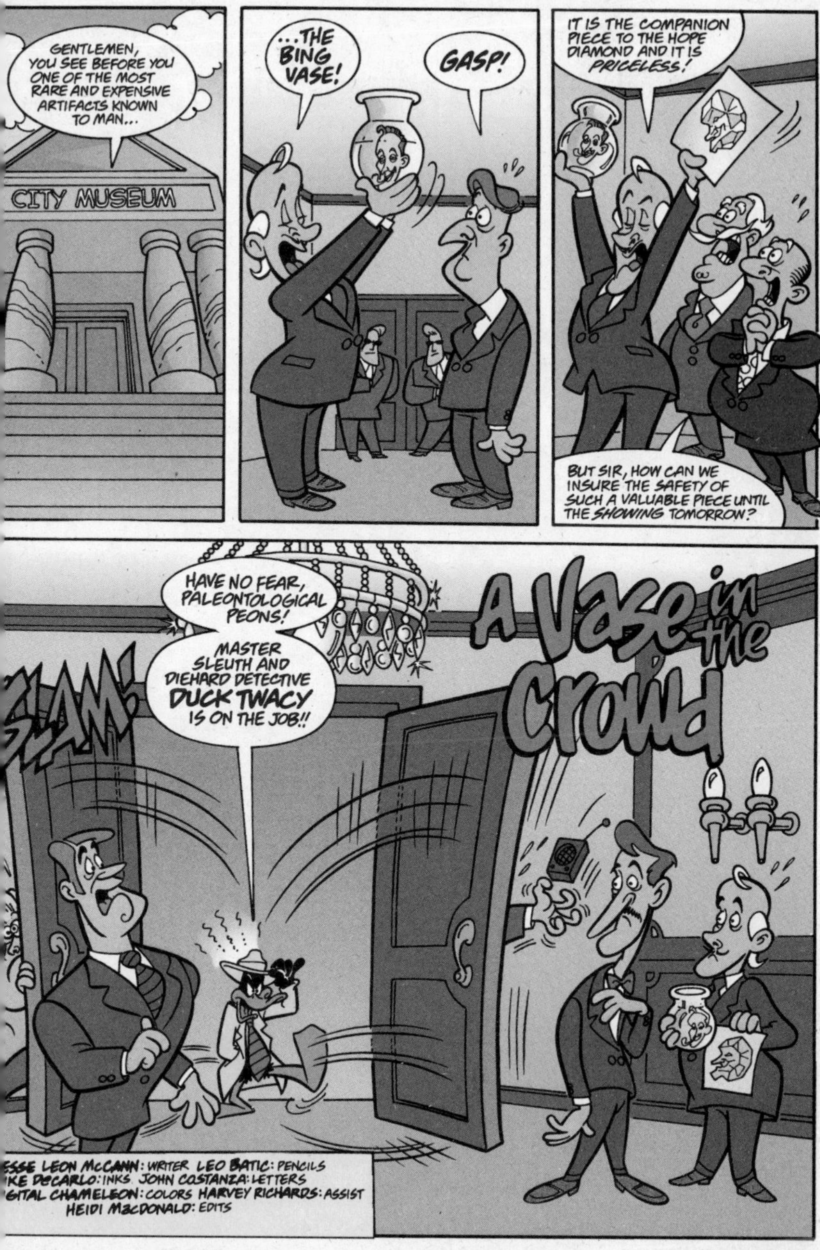
GENTLEMEN, YOU SEE BEFORE YOU ONE OF THE MOST RARE AND EXPENSIVE ARTIFACTS KNOWN TO MAN...
CITY MUSEUM
...THE BING VASE!
GASP!
IT IS THE COMPANION PIECE TO THE HOPE DIAMOND AND IT IS PRICELESS!
BUT SIR, HOW CAN WE INSURE THE SAFETY OF SUCH A VALUABLE PIECE UNTIL THE SHOWING TOMORROW?
HAVE NO FEAR, PALEONTOLOGICAL PEONS!
MASTER SLEUTH AND DIEHARD DETECTIVE DUCK TWACY IS ON THE JOB!!
SLAM!
A Vase in the Crowd
ESSE LEON McCANN: WRITER LEO BATIC: PENCILS
IKE DeCARLO: INKS JOHN COSTANZA: LETTERS
GITAL CHAMELEON: COLORS HARVEY RICHARDS: ASSIST
HEIDI MacDONALD: EDITS

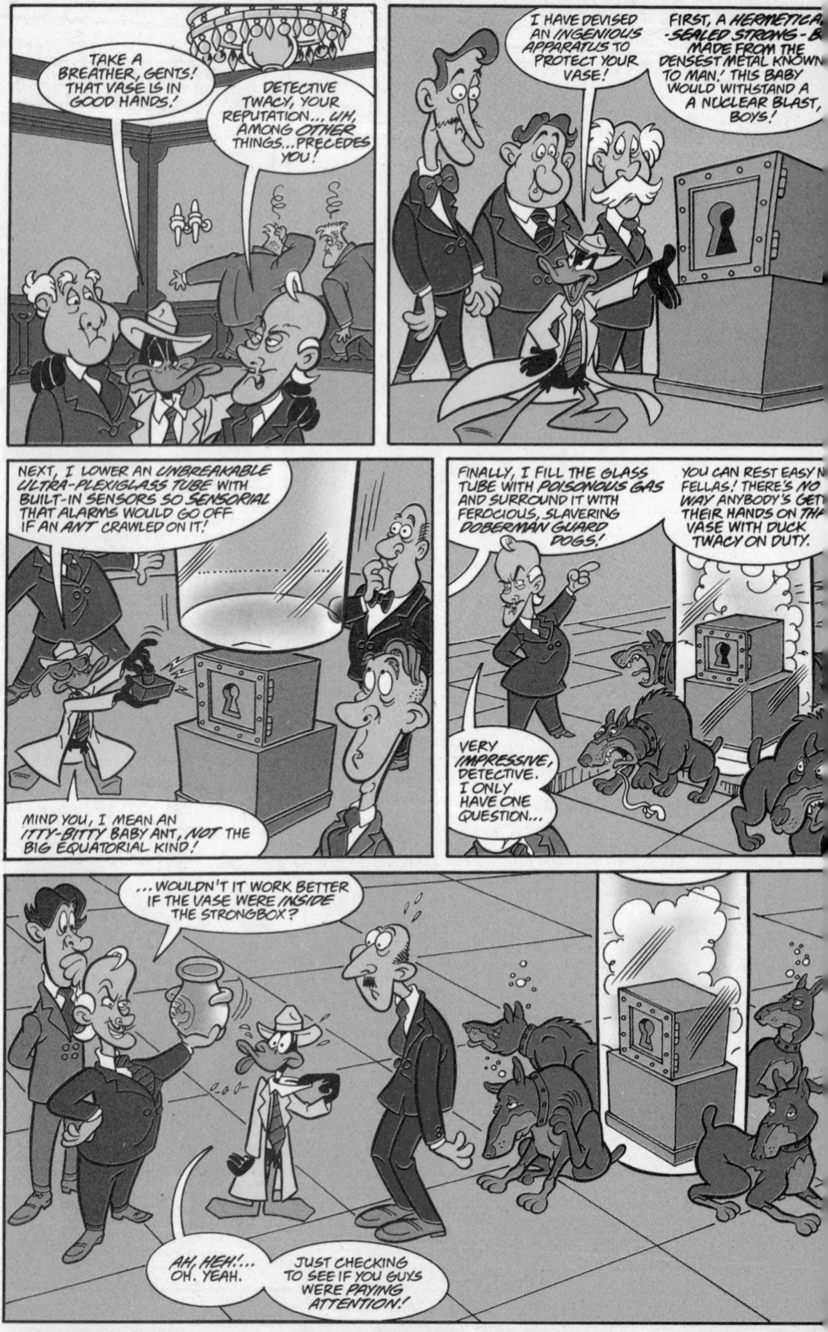
TAKE A BREATHER, GENTS! THAT VASE IS IN GOOD HANDS!
DETECTIVE TWACY, YOUR REPUTATION... UH, AMONG OTHER THINGS... PRECEDES YOU!
I HAVE DEVISED AN INGENIOUS APPARATUS TO PROTECT YOUR VASE!
FIRST, A HERMETICA -SEALED STRONG-B MADE FROM THE DENSEST METAL KNOWN TO MAN! THIS BABY WOULD WITHSTAND A A NUCLEAR BLAST, BOYS!
NEXT, I LOWER AN UNBREAKABLE ULTRA-PLEXIGLASS TUBE WITH BUILT-IN SENSORS SO SENSORIAL THAT ALARMS WOULD GO OFF IF AN ANT CRAWLED ON IT!
MIND YOU, I MEAN AN ITTY-BITTY BABY ANT, NOT THE BIG EQUATORIAL KIND!
FINALLY, I FILL THE GLASS TUBE WITH POISONOUS GAS AND SURROUND IT WITH FEROCIOUS, SLAVERING DOBERMAN GUARD DOGS!
YOU CAN REST EASY FELLAS! THERE'S NO WAY ANYBODY'S GET THEIR HANDS ON THA VASE WITH DUCK TWACY ON DUTY.
VERY IMPRESSIVE, DETECTIVE. I ONLY HAVE ONE QUESTION...
...WOULDN'T IT WORK BETTER IF THE VASE WERE INSIDE THE STRONGBOX?
AH, HEH!... OH. YEAH.
JUST CHECKING TO SEE IF YOU GUYS WERE PAYING ATTENTION!

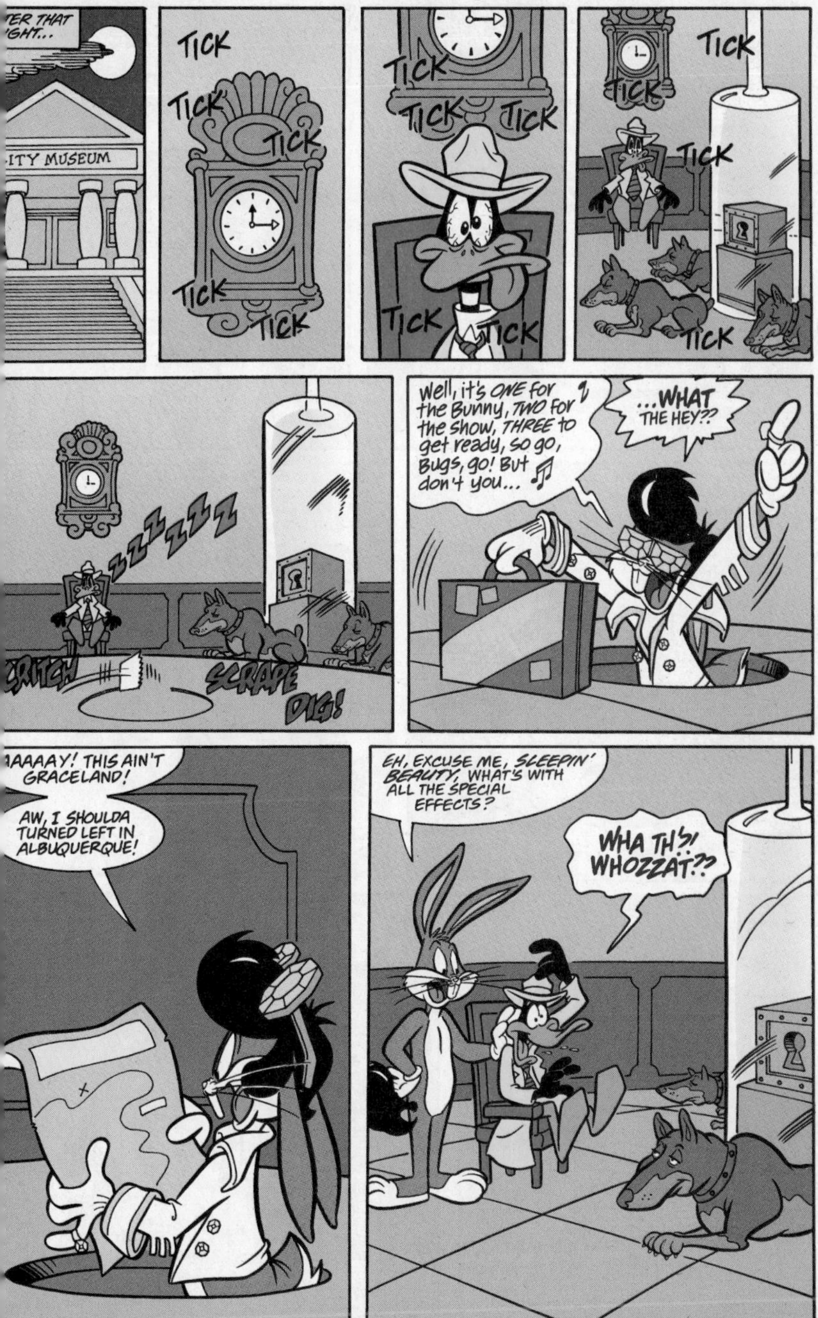
ER THAT
GHT...
ITY MUSEUM
TICK
TICK
TICK
TICK
TICK
TICK
TICK
TICK
TICK
TICK
TICK
TICK
TICK
TICK
TICK
ZZZZZZZ
CRITCH
SCRAPE
DIG!
Well, it's ONE for the Bunny, TWO for the show, THREE to get ready, so go, Bugs, go! But don't you... ♫
...WHAT THE HEY??
AAAAY! THIS AIN'T GRACELAND!
AW, I SHOULDA TURNED LEFT IN ALBUQUERQUE!
EH, EXCUSE ME, SLEEPIN' BEAUTY, WHAT'S WITH ALL THE SPECIAL EFFECTS?
WHA TH?! WHOZZAT??

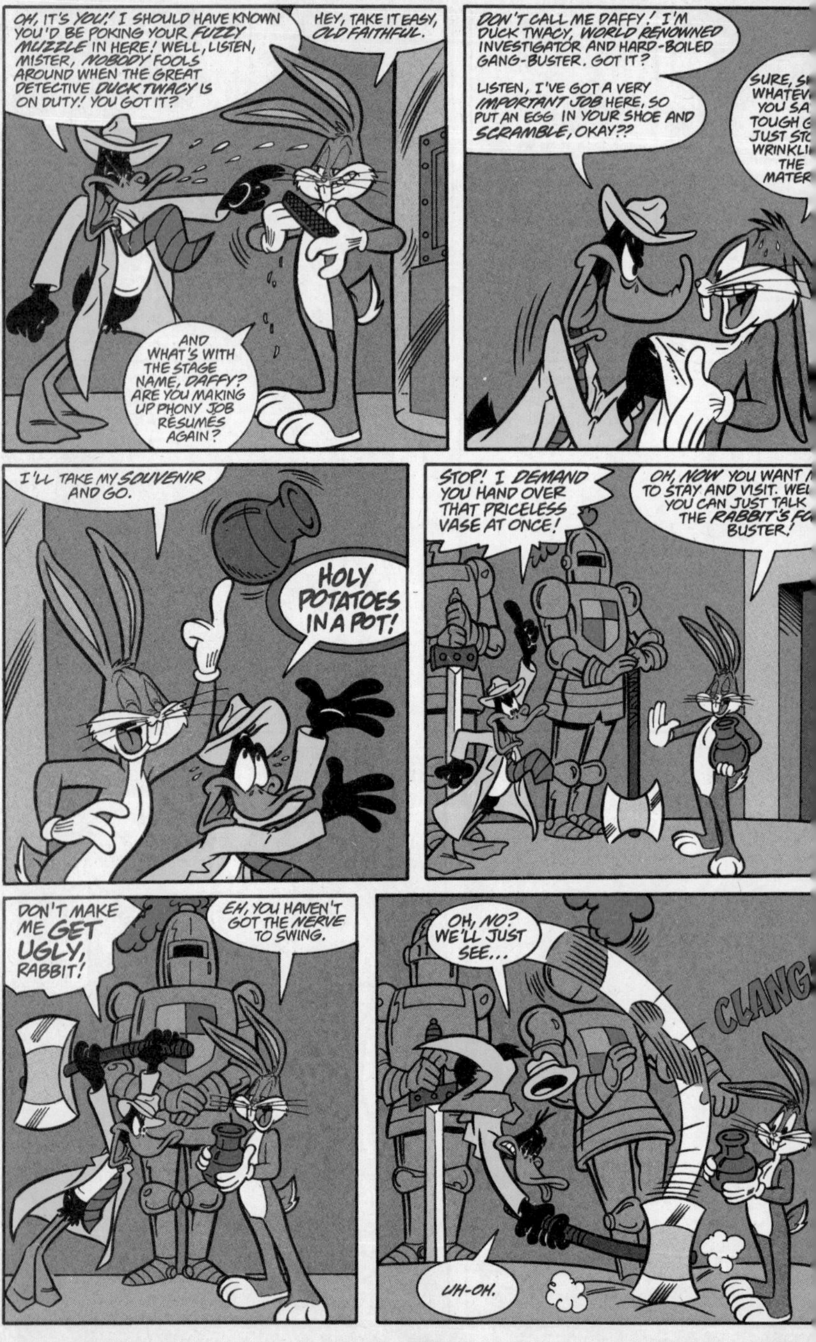

OH, IT'S YOU! I SHOULD HAVE KNOWN YOU'D BE POKING YOUR FUZZY MUZZLE IN HERE! WELL, LISTEN, MISTER, NOBODY FOOLS AROUND WHEN THE GREAT DETECTIVE DUCK TWACY IS ON DUTY! YOU GOT IT?
HEY, TAKE IT EASY, OLD FAITHFUL.
AND WHAT'S WITH THE STAGE NAME, DAFFY? ARE YOU MAKING UP PHONY JOB RÉSUMÉS AGAIN?
DON'T CALL ME DAFFY! I'M DUCK TWACY, WORLD RENOWNED INVESTIGATOR AND HARD-BOILED GANG-BUSTER. GOT IT?
LISTEN, I'VE GOT A VERY IMPORTANT JOB HERE, SO PUT AN EGG IN YOUR SHOE AND SCRAMBLE, OKAY??
SURE, S WHATEV YOU SA TOUGH G JUST STO WRINKLI THE MATER
I'LL TAKE MY SOUVENIR AND GO.
HOLY POTATOES IN A POT!
STOP! I DEMAND YOU HAND OVER THAT PRICELESS VASE AT ONCE!
OH, NOW YOU WANT TO STAY AND VISIT. WEL YOU CAN JUST TALK THE RABBIT'S F BUSTER!
DON'T MAKE ME GET UGLY, RABBIT!
EH, YOU HAVEN'T GOT THE NERVE TO SWING.
OH, NO? WE'LL JUST SEE...
CLANG
UH-OH.

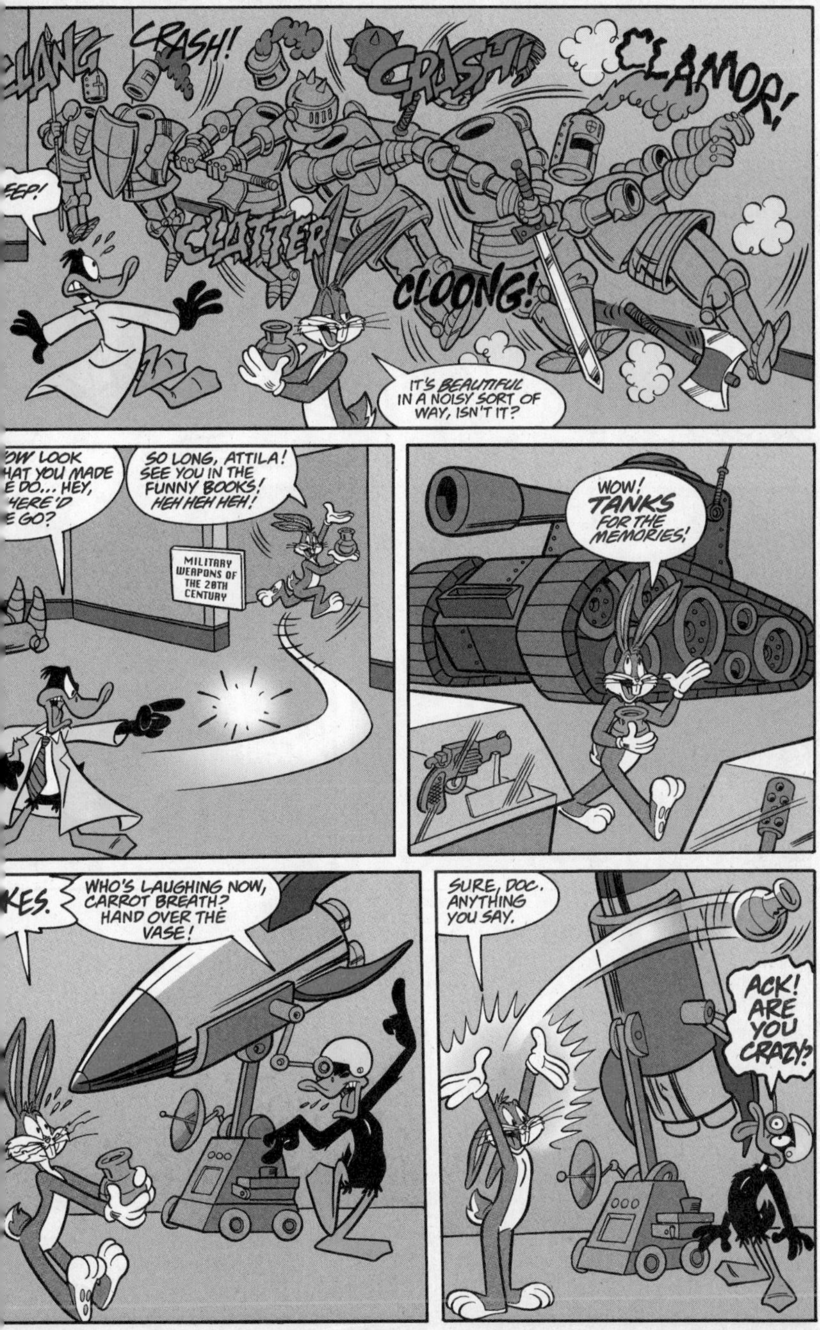
CLANG
CRASH!
CRASH!
CLAMOR!
EEP!
CLATTER
CLOONG!
IT'S BEAUTIFUL IN A NOISY SORT OF WAY, ISN'T IT?
OW LOOK HAT YOU MADE E DO... HEY, HERE'D E GO?
SO LONG, ATTILA! SEE YOU IN THE FUNNY BOOKS! HEH HEH HEH!
MILITARY WEAPONS OF THE 20TH CENTURY
WOW! TANKS FOR THE MEMORIES!
KES.
WHO'S LAUGHING NOW, CARROT BREATH? HAND OVER THE VASE!
SURE, DOC. ANYTHING YOU SAY.
ACK! ARE YOU CRAZY?

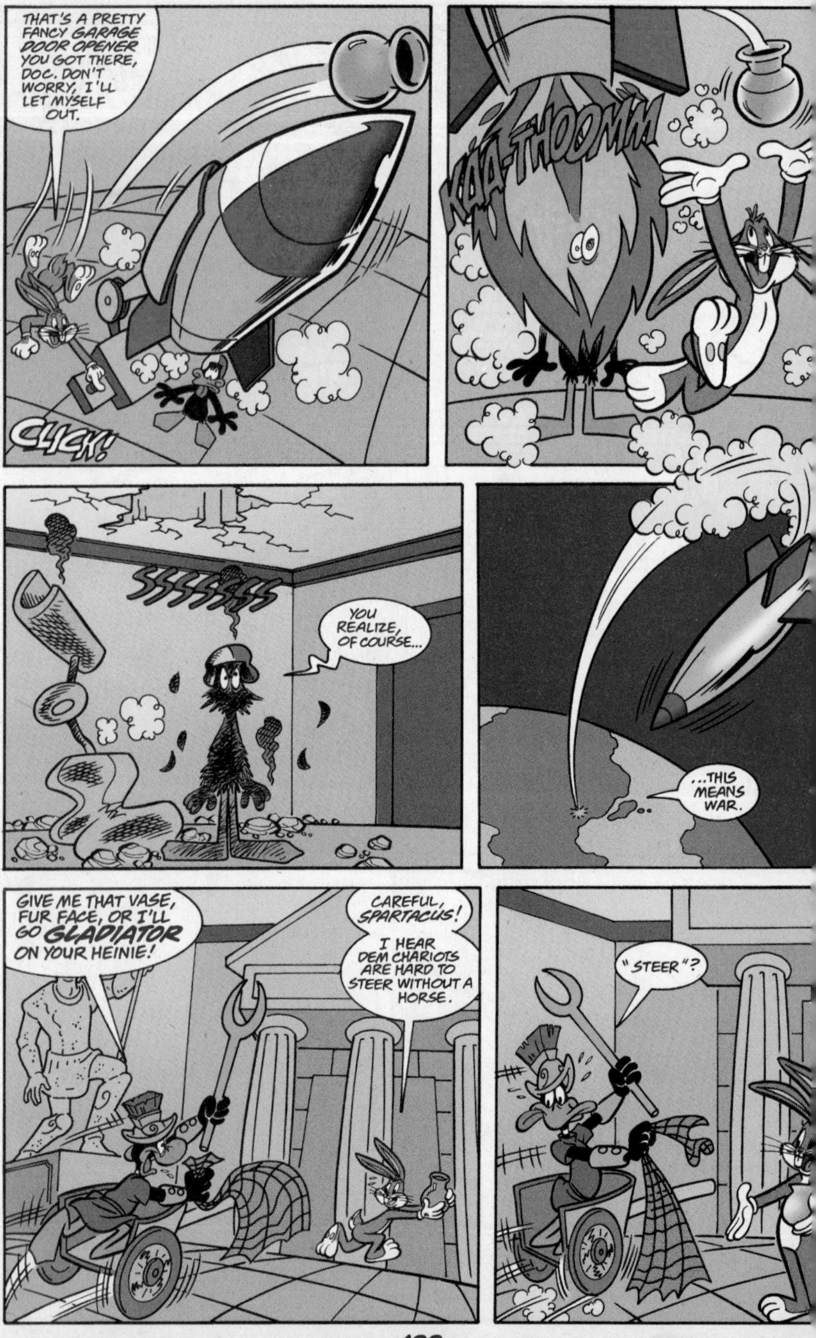
THAT'S A PRETTY FANCY GARAGE DOOR OPENER YOU GOT THERE, DOC. DON'T WORRY, I'LL LET MYSELF OUT.
CLICK!
KAA-THOOMM
SSSSSSS
YOU REALIZE, OF COURSE...
...THIS MEANS WAR.
GIVE ME THAT VASE, FUR FACE, OR I'LL GO GLADIATOR ON YOUR HEINIE!
CAREFUL, SPARTACUS!
I HEAR DEM CHARIOTS ARE HARD TO STEER WITHOUT A HORSE.
"STEER"?

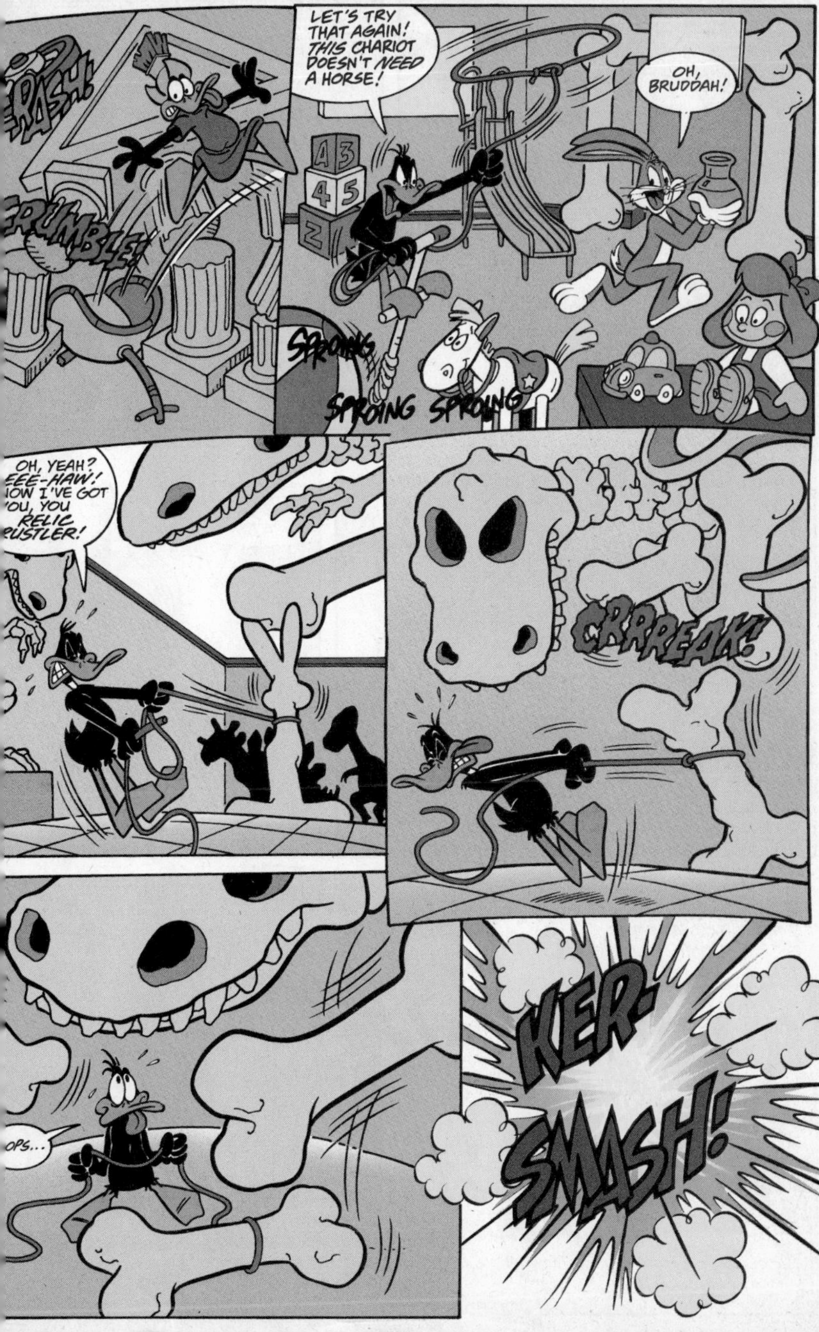

CRASH!
CRUMBLE!
LET'S TRY THAT AGAIN! THIS CHARIOT DOESN'T NEED A HORSE!
OH, BRUDDAH!
SPROING
SPROING SPROING
OH, YEAH? EEE-HAW! NOW I'VE GOT YOU, YOU RELIC RUSTLER!
CRRREAK!
OPS...
KER-SMASH!

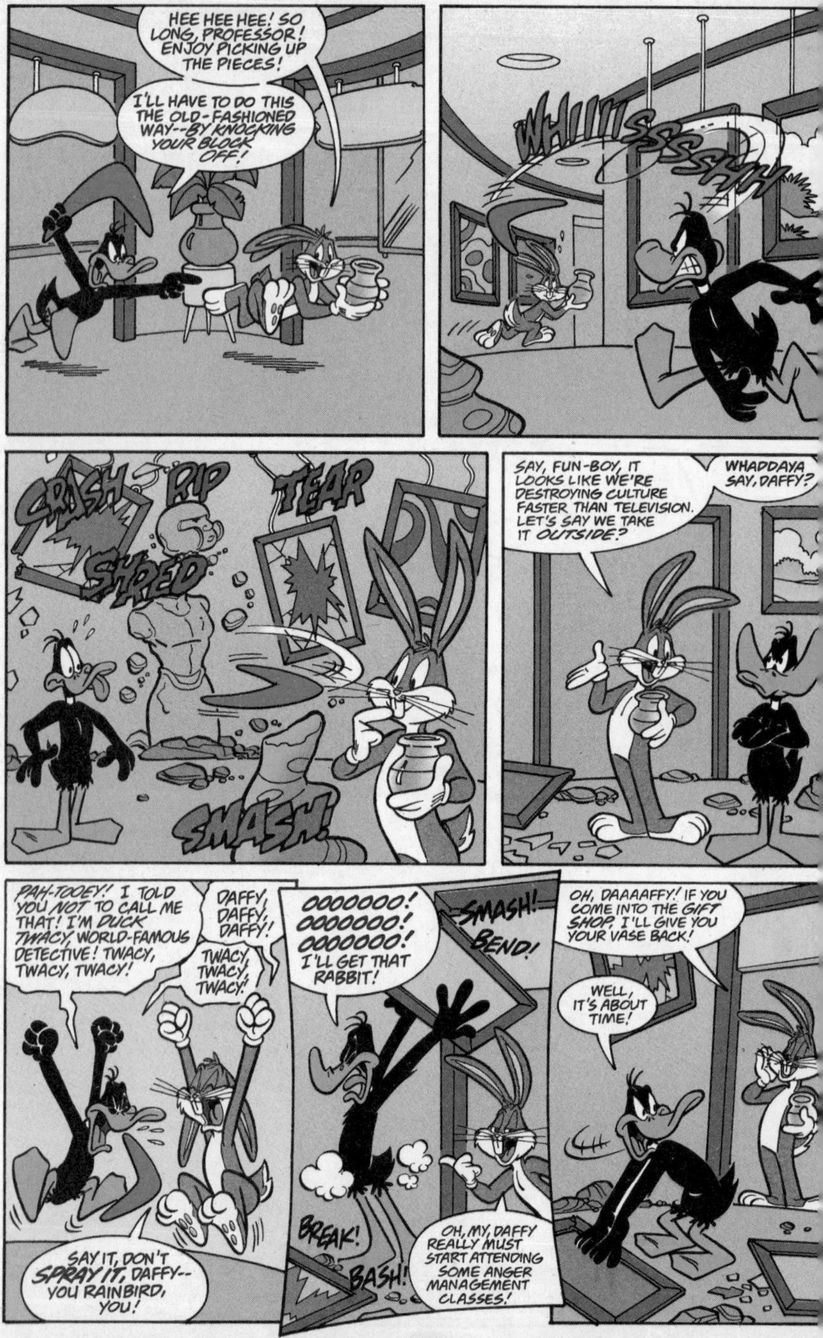
HEE HEE HEE! SO LONG, PROFESSOR! ENJOY PICKING UP THE PIECES!
I'LL HAVE TO DO THIS THE OLD-FASHIONED WAY--BY KNOCKING YOUR BLOCK OFF!
WHIIIISSSSHH
CRASH
RIP
TEAR
SHRED
SMASH!
SAY, FUN-BOY, IT LOOKS LIKE WE'RE DESTROYING CULTURE FASTER THAN TELEVISION. LET'S SAY WE TAKE IT OUTSIDE?
WHADDAYA SAY, DAFFY?
PAH-TOOEY! I TOLD YOU NOT TO CALL ME THAT! I'M DUCK TWACY, WORLD-FAMOUS DETECTIVE! TWACY, TWACY, TWACY!
DAFFY, DAFFY, DAFFY!
TWACY, TWACY, TWACY!
SAY IT, DON'T SPRAY IT, DAFFY-- YOU RAINBIRD, YOU!
OOOOOOO! OOOOOOO! OOOOOOO! I'LL GET THAT RABBIT!
SMASH!
BEND!
BREAK!
BASH!
OH, MY, DAFFY REALLY MUST START ATTENDING SOME ANGER MANAGEMENT CLASSES!
OH, DAAAAFFY! IF YOU COME INTO THE GIFT SHOP, I'LL GIVE YOU YOUR VASE BACK!
WELL, IT'S ABOUT TIME!

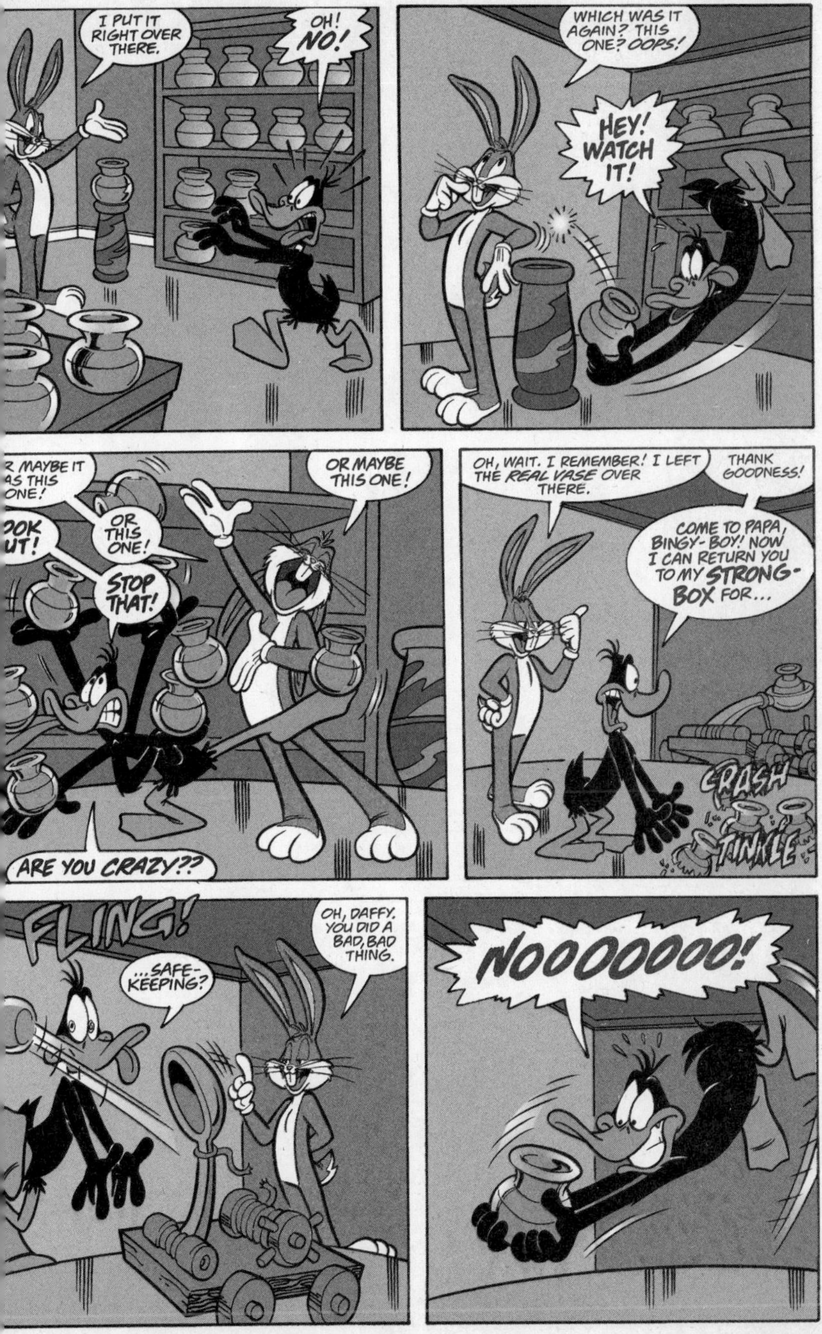
I PUT IT RIGHT OVER THERE.
OH! NO!
WHICH WAS IT AGAIN? THIS ONE? OOPS!
HEY! WATCH IT!
R MAYBE IT AS THIS ONE!
OOK UT!
OR THIS ONE!
STOP THAT!
OR MAYBE THIS ONE!
ARE YOU CRAZY??
OH, WAIT. I REMEMBER! I LEFT THE REAL VASE OVER THERE.
THANK GOODNESS!
COME TO PAPA, BINGY-BOY! NOW I CAN RETURN YOU TO MY STRONG-BOX FOR...
CRASH
TINKLE
FLING!
...SAFE-KEEPING?
OH, DAFFY. YOU DID A BAD, BAD THING.
NOOOOOOO!

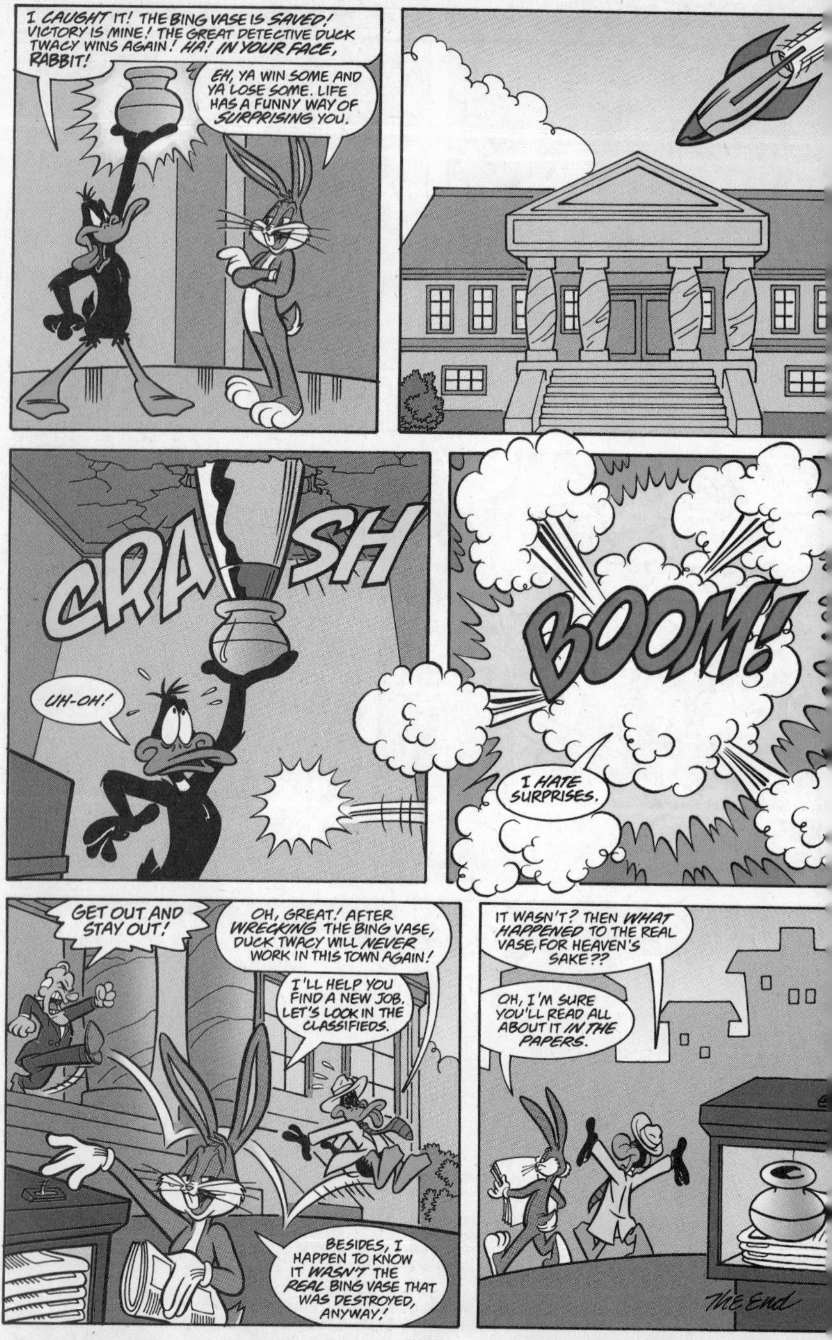
I CAUGHT IT! THE BING VASE IS SAVED! VICTORY IS MINE! THE GREAT DETECTIVE DUCK TWACY WINS AGAIN! HA! IN YOUR FACE, RABBIT!
EH, YA WIN SOME AND YA LOSE SOME. LIFE HAS A FUNNY WAY OF SURPRISING YOU.
CRASH
UH-OH!
BOOM!
I HATE SURPRISES.
GET OUT AND STAY OUT!
OH, GREAT! AFTER WRECKING THE BING VASE, DUCK TWACY WILL NEVER WORK IN THIS TOWN AGAIN!
I'LL HELP YOU FIND A NEW JOB. LET'S LOOK IN THE CLASSIFIEDS.
BESIDES, I HAPPEN TO KNOW IT WASN'T THE REAL BING VASE THAT WAS DESTROYED, ANYWAY!
IT WASN'T? THEN WHAT HAPPENED TO THE REAL VASE, FOR HEAVEN'S SAKE??
OH, I'M SURE YOU'LL READ ALL ABOUT IT IN THE PAPERS.
The End

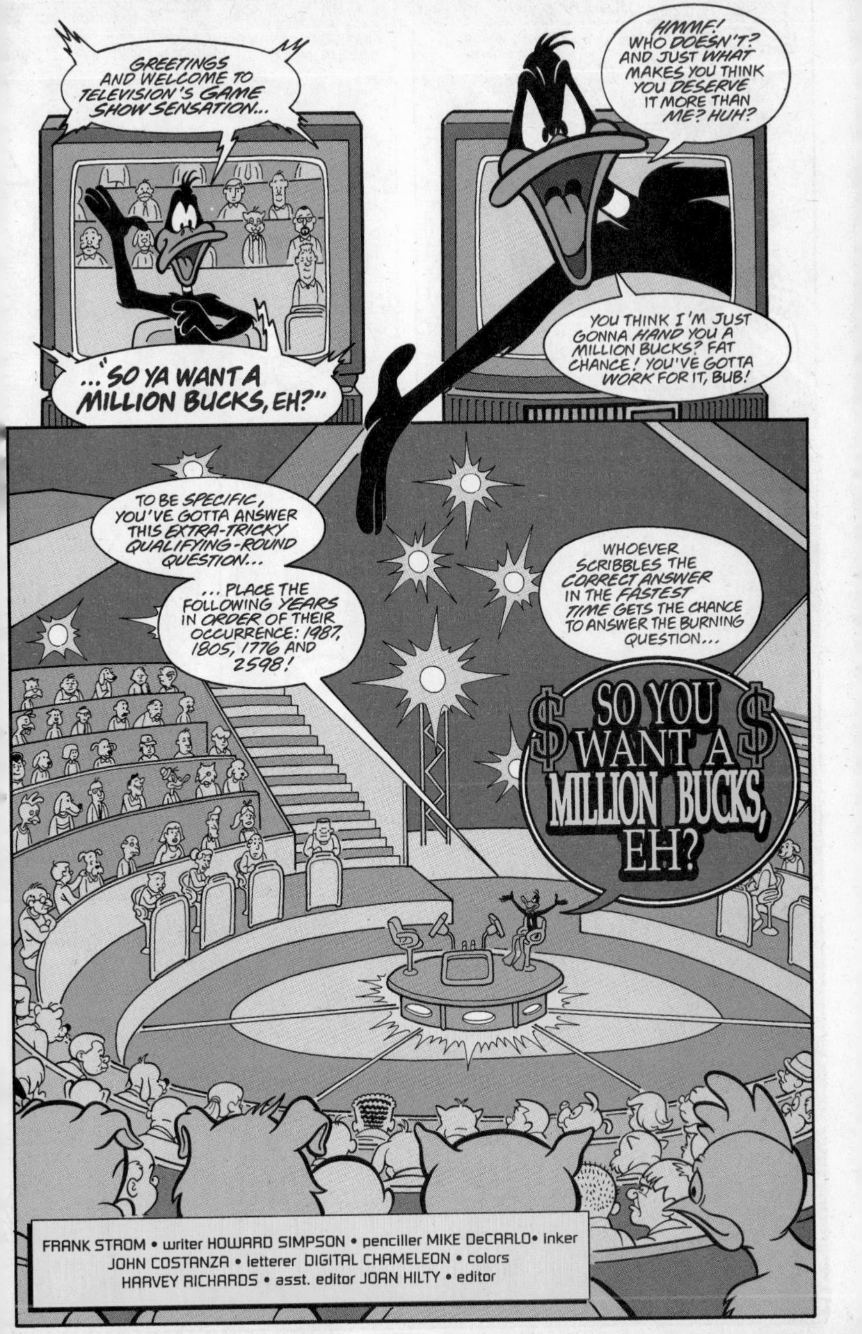
GREETINGS AND WELCOME TO TELEVISION'S GAME SHOW SENSATION...
..."SO YA WANT A MILLION BUCKS, EH?"
HMMF! WHO DOESN'T? AND JUST WHAT MAKES YOU THINK YOU DESERVE IT MORE THAN ME? HUH?
YOU THINK I'M JUST GONNA HAND YOU A MILLION BUCKS? FAT CHANCE! YOU'VE GOTTA WORK FOR IT, BUB!
TO BE SPECIFIC, YOU'VE GOTTA ANSWER THIS EXTRA-TRICKY QUALIFYING-ROUND QUESTION...
...PLACE THE FOLLOWING YEARS IN ORDER OF THEIR OCCURRENCE: 1987, 1805, 1776 AND 2598!
WHOEVER SCRIBBLES THE CORRECT ANSWER IN THE FASTEST TIME GETS THE CHANCE TO ANSWER THE BURNING QUESTION...
$ SO YOU WANT A $ MILLION BUCKS, EH?
FRANK STROM • writer HOWARD SIMPSON • penciller MIKE DeCARLO • inker
JOHN COSTANZA • letterer DIGITAL CHAMELEON • colors
HARVEY RICHARDS • asst. editor JOAN HILTY • editor

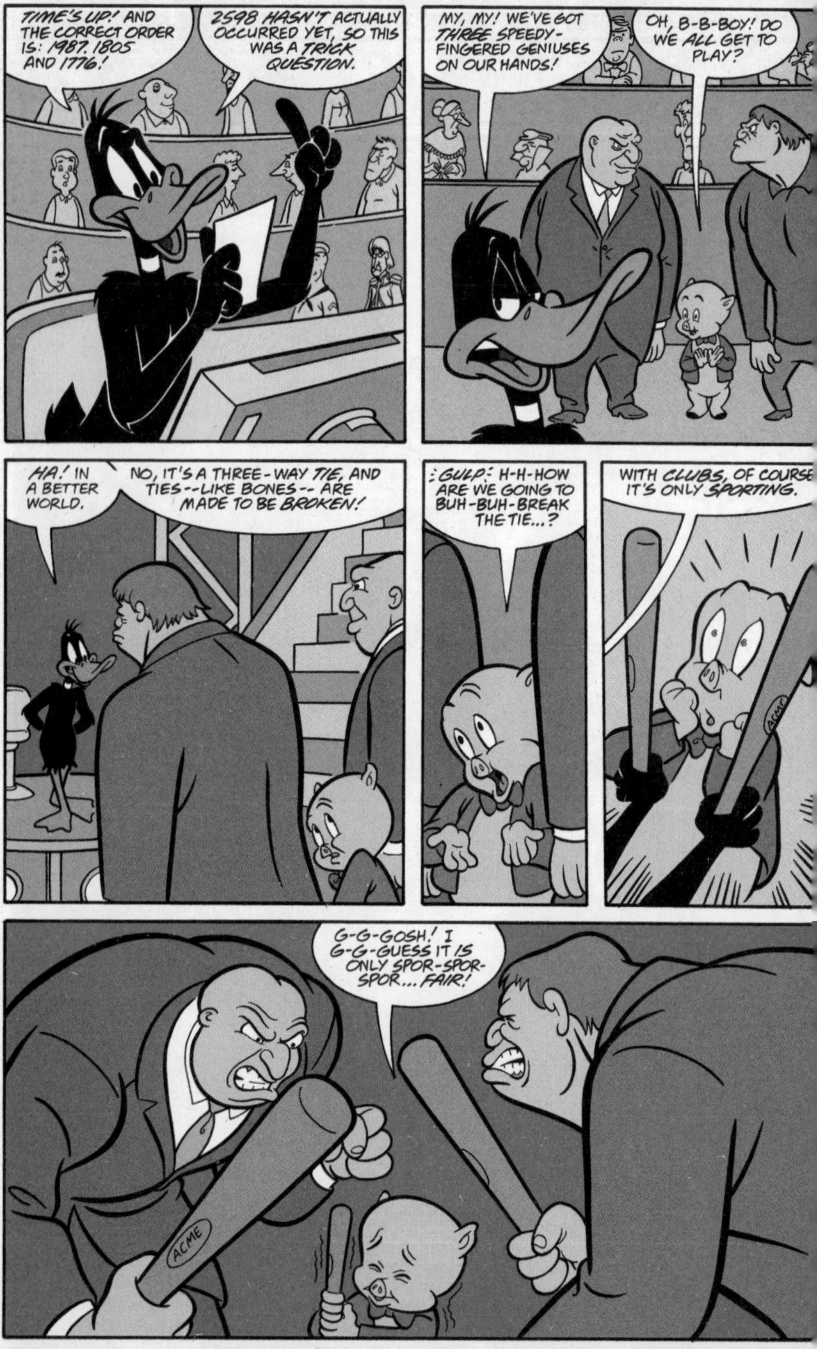
TIME'S UP! AND THE CORRECT ORDER IS: 1987, 1805 AND 1776!
2598 HASN'T ACTUALLY OCCURRED YET, SO THIS WAS A TRICK QUESTION.
MY, MY! WE'VE GOT THREE SPEEDY-FINGERED GENIUSES ON OUR HANDS!
OH, B-B-BOY! DO WE ALL GET TO PLAY?
HA! IN A BETTER WORLD.
NO, IT'S A THREE-WAY TIE, AND TIES--LIKE BONES--ARE MADE TO BE BROKEN!
:GULP: H-H-HOW ARE WE GOING TO BUH-BUH-BREAK THE TIE...?
WITH CLUBS, OF COURSE IT'S ONLY SPORTING.
G-G-GOSH! I G-G-GUESS IT IS ONLY SPOR-SPOR-SPOR... FAIR!
ACME

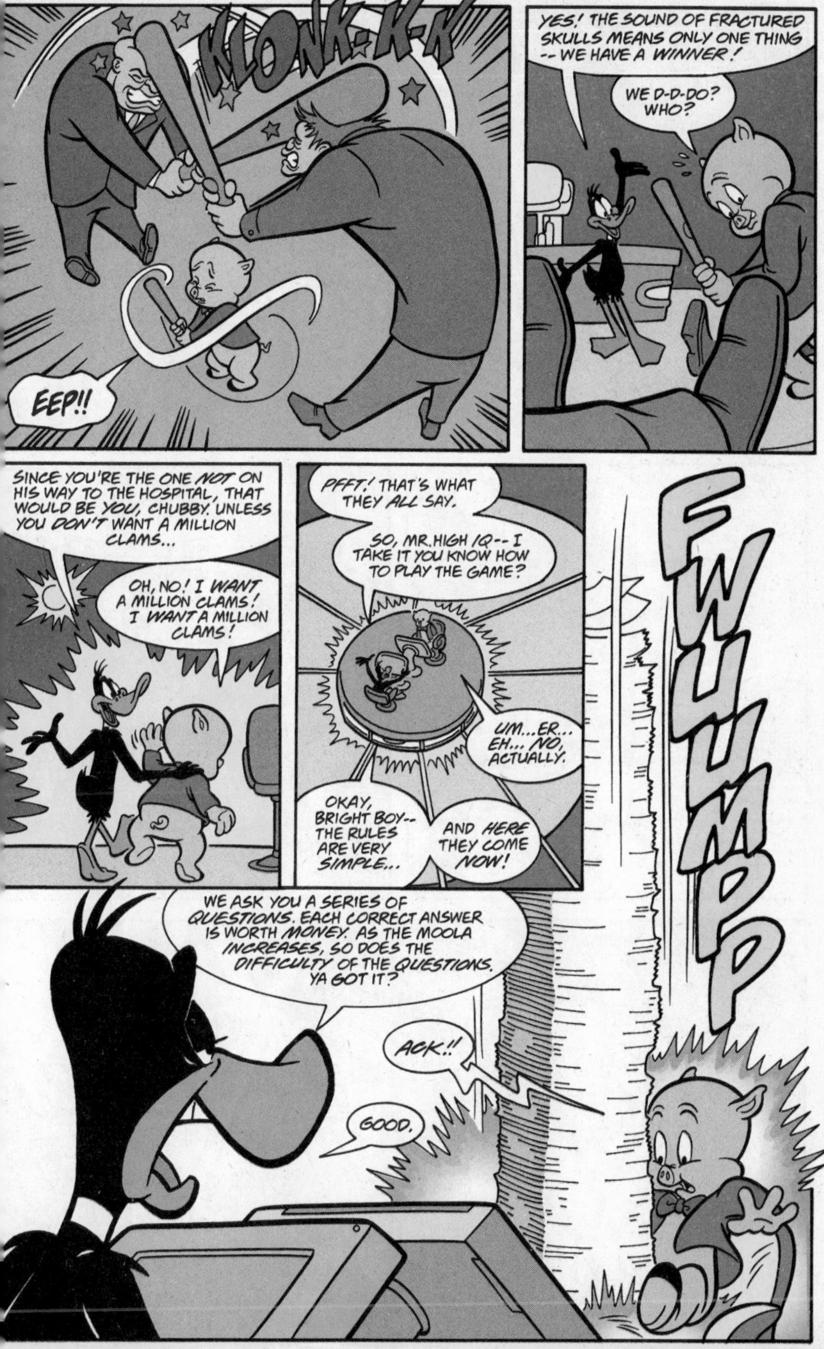
KLONK-K-K!
EEP!!
YES! THE SOUND OF FRACTURED SKULLS MEANS ONLY ONE THING -- WE HAVE A WINNER!
WE D-D-DO? WHO?
SINCE YOU'RE THE ONE NOT ON HIS WAY TO THE HOSPITAL, THAT WOULD BE YOU, CHUBBY. UNLESS YOU DON'T WANT A MILLION CLAMS...
OH, NO! I WANT A MILLION CLAMS! I WANT A MILLION CLAMS!
PFFT! THAT'S WHAT THEY ALL SAY.
SO, MR. HIGH IQ-- I TAKE IT YOU KNOW HOW TO PLAY THE GAME?
UM...ER... EH... NO, ACTUALLY.
OKAY, BRIGHT BOY-- THE RULES ARE VERY SIMPLE...
AND HERE THEY COME NOW!
FWUMP
WE ASK YOU A SERIES OF QUESTIONS. EACH CORRECT ANSWER IS WORTH MONEY. AS THE MOOLA INCREASES, SO DOES THE DIFFICULTY OF THE QUESTIONS. YA GOT IT?
ACK!!
GOOD.

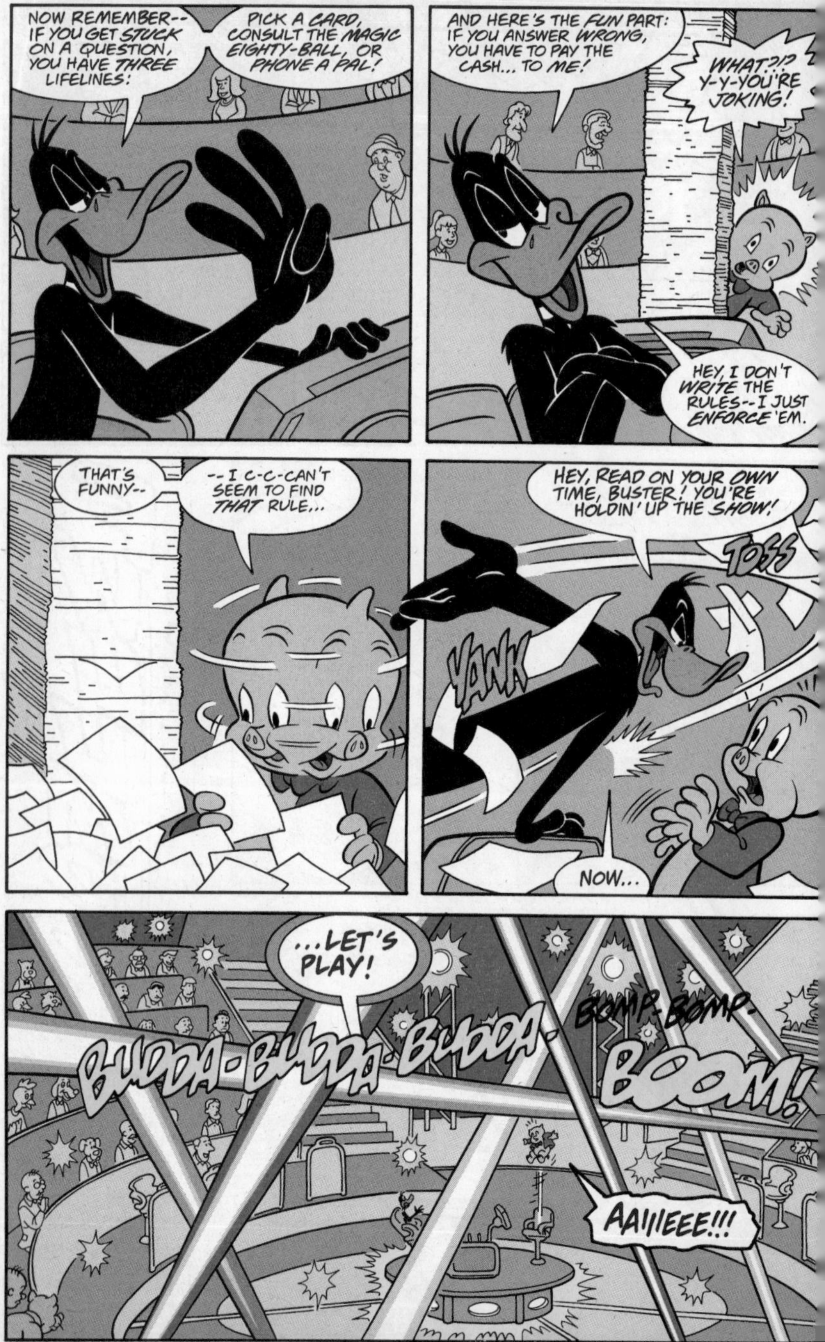
NOW REMEMBER-- IF YOU GET STUCK ON A QUESTION, YOU HAVE THREE LIFELINES:
PICK A CARD, CONSULT THE MAGIC EIGHTY-BALL, OR PHONE A PAL!
AND HERE'S THE FUN PART: IF YOU ANSWER WRONG, YOU HAVE TO PAY THE CASH... TO ME!
WHAT?!? Y-Y-YOU'RE JOKING!
HEY, I DON'T WRITE THE RULES--I JUST ENFORCE 'EM.
THAT'S FUNNY--
--I C-C-CAN'T SEEM TO FIND THAT RULE...
HEY, READ ON YOUR OWN TIME, BUSTER! YOU'RE HOLDIN' UP THE SHOW!
TOSS
YANK
NOW...
...LET'S PLAY!
BUDDA-BUDDA-BUDDA-
BOMP-BOMP-
BOOM!
AAIIIEEE!!!

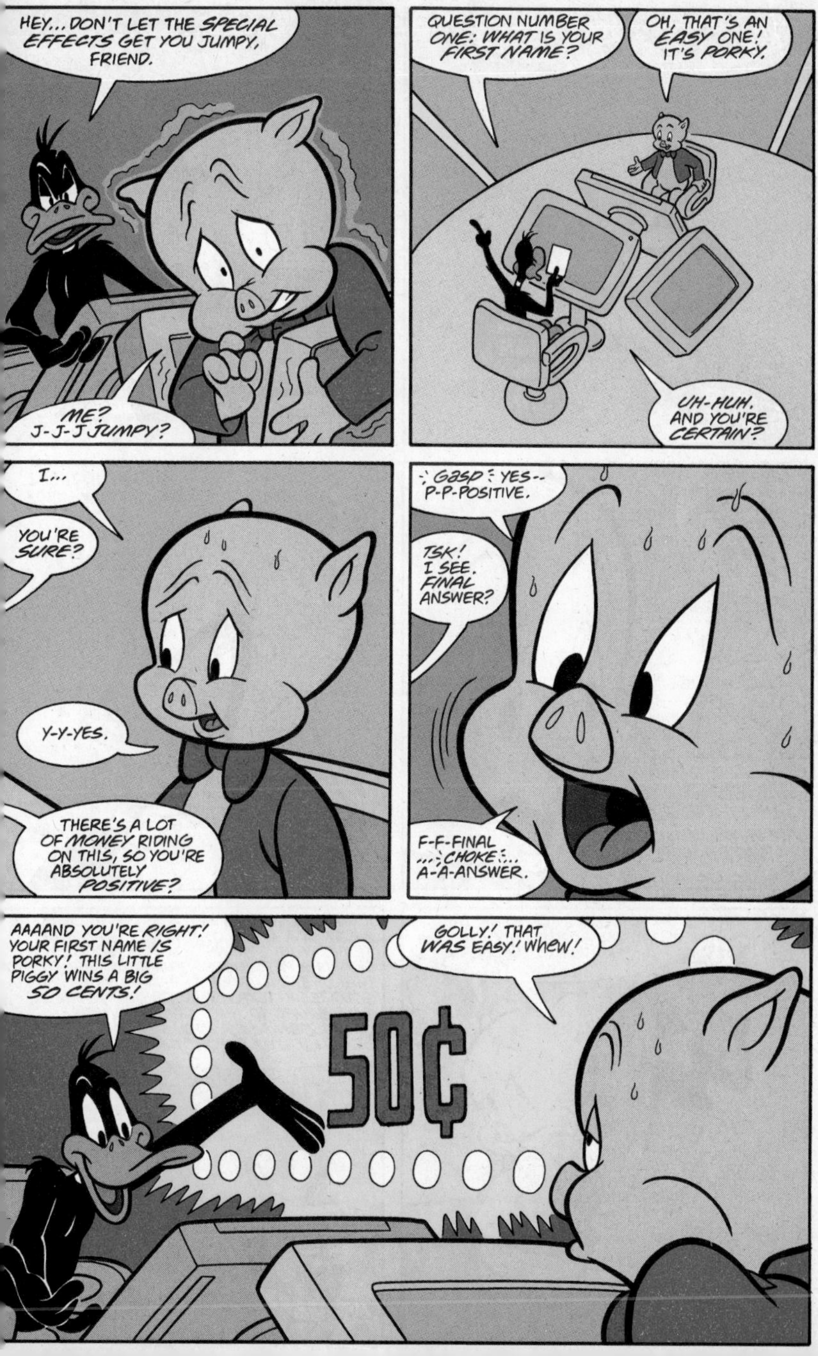
HEY... DON'T LET THE SPECIAL EFFECTS GET YOU JUMPY, FRIEND.
ME? J-J-J JUMPY?
QUESTION NUMBER ONE: WHAT IS YOUR FIRST NAME?
OH, THAT'S AN EASY ONE! IT'S PORKY.
UH-HUH. AND YOU'RE CERTAIN?
I...
YOU'RE SURE?
Y-Y-YES.
THERE'S A LOT OF MONEY RIDING ON THIS, SO YOU'RE ABSOLUTELY POSITIVE?
:GASP: YES-- P-P-POSITIVE.
TSK! I SEE. FINAL ANSWER?
F-F-FINAL ...:CHOKE:... A-A-ANSWER.
AAAAND YOU'RE RIGHT! YOUR FIRST NAME IS PORKY! THIS LITTLE PIGGY WINS A BIG 50 CENTS!
GOLLY! THAT WAS EASY! Whew!
50¢

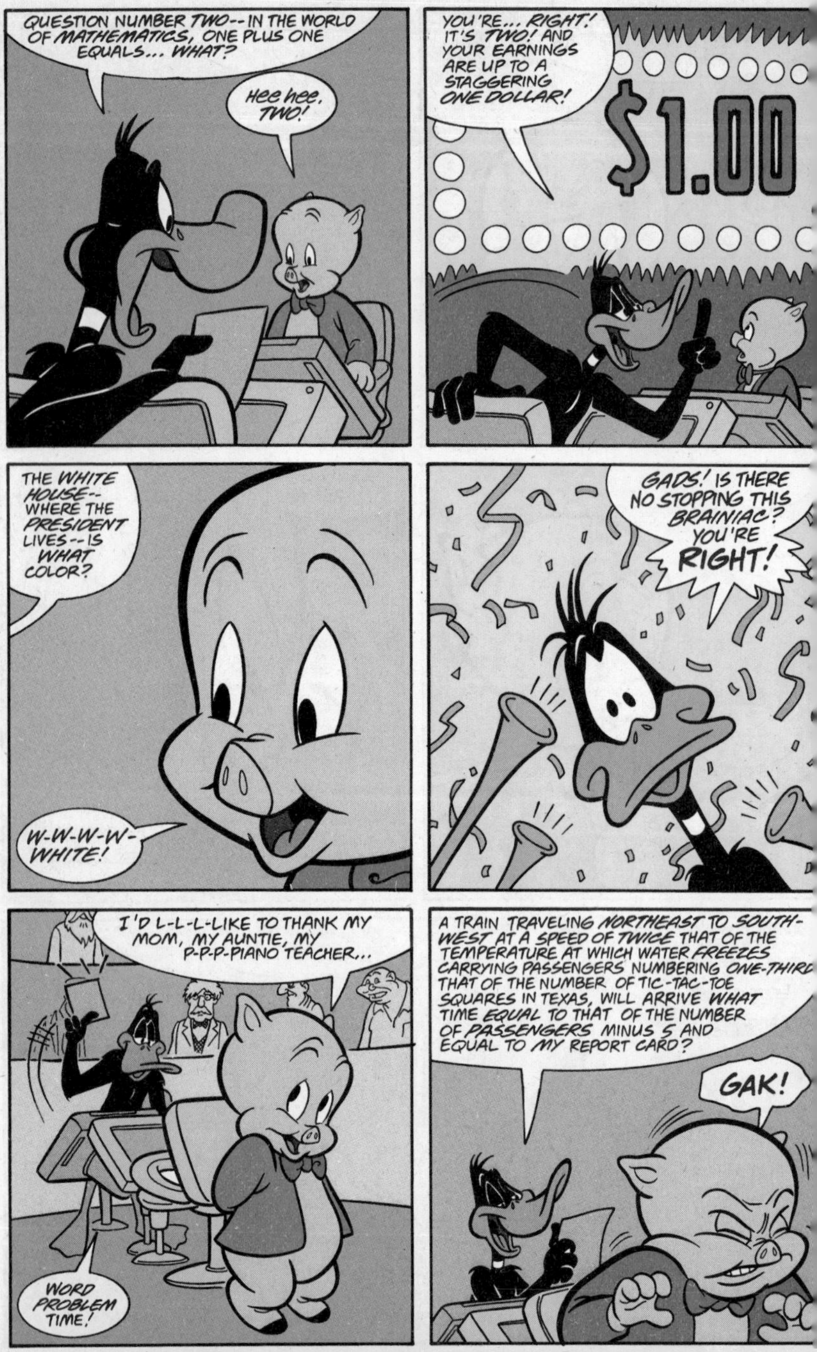
QUESTION NUMBER TWO-- IN THE WORLD OF MATHEMATICS, ONE PLUS ONE EQUALS... WHAT?
Hee hee. TWO!
YOU'RE... RIGHT! IT'S TWO! AND YOUR EARNINGS ARE UP TO A STAGGERING ONE DOLLAR!
$1.00
THE WHITE HOUSE-- WHERE THE PRESIDENT LIVES-- IS WHAT COLOR?
W-W-W-W-WHITE!
GADS! IS THERE NO STOPPING THIS BRAINIAC? YOU'RE RIGHT!
I'D L-L-L-LIKE TO THANK MY MOM, MY AUNTIE, MY P-P-P-PIANO TEACHER...
WORD PROBLEM TIME!
A TRAIN TRAVELING NORTHEAST TO SOUTHWEST AT A SPEED OF TWICE THAT OF THE TEMPERATURE AT WHICH WATER FREEZES CARRYING PASSENGERS NUMBERING ONE-THIRD THAT OF THE NUMBER OF TIC-TAC-TOE SQUARES IN TEXAS, WILL ARRIVE WHAT TIME EQUAL TO THAT OF THE NUMBER OF PASSENGERS MINUS 5 AND EQUAL TO MY REPORT CARD?
GAK!

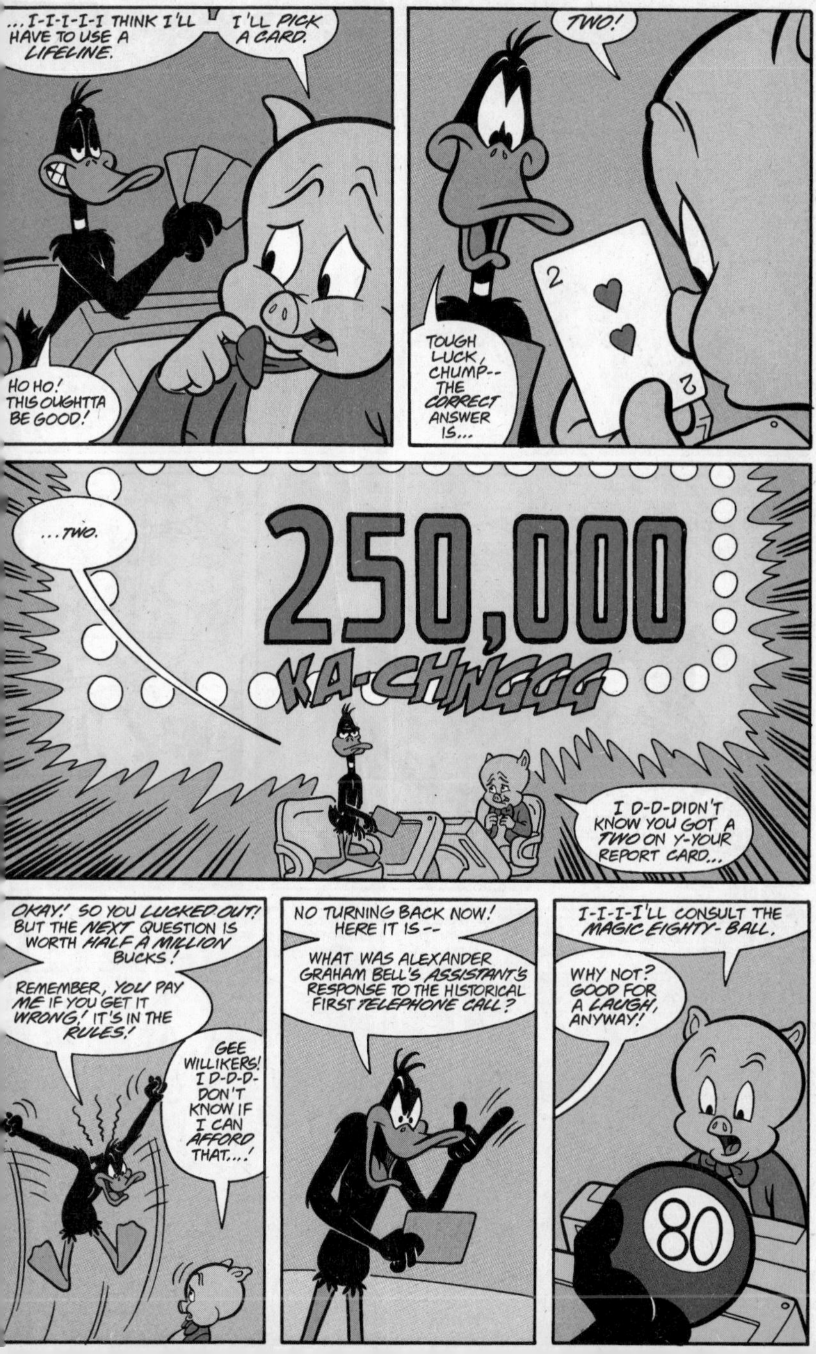
...I-I-I-I-I THINK I'LL HAVE TO USE A LIFELINE.
I'LL PICK A CARD.
HO HO! THIS OUGHTTA BE GOOD!
TWO!
TOUGH LUCK, CHUMP-- THE CORRECT ANSWER IS...
...TWO.
250,000
KA-CHNGGG
I D-D-DIDN'T KNOW YOU GOT A TWO ON Y-YOUR REPORT CARD...
OKAY! SO YOU LUCKED OUT! BUT THE NEXT QUESTION IS WORTH HALF A MILLION BUCKS!
REMEMBER, YOU PAY ME IF YOU GET IT WRONG! IT'S IN THE RULES!
GEE WILLIKERS! I D-D-D-DON'T KNOW IF I CAN AFFORD THAT...!
NO TURNING BACK NOW! HERE IT IS--
WHAT WAS ALEXANDER GRAHAM BELL'S ASSISTANT'S RESPONSE TO THE HISTORICAL FIRST TELEPHONE CALL?
I-I-I-I'LL CONSULT THE MAGIC EIGHTY-BALL.
WHY NOT? GOOD FOR A LAUGH, ANYWAY!
80

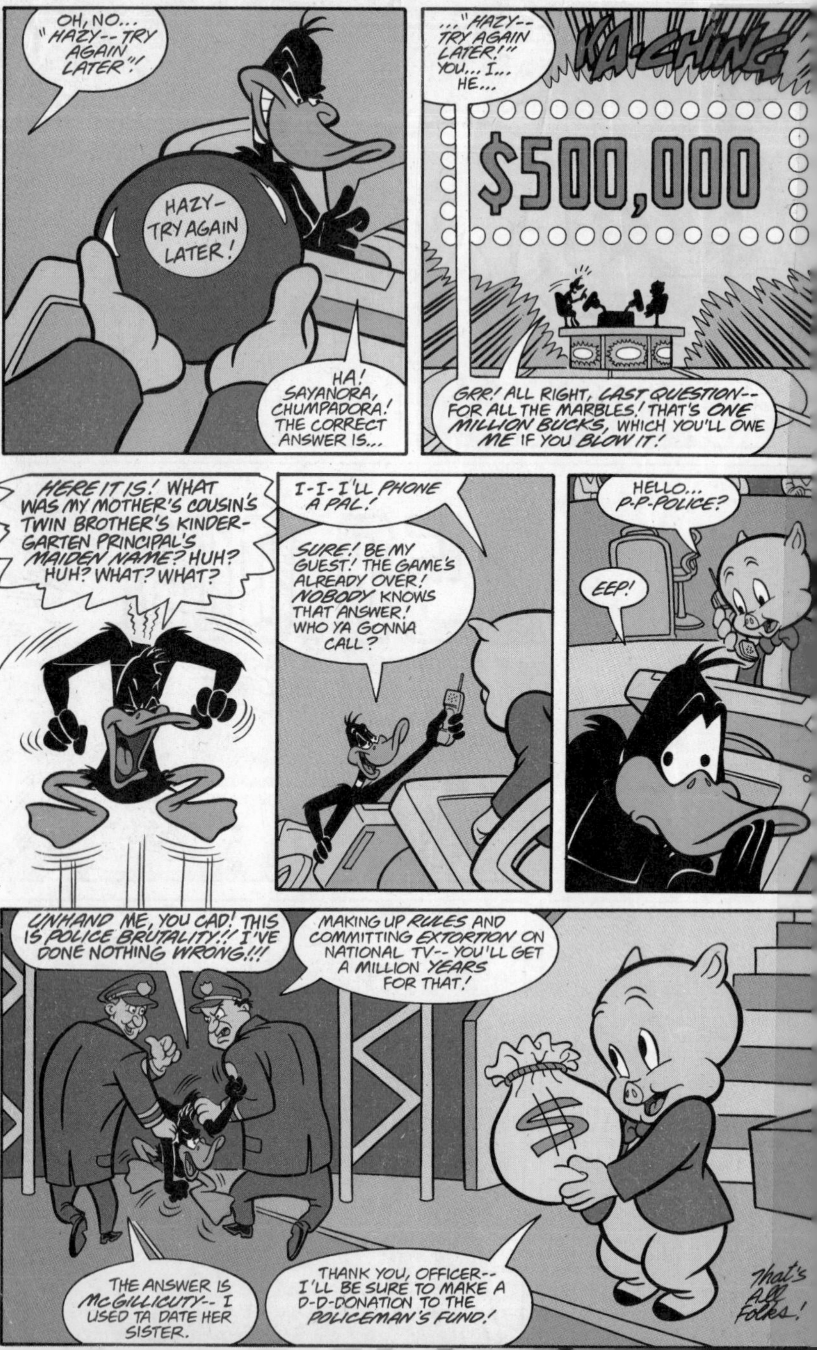

OH, NO... "HAZY-- TRY AGAIN LATER"!
HAZY- TRY AGAIN LATER!
HA! SAYANORA, CHUMPADORA! THE CORRECT ANSWER IS...
..."HAZY-- TRY AGAIN LATER!" YOU... I... HE...
KA-CHING
$500,000
GRR! ALL RIGHT, LAST QUESTION-- FOR ALL THE MARBLES! THAT'S ONE MILLION BUCKS, WHICH YOU'LL OWE ME IF YOU BLOW IT!
HERE IT IS! WHAT WAS MY MOTHER'S COUSIN'S TWIN BROTHER'S KINDER-GARTEN PRINCIPAL'S MAIDEN NAME? HUH? HUH? WHAT? WHAT?
I-I-I'LL PHONE A PAL!
SURE! BE MY GUEST! THE GAME'S ALREADY OVER! NOBODY KNOWS THAT ANSWER! WHO YA GONNA CALL?
HELLO... P-P-POLICE?
EEP!
UNHAND ME, YOU CAD! THIS IS POLICE BRUTALITY!! I'VE DONE NOTHING WRONG!!!
MAKING UP RULES AND COMMITTING EXTORTION ON NATIONAL TV-- YOU'LL GET A MILLION YEARS FOR THAT!
THE ANSWER IS McGILLICUTY-- I USED TA DATE HER SISTER.
THANK YOU, OFFICER-- I'LL BE SURE TO MAKE A D-D-DONATION TO THE POLICEMAN'S FUND!
That's All Folks!